NIGHTINGALE

ALSO BY DAVID FARLAND

On My Way to Paradise

The Serpent Catch Series:

> *Serpent Catch • Path of the Hero*

The Golden Queen Series:

> *The Golden Queen • Beyond the Gate • Lords of the Seventh Swarm*

Star Wars:

> *The Rising Force • The Courtship of Princess Leia*

The Mummy Chronicles

The Runelords Series:

> *The Runelords • Brotherhood of the Wolf • Wizardborn • The Lair of Bones • Sons of the Oak • Worldbinder • The Wyrmling Horde • Chaosbound*

You can check out all of David's Books and even sample some free short stories at:

www.davidfarland.com

Nightingale

David Farland

East India Press

DELUXE HARDCOVER EDITION

TEXT © 2011 BY DAVID FARLAND

COVER PHOTOGRAPH © 2011 BY LUC COIFFAT

COVER DESIGN © MILES DAVID ROMNEY

ISBN: 978-1-61475-787-0

INTERIOR DESIGN BY BOOK LOOKS DESIGN
WWW.BOOKLOOKSDESIGN.COM

PUBLISHED BY EAST INDIA PRESS LTD
EMPIRE STATE BUILDING
350 FIFTH AVENUE, 59TH FLOOR
NEW YORK, NY 10118
WWW.EASTINDIAPRESS.COM

This is a work of fiction. All of the characters and scenarios portrayed in this novel are either the imaginings of the author or are used fictitiously.

DEDICATION

To Mary and Spencer
for their continued help and support.

WITH SPECIAL THANKS TO:

Buddy Bracken, who took me and my son Forrest on a night tour of the swamps at Black River in the Louisiana Bayou;

Christy Hall, who was so kind as to give me the guided tours of Tuacahn High School as I prepared for this novel;

Danielle Wolverton, who provided insights into Tuacahn High School along with editorial support;

Joshua Essoe for providing a fine edit;

Miles Romney and all of his team for their work in illustrating, and composing for the enhanced novel.

A number of people gave excellent critical help, and I'd like to thank all of my readers. It's difficult to express just how grateful I really feel to all of you, especially Day Leclaire, romance author, whose insights into plotting were invaluable. I also got wonderfully detailed feedback from Gray Rinehart, editor at Orson Scott Card's Intergalactic Medicine Show Magazine, who has an uncanny ability to spot every kind of typo imaginable.

There are so many people who offered valuable comments. Very often, something as simple as "I felt like this" allows an author to get a better handle on a reader's emotional response, and that's a tremendous help. I can't get into much detail, but let me just mention a few: Sabine Berlin, Heather Clark, Lisa Devers, Jared Garrett, John Harper, David Hill, Jennifer D. Lerud, Juliana Montgomery, Joe Romano, and Robin Weeks.

PROLOGUE – 16 YEARS AGO

Sommer Bastian had fled her safe house in North Carolina, and now nowhere was safe.

She raced through a thick forest, gasping in the humid air. Sweat drenched her, crawling down her forehead, stinging her eyes. Dogs barked a quarter mile behind, the deep-voices of mastiffs. Her vision reeled from fatigue, and she struggled to make out a path in the shadows.

Fireflies rose from the grass ahead, lugging their burden of light, lanterns in shades of emerald and citrine that pushed back against the gathering night. Eighty thousand stars wheeled through otherwise empty heavens. Without even a sliver of moon or the glow of a remote village, the stars did not shine so much as throb.

She could run no faster. With every stride, Sommer stretched her legs to the full. A mastiff keened, not far back now. It was almost upon her.

Her pursuers were faster than any human, and stronger than her. At nineteen, Sommer was in the prime of her life, but that made no difference. A desperate plan was taking form in her mind.

The dogs were trained to kill. But she knew that even a trained dog can't attack someone who surrenders. Nature won't allow it. And when a dog surrenders completely, it does so by offering its throat.

That would be her last resort—to lie on her back and give her throat to these killers, so that she could draw them in close.

She raced for her life. To her right, a buck snorted in the darkness and bounded away, invisible in the night. She hoped that its pounding would attract the dogs, and they did fall silent in confusion, but soon snarled and doubled their speed.

The brush grew thick ahead—blackberries and morning glory crisscrossing the deer trail. She heard dogs lunging behind her; one barked. They were nearly on her.

Sommer's foot caught on something hard—a tough tree root—and she went sprawling. A dog growled and leapt. Sommer rolled to her back and arched her neck, offering her throat.

Three dogs quickly surrounded her, ominous black shadows that growled and barked, baring their fangs, sharp splinters of white. They were huge, these mastiffs, with spiked collars at their throats, and leather masks over their faces. Their hooded eyes seemed to be empty sockets in their skulls.

They bounded back and forth in their excitement, shadowy dancers, searching for an excuse to kill.

I can still get away, Sommer thought, raising a hand to the air, as if to block her throat. By instinct she extended her sizraels—oblong suction cups that now began to surface near the tip of each thumb and finger. Each finger held one, an oval callus that kept stretching, growing.

Though she wasn't touching any of the dogs, at ten feet they were close enough for her to attack.

She reached out with her mind, tried to calm herself as she focused, and electricity crackled at the tips of her fingers. Tiny blue lights blossomed and floated in the air near her fingers like dandelion down. The lights were soft and pulsing, no brighter than the static raised when she stroked a silk sheet in the hours before a summer storm.

She entered the mastiffs' minds and began to search. They were supposed to hold her until the hunters came, maul her if she tried to escape. Their masters had trained the dogs well.

But a dog's memories were not like human memories, thick and substantial.

Sommer drew all of the memories to the surface—hundreds of hours of training, all bundled into a tangle—and snapped them, as if passing her hand through a spider's web.

Immediately all three mastiffs began to look around nervously. One lay down at her feet and whimpered, as if afraid she might be angry.

"Good dogs," Sommer whispered, tears of relief rising to her eyes. "Good!" She rolled to her knees, felt her stomach muscles bunch and quaver. She prepared to run.

"Where do you think *you're* going?" a deep voice asked.

There are more dangerous things than mastiffs, Sommer knew. Of all the creatures in the world, the man who spoke now was at the top of the list.

She turned slowly. A shadow loomed on the trail behind her. In the starlight, she could make out vague features. She knew the man well. He was handsome—not as in "pleasing to look at," but so handsome that it made a woman's heart pound. His beauty, the clean lines of his jaw, the thoughtful look to his brow, hit her like a punch to the chest even now, though she knew he was a killer.

His name was Adel Todesfall, and he served as the head of security for the man who had held her captive for most of the past year, Lucius Chenzhenko.

"Don't hurt me," Sommer's hand raised protectively. "Please don't hurt me. Tell Lucius that I'll be his poppet. I'll be his toy. I'll do anything."

Adel drew a gleaming piece of metal from a shoulder holster, a pistol. Sommer was powerful in her way. Even at ten feet she presented a danger, but Adel remained outside her range.

"You're ill-suited to be a poppet," Adel argued. "Nor would you be very entertaining as a toy. Besides, we have a problem here, one not so easily solved. You stole something from him...."

She peered up, bewildered. "No," she begged. "I took nothing from the compound, not even spare clothes."

Adel smiled, amused. "You don't remember?" She shook her head. "You don't recall carrying a child in your womb for these past *eleven* months?"

"I've never—" *had a child,* she thought. But she remembered Lucius, that sadistic monster, forcing himself upon her....

Sommer's people, the masaaks, took longer to gestate than humans did. Sommer could not imagine having carried a child to term, much less forgetting about it, unless ...

Adel offered, "You've had the memory ripped from you."

"I don't recall *having* a child!" she said. She hoped to stall while she gathered her wits. Sommer could not reveal information that she didn't know. Yet if another memory thief had pulled vital information from her, Sommer knew that they might not have been thorough. Each memory in a person's brain is laid down tens of thousands of times, through multiple connections between neurons. Stray thoughts, random feelings, might still be hiding in her skull— clues to the mystery of her missing child.

A moment ago she'd thought that she would have done anything to get her freedom, but she couldn't betray an innocent babe.

Adel stiffened, and as his composure vanished, a snarl escaped his lips. Frustrated, he took aim quickly and the muzzle of his pistol flashed three times in rapid succession. Dogs yelped and dropped to the ground, muscles quivering. The odor of blood and burning flesh arose. Dogs kicked and whimpered as they died.

Sommer cringed.

"You!" he growled, "you *ruined* my dogs!" Adel's eyes widened as he pointed the gun at her face, steadied his aim. Sommer prepared to die. Adel had been an excellent shot for at least five hundred years, since the very invention of the hand cannon.

Adel gritted his teeth.

Suddenly a fierce protective instinct took over. Sommer argued, "I heard ... I heard a few weeks ago, that Lucius killed one of his own sons. He didn't like the child's ... features." She said it accusingly, incensed.

At least she knew now why she had run.

Adel shrugged. "He didn't like its nose. A good eugenics program requires that we cull ... defectives."

Sommer knew that Adel considered her to be "defective." She was a masaak, like him, but she wasn't one of Lucius's well-bred Draghouls. She was from "feral" stock. She was an Ael. Her ancestors had been hiding from Lucius and his Draghouls for hundreds of years.

An image flashed through her mind, an ancient memory. It was from an incident that had occurred eighteen hundred years before she was born. She didn't recall who had given the memory to her.

She saw Lucius, dressed in a fine red-silk toga, sitting in the balcony at the Roman Coliseum. He conversed with a general as he devoured a breast of swan. Down in the arena, a brutish Christian with a crude ax was trying to defend himself while a pair of hungry lions circled. It was only a minor pre-show, before the gladiatorial combats began. The Christian was a missionary named Titus who had preached in the streets of Rome, hounding the philosophers.

"*Ego dont 'have ullus problems per homines,*" Lucius jested, "I don't have any problem with humans," he waited before delivering the punch-line, "hunting them is such fine sport." He laughed.

Just then, the crowd roared as a lion lunged. With one swipe of its paw it jerked the Christian's feet from under him, while its hunting partner pounced.

In those days, Lucius looked much as he did now, but there was a vitality to him, a light in his eyes, that had since burned out.

Lucius no longer had that "fire in the belly" one needs to be a global dictator. Sommer hoped that Lucius and his empire would soon crumble like a log that has turned to ash.

"Sommer," Adel said softly. He crouched. "I'm not angry. But I need you to make this right. We must find this child. Perhaps you cannot recall what you have done, but you should be able to tell me what you *might* do. Where would you take him, given the proper provocation?"

Sommer shook her head. She couldn't imagine. "Home?" she moaned, guessing. Immediately she wished that she'd held her tongue. She wouldn't want to lead them toward her family.

"We've checked," Adel said.

Sommer's heart pounded. They'd been to her house? They'd found her mother? Her father and sisters? What would Lucius have done to them?

Gone, she realized. *They're all gone.* The news left her sickened, shocked. Her mind seemed to shut down.

"I have an offer," Adel suggested. "Cooperate. Help us find the child. You can have ... money. A few million? And life. We'll give you a thousand extra years. Imagine what you could do with both?"

"I don't want your money," Sommer fumed. She set her jaw. "And I'd rather die than live among you."

"Then ... perhaps you'd barter for your sisters' lives," Adel suggested, as if he'd grown tired of her games.

15

"They're still alive?" she asked. She wasn't sure if she believed him. She certainly didn't trust him. But she realized that she had no choice. In order to earn mercy for her family, she'd have to do both.

The gun in Adel's left hand flashed as he waved it in the moonlight. Such was his skill that Sommer did not see the Taser in his right hand until the electric arc shot toward her, and she fell into darkness.

Three thousand miles away, an infant woke in the night, and cried for his mother.

CHAPTER 1

INTO THE DESERT

"We all become lost *children at one time or another. When no one else can find us, we must find ourselves."*

– Monique

Bron Jones wasn't afraid when Jenny called him in to speak with his foster mother. He hadn't done anything wrong. Still, sometimes people will knock you down even if you don't deserve it.

"Bron," Jenny said loudly enough to be heard over the roar of the lawnmower, in a tone of both care and warning, "mom wants you."

At eleven years old, Jenny Stillman was savvier than other kids. With a mom like hers, she had to be. Jenny could smell trouble coming a week in advance.

Bron cut the gas to the mower, wiped the sweat from his brow with the back of his hand, and tried to steel himself for whatever might come.

With his foster mother, Melvina Stillman, you could never tell what it might be. He imagined that she would gripe about his mowing. Bron had begun at eight in order to beat the heat of the day. Here in

Alpine, Utah, it might get into the hundreds in late August, and the huge lawn needed to be done by ten.

But Melvina suffered from aches and pains, and she didn't sleep well at night. Bron figured that she'd want him to put off the mowing for a couple more hours while she slept, but he could never tell what the crazy woman might want.

He gave Jenny a questioning look, and she whispered, "You're in serious trouble!" while holding her hand up to her mouth to signal that Melvina was on the phone.

Great, Bron thought, *she's talking to social services.* He'd been living in the system from the time he was an infant, getting bounced from home to home. He was used to being talked about, prodded, and torn apart.

What's the worst that could happen? he wondered. He knew the answer. *They could send me to another home, somewhere terrible.*

Bron had almost hit rock bottom. Melvina hated him. To her, he was just a paycheck worth $518 a month in "maintenance fees." If she controlled her costs, she could feed him for $150 per month and dress him in hand-me-downs from the neighbors. That left $368 in profit that she could use to feed her own seven kids, with the bonus that she could work Bron like a house servant, cooking dinners, mowing lawns, and changing diapers.

Melvina got paid to keep Bron as her slave.

Bron wiped the sweat from his brow with the back of his hand and turned toward the house, a grand old yellow Victorian with a pair of turrets on each end and green gingerbread trim around the windows. It looked like a place that should be throwing parties, not a home so filled with poverty and despair.

He stopped for a moment, peering up. Crouched on the chimney was a crow, just watching him, its black feathers ruffled against an invisible wind. The crow cawed once, and then leapt into the sky, beating its midnight wings, feathers extended like fingers to rake the heavens.

Bron slipped off his shoes on the porch, brushed the grass clippings from his pant cuffs, then went through the door and down the bright hall to Melvina's bedroom. He opened her door softly. After being in the bright sunlight, the place was as oily dark as an octopus's den.

Melvina was a hoarder. She had boxes full of food stacked all around the bed, blocking the windows, forbidding all light. With a box of peaches ripening in the shadows, the place had an earthy odor, like an animal's cage.

Something flew out of the darkness, slapping Bron lightly. A red sandal dropped at his feet. He saw Melvina there now, a shapeless mass on the bed, a box of shoes at her side. She grabbed a second shoe and tossed it. Bron leaned away.

"You stop that!" Melvina screamed. "You stay right where you are." She growled and tossed a slipper, missing wildly. "You got into my peaches! I can't even get up to use the bathroom without you stealing something!"

"I didn't take your peaches, Melvina," Bron said softly, but she continued to glare. She was having one of her fits. Talking to her would be a waste of breath.

"You liar!" she screeched, and then hunted vainly in her box for a heavier shoe. She was too fat to get up and chase him. Every day she lay in bed, growing plump as a melon. In the past couple of months, shoe-throwing had become her favorite method of discipline.

She made a moaning noise, stopped rummaging, and grabbed her phone. For a moment, Bron thought she'd throw that, but she hit the speed dial and warned, "The welfare people are going to want to talk to you!"

She thought that would terrify him.

She spoke to Bron's caseworker for a moment, James Bell, and then shoved the phone toward Bron.

Here it comes, Bron thought: *the vague accusations, the grilling questions*. His heart pounded, and he fought his outrage by telling himself, I can handle it. I'm used to it.

Bell's tranquil voice came over the phone. "So, it seems that there is a problem...."

He waited for Bron to say something. So often, Bron found that adults tried to twist his words, so he hesitated, but then realized that it was Melvina who always twisted his words, not Mr. Bell.

"I don't know what's going on," Bron said. "Melvina's mad. She thinks I stole a peach or something."

There was a long silence, and Bell said, "Nine peaches. She thinks you ate nine. Oh, and some chocolate is missing. She can't admit that any of her own kids might sneak in and take them."

The little ones would have done it, Bron knew. Melvina kept her favorite foods in her bedroom, where she could guard them—fresh peaches, Cap'n Crunch cereal, Hershey's Symphony bars, Mountain Dew. The children rarely got such fare, unless she was in a generous mood. But the peaches had been filling the house with their sweet aroma for days. The temptation must have become too much.

"Pack your bags, Bron," the caseworker said. "It's time to get you out of there. I'll be by to pick you up in a few minutes."

"Okay," Bron said, feeling like he'd been punched.

It wasn't fair, but then getting shuffled from home to home never had been fair.

How am I going to break the news to the little ones? he wondered. *Caleb and Sarah won't understand.*

At three and four, the little ones had relied upon Bron most of their lives. Their father worked driving long-haul trucks across the country, while their mother hid in her room.

Bron didn't have time to think about it. He needed every minute to pack. He pushed the *off* button on the phone.

"Did he tell you?" Melvina demanded. "You're out of here." She waited a moment, as if hoping that he would start to sob and beg her to let him stay. There was a tone of triumph in her voice, tinged by contempt. He wasn't going to give her any satisfaction.

"I can't tell you how glad I am, either," Melvina gloated. "Ever since you got here, you've just drained the joy out of this family."

He could see her better in the shadows, now that his eyes had adjusted. His eyes were good in the dark. She was a sickly thing, pale and blubbery and sad, with frizzled hair going gray. But right now there

21

was a gleam in her eyes, a gleam of conquest and retribution.

"I'm sorry that you're not happy, Melvina," Bron said. "Maybe you'll like your next foster child better."

Bron went to his bedroom and quickly emptied his dresser, shoving his worn clothes into the old backpack that he'd gotten for school.

Now it starts all over, he thought. The state would look for a new home, and he'd get all of the questions: "What's wrong with him? Is he a crack baby? Does he steal? What's his criminal history? Is it safe to have him near our daughter?"

People had a right to ask those questions, Bron knew, but the answers hurt. There was nothing wrong with him. He was just unwanted.

When the backpack was full, he took the pillowcase from his bed and began to stuff clothes into it, but Melvina plodded into the room, the floorboards creaking beneath her weight. Bron was surprised to see her up. Melvina said, "Don't you steal my pillowcases!"

The children all began watching now, the little ones peeking out from between Melvina's legs, sobbing, while the older ones paced at her back. Melvina blocked the door, as if to keep any of the children from coming to hug him or say goodbye.

Bron wondered if he should tell her the truth: that her own kids had taken the food, that even a child knew it was wrong for a woman to make her kids go hungry, but he decided to let it go. He wouldn't gain anything by placing the blame where it belonged. In his mind, the children had done nothing wrong. They shouldn't be punished for Melvina's mental illness.

He put his clothes on the floor, used a t-shirt like a sack and filled it. Melvina glared at him the whole time. He went to the bathroom and threw in his toothbrush and shaving kit. Melvina wouldn't let him take the toothpaste.

"You think you can get by in life just on your good looks," she complained. "Well not anymore, buster! I hope they send you to jail!"

Bron shook his head. Her ranting hardly made sense. He'd never considered himself to be good-looking, and it wasn't as if he tried to skate through life. Nobody worked harder on his studies, and Bron was constantly toiling once he got home from school, fixing meals for the kids, cleaning house, settling disputes.

When he was all finished, he looked around his room. He had some cheap movie posters on the wall: Harry Potter and Transformers, but he knew that he'd just rip them if he tried to take them down. He left them for Melvina's next slave.

He grabbed his guitar, an old one that he'd had for a year. He'd hardly had time to learn to play it, between school and housework.

"Leave the guitar," Melvina demanded.

Now it was his turn to glare. Being mentally ill didn't give Melvina the right to be cruel and petty. "I bought it with my own money," he reminded her. He'd gotten it second-hand last spring for $400, which he'd made by helping the neighbors build a water fountain in their yard.

Melvina growled, "You owe me for the peaches!"

Bron suspected that at some level, she realized that he hadn't taken them. It was only pride that kept her making stupid accusations. Bron had never tried to make her angry before, but he didn't have much in this world, and he wasn't going to give up all he had.

"Are you sure that you didn't eat them in your sleep?" Bron asked. "Your butt is growing fatter by the day."

She gasped in astonishment, her mouth working like a fish's, her chins quivering. Melvina looked as if she was in the throes of preparing to say something monumentally devastating. "After all I've done for you—you little hoodlum!"

"Is that the best you can come up with?" he asked. "I've been called worse by better people than you." He shoved past her and headed for the front door.

Melvina lunged for the guitar, and he simply lifted it over her head. She went crashing against his dresser.

"You pushed me!" she screamed.

"I would never do that," he said gently. He worried. If she claimed that he'd hit her, she might get him arrested.

He hurried from the room. He found Jenny in the hall, and he felt a surge of relief. She'd seen what had happened.

"I love you," she mouthed.

Bron smiled sadly. He didn't want to encourage her, or hurt her feelings. He just wanted to leave. He didn't know where the state would send him next, but he was eager to get out of this place.

The little ones were crying, and Sarah, stricken, called at his back, "Where are you going, Bron? When will you come back?"

He knew the truth. Leaving a foster home was like dying. You never got to go back.

"You'll be all right, Sarah," he said. "I'll come visit you when I can." *Most likely,* he thought, *that won't be for a couple of years, and by then you won't know who I am, or care.*

He stepped out the front door. Here so close to the mountains, the land was still in shade, even at nine in the morning, and so he stood in the shadow of Mount Timpanogos, and waited until the social worker's dusty-green car pulled into the driveway.

Bron threw his things into the back, and then slid into the front passenger seat.

Mr. Bell was talking on the phone. He was a handsome black man with a voice as soothing as a massage.

He finished the phone call abruptly and went to the house to have Melvina sign some papers. Mr. Bell stood talking to her on the porch. All seven Stillman kids came and peeked over her shoulders or between her legs, watching Bron, but too afraid to approach. Doug, the oldest boy, was only fourteen. He'd have to be the man of the house. The other kids were too young to take care of themselves, much less anyone else. They all milled nervously, wanting to say good-bye, but they didn't dare try to pass Melvina's barricade of flesh and incur their mother's wrath.

Bron closed his eyes, trying to shut them all out. He wanted to feel nothing for Melvina. He fought back his hurt and his rage, until he felt able to stare at her as if she were an object, a chair or a melon. He felt nothing for her. It was that way with all of his foster parents. He'd learned to feel nothing long ago.

The children were different, though. Seeing the kids in pain, that hurt.

Mr. Bell finished talking and ambled back to the car, waving to the kids cheerfully, as if this was just another day's work. He was short, with a build that had once been athletic, but was now going soft.

There had been a time when Mr. Bell was just a naïve caseworker, but over the years, he'd grown wise. In the past dozen years he'd placed Bron with six different families. Now he acted casual as he put the key in the ignition, turned it, and the engine came alive. "You all right?"

"I'm fine."

"You're not fine. Your face is pale, breathing shallow. You feel like you been punched in the gut?"

"A little," Bron admitted.

Mr. Bell didn't put the car into gear, just let it run for a second. He gave Bron a gentle look. "You wave goodbye to them kids now. I know it's not a proper goodbye, but if you don't give them at least that, you'll regret it for the rest of your life."

Bron had been wondering about that. He'd never see the Stillman kids again. He wanted the little ones to forget him quickly. It's easier, he knew, to let go of your feelings, if someone leaves you with a little hurt.

Bron gritted his teeth. He waved and forced a smile, and Jenny lit up like she'd just been touched by a ray of sunshine. All of the sudden, the kids began shouting, "Goodbye," and waving like mad. Melvina grimaced and herded the kids inside. For an instant, four-year-old Sarah had a clear view. She blew Bron a kiss, as if he were just heading off to school.

Then the blue-gray door slammed shut, and they were gone.

Bron sat for a moment, clearing his mind, letting them all go away forever, purging his feelings. In a moment, he reached a comfortable, hollow state.

Mr. Bell pulled out onto the road, driving through the picturesque neighborhood that made up Alpine, with its expansive yards and custom homes. Mr. Bell weighed his words. "Leaving those kids has got to be hard."

"Not really," Bron said. "You learn not to get attached. I could tell that it was time to go."

Mr. Bell gave him a long look, his nostrils flaring just a bit. "After three years, I'm sure that you love them."

"I was never part of their family. I never could be."

Mr. Bell's dark eyes bored into Bron. "You can't really be so cold."

Bron didn't dare speak his thoughts. *If I am a monster, it is because you—and the world—have made me that way.* He joked weakly, "Hey, it's a talent."

Mr. Bell waited for Bron to say more, but he just let the silence hold as they rolled past the Kencraft Candy Factory, the little town's only manufacturing plant.

Alpine was a pretty place, nestled between the folds of the Wasatch Mountains. Most of the storms blew in from the south, and when they butted up against the mountains, they hit an impenetrable wall and were forced to release their moisture.

So Alpine had a lushness to it that was perhaps unmatched for hundreds of miles in any direction, and it remained verdant most of the year, but the green zone was small—only about a dozen miles square. They began driving away from it now, along fenced pastures where golden grass graced the fields and cottonwoods lined the banks of the American Fork River.

Now, in mid-August, the black-eyed Susans grew wild in the fields on the outskirts of town, reaching heights of eight or ten feet, becoming huge bushes with hundreds of enormous golden sunflowers bobbing in the wind, the dark hearts at their center as deep brown as a doe's eyes.

Mr. Bell broke the silence and finally demanded, "Did you really tell Melvina that it looked like she was hiding those peaches in her butt?"

Bron admitted, "Something like that. It was kind of a ... metaphor." He waited for Mr. Bell to chew him out.

"Good one," Mr. Bell said after a second, and laughed.

As they drove west toward I-15, the number and size of the flowers dwindled, and the cottonwoods along the creek surrendered to fields of stubby tan salt grass that rolled on for miles.

"Most people are crazy, you know," Mr. Bell said absently. "I mean, most people are just a little bit crazy. They'll admit it, if you ask." Bron nodded, suspecting where this was going. "But most crazy people are pretty harmless, you know? Like we have this one foster mother, she believes that crystals carry encoded messages left by the people of Atlantis. She'll hold them up to the light and meditate, and she'll 'read' all kinds of messages from them—things like 'Go buy celery today.' It doesn't matter if I dug up the crystal out of my backyard, she's convinced that all crystals have hidden messages in them, and that the Atlanteans just left them lying around for our benefit."

"But not all crazy people are harmless," Bron said. "Melvina is getting mean."

"That they are not," Mr. Bell agreed. "You and I have both seen this coming—Melvina hiding in her room with all of that food, getting fatter by the hour. Do you know what she told me?"

"What?" Bron asked, glad to hear him confide such secrets.

"She said that she was hiding from *you*. She said that from the day you moved into that house, you started sucking the energy out of her."

Bron shook his head, pained by the thought. He knew that the accusation would end up on his personal record, and such words—no matter how incoherent or crazed—could cost him dearly.

When he was a child, a preschool teacher had said that Bron was "dreamy," and one of his foster parents, Mr. Beardley, had demanded that the state run a battery of tests for schizophrenia. The tests had come up negative, but the Beardleys had given Bron back to social services. Because of their concerns, he'd had a hard time finding another home. That had been what? When he was four or five?

Bron didn't remember much from that time in his life. It was just another home where he hadn't been wanted. As an infant, he'd been dropped off at a hotel in Brigham City. A note pinned to his chest said, "If you want him, Bron is free!"

Often, Bron thought about that wistfully. He won-dered where he came from, why his mother had abandoned him. He asked himself, *When have I ever really been free?*

Sometimes Bron used to pester Mr. Bell for news. Bron would ask if anyone had ever made an anony-mous call, saying something like, "I just wondered if that baby that I abandoned sixteen years ago is okay?" But Bron had given up asking.

"You know what I think?" Mr. Bell went on. "I think that when you got to the Stillman's, you began doing dishes and helping out a lot...."

Bron remembered it well. He'd wanted so badly to make that home work, to live in a little gingerbread house with that big family. So he'd mopped floors and washed dishes that winter until his hands were raw. Even with all that, he'd never really felt connected to them.

"When Mrs. Stillman saw what you could do, she decided to take a break for a bit, let you do most of the work. After twelve years of spittin' out kid after kid, it probably felt good. She was always heavy, but the more she rested, the fatter she got, and getting up to work just took more and more energy—until now she can hardly climb out of bed."

"That sounds about right," Bron said, "though I never thought that much about it. Did you tell her what you think?"

Mr. Bell laughed. "I told her that I doubted that you had such powers."

"If I had a super power," Bron admitted, "I'd like the power to hear people's thoughts. Not everyone's, just the thoughts of girls."

"Why's that?"

"Cause I'd really like to know what they're thinking."

Mr. Bell chuckled. He got into the HOV lane, and then headed south, but Bron had imagined that they'd go north, toward the group home in Salt Lake.

"Where are we going?" Bron asked.

"Where do you want to go?" Mr. Bell gave him a sidelong glance, and Bron knew that it wasn't a rhetorical question. "Look," Mr. Bell said, "I checked into this charter school that I heard about last year, one for kids who want to be singers and actors and artists...."

Bron's heart suddenly pounded. He'd never told Mr. Bell about his dreams. He hadn't wanted to sound stupid.

"It's called Tuacahn," Mr. Bell said, pronouncing it carefully so that Bron would learn it: Two-uh-con. "It's a Mayan word, and means 'Canyon of the Gods.'"

Bron had heard television commercials advertising musicals at Tuacahn, but it was hundreds of miles south of here, down in the hottest corner of the state. Bron fought back an irritating fear.

"Townsfolk down south," Mr. Bell added, "take a lot of students there on placement from around the whole country, so I checked to see if any of them are certified foster parents. I found a teacher at the school who has been certified for three years, though she's never taken a child. The Hernandez family. They're good folks: middle-aged, can't have kids of their own. For the past three months we've been phoning back and forth. I didn't tell you about them because I didn't want to hold out any false hopes, but the long and short of it is, I called her not half an hour ago, and she is willing to take you in."

Bron let out a breath that he hadn't realized he'd been holding. "I don't know these people. We haven't even met!"

"They know a little about you. They know you're an artist."

Bron's head was spinning. He loved art, but that didn't make him an artist. He worried that he wouldn't fit in at such a school. He imagined that Tuacahn would be filled with poor-little–rich-kids. Then there was the family name.

"Hernandez?" he asked. "She's a Mexican?" He worried that he might have to eat enchiladas all the time, or deal with weird cultural issues.

"Not that you could tell," Mr. Bell said. "Her husband might be third generation."

"What about the heat?" Bron said. "I heard that it gets up to 120 down there?"

"They have this thing called 'air conditioning' at the school," Mr. Bell said dryly.

The man was trying to put Bron at ease, but the truth was that the idea of going to a new area, to this special school, unnerved Bron, despite its attractions.

Bron desperately wanted to spend more time working on his art. But it all sounded too ... fortuitous. Bron had learned young that good luck never lasts. You can never let your hopes get too high. Something was bound to go wrong.

"What if I don't like it?" he wondered.

"There's two girls for every boy in that school," Mr. Bell said, as if offering a tempting dish, "and every one of them wants to be an actress or a supermodel. What's not to like?"

"How long do I have to think about it?" he asked. He figured that he'd be a couple of weeks in a group home down south before all of the paperwork was done. There would be phone calls with his potential foster parents, then maybe a personal "meet-and-greet."

Mr. Bell gave him a sideways smile as they rounded a bend. "Where do you think we're going now?"

"Today?" Bron asked.

"School starts on Monday. Mrs. Hernandez, Olivia, thought it would be best to get you settled in."

Bron didn't know how to respond. He'd seldom just been dumped into a new family. He usually had at least one meeting first, sometimes three or four.

So he merely stared out the window, aware that he might never come back to this place again.

Bron gazed off into fields of golden grass and golden flowers, and fought the urge to jump out of the car.

New city. New school. New family. He hadn't had even an hour to get ready for this.

I don't have to bail out here on the highway, he told himself. *If I don't like the school, I'm old enough so that I could walk away from it—and the Hernandez's.*

No one would ever miss me. No one would bother to come looking.

CHAPTER 2

FINDING THE FLEDGLING

"Some sing to drive away the darkness. Others sing to beckon it. I always imagined that I sang at night because I felt at one with it."

– Bron Jones

A message came over the intercom, "Olivia Hernandez, your *son* is here." Olivia glanced up from the computer at her desk, peeved at the administrative secretary. She hadn't wanted anyone to know that she might be hosting a foster child. Now every teacher in the high school would find some reason to visit the office in the next five minutes.

Today was supposed to be a prep day, but Olivia didn't have anything to prepare for. She had her curriculum planned for the fall, had studied the upcoming plays, and she knew all of the returning students and had read the bios of the incoming freshmen. Still, bios sometimes revealed more about prejudices and phobias of teachers and school administrators than they actually did about the students. You had to read between the lines.

That's what she was doing as she studied the case files for Bron Jones. She didn't like what she saw.

Bron had been abandoned at less than a week, and had been given into the care of a young couple. But Child Welfare Services had removed him at the age of two and a half. His foster mother, they'd found, refused to touch him, often put him on a dog leash, and had been keeping him sedated during much of the day in an effort to avoid contact.

Children who suffer touch deprivation at an early age, Olivia knew, tended to withdraw, grow cold, and become prone to sociopathy.

His next foster parents, though, loved him dearly, and had asked to adopt. But the State of Utah, in its wisdom, did not want to encourage a child to bond to foster parents when the biological parents might return to stake a claim. Though his mother had abandoned him, a memo at the time showed that someone in the state hierarchy was worried that a father might still appear—and so Bron had been moved again.

Olivia didn't believe that this had been done maliciously, only that the administrator had made a terribly bad call. Similar policies had been the norm for state adoption agencies throughout the 60's, 70's and 80's. The administrator's memo showed that her attitudes were unfortunate holdouts from an unenlightened age.

Strike two for Bron.

A third family kept him only for a few months before rejecting him, claiming that he was "strange" and "possibly schizophrenic." A battery of tests showed that Bron was only a normal five-year-old who was retreating into a dream world to escape reality.

He stayed with his next family until he was eight, at which time his father apparently committed suicide after a fight with the mother.

The next family had complained of a child who was distant, "spooky." He'd gone through an EMO phase, dressing in black and secretly piercing body parts, before he was eventually sent to the Stillman's, where initial letters referred to him as a "good hard worker" and a "lone wolf."

That combination of descriptions terrified Olivia.

Bron had gone through a string of terrible bad luck when it came to foster care.

Here was a broken child, someone who needed to be fixed.

Olivia took one last look at the distant, poorly focused image of what her husband Mike was calling her "mail-order" son, and then turned off her computer monitor.

She felt ready for school; she just hoped that she was ready for Bron. Mike hadn't even wanted to come meet the boy, but Olivia knew that Bron needed them both. She couldn't turn this one away.

So she hurried down the familiar beige halls, past the tastefully decorated atrium. She halted outside the office door, smoothed her tan skirt, and listened as Allison, the administrative secretary, recited the school's praises. "You're just going to love this school," she told Bron. "You know we won an award for Charter School of the Year, last year? And Olivia is everyone's favorite teacher. All of the students adore her—"

Olivia felt embarrassed by that word, *adore*. Yet it was probably close to the right word. There would be

274 students at the school, and Olivia believed that each one was important. Puberty was perhaps the roughest time that any of them would have in life. They suffered through raging hormones, love affairs, manic episodes, teen pregnancies, drug addiction. Olivia helped kids "grow through" their problems. She believed in them, she loved them, and in return most of them would respect and care for her the rest of their lives.

Olivia spotted Bron standing taller than the social worker, Mr. Bell. Bron instantly made the hair stand up on the back of her neck. Though she'd only seen five other people like her in her entire life, she recognized him as one: he was a masaak.

She felt bewildered. The fuzzy photograph hadn't let her see him well enough. She realized now that his long hair hid the odd boxlike shape of his skull.

He was taller than she'd imagined, or perhaps a thick head of wavy hair made him seem taller than five-eleven. His hair was the same shade as hers, when she didn't bleach it blonde. He was broad-shouldered, with an impressively wide chest. His skin was supernaturally smooth, almost luminous, and he had a strong chin, pronounced brows, and a face that was perfectly symmetrical.

Olivia found her heart pounding. He looked more than human. She was all but certain.

He spotted her through the glass, and Olivia stopped. She held up her left hand, fingers splayed wide, as if to say "Hello!" then counted to three.

Among the masaaks it was called a "display," and was a way of identifying one's species.

Bron just smiled weakly in return, like a naïve human.

Am I wrong? Olivia wondered, doubt twisting her stomach. *Is he one of us, or one of them?*

She strode up to him, feeling unsure how to treat him—as a new student, as a stranger, as a masaak ... or as a son?

She decided that there shouldn't be any difference.

Mr. Bell was muttering pleasantries when Olivia reached out to shake Bron's hand. As she grasped it, she folded her left hand over the top of his, so that she held his hand with both of hers. It was also an old sales trick: by touching a person in a way that was both modest yet familiar, it helped build trust quickly. If this boy had been deprived of touch all of his life, she'd need to break down his walls.

Allison sat behind her desk, staring at Bron through thick glasses, smiling as if at a shared joke. He was handsome, her smile said. If he'd been a puppy, he'd have been a keeper.

Bron finished shaking, and tried to pull away, but Olivia took his hand more firmly.

It was big-boned, and she felt roughness along the ridge of his palms, calluses that could only come from hard labor—digging in a garden or mowing lawns. She touched the inside of his fingertips, pressed into them firmly, and found some harder lumps, ones that were more interesting.

She turned his palms up to get a better look. The thick skin on his fingertips was as hard as pebbles. "You play the guitar?" She studied his calluses, looking for something elusive.

"A little," Bron admitted.

"Not enough," Olivia said. She flipped her own hand up for him to see. Her calluses were heavier, more rigid. He peered at them in surprise. "I teach musical theater," she said, "but I also teach guitar. We're starting classes in it this year."

Bron opened his mouth a fraction in surprise. She suspected that he was beginning to understand just how perfect she might be as his foster mother, but if her guess was right, even he didn't have a clue *how* perfect they might be together.

"I want to thank you for agreeing to meet with Bron," Mr. Bell said. "He's one of my favorite kids, and I know that this could be a great opportunity."

Bron smiled weakly, like a patient preparing for heart surgery. Olivia flashed a reassuring smile.

She needed to be sure of this boy. She reached up and tilted Bron's chin high, appraised him. It was an eccentric thing to do, but she'd had acting teachers study her this same way in college.

Yes, she could see the slightly enlarged brain cavity in the anterior, with the pronounced bulge, creating a "box-like skull." His skin color had an olive cast, with a bronzed look that made his ancestry hard to classify. Mediterranean, one might guess, with a hint of Arab blood? Olivia sometimes saw humans who could pass as masaak, but this boy....

When guaging an actor's look, most directors looked for opportunities to praise their features so that the actor wouldn't feel defensive. She asked the secretary, "What do you think, Allison? He's got nice thick lips. A lot of girls will want to play Juliet to his Romeo. The hair and chin gives him a Greco-Roman look. I can't decide which features I like better."

His nose was a bit hawkish. With his distinctive chin, he looked like he might someday become a banking magnate or a politician. Or a movie star.

"Where do you think your people come from?" Olivia asked.

Bron shrugged. "I've never met my parents."

He tried to sound bored, as if he had no interest.

Olivia knew that masaak mothers sometimes abandoned their children, much as a cuckoo will abandon its eggs in another's nest. It was called brood parasitism. They'd leave their children for humans to raise, hoping that the children would learn to mimic human behavior, pass themselves off as humans. From ancient times, such children had been called "nightingales."

Olivia couldn't imagine a loving mother doing such a thing.

By now, Olivia suspected, *Bron's beginning to sense that he's different from others–stronger, more cunning, more dangerous.*

She asked, "Do you like to act at all?" She was an acting teacher, after all, specializing in musicals. So it was a natural question.

"I've never tried," he said shyly.

Olivia had him. "We all act, Bron," she said. "We're all playing roles, all of the time. Do me a favor. Imagine for a moment that you are a king. How would you stand?" Bron had been hunched over just a bit, trying to hide the fear that he must have felt at making this introduction.

Now he straightened his back, thrust out his chest, raised his chin. He still seemed nervous, but it was an improvement.

"Very good," she said. "Now imagine that you're not just a king by birth, but by nature. You're not a conquering hero—you're a kindly lord, one who seeks to rule with benevolence and wisdom."

Bron dropped his chin by a quarter of an inch, and the sparkle left his eyes. His irises widened just a fraction, and his entire expression softened. He transformed from a reluctant warrior to ... something else, a wise and noble man, with just a hint of mirth.

The change was so complete that Olivia was taken aback. "Well," she smiled. "You *do* know how to take direction!" From a director, that was a huge compliment.

She had known of course that children who came from troubled backgrounds often had to learn to act. They learned to lie, to conceal their emotions. For them it wasn't just play, it was a survival skill. Bron had suffered more than a child should.

She felt more entangled by the minute. Bron wasn't just an abandoned and abused child, he was one of her own kind. Every mothering instinct in her was screaming. She wanted to pull him in, to gather him, *as a hen gathereth her chicks,* she quoted.

She continued peering into his eyes. "Now, Bron, you look like a king. You look as if you were born to rule here in this school. So here's a trick I want you to learn, for your own benefit: when you come to school on Monday, none of the students will know who or what you are. This is your chance to start over, to make an impression. So I want you to try something: I want you to hold the stance that you have now. I want you to act as if you were the king here, the rightful ruler, and I want you to carry yourself that way for the first three days. Stay in character!"

Bron dropped his chin a little, raised an eyebrow. "You want me to act like I'm the king of the school?"

"Something like that. You won't believe how much it will help. Long ago, there was once a playwright in Spain who worked as a political advisor. The king was a corrupt and wicked old man. So one day a merchant came to the playwright and asked for ideas on how to make himself look as if he were the rightful king—not because he wanted to *be* king, but because he loved his country. The playwright told the merchant, 'If you want to be a king, first act the part of the king. In time, the people will see you as such and grant your desire.' So the merchant acted the part, and eventually overthrew the king. The merchant's rule was long and prosperous."

"What if I don't want to be a king?" Bron asked.

"Well," Olivia said. "I suppose you could be the class jester, if you like, or you could play the part of a glum loser who doesn't have a future, or perhaps the dreamer—but if you do, you'll just be part of the crowd."

Bron looked thoughtful, bit his lip.

There was something worrisome about nightingales, Olivia remembered. She'd talked with her mother about them when she was very young. "None of the Aels would abandon a child like that," her mother had said, holding Olivia on her knee. "If you see a nightingale, you can be sure that it was left by a Draghoul."

Olivia tried to still her breathing. Was Bron a Draghoul, one of the Aels' ancient enemies? Could this be a trap?

She didn't doubt that he was born of the Draghoul, but being born to an enemy does not make one an enemy. Nor did she believe that this was likely a trap. Bron didn't have the superior smirk of a Draghoul, the dangerous swagger, the hungry gleam in his eye. He was all innocence and nerves.

He's just a nightingale, she thought. *It's an accident that brought him to me, a fortunate accident.*

She'd learned later in life that even the Aels sometimes had abandoned their children. In the old days, when they were burned as witches, the Aels had often hidden their young among humans, as a way to protect them.

As she had expected, a couple of teachers had found excuses to wander to the principal's office. As they came in behind, she was forced to crowd.

"Let's go down to my room," she suggested to Bron and Mr. Bell, thinking furiously. "I'll give you a tour."

She brushed past the other teachers without making introductions. There wasn't much to see on their school tour at this time of the year, just empty classrooms. Olivia pointed out the bulletin board where auditions for various clubs would be listed, while other boards would be filled with art projects. There were a lot of posters for plays, rooms for dance rehearsals, and the school featured four separate theaters.

At the center was the school's atrium. Its high windows let light shine in as if through crystal, accenting the southwestern art that graced the walls. It

looked tasteful, and expensive. They strolled downstairs to Olivia's office, just off the stage area of the
Hafen Theater. As they walked, Mr. Bell offered comforting assurances about Bron, as if to close the sale.

When they reached Olivia's office, she went to her
computer. With a click of the mouse she opened a
file. It showed a picture of a sculpture that Bron had
made in white clay, a "self-portrait."

"You sculpted this?" she asked.

Bron nodded. He'd obviously spent weeks on the
piece. It showed a human face from the front, flawless and serene: Bron, as he would have appeared at
fifteen, eyes closed, lips pursed.

"You look like a Greek god in that sculpture," Olivia said. "You perfected your features." He'd also made
himself look more human, creating a smoother skull.

"Thanks," Bron said. "So Mr. Bell sent you that
one?"

She nodded. "What do you call the piece?"

"It was called 'Becoming.'"

She grinned at the double-entendre. His face in
the sculpture was indeed 'becoming.' She scrolled her
pictures to a side image of the bust. In it, one could
see that Bron's head had something grotesque coming out the back, an oily alien with long tentacles that
had appeared to be hair from the front. She scrolled
to the complete back, and one could see another
face—that of a strange squid-like creature, cruel and
malicious.

"Is this how you see yourself?" she asked.

"Sometimes," Bron admitted.

Mr. Bell shifted on his feet, looking as if he was
afraid that Olivia would send Bron packing.

Olivia sighed. No, she definitely couldn't turn this one away. Not with his tremendous potential. Not when she didn't even know what gifts he had yet.

She did know one thing: Draghouls were not like other brood parasites. They didn't abandon their offspring. They only loaned them out, letting humans do the hard work of raising them. In time the Draghouls would come to claim Bron, and if Olivia took him, the state's paperwork trail would lead them straight to her.

She tried to snap back into teacher mode, and asked Bron, "I noticed that you used the word 'was,' when you described your sculpture. Did you sell the piece, or give it away?"

Bron shook his head regretfully. "It got busted at my old school. Some kid busted it."

"But you have other pieces?"

Bron shook his head. "They always got busted. I quit sculpting."

"Jealousy," Olivia explained. "It happens often at other schools. You won't find it at Tuacahn. All of the students are creative, and they'll respect your paintings and sculptures."

Do I dare take him? she wondered. *Do I dare risk it?*

Her people had been in hiding from their enemies for more than a thousand years. If a tenth of the stories that she'd heard were true, the Draghouls were unimaginably evil.

I could get myself killed, she thought, *but only if I'm lucky. The Draghouls can do things that are far worse than just killing you.*

I should let him go. I should let them have him.

She swallowed hard, made her decision.

She glanced at the social worker. "I like Bron's honesty. An artist needs that. I like his talent, too.... I want to adopt. I don't want anyone else to have him."

Mr. Bell smiled. "I'd love for you to adopt, but it will take time: your husband needs to meet Bron. There will be a hearing before a judge, a mandatory waiting period...."

"I understand," Olivia said. "E-mail the forms. Mike and I will fill them out...."

Yet every instinct in her warned: this could be the biggest mistake you'll ever make.

CHAPTER 3

MOTHER AND CHILD

"Love can be nurtured, but it must never be forced. To try to force it is to destroy its very foundation."
                                    – Olivia Hernandez

Mr. Bell had Olivia sign some papers which gave her temporary parental rights.

Bron noticed that she was left-handed, just like him.

"There will be a lot to do," Mr. Bell offered as the three of them began walking toward the front door of the school. She'd want to get Bron on her insurance, set up ground rules for him so that he'd know what was expected. Mr. Bell assured Olivia that it was always difficult for kids to adjust to a new school, new family. He promised counseling services to help them through this "initial phase."

Bron figured that Olivia was going to need some counseling. He'd met women like this before, women so desperate for a child that they'd latch onto the first one they could.

Where the hell is her husband? Bron wondered. *Doesn't he even want to see me?*

The fact that Olivia had gone kid-shopping without Mike told Bron that his new foster parents weren't in this together. They might fight if Olivia took him home. At the very least, Mike would spend time pouting. Yeah, Olivia needed counseling.

Yet Bron didn't dare object. The school, he decided, was pretty cool. Olivia seemed generous, and Bron wouldn't have to slave to take care of other people's children.

If he had to spend the next two years someplace, this might be a good one. He didn't want to mess up this chance.

He could put up with a cold foster father, or with a woman who was dumb enough to think that in two years she could become a real mother to him.

Mr. Bell assured Olivia, "You're going to like Bron. I think that he's going to be perfect for your little family. You know, a lot of times, I do my best to match people up, and it just doesn't work. But sometimes this is a great job. Sometimes I find a kid and a family, and they fit perfectly."

Once the three passed out the door, the scenery smote Bron again. Tuacahn High School was situated on the edge of a state park. Overhead on either side of the school were gorgeous rock walls that rose fifteen hundred feet almost straight up, in columns of hoodoos that, in the angled light, seemed like giant sculptures of ancient kings, their faces eroded by wind and rain. The rock walls formed a canyon that wound back behind the school in a V for more than a mile. Lush green trees and brush lined the rocky creek bed, until gradually the creek climbed up into the hills.

The lawns on campus were vibrant green, and next to the high school was a professional theater, the Tuacahn Center for the Performing Arts. The architecture had been fused into something of a modern Aztec flavor, made of stone colored to match the reds and tans of the native sandstone in the region. Much of the area between the schools was left open to the air, but soon gave way to a covered area for picnic tables, snack booths, and some shops that sold knickknacks to tourists.

Along the walls of the buildings, huge posters announced the summer season's plays at the theater: "Tarzan," "Cats," and "Crazy for You."

As the grounds transformed gracefully from the school building to the courtyard and theater, it seemed as if the school and Broadway were somehow physically connected. Though it was early afternoon and the next play wouldn't be starting for hours, a snack shop was open. He could smell fresh popcorn.

Bron stood just peering around. Something was missing.

Mr. Bell asked, "What are you looking for?"

"Litter," Bron said. "There's no litter anywhere. It's not like some of my old schools."

"Hey," Olivia teased, "we can sprinkle some around, if you feel homesick."

He smiled, and they walked to Mr. Bell's car. Bron pulled out his guitar, and then flushed with embarrassment as he withdrew his battered Army-green backpack and the t-shirt stuffed full of clothes, like the torso of a scarecrow.

Olivia glanced at the t-shirt. "Looks like you could use some better luggage."

Bron smiled sheepishly.

She thought, then asked, "Is there anything in here that you really feel ... emotionally attached to?"

Bron shook his head no.

"Do me a favor then," she said. "Toss this in the garbage. We'll do some shopping before we go home."

Bron hesitated. Some foster parents would come on strong at first, be so happy to have him. But it didn't last. He wanted new clothes, but he didn't want to risk throwing his old ones away and then not having anything at all.

"Go on," Olivia said. "Scoot."

Bron nervously wrestled the lid off the nearest trashcan. Stuffing in the t-shirt was like trying to dispose of a body. Bron manhandled it in, and Olivia threw the pack on top, then replaced the lid.

As he prepared to leave, Mr. Bell gave his standard warning to Olivia, "I'm sure that Bron will work out wonderfully, but if you have any problems, give me a call. You've got my card. Call anytime, day or night. If you are ever faced with a situation that you don't know how to handle, let me handle it with you."

Mr. Bell shook hands firmly, and stared Olivia in the eye, as if he were sure that trouble would come.

They waved goodbye as Mr. Bell drove off. Bron watched him go with a mounting sense of loss. As Mr. Bell's car receded into the distance, Bron felt more and more ... abandoned, resigned to his fate.

Olivia took Bron back into the school. As they got online, she said, "It's a shame that we didn't get you registered a couple of months ago. I'm afraid you won't have much choice of classes, but I'll see if I can call in a few favors."

Students at Tuacahn got to choose areas of specialty—such as visual arts, dance, or musical theater. Depending upon the specialty, the student was put into an "academy" with a tailored track for graduation, one that prepared the student for training or employment in his or her specialty.

Bron hesitated for a long time, trying to choose his academy—visual art or music. He settled on music.

Olivia smiled. "You can try them all, you know. We encourage students to experiment. In fact, you might want to enroll in an acting class this fall, or theater tech. We have drama rehearsals each night after school, so I'm often here until midnight. You'll have your own car to drive, of course, but you'll be free to drive home with me after rehearsals, if you like."

That perked Bron up. He had his driver's license, but hadn't driven much since his driver's education class. "I'll have a car?" She nodded. "What kind?" He imagined an old car moldering in her garage.

"We'll have to go to a dealer and pick one out."

That was extravagant for any foster parent, and even more so in these tough times, what with the recession. Between clothes, school supplies, and a car, this was going to put a monumental dent in the Hernandez's savings.

"Are you sure?" Bron asked. "Don't you need to talk to your husband about it?"

Olivia smiled. "Well, there are some costs that you can't really get around. Raising a son is expensive. Mike knows that. It's sort of like getting a hamster. Even if you get the hamster for free, you still have to buy food for it, and a cage. Even a free hamster is expensive."

Bron wasn't sure how he felt about being compared to a hamster, but he got the point.

Olivia smiled eagerly. "Let's get started."

She took him back into the office to see the secretary, Allison, and said, "We're going to need school shirts for Bron."

Allison led him into a storage room, where the uniforms were laid out—shirts in seven colors, with Tuacahn's logo on the chest, a golden sunrise casting rays of light toward heaven as it climbed over a mountain.

"So," Bron asked, "all of the creative people in this school dress exactly the same?"

"We want you to worry about your art," Allison groused, "not what kind of rags to wear." He'd struck a nerve.

"If we're all dressed the same," Bron asked nervously, "how are the rich kids going to know who's best?"

"Talent," Olivia replied. "Here at Tuacahn, the guy with the most talent is the biggest stud."

"Let's try a large." Allison tossed Bron a shirt. He turned away, stripped off his shirt, and caught a glimpse of Allison grinning at his washboard abs, shooting a look toward Olivia, and mouthing the word, "Nice!"

"Are you into sports?" Olivia asked.

"I did a little wrestling last year," Bron said. "Mostly I just like to run."

"That's the one problem with Tuacahn," Olivia said, "we're too small to support sports programs."

They took Bron's shirts and dropped them in Olivia's car trunk. It was still early afternoon, and it was in the low-hundreds. Olivia gave Bron the nickel tour of the grounds—showing him the green theater beside the school, the tables out under the pavilions where he'd eat lunch, the outdoor lockers used only by freshmen. Older students like Bron would have to carry their books in backpacks. Olivia led him under some awnings. Light rock music was playing. A couple of the little shops were selling souvenirs for plays, along with wall decorations, statuary, and exotic treats.

"This is the professional side of the complex," Olivia explained as she led him to the outdoor amphitheater where plays and concerts were held.

In the background above the stage loomed a massive wall of red rock. The ceiling was an azure sky filled with glorious sunlight, and Bron imagined it lit by smoldering stars at night. As he walked toward the open-air seats, he felt humbled.

Olivia explained, "There's something showing almost every night, mostly plays, but sometimes music concerts. Next week we have Styx playing."

"Will J.Y. Young be there?" Bron asked.

"You've listened to his music?"

"A little. He plays on a Stratocaster, with a special pre-amp."

"Do you know what it's called?" Olivia asked.

Teachers like to test you, Bron knew. They liked it even better when you knew the answers. "It's called a Yoshironator. It was hand-made for that guitar, and it's the only one in the world."

"Wow," Olivia said. "You do know your guitarists. Who's your favorite?"

"Living or dead?"

"Let's stick with the living."

"Joe Satriani."

"He's pretty avant-garde."

"He pushes the instrument," Bron said. "I like that. A lot of people can handle a classical style, but I like to hear artists do new things."

Olivia smiled. "I met Joe once, years ago. I even gave him a couple of lessons, down in L.A."

"No way!" Bron said.

"I make it a point to meet guitar players, listen to them seriously. I'll tell you what. I'll get an extra ticket for you for the Styx concert. Heck, you can probably have Mike's. He usually falls asleep at rock concerts anyway."

Bron didn't trust his luck, but since Olivia was in a giving mood, he kept quiet. Olivia waved down at the amphitheater.

"Tuacahn keeps three theatrical performances running each season. The stars of the shows are hired out of New York or London, but if our high-school actors are good enough, some get parts. Every year, we have several students who go straight to Broadway. Talent scouts come and look them over. Disney makes a trip out each year looking for talent, too. That's how we got the contract to have the first performance of the new 'Tarzan' musical. Disney thought that our outdoor theater, with its unique backdrop, made it the most perfect place in the world for an opening."

With that, Olivia led Bron back to her white Honda CRV. As he was about to get in, she tossed him the keys. "You drive?"

"Me?" he asked. "Now?"

"It's a good way to learn the roads. Besides, I'm going to need to see how much I trust you with a car."

Bron got in nervously, adjusted the seat and mirrors, turned the key, and headed out of the theater complex. The road led down past a gate into a desert. Nothing grew here but mesquite bushes and a few Joshua trees. The road was empty, lazy.

"That sculpture you made," Olivia said as he drove, "'Becoming.' Are you afraid of what you're becoming, Bron? Do you feel torn between being a god or a monster?"

"I wouldn't quite put it that way," Bron said. It sounded so pretentious, talking about monsters and gods. "Every decent person ought to be worried about what he is becoming."

"You know," she said, "I'm not worried about you becoming a monster. I think ... we should let our passion shape our lives. We decide that we want to do something grand, and then shape our lives with our will and wit."

Nice sentiment, he thought. *Let's see if it lasts.* New parents often went through a "sweet phase," where they'd ask about his favorite foods and television shows. If he was lucky, they might buy him something.

It had been too many years since he'd been in the sweet phase, though. Melvina had never had one. She'd announced when they first met, "You'll eat what's put in front of you and wear what you're told."

Bron had admired her refreshing honesty. He'd learned long ago that you can never trust the sweet phase. All that niceness, that pandering, would fade in a week.

Pretty soon, he thought, *Olivia will figure out that she can't make me love her.*

Yet he'd missed having anyone care for him. Melvina hadn't spent any money on him in years; getting a few new clothes would be welcome. Bron didn't expect Olivia to deliver on everything she promised.

She'd take him home, talk with Mike, and he'd say something like, "Why spend all of that money on some kid that we might end up shipping off next week?" The promises would blow away like dying cinders riding the night's wind.

If Bron had been a different kind of person, he would have made sure to get as much as he could from Olivia, as fast as possible. But he didn't need much to get by. So he'd let them give what they wanted, and they could take it back to the stores later, if they felt like it.

"Bron ..." Olivia began in a tone that was both confidential and serious.

Ahead, a cottontail bunny raced onto the road. "Slow down," Olivia said. "We have a rule in our house. You kill something, you get to eat it."

Bron tapped the brakes. The rabbit peered at the car, dashed for cover. It was cute, and reminded him of something....

When he was a child, he'd lived with a family who seemed all warm and caring at first. The Golpers. They'd smothered him with affection. But then one Christmas Eve they'd been on the way to the store to buy a turkey and some pumpkin pies, and some old gray-haired women had been sitting out in front with a box of kittens. One kitten had been striking—with long smoky-gray hair and white paws. Mrs. Golper fell in love with it instantly, and got it "for Bron."

He'd loved that kitten, had slept with it every night, but after a week, it still hadn't managed to get trained to go in its litter box. So on New Year's morning, Mr. Golper had taken Bron to "get rid" of the kitten. He'd tied it into a burlap bag and carried it to a bridge that overlooked the Provo River. Then he'd told Bron to throw it in.

The kitten meowed plaintively in its bag, and the gray swirling waters roared and thundered over the rocks. Snow and ice crept down to the bottom of the gorge, and Bron's timid breaths came out in little wisps of fog.

"No one wants a kitten like this," Mr. Golper explained, scratching his balding head, "one that's too stupid to poop in the right place. So we have to get rid of it. We can't just pawn our problems off on someone else. Since it's your kitten, it's your job to do it."

Bron had cried and refused to throw his kitten off the bridge, promising to work harder to teach it, and Mr. Golper had spanked him and told him to "cowboy up." After twenty minutes of beatings, when Bron refused again and again, Mr. Golper had finally let out a string of profanity and tossed the bag into the river.

The kitten's meowing was frantic for a few aching seconds, and then the floating bag had tumbled over a rock and gotten swallowed by the dark flow.

Bron had stood in disbelief, watching the kitten disappear, and he seemed to have an epiphany.

I'll be smart, he told himself. *I'll study harder than anyone in school, so that no one throws me away.*

So he'd learned to read that year, better than anyone in kindergarten, and he came up with the coolest art projects, and began to learn how to add and subtract.

It didn't matter. The Golpers, so loving when they took him in, junked him at the end of the school year.

Now Olivia was buying him a new wardrobe.

Bron smiled weakly and told himself, *Enjoy it while it lasts. She'll junk you soon enough.*

CHAPTER 4

DISCOVERED

"The day comes when each of us must gaze into the face of evil. I only pray that I do not see it when I am looking into a mirror."

– Olivia Hernandez

How do you tell someone that they're not human? Olivia wondered.

There was no easy way to reveal that kind of information. Ancient laws among the Ael governed *what* she could tell him and *how* she could tell.

She let Bron drive through Ivins, passing picturesque housing developments where rock walls encircled sandstone-colored homes with tile roofs. The landscaping was often natural–with cactuses, Joshua trees, palms, and desert bushes that featured tiny leaves and huge yellow blossoms. While each development conserved water by avoiding lawns, they all had ponds with waterfalls and streams and water springing up out of the ground, as if to demonstrate their wealth by how much water they could waste.

At Highway 89, they turned south into Saint George. Olivia seldom traveled into town. It was too dangerous. Two million tourists passed through each year, off to see the wonders at Zion Canyon, or Bryce, or Moab. Some of them would be masaak. Most of those masaak would be Draghouls.

She directed Bron to an outlet store where he selected a backpack that happened to have a little pocket for his iPod.

Olivia asked, "What kind of iPod do you have?" Most kids at Tuacahn had a shuffle at least.

He shrugged as if it didn't matter.

Olivia studied him. He didn't have one. The Stillmans had been so damned cheap. She brushed back a few strands of blonde hair. "You'll need a Touch if you're going to be cool, along with a cell phone, and a laptop."

She hadn't considered all of the accouterments that a teenager required. This was going to cost. Her bank account wasn't bottomless. Three years ago she'd had nearly fifty thousand in savings. The recession had eaten through all but ten of it.

Olivia set her teeth, remembering something another masaak had taught her, an old man called "The Preacher." He'd said, "In order to give something away, one must first possess it. The virtue of largesse becomes strained in poverty."

A lot of virtues become strained when one is in want, Olivia thought.

Because of his battered clothing, Bron had probably never been considered "cool." He had been an orphan, a wanderer, rejected by those who were supposed to love him, damaged by the system that was supposed to protect him and provide for his needs.

Damn it, Olivia thought. *Every kid deserves better than that.*

She studied his face, hope warring with skepticism. Yeah, here was a kid who was used to getting nothing. "Okay, we'll go to the electronics store, but clothes come first."

The dress code at school didn't allow for much of a selection, but Olivia bought him some underwear, and then looked for a couple of outfits for the weekends.

As they shopped, Bron couldn't help but notice several women, their faces completely plain and free of makeup, their hair all braided and tucked back in an identical style. They wore modest dresses in solid shades of blue or green.

"It's not polite to stare," Olivia said. "Those are polygamists. You'll see a lot of them here in Saint George. They live in little towns nearby—Colorado City, Orderville, and such. They come to shop or go to the doctors."

"Are there any at our school?"

"They have their own schools," Olivia said. "They keep to themselves."

Bron picked out an outfit to wear home, some new running shoes, a shirt.

"Of all the pants you can wear at school," Olivia said, "the Dickies are the most expensive." She grabbed him five pair. "You are now officially as cool as your clothes can make you. But there's more to your appearance than clothes. For example, we could do something about your hair...."

"My hair?"

"Yeah," she squinted, trying to envision him with a new look. His hair was dark brown, almost black—an odd color among humans. But among the masaak—

both the Ael and the Draghouls—it was the norm. Olivia lightened her own hair every two weeks, in an effort to camouflage herself. He'd need to do it, too. "You game?"

"I don't know," he said. He looked miserable.

"Tell you what, we'll ask the stylist to make you look as hot as Zak Efron. If you don't like it, you can change it back."

He nodded, but hung his head as if he was about to get whipped.

So the next stop was a styling salon where she had his hair cut, bleached to a pale blonde, and then streaked with black. When she finished, she talked Bron into getting his left ear pierced, and let him pick out an earring—a $90 black quartz stud—to complete the disguise.

He looked like a rock star. She gave him a fist bump. Between clothes, accessories and hair, she was up to $800 for the day so far. That didn't seem too bad.

Saint George was small enough that it didn't have a huge selection of electronics stores. Best Buy was going to have to do. She had him drive.

As he did, she asked, "So have you given any thought to which clubs you'll join?" He shot her a vacant stare. "You asked how people will know whether you're hot at school? The answer is, by the clubs you join. You don't have to audition to get into Tuacahn, but you do for most of the *clubs*. So if you want to sing, you audition for the Madrigals. If you want to play guitar, you join the Small Band Club. The most talented students make it into three or more clubs. Auditions start Tuesday."

She left the rest unsaid. Bron peered forward with a certain dread. Olivia knew that it wasn't just that this was a strange school, it was a *strange* school. Everyone in it was some kind of band nerd or theater geek. It put a lot of pressure on new kids, but the pressure drove them to excel.

"You nervous?" Olivia asked.

Bron nodded.

"Don't worry. There's a lot of competition, but most kids have more hope than skill, more delusions of grandeur than real talent. You'll do well."

"What makes you think so?" he asked.

She smiled secretively. "I can spot talent."

Bron gritted his teeth. "When you say that they have 'more delusions than talent,' I'm worried that it sounds like me."

"Everyone worries a little," Olivia said, trying to ease his tensions. "If you just want to have fun, some clubs are easy to get into. For example, everyone joins the Star Wars club."

"I don't know much about Star Wars," Bron admitted. "I think Spock is cool."

Olivia smiled. "It's not so much a 'Star Wars' club as a movie-appreciation club. They watch films and critique the acting, directing, and writing. Mostly they eat a lot of snacks and have fun."

Bron nodded. "Sounds easy."

Olivia had Bron take the freeway to Washington, past the signs that invited them to see the dinosaur tracks at Johnson Farm. Bron grew excited about the prospect of seeing real dinosaur tracks, but Olivia wanted to make this a quick stop.

At Best Buy she picked up an iPad Touch and a 3G cell phone for just under $400 dollars. The computer took a little more time.

She imagined that Bron would want to compose on his computer, and her favorite program for that was Finale. Apple had a similar program, Garage Band, but it wasn't as robust, and it cost more.

Still, most kids considered the Apple to be cooler. But was it worth $500 to have an apple glowing on the back of his screen?

She glanced to her left out of long habit and spotted an elderly man staring at her. With him were four teenagers—three boys and a girl. All five were masaak.

The Ael would never travel in a pack like that, Olivia knew. They had to be Draghouls.

Instantly Olivia's heart began to pound and her throat went dry. In all her life, she'd only seen five other masaaks, and the Draghouls had never spotted her. Now, here was a pack of her ancient enemies.

Had she been alone, she might have escaped their notice. But one teen was pointing to Bron, whispering in the ear of the elderly man.

He was the pack leader, Olivia knew. The teens had to be acolytes, training in his dark ways.

Immediately the Draghouls strode toward them. The old man's eyes fixed on Olivia, the eyes of a hunter that has spotted prey. His face was determined. He walked with a rolling gait, like a trained martial artist.

Olivia turned to Bron and said softly, "Some people are coming to talk to us. No matter what, don't you dare speak to them! Remember, you're a king, a cruel and sadistic king."

She glanced in his eyes, tried to make sure that he understood her warning, and squeezed his right bicep.

He gave her a questioning look, then a smile spread across his lips, and he raised his chin proudly. Olivia turned to meet the Draghouls.

The leader halted ten feet away, raised his left hand, and made his display. A suction cup suddenly showed briefly at the tip of each finger.

If Bron noticed, he did not gasp, as Olivia expected that he would. From that she surmised that he had been looking at the people's faces, perhaps distracted by the girl, who was quite attractive, with long dark hair tinted purple.

Olivia raised her chin, mirrored the expression of the killer before her, and flashed her sizraels.

I'm their master, she told herself, *and these people are beneath me.* She hoped that they believed the act. Her life depended upon it.

One teenage boy, a little younger than Bron, spoke. He had blond streaks in his hair and wore a stylish shirt and gold chains. "Bron?" the boy asked. "Bron Jones? Is that you?"

Olivia shot the boy a contemptuous gaze. "You are mistaken, acolyte." She glanced at the old man and warned, "Keep your charge in line. Acolytes should not speak unless spoken to."

Their leader looked back and forth between Olivia and Bron, clearly worried. Olivia hoped that the Draghouls would believe her act. Their leader was trained to attack a feral masaak on sight, but Bron ... confused him, possibly even unnerved him.

"Who *are* you?" their leader demanded.

"That's Bron Jones," the acolyte affirmed. "We were in a group home together, up near Nephi."

So, Olivia realized, the boy had also been a nightingale.

Their leader looked to Bron for confirmation. Olivia gave Bron a warning glance. With his hair freshly cut and dyed, wearing his new outfit, she almost didn't recognize him from earlier in the day. She hoped that even the Draghoul boy might feel unsure.

Bron glared at the boy. "You are mistaken," he said, deepening his voice. "If we had met, I would remember."

Their leader's face paled, and he licked his lips. Bron's manner unnerved him. He turned to Olivia. "And who are you?" he demanded again.

Olivia wasn't sure of Draghoul etiquette. They were a military organization. Did they share names, ranks? She feared that she knew too little to fake it.

Their leader recognized her as a *feral*, someone who had not been spawned by their vaunted breeding program. Yet even feral masaaks could be of great value to the Draghouls, if they converted. She had to convince him that she was a convert, or at least a poppet—an Ael whose memories had been hollowed out and replaced with Draghoul propaganda.

She saw uncertainty in the stranger's countenance. Bron had the strong shoulders of a Draghoul lord, the jutting chin, the perfect symmetry to his face. He was too beautiful to be a feral.

"When the serpent roars," Olivia said on a hunch, "do not the foxes scatter?" She had all but announced that Bron was of royal lineage, comparing him to a dragon, the ancient symbol for their shadow lord.

The elderly leader recoiled as if he had been slapped. He bowed. "Forgive me, my...." He waited for Bron to insert a title.

The teens shied back en masse, as if Bron might lash out.

Now Olivia dismissed them. She glanced down at the Toshiba. "So this one does not please you, my lord?" she asked Bron.

"No," he said imperiously, "it does not please me."

The Draghouls immediately sped for an exit, and Olivia stood, heart pounding in her throat, and fought the urge to grab onto Bron for support.

When the pack was out the door, Bron whispered savagely, "Who the hell were those people?"

Olivia turned to Bron, peered into his face. "You knew one of the boys? He was in foster care, too?"

"Yes," Bron said. "His name is Riley O'Hare—only...."

"What?"

"He looked different from when I knew him," Bron said. "It's like ... he joined the Nazis or something."

"What do you mean?" she demanded. She was shaking, in shock, and she could feel her face drain of blood. He shook his head, as if he couldn't explain. "What did you see when you looked into his eyes?"

"It was like a different person staring out at me," Bron said. "It was like rage, and hunger and ... madness all rolled into one."

Olivia nodded.

"But he wasn't that way as a child?"

"Hell, no!"

He'd seen the face of a Draghoul, she realized. "Nazis," she chuckled. "You don't know how close you are to being right." Except that a Nazi would have been so much easier to handle.

Olivia's head was spinning. Bron was a Draghoul by birth, she had suspected, and she rightfully feared that the Draghouls would come to collect their nightingale. From the ages of the teens she had just seen, she expected that a visit was overdue. Riley had obviously been collected.

Had they come searching for Bron?

She couldn't imagine how they'd know where to look. Besides, there had been surprise in the enemys' faces. No, it was all just a coincidence.

Something that her mother used to say came to mind. *If you play games of chance, chance will betray you in the end.* That's what had happened. Each time she'd ever gone to the city, it was a game of chance, and now it had caught up with her.

Yet even if she'd bumped into the Draghouls by coincidence, she worried that this sighting would get reported, and the Draghouls' attention would be drawn to this area.

She found herself struggling for breath, as if a garrote was tightening around her throat.

"Are they some kind of cult?" Bron asked. "Are they polygamists?"

Olivia considered the mating habits of Draghoul males. She couldn't explain the truth—not here, not now, so she said, "A cult? Yes—something like that."

CHAPTER 5

GUNFIRE

"I discovered too early in life that the only thrill greater than that of the hunt, comes from being the hunted."

– Bron Jones

Blair Kardashian shook with excitement as he punched the numbers into his cell phone. It had only been a few minutes since his encounter in Best Buy, and he had to report a sighting of two masaaks. Humans outnumbered the masaaks by well over 200,000 to one. To spot a masaak every five years was not uncommon. To spot two in a day was nearly unprecedented. It had been a good forty years since he'd last collected two masaaks at once.

In the back seat, Riley said, "I've got a bad feeling about this. That really looks like Bron. Maybe he's been captured. Maybe he's possessed."

Blair glanced at Riley, then pressed the Send button, and sat staring at the door of the Best Buy, in case the masaaks tried to escape.

I nside the store, Olivia pulled a Kleenex from her purse and wiped her fingerprints from the Toshiba, rubbing frantically.

Bron stared in surprise. "What are you doing?"

She handed him the items they had already picked out—the cell phone and iPod. "Go put those back. We can't buy anything here today."

Bron thought he knew why, but he couldn't believe that she would be *that* afraid. "Why not?"

"We don't want to leave an electronic signature leading them back to our house," she said. She pleaded. "You don't know who those people are.... Bron, they'll be waiting for us outside. They're probably already contacting their superiors...."

Bron felt stunned. "I don't get it. What's going on?"

Olivia shook her head roughly. "There's no time to explain. Just come with me!" She grabbed the two items, dusted off her fingerprints from the packaging, and tossed them behind a computer. She took Bron's hand and pulled him toward the door, racing as fast as she could.

Bron wasn't sure if he should follow. He's never been around anyone more paranoid than Melvina Stillman, but he thought, *Man this chick is out there!*

Olivia hit the front door at a near run, and they exited into the stabbing daylight....

T he phone beeped three times before Blair's contact picked up. For security reasons, Blair didn't know the man's name. The contact asked, "Blair?"

At that instant, the two masaaks hurried from the store. Blair prodded a young acolyte, who raised his own cell phone and began snapping pictures.

"We may have a situation," Blair reported. "I've spotted two masaaks in an electronics shop in Saint George, Utah. One is an adult female—of feral heritage. The other is obviously of superior breeding, a young man."

Every instinct told Blair that he should accost these two, capture them before they had a chance to escape, but he dared not attack, lest the young man be a Draghoul lord. Blair couldn't even stop them as they hopped into a Honda CRV.

The contact pondered for a long moment. Blair almost worried that he'd left the phone, but Blair could hear steady breathing and fingers clacking on a computer's keyboard...

B ron slid into his seat.

"Fasten your seatbelt," Olivia warned as she turned the key. Bron was still buckling in when she urged, "Open the glove compartment. Hand me the gun."

"What?" he yelped.

"Give me the gun—" Olivia urged. "And the spare clip!"

Bron hit the latch. The glove compartment dropped open. Sure enough, he found a pistol there, on top of two paper bags. He took it carefully, afraid it might discharge. He'd never touched a handgun before. "Is this thing loaded?"

"It wouldn't be any use if it wasn't," Olivia said. Her face was pale, drawn into a frown. She grabbed the gun and set it in her lap. Her hands shook. "Get me the spare clip."

"What are you doing with a gun?"

"Mike bought it for me, to shoot at coyotes or intruders."

Bron pawed around in the glove compartment, but didn't see a spare clip.

"It's not here," he said. His heart pounded. He'd thought that Olivia was such a nice woman, and now he wondered if she was even sane.

"Damn," she whispered, "I wish that Mike would put things back where they belong!" Olivia threw the car into gear and backed out of her parking stall. She shoved the car into drive, hit the gas, and went speeding toward the exit onto the street.

B lair was waiting on the phone as his quarry left their parking stall. Over the phone, he could still hear keys clacking.

He didn't dare just let the masaaks wander off, so he put his own car into gear and followed discreetly. The quarry turned onto the main boulevard before his master finally said, "I don't believe that we have any operatives in that area. You think that a feral has what ... co-opted one of our own?"

Blair's heart thrilled as adrenaline flooded his system. This was going to turn into a hunt!

"Yes—a young man, just a little older than a songbird."

Blair's superior breathed heavily as he considered. After a moment he said, "You're training your apprentices as hunters, are you not? Let the hunt begin."

"Let me verify: we have authorization to apprehend these two?"

"Absolutely. Do so immediately."

"And once we have them? What would you have done?"

The voice on the other end went cold. "I'll have the Dread Knights take it from there."

Olivia gripped the steering wheel. Her knuckles went white as she slid down West State, until she hit the red light at Telegraph Road. To the right was the underpass and ramp to the freeway. To the left were the guts of the city.

She took a heavy breath, as if she might hyperventilate.

"You aren't going to shoot anyone, are you?" Bron asked.

"Not if I don't have to," Olivia said.

"There's no reason for that!" Bron said, heart hammering.

Olivia glanced into the rearview mirror. "They're coming for us."

Bron glanced back. A black Mercedes Benz S600 sedan with tinted windows had pulled up behind them. Bron once had a friend who was a car geek, and Bron had learned a lot more than he wanted to know about such vehicles.

In the Mercedes, the elderly man was just pocketing his cell phone. Bron could see determination in his cold eyes.

Olivia stopped at a red light, and behind them the Mercedes lurched to a halt. Instantly, all four teens lunged out their doors, rushing toward Olivia's car.

One young man grabbed Bron's door handle and pulled, but the doors were locked. "Get out!" he shouted. Bron looked up at Riley O'Hare, face twisted in rage.

Bron heard a click, and suddenly Olivia's gun was near his face, aimed at Riley's chest.

"No!" Bron shouted, pushing Olivia's hand. The gun discharged. The sound was deafening. The window shattered. Bron saw that Olivia had missed. The bullet had gone wide and to the left.

Olivia punched the gas just as Riley reached through the window, fumbling with the door lock. He grabbed onto the door post and just clung to it.

A truck honked and swerved as Olivia raced through the red light. Riley was still grasping onto the latch. He clung and cursed as the Honda dragged him.

Riley shouted in a foreign language, perhaps Russian, and Olivia sped up as she raced a couple hundred yards, hitting the next red light just before the freeway entrance.

Cars were coming from the opposite direction. She slammed the brakes, and Riley was thrown forward, onto the pavement, where he lay groggily. He had blood on his face.

Bron suddenly remembered when they were kids at the group home, Riley eating a ton of stuffing at a Thanksgiving dinner, laughing, with his mouth full.

He'd looked so completely different from now.

What the hell is going on? Bron wondered. He glanced back. The other three teens had returned to their Mercedes, which rushed toward them.

Olivia hit her horn and sped through crossing traffic, dodging a pair of cars.

"Get those paper bags out of the glove compartment!" she shouted. There was no way that Olivia could beat the Mercedes, but she floored the gas as she sped up the freeway's on-ramp.

Bron reached in the glove compartment. There were two paper bags. He grabbed one, and spikes poked through the paper and cut into his hand. He pulled the bag out. The thing was surprisingly heavy—perhaps eight or ten pounds—and was filled with little metal spikes of some kind. Olivia rolled down her window as she took the bag. She hurled it so that it lofted over the CRV and landed on the road behind them, breaking open. Little pieces of gray metal scattered like shards of glass.

Bron heard horns blare as the Mercedes barreled onto the onramp, accelerating. With over 550 horsepower in its engine, the Mercedes streaked toward them like black lightning.

The front tires on the Mercedes exploded, pieces of rubber flying like shrapnel. The car began to spin, then slewed off the embankment in a cloud of sand and dust. It rolled twice before settling on its hood.

Bron looked back at the flying dust, the battered vehicle, a side-mirror rolling down the on-ramp. He was scared and elated and confused, and found himself shouting inanely, "Epic failure!"

Olivia laughed in what sounded like pure relief, then punched the gas and raced ahead at eighty miles per hour until they reached the next exit. She was panting, her face stark with terror.

Bron's heart hammered, and his stomach twisted into a knot from adrenaline. His ears still rang from the gunshot.

He couldn't deny that those freaks had been chasing them. Olivia wasn't crazy. She had a right to be afraid. But pulling a gun?

"What the hell?" Bron demanded. He wasn't used to swearing in front of adults, but the situation seemed to demand it. "Who were those people?"

Olivia merely handed the gun to Bron, and nodded toward the glove compartment. He glanced down. The barrel said that it was a Glock 35, a .40 caliber. Bron didn't know much, but this looked like serious firepower. He laid it gingerly into the glove compartment, on top of the second bag of metal bits.

"Later," she said. "I'll explain later."

B lair crawled out of his overturned Mercedes, clutching at his chest. He felt a sharp and intense pain, one that nearly bowled him over, left him feeble and weak.

It's a heart attack, he thought, *caused by the exhilaration.* He knew that a heart attack was tricky to diagnose based on pain alone.

He worried. As a masaak, it was not wise to go to a hospital, expose himself to human doctors. With a careful examination, they'd recognize that he wasn't human.

Riley came limping up, nodded toward one of the acolytes. "I think Fields is dead."

Blair glanced back. Fields was lying on his back forty feet off the road. His eyes were fixed and staring. The boy's feet spasmed. His face was crushed and misshapen.

Blair, clenching his teeth in rage, called in his report.

"We've lost our quarry," he said.

"Lost them?"

Blair peered back. Another car pulled onto the ramp. Its tires exploded. It swerved to the left, into the median, completely blocking the road. The police would arrive soon.

"One of my apprentices was killed in the chase," Blair asserted. "And I'm not feeling well. It may be my heart."

There was a long silence. His superior would be trying to figure out how to remedy the situation.

"Take a hotel in town," his master said.

He's decided to let me die rather than letting the humans risk discovering us. If I'm to make it, I'll have to do it on my own.

He felt lost and alone, but among the Draghouls, to show weakness was worse than death. After all, everyone succumbs to death, but only cowards succumb to fear.

"Have your apprentices scour the area," his master ordered. "When you find your quarry, hobble them...."

"With pleasure," Blair said. *Hobbling* was a cruel thing to do. Stripping a captive of the knowledge of how to walk or crawl left prisoners as helpless as slugs, but it was effective.

They would not escape....

O livia drove to exit four, then turned right, as if she'd head back into the mountains, to the little town of Pine Valley. Instead she turned into a crowded parking lot at a McDonald's and collapsed, resting her forehead on the steering wheel, gasping.

"You know those guys?" Bron accused.

"No," Olivia said. "I've never met them personally. But I've heard about them."

"Who are they? What have you heard?"

Bron felt desperate for answers.

Olivia picked her head up off the steering wheel and gazed into Bron's eyes steadily, as if wondering whether she could trust him to keep a secret.

"I'll tell you sometime," she promised. "Soon."

"I want to know now!" Bron demanded. He tried to reason more slowly. "In six months I'll be old enough to join the Marines. If there are dangerous cultists in town, you should tell me."

Olivia shook her head, as if she couldn't find the words. "Trust me, Bron. I just want to go home."

Her tone was pleading, but Bron didn't dare let her off the hook. He came to a decision. "I'm bailing,"

Bron said as he opened the car door. "I'm out of here."

He didn't know where he would go, or what he would do. He just knew that he had to force her to tell the truth.

"Wait!" Olivia focused on him. "Haven't you ever wondered *who* you were?" she asked. "Haven't you ever wondered why your mother abandoned you?"

Her words stopped him, yanked him as surely as if they were a chain around his neck. He felt like a child, again, a toddler whose world was defined by a dog collar and a length of rope.

He turned to her slowly, unbelieving. "You *know*?"

"I know," she whispered as if her heart would break. "I swear to god I know."

"Tell me," he said, settling back.

"I can't," she said. "Not yet. I'm not allowed to tell you."

"Is Mr. Bell behind this?" Bron demanded.

"No, he doesn't know anything," Olivia said. She held her arm next to his. "Do you see the color of our skin, the similarities in our hair, the shapes of our eyes? I can't tell you *exactly* who you are, but I know *what* you are."

"I'm listening," Bron said, and unexpectedly, his voice cracked. His eyes stung. "Tell me. Please."

"I'll make a phone call, as soon as we get home. By law, I can't tell you. But there's someone who can. I was going to call anyway, once I realized the truth, to get the process started."

"How long will it take?" Bron asked.

"A week, maybe two," Olivia said. "I can't be sure."

Bron leaned back in his seat and drew a long breath. He tried to block out his excitement, cast away all hope, until he felt comfortably numb.

"Make the call now," he dared her. He didn't think she'd do it.

Olivia studied him, pulled out her cell phone, and punched in a number. "Father Leery?" she asked.

Bron could hear a voice on the other end, solemn and grave. "Yes?"

"This is Olivia. I have a problem. I found a song-bird."

"Oh ... bloody ... hell! A nightingale?"

"Yes," Olivia said.

"Black or white?"

"Black."

"Oh ... bloody ... hell!"

"There's more," Olivia said. "We went to a store. The enemy spotted him. We got away, just barely."

Bron had to lean close in order to hear the priest.

"Enemies? How many?"

"Five. A master hunter, I think, and four acolytes."

"They'll be after you," Father Leery warned.

"I don't know what to do," Olivia said. "I'm thinking we should leave town...."

"That's just what they'll expect," Father Leery said. "They'll be watching the freeways for suspicious activity."

"So what should I do?"

"You live what, forty miles out of the city? Go home, Olivia. Go home and hide. I'll see if I can handle this."

"There's another thing," Olivia said. "Our song-bird, the boy, wants to know what's going on."

"He *needs* to know," the priest said, "but you can't tell him. The law protects him as much as it does us."

"He needs to know *soon*," Olivia urged.

"I'll alert the Weigher of Lost Souls," the priest said, and the phone clicked off.

Olivia sat for a moment, breathing hard.

"He sounds as crazy as you," Bron said.

She grinned. "We're not crazy, Bron. We're in more trouble than you can imagine. There are good reasons for our laws, profound and important reasons. You're special. You don't know how special yet. But your world is about to grow very large indeed."

Bron studied her, made his decision. He wanted to know now, but he knew that he wouldn't get that. Still, he knew that if he put it off indefinitely, Olivia might hold out on him. "Two weeks," he agreed. "I'll give you two weeks."

Olivia smiled a terse grin, appraised Bron's broken window, and shook her head regretfully. There was a bit of jagged glass edging up near Bron, and she leaned forward, hit it with her fist, breaking it off. Now the window looked as if it were rolled down instead of as if it had been shot out.

She checked behind to make sure that they weren't being followed, then eased back onto the road and drove slowly through Saint George, heading out through the desert into the mountains.

"Bron," Olivia said when she'd settled down a bit. "You mustn't ever tell anyone what just happened. If this gets into the news, or even if the police hear about it, those people will hunt us down. You can count on it. Promise that you won't tell anyone. Not the police, not social services, not even Mike!"

Bron weighed the alternatives. "Are you sure that we shouldn't go to the police?"

"Very sure," Olivia said. "The police aren't equipped to handle people like these." She seemed convinced that she was being honest.

But why would they want us? he wondered. A more pressing concern struck him. "What about our license plates? They had to have gotten a good look!"

"If they check the plates," Olivia said, "they'll find that the plates are registered to another car. I've been afraid that something like this would happen. So the plates are stolen. I've got my real ones in the barn. We can switch them out in the morning."

Bron's head did a little flip. Certainly witnesses in other cars had seen the altercation, but what would they have seen? A bunch of freaks attacking Olivia's car? Anyone in their right minds would have been writing down the license plate number to the Mercedes, not to the Honda.

With Olivia's tinted windows, no one would have gotten a description of Bron or Olivia.

"So what's in the paper bags," Bron asked, "the things that you threw on the road?"

Olivia shook her head, as if to clear it. "They're called *caltrops.* A thousand years ago, in the midst of the Crusades, peasants were often forced to fight mounted Arabs armed with scimitars. So during the night before a battle, they would take pieces of metal welded together and armed with barbed spikes, and hide them in the grass on the battlefield. When the cavalry charged, the warhorses would step on them and ruin their hooves. They were called 'cavalry traps,' but the name got shortened to caltrops. They work well on tires, too."

For a long moment, Bron thought about this. You couldn't just go down and buy caltrops at Home Depot. You probably couldn't buy them anywhere. Olivia had either made them herself, or had them made.

And she kept a loaded pistol in her car, a big heavy one.

What kind of person did that?

She obviously wasn't your average mousy little school teacher.

Olivia was so rattled that she didn't speak at all anymore. Instead she followed Highway 18 past a small, perfectly conical volcano near the town of Diamond Valley, then past two more volcanoes and the towns of Dammeron and Veyo, until they turned off the highway, following signs that directed them toward Pine Valley.

The ringing in Bron's ears faded and his heart slowed to a steady thump. He decided that maybe Olivia knew what she was doing. He'd just have to pretend that this was "life—as usual."

He settled back, determined to remain calm.

"What are you going to tell Mike when he sees the window?" Bron asked.

"We'll say that we went to the store, and someone broke into the car—maybe a burglar, even though nothing got stolen."

It sounded believable.

"Do you lie to Mike a lot?"

Olivia flinched, as if Bron's words were a slap in the face.

"Not if I can help it," she said. "I love Mike. He's a good man. I'm sorry that he wasn't able to come meet you today. But there are some things that he doesn't know about. Some things that he'd never understand."

"He's not like ... us?"

Olivia smiled secretively. "He's not like anyone."

Bron decided to let the matter go, for now.

"You live way out here?" Bron asked. In the middle of nowhere?

"It's quiet, and pretty," Olivia said.

Bron didn't think it was pretty. The only vegetation had been sagebrush until they turned onto a smaller road. Big trees that looked like pines, except that the bark had a yellowish cast to it, backed some houses on the turn. Then they drove through a dense forest of juniper trees, with their sharp scent and tiny blue berries.

It wasn't pretty, Bron decided. It was *remote*, so removed from civilization that Bron suspected Olivia was in hiding.

He felt nervous about that, and about her husband Mike, who had not bothered to come meet him.

A dozen miles down the road, the car dropped into a small valley where a silver stream wound through emerald fields. A tiny town grew in the shade of a few pine trees on the far side of the valley. The town was dominated by a picturesque old church painted such a bright white that it was like a pearl lying upon green velvet.

Pine Valley didn't have more than a hundred homes, Bron guessed. The car reached the first and only intersection, then turned left and headed farther up into the hills.

"We live in this little town?" Bron asked. He'd never lived in the country before.

"Actually, we don't live *in* town," Olivia said. "We live outside of it." Her voice sounded more normal now, and her color had returned. She glanced back over her shoulder, searching the road behind. No cars were following.

She drove through town, past a couple of rustic restaurants decorated in western motifs. The homes were eccentric. A sagging pioneer log cabin crouched next to a modern mansion, followed by a vacation home from the 1980s.

People had built whatever they wanted. Olivia passed a little pine-shaded park where a sign announced "Mortensen Reunion." Perhaps a hundred cars crowded around.

Olivia stopped at a restaurant next to a gaudy statue of a giant horse and purchased dinner. It came in a brown paper bag that smelled heavenly. Moments later they reached the entrance to the campground for Pine Valley Reservoir.

A ranger's hut squatted in the middle of the road; a tourist had stopped his car at the hut's window, and he was buying a permit to enter. Bron wondered if Olivia lived in the park—maybe in a ranger's cabin, or in a camping trailer?

But Olivia turned onto the very last driveway before the park. Cedar poles formed a gate on each side of the driveway, and a huge log overhead, split down the middle, served as the backdrop for a sign that read "Heaven's Gate Ranch."

"Great," Bron said, eying some black-and-white cattle grazing in the distance. "Am I going to have to milk those things?" For a moment, he almost longed to be slaving away for the Stillmans. At least they didn't have barns to clean and stinky cows to milk.

"Those are beef cattle," Olivia said. "No one milks them. Mike takes care of them—though he might need you to help chase one down if it breaks through a fence."

A ranch, huh? Bron wondered. Ranches were big pieces of land, and he wondered idly if maybe Olivia was richer than he'd thought.

Bron studied the herd, and couldn't help but feel that something was odd. "What's wrong with those cows?"

"They're called Oreo Cookie cattle," Olivia said. "They're black on each end and white in the middle." Now that she'd mentioned it, Bron could see that it was true. Each of the cattle had a band of white around the middle of its stomach, and was a dark-chocolate brown, almost black, on each end. He'd never seen anything like it.

Olivia continued, "Their real name is 'Belted Galloways.' They're a rare breed out of Scotland. Their fur is shaggy, so they take the snow in the winters here pretty well."

She was trying hard to talk about normal things, he decided, to avoid discussing the attack. Bron gave in.

"Snow? I thought we were in the desert?"

"Sure, down in Saint George, but we've climbed a couple thousand feet into the mountains here." She jerked her chin toward some homes off to the left.

"Most of these houses are just summer cabins for families from Saint George. People come up here to get out of the heat, or maybe do a little sledding in winter. Once the snow flies, the locals all huddle in. The driving gets dangerous then—between the ice, and the deer and elk leaping across the roads."

Bron glanced at the neighbors' houses, and caught sight of a young woman in a red one-piece bathing suit. She had beautiful long blonde hair, and she was walking around with a hose, spraying down a deep-red Lexus LX that couldn't have cost less than $85,000.

"Nice scenery," Bron said without enthusiasm. A girl that gorgeous, he'd never even get up the nerve to talk to her, and girls that rich wouldn't bother talking to him.

Olivia honked the car horn as she neared her house, and a huge man came walking out from the barn dressed in blue jeans, boots, and a red-and-white checkered work shirt.

"That's Mike," Olivia said. A black Labrador retriever danced about, wagging its tail, at Mike's side.

To say that Mike was a massive man was an understatement. He was huge—probably six-eight, three feet across the shoulders, maybe three hundred and fifty pounds. His fists were so big that Bron imagined that they could drive fence posts into the ground.

Bron suspected that this was the custom for the Hernandez family—buying dinner on the run, honking the horn to let Mike know that it was time to eat.

Olivia drove down to a little single-story ranch house that looked as if it had been there for a hundred years, and pulled into the shade of a butterfly bush. Hummingbird feeders hung beside the window, and wind chimes made of stained glass tinkled by the backdoor. Bron got out and smelled the clean mountain air and listened. Not a human sound came to his ears—no racing engines, no police sirens, no honking of horns. The only noise came from cicadas in the fields, distant birds. The quiet settled over him like a dead weight.

So this is home.

Mike trudged close, and stood with a smile across his face. "Hi," he said. "You must be Bron?" The black lab raced up to Bron, wagging her tail and sniffing for danger.

Mike reached out to shake, and Bron's hand disappeared into his grasp.

Mike wasn't a Mexican, Bron decided. Mexicans just don't come that big. His face was as broad as a catcher's mitt, and more the bronze that Bron associated with Indians. Mike had blackish-brown eyes, dark-brown hair, a day's stubble. He smiled at Bron and tried to nod cordially enough, but his movements were uneasy.

"I'm sorry that I couldn't make it to the school to meet you," Mike said. "I have a breeder coming in from Australia tomorrow, and I had to spruce things up."

Bron studied Mike. He dwarfed Olivia, and she wasn't a petite woman. Bron had seen Mike's unhappy expression on other people before: disappointment. He was displeased that his wife had picked out a son who was practically grown; he probably felt jealous of the stranger in his house. In Bron's experience, every family had one person who felt that way.

Mike might even be worrying about how much Bron would eat, or whether he'd steal the family silver.

Bron nodded. "Thank you for letting me stay, Mr. Hernandez. You've got a beautiful place here."

Mike grinned broadly at the compliment. He was that easy to please. He eyed the car. "What happened to the window?"

"Someone broke in while we were at the store," Olivia said. "Must have gotten scared off. They didn't take anything."

"We'd better move it into the barn until I can get that glass replaced," Mike said. He scratched his head thoughtfully, as if planning the job. "Well, Bron," he changed subject, "come on in and make yourself at home, I guess." Mike trundled into the house. Bron followed in the giant's shadow.

"How do you think you'll like the farm?" Olivia asked. "I mean, I know that you're new to the idea still...."

"Seems kind of lonely out here," Bron said. "I don't imagine that there are many kids to hang out with."

"It's not so lonely if you know where to look," Mike said. "One house down, big log mansion?" He jerked his chin toward the three-story log house, gleaming of lacquered white pine, with the blonde scrubbing the LX beside it. "That's the Mercer place. Their daughter, Galadriel, is cute."

"Please, Mike," Olivia cut in. "She's an idiot."

"When she's hosing down that car in her swimsuit," Mike laughed, "she sure looks brilliant to me."

Galadriel Mercer was hosing dust off the Lexus when Olivia's white Honda CRV rolled in. Galadriel almost waved as Olivia got out of the car. They weren't great friends, but Pine Valley was lonely. If you saw someone you knew, you were expected to watch out for them, and say hello.

A fat mosquito landed on Galadriel's arm. She brushed it off. Washing the car in a swimsuit kept her from getting her clothes wet, but it left her exposed to mosquitoes that sometimes drifted up from the marsh out in the back field.

She glanced up and saw a boy climb from Olivia's Honda, and Galadriel's heart began to pound.

She tried not to stare. From this distance she couldn't really see him well, but he looked hot, maybe even super-hot.

Galadriel remembered the binoculars in the living room.

She set down the hose and turned off the water. As she did, the phone rang in the house. Her mom picked up. By the time that Galadriel reached the front door, her mom was already opening it.

"Olivia Hernandez got a new son!" her mom said. Marie Mercer wasn't the town gossip—far from it— but news traveled fast in Pine Valley.

Galadriel went to the binoculars that her dad kept by the bookshelf. Usually he used them to look at the elk that often came down from the hills to graze in the fields, or to appreciate the bald eagles that nested nearby. For once, Galadriel found them useful for spotting her own quarry.

Galadriel didn't even have to move the focus rings. Bron's image popped right out at her. He had on a t-shirt, and she could see his six-pack right through it. His hair was stylishly cut, his jaw strong. But it was the sensuousness of his lips that left her weak—that combined with the sensitive expression in his eyes.

She studied him. He looked ... frightened, shell-shocked, alone. She wondered how long he had known that he would be moving. She figured that this was all a big surprise for him.

His eyes seemed to say, "I've known pain, and I know your pain. Speak softly, and I will comfort you."

Marie trembled at Galadriel's side. It was unusual for Galadriel's mom to get so excited.

"Well?" Marie demanded.

"Yummy!" Galadriel said.

Her mom instantly went cold. Galadriel glanced to her left. Her mother's brow was pinched with worry, and the excited smile had fled.

Galadriel enjoyed the reaction. Anything to get a rise out of mom.

"I don't think," Marie said, "that one should discuss boys as if they were comestibles."

Where do you get those words? Galadriel wondered for the ten-thousandth time. Her mom was always so critical.

"Why not?" she asked.

Galadriel pulled up the binoculars again, heart pounding. The neighbors wouldn't see her, she knew, behind the glare of the window. The boy looked even better the second time around. She wanted to stand there forever, to really appreciate his beauty. *I want to chew those lips.*

Galadriel's mother waited for her to say something more.

"I think we should go welcome him to the neighborhood," Galadriel suggested.

"Not dressed like *that,* you won't!" Marie said.

Marie didn't approve of flirting, even among animals. Galadriel remembered a few months ago, her mother had been watching some elk out in the fields. Snow had been falling, and the young calves were loping about with their tongues out, trying to catch fat snowflakes. They were having so much fun. But then one young female had gone near a large bull, her tail up, and had nonchalantly begun to graze just a few feet in front of him. The bull's nostrils had flared, and he immediately took interest.

"See that," Marie had said angrily, as if she wanted to spank the elk. "She's such a flirt!"

It was just nature. At the time Galadriel had thought of her parents' daily motivational speeches. They were always telling her how, "If you want something in life, you have to go out and *take* it."

That's what the elk cow had done.

Now as Galadriel watched Bron head into the house, she knew what she was going to do.

"Yummy, yum-yum," she said.

The house was ranch style. The outside was covered with siding, but inside Bron could see that this was an old log cabin. The bare walls displayed varnished wood, bronzed with age, with calking between the logs. The house had a solid feel to it, but the walls were sagging. It was only a matter of time before the logs settled so far that it needed to be torn down. The ceiling was only slightly vaulted, and perhaps in its day the exposed pine rafters had seemed chic, but compared to the gleaming new extravagant cabins in town, the place looked antiquated. The ancient atmosphere was confirmed by a wood-burning stove in the living room, and a pair of muzzle-loaders with powder horns hanging above it.

The family sat down to a picnic table just off the kitchen. Mike took a bench all to himself, and Bron felt that he probably liked the picnic table just for that reason: he could fit on it.

Mike sat quietly, looking at the food. Bron couldn't have felt less welcome at the dinner table if he'd been a raccoon. No one acted as if they were hungry. Bron's stomach was still queasy from all the excitement, and Olivia seemed lost in thought.

Bron tried to break the silence with an innocent question. "So, Mike, you don't look much like a Hernandez?"

"I'm not," Mike said. "My great-grandfather was Navaho. When he left the reservation, he took the name Hernandez. He thought that trying to pass himself off as a Mexican would give him a leg up in the world."

"What made him leave the reservation?" Bron wondered. It seemed to him that a place that offered free land would have its attractions.

"Ah," Mike said, as if to say, "thereon hangs a tale." He took a deep breath and launched into the story in a voice both soft and deep, like distant thunder. "When he was nineteen, he became a brave, and a few weeks later, the tribal elders caught a skinwalker. Do you know what that is, a skinwalker?"

Bron shook his head. He'd heard of them, of course, but he wanted to draw Mike out, let him establish his expertise.

"It's a man who uses sorcery to change into monsters, creatures half animal and half human. This man kept the hide of a puma, along with its claws and teeth. The sorcerer used magic to turn himself into a cat, and he attacked a woman and tried to kill her, but some men in the camp heard her cries and stabbed the cat, and drove it off.

"Later, the sorcerer was found in a cave with a spear wound to the chest, and his animal furs lying on the ground beside him."

"So the elders of the village put him on trial, and executed him. According to the law, he was executed at dawn and his body was cut up into four pieces.

"When you kill a skinwalker, you have to be careful. You have to carry the pieces far away from each other, so that the skinwalker doesn't rise from the dead. The heart cannot be near the head, and liver cannot be near the gonads. My great-grandfather, being a young brave, was given the honor of taking one of the sorcerer's quarters, and he rode off on his horse. The village Medicine Man warned him to ride far that day, at least twenty miles, and then to bury the leg at sundown, covering it with rocks, so that no one would ever find a trace. The goal was to make the evil sorcerer disappear forever.

"So my grandfather rode up out of the Grand Canyon and into the desert. The sun was very hot, and often he was tempted to stop and take a nap, but he did as the Medicine Man told him."

Bron glanced over to Olivia, who sat with her hands folded, eyes half closed, with a knowing smile. She'd obviously heard this story before.

"At last, at sunset, he was more than thirty miles from the village, out in a lonesome wash. He spent an hour digging a hole, and would have kept digging longer, but the leg began to jerk and kick in its sack, so he tossed it into the hole and buried it quickly, weighing it down with stones."

Mike sat back in satisfaction for a moment, letting Bron think. Outside, the evening was utterly quiet. There was no road noise. Bron heard a clank on the window and looked out. A moth had batted against the window, and smaller bugs were covering it, drawn to the light.

Here in Pine Valley, nightfall did not come all at once. The sun had dropped behind the mountains half an hour ago, and the sky was tinged with a hazy smoke from California wildfires. The setting sun left a band of violet on the horizon, with a touch of rose overhead, filling this little bowl of land with cold shadows that shut out all sound, like a hand clasped over a mouth. Bron shivered.

"My grandfather danced above the site and sang prayers, trying to force the skinwalker's soul to rest, and when the moon rose, grandfather began to lead his horse home.

"But a burrow owl screeched and rose up out of the ground at his feet. That is an evil portent, for the owl warns against death, and my grandfather did not dare return home. Instead, he stopped at that very spot, and he worried that something had gone wrong.

"He did not sleep all that night. Instead, he danced within a magic circle, and at dawn a girl from the village came for him, running and crying, so weary that she often stumbled. He was in love with her, and hoped to marry her someday, and she felt the same for him.

"She told him that one of the other warriors was dead. He had not carried his portion far from the village, but instead had stopped beside the river to take a rest through the heat of the day, and he must have fallen asleep. The young brave had been carrying the sorcerer's head and right arm, and the brave was found dead—strangled and covered in bite marks from human teeth.

"The skinwalker had survived!

"So my grandfather turned away from the reservation and rode north, and made his home here—far away, where the sorcerer would not look for him."

Something about the story left Bron shivering in fear. It wasn't just the tale of the skinwalker, it was the strangers in town, Bron's worries about the school—a mounting pile of things.

Mike fell silent, then asked in a happy tone, "Who wants chicken?"

He grabbed the bucket from Olivia and began to fill up plates. Olivia just sat with her hands folded. She looked to Mike, "But we don't believe in skinwalkers in this house, do we?"

She said it as if it were an old argument, as if she had trouble with Mike's superstitions.

Mike stopped grabbing food and stared up at her guiltily. "Well, I don't know...." he said. "I've heard a lot of strange stories. Doctor Carnaghan used to work down on the reservation, and he saw one once when he was getting ready to land his bush plane. He said it looked like half-man, half black bear, and it ran on all fours. He clocked it at forty-five miles an hour!"

"But *we* don't believe such stories, do we?" Olivia urged.

"You know what I believe?" Mike said, not to be cornered. "I believe that the world is stranger than we know, and we should eat this chicken before it gets any colder!"

After dinner, the Hernandez family didn't watch television like normal people do. Olivia got out her guitar and showed Bron her fingering techniques. She played a song that she had composed, using picks on each finger, thumping the guitar like a drum, humming a counter-melody.

It was a song about wind rushing over water, and pine trees creaking in the hills, and a bold elk coming out of the forest at dawn, with its rack held high, as it smelled the world of men for the first time.

At least, that's the picture that formed in Bron's head, and the music was just like that—sounds turning to pictures and colors and emotions all rolled into one.

Olivia wasn't just good, Bron decided within a minute. She was phenomenal—too good to be hiding her gift out here in the woods. He'd thought that she was exaggerating when she said that she'd once given a lesson to Joe Satriani. Now he realized that she had probably told the truth.

Yet if she was one of the best guitarists in the world, Bron wondered, what was she doing hiding up here in the mountains, in the middle of nowhere, wasting her time teaching kids? She should be working in music studios. She could be playing guest leads for major vocal talent. She could be making millions!

As he frowned at these thoughts, he glanced up into Olivia's eyes. She wasn't even watching her hands! She was staring right into Bron's face, as if daring him to ask her, "Why?"

Yet he knew from her expression that she wouldn't answer.

She played a couple of songs, then Mike began to sing, and she accompanied. Bron suspected that they did this every night.

But on the third song, Olivia asked Bron, "Why don't you get out your guitar? I'll be happy to teach you a few tricks, maybe even a few that Joe Satriani doesn't know."

Bron ducked his head shyly. Olivia was so much better than him. It would be like a concert pianist playing chopsticks with a six year old.

"I've never played in front of other people," he apologized.

"At least you could sing with us," Olivia suggested, but Bron shook his head. His singing was even worse. A knot of alarm coiled in his stomach.

"You don't sing or play in front of others?"

He shook his head. "At my last home, I wasn't allowed to do it in the house."

"No one's that bad," Olivia said.

"Mr. Stillman worked as a trucker," Bron explained. "When he got home, he needed to sleep. Melvina, his wife, had a touch of tinnitus. She didn't want me making noise in the house."

"Music is never 'noise,'" Olivia said. "Even when it isn't played well. There's more going on here than it seems. This Melvina sounds as if she has a cruel streak."

Bron shrugged. "I've known worse."

"You're starting in a school for the performing arts on Monday," Olivia said in exasperation, "and you don't perform?"

"Not in public," Bron said.

Mike teased, "Dude, you got to grow a set on you, and fast!"

Bron fell silent, thoughtful, and got his guitar. He picked one of his favorites, Green Day's "Boulevard of Broken Dreams," and for the first time ever, he dared sing the lyrics in front of others.

It wasn't great. He wasn't used to singing and playing at the same time, and he fumbled in a couple of places. When he finished, he felt queasy.

Mike didn't say anything, simply smiled, but Olivia offered, "Good job, Bron. Tomorrow we'll start practice."

Bron fell silent, thoughtful. "Olivia, can you show me my room now?" he asked. He felt wearier than he'd imagined. It was as if he'd been running on adrenaline all day, and now he just wanted to collapse.

She and Mike took him to a large room at the back of the house. It had once been a woodshed, in the old days when the house was heated by the fireplace, but now it was insulated and boarded in. A single window with no curtains let in the starlight. The bulb, a 40-watt, hardly chased back the shadows. There was a dresser in the room, and a closet, but the whole place smelled of dust.

A back door to the house was at the far end of the room, locked with an ancient-looking deadbolt.

"We'll have to clean up in here tomorrow," Olivia apologized. "We hardly ever use the guest room. We could try opening the window to let in some fresh air, if you like?"

She went to open the window, but Mike stopped her. "Wait until we're gone, and turn out the lights first. There's no screen in that window, and the light will attract moths."

Mike said goodnight, and Bron sat on the bed for a moment. Olivia just stood, staring at him, as if she wanted to speak but didn't dare.

He felt that she was on the verge of opening up, so he asked, "What is it that you're hiding from, Olivia?" She paused in thought. "Is it just those people who chased us?" Bron suggested. "Or are you afraid of the cops, too?"

Olivia smiled sadly. "Not now. Not so close to sleep."

To his surprise, she grabbed him by the shoulders, leaned down and kissed him on the cheek. "My mother kissed me goodnight when I was young," she explained, "every single night. Even the last night that I saw her in the hospital, dying from cancer, she did it. It was comforting. I miss my goodnight kisses."

The closeness, the tenderness that she showed, had an effect on Bron. It was warm and comforting, and he wanted to try it again. She turned out the light, then went to the window and opened it a crack, and he could not help but notice how shapely she was in the starlight. She had a dancer's figure. She probably had to do a lot of dancing if she taught musical theater. He felt creepy being attracted to her.

He'd never loved any of his foster parents. He knew the danger of getting too close. He suspected that she sensed that, and so she was working to break through his barriers.

He blinked away his thoughts.

She left the room, and Bron lay wide awake. A mosquito entered through the open window and buzzed around his head. Bron didn't kill it. For some reason, mosquitoes never bit him.

He wondered if Olivia's kiss was more than a kiss. Was Olivia flirting with him? He'd heard of women like that. A teacher in Highland, a town near his old home, had just been sentenced for abusing a boy.

How old is Olivia? he wondered. Mr. Bell had said that she was in her early thirties. But she could have been in her late twenties.

No, he decided, she wasn't flirting. But there was something going on here.

There was something odd about Olivia. She looked a lot like Bron did, at least in the strange color of their skin, and the slightly off shapes of their heads. Her eyes were more hazel, where his were gray.

They looked so much alike that he could almost imagine that she *was* his mother. He got an odd notion: what if she'd had a child when she was young, and had abandoned it?

Mr. Bell had said that she had applied to become a foster parent three years back. Could she have just been waiting for him, hoping to reunite?

It sounded crazy, but this woman with her touchy-feely attitude, her instant bonding, her fear of ... something—Bron had never met anyone like her.

He wondered about his real parents. He wondered if they ever lay awake at night like this, speculating on what had become of him.

So he lay on his bed, in utter turmoil, wonders whirling like autumn leaves caught in a dust devil, until he finally settled down to sleep.

CHAPTER 6

EVIL NEVER SLEEPS

"With cunning comes the prize."
                                        – Lucius Chenzhenko

Blair Kardashian stalked into a seedy motel on Saint George Boulevard, one that advertised rates at $24.95 per night. The sharp odor of Lysol permeated the floor tiles, covering the scent of dust and decay. An outdated television played a Spanish soap opera. No one bothered to sit at the front desk. It was too late at night. Blair punched a call button on the counter, and heard a buzz in a back room.

Sixty years ago, this would have been a decent motel. Millions of tourists passed through Saint George each year on their way to some of the bigger parks—Zion, Bryce, Arches. The hotel had been built to service such tourists.

A dull twinge struck his stomach, and Blair wondered at it. The pains had eased. Blair had purchased a stethoscope a few hours earlier. A quick check showed that his heartbeat was strong and regular. After years of running marathons, it was as strong as a teen's. So he had to ascribe these phantom pains to a pulled muscle, or perhaps a deep bruise to the sternum. He *had* hit the steering wheel hard when the Mercedes rolled.

The memory filled him with rage. He had a dead acolyte, and no clues. His superiors had run the plates on the Honda CRV. Someone had reported them stolen eighteen months ago.

The Ael frequently drove cars with stolen plates.

An elderly Mestizo woman came from the back, walking carefully, as if to make sure that her considerable bulk did not accidentally knock over the office chair. "Hello?" she asked with a thick accent.

Blair immediately launched into Spanish, which he spoke with a distinguished, Castilian accent. "I am looking for a woman and a young man. They may be visitors to the area."

He pulled out his cell phone and showed the picture that his acolyte had taken of the boy they called "Bron." The night manager squinted as she studied the image.

Blair waited for her answer.

After the crash, he had told the police that a car had scraped his in the parking lot. He'd claimed that he'd tried to exchange insurance information, but the female driver had fled. He hadn't thought to get her license number. "She sped away too quickly," he told them, "and when we tried to follow, she threw tire spikes out the window."

The police had been mortified. They would make eager allies. The caltrops were obviously home-made. This implied forethought on the part of those who threw them. The fact that Blair's vehicle had rolled, and that someone had died, elevated the charges: fleeing the scene of an accident. Battery. Homicide.

The police would have a field day.

"Such a handsome boy," the woman said in an atrocious Mexican accent. She leaned forward, resting her bulk against the counter. "What do you want him for?"

Immediately Blair sensed that she was evasive. She was the kind who helped her friends hide from the immigration police, and rented rooms to hookers by the hour.

"He threw some tire spikes out the window of a car earlier tonight," Blair said. "My son was killed."

"Oh, I heard about that on the news!" she said. She shook her head. "I haven't seen him."

Blair didn't trust her to tell the truth. He had little use for humans. They were inferior creatures. He had even less respect for this woman.

"Thank you," Blair said, reaching casually for the phone. Just as he nearly had it, he raised his hand and grasped the right hemisphere of her cranium. The sizraels on his fingers extended. His sizraels had extremely long, articulated ridges, when compared to those on others of his species. They would have looked fake, like plastic suction cups, except that they stretched out eagerly when he attacked.

With a single touch, electricity arced down his arm and shot pale blue-white faerie lights. The woman spasmed and fell forward. He gripped her, his fingers probing her greasy hair. He reached out with his other hand, grasped her firmly, and peered into her mind.

He did not fear getting caught. It was late enough that most of the humans slept. The few people cruising the strip would not be able to see into this dim office.

Her name was Imelda, a vile woman, a murderess who had crossed the border years ago to escape prosecution for killing a marijuana farmer and stealing his crop. The fruits of her theft had purchased this seedy motel, which grew more worthless by the minute.

But that did not interest him.

He looked for an image of Bron in her mind. The woman had six runaways living in one of her rooms, teens who barely scraped enough money together to pay for their rent and their drug habits, but otherwise the hotel did not harbor any teens.

Blair growled in consternation, then ripped the memories of his visit from Imelda's mind, every trace, so there would be no record. The hotel office had a security camera, but he learned by peeking into Imelda's memory that it did not work. She only used it to keep would-be robbers at bay.

He let Imelda go, and the woman sagged against the counter for a moment, then dropped to the floor with a *whuff*. When she woke in a few minutes, she would remember nothing, and Blair would be gone.

He went into the parking lot and got into his rental, confident that all over town, his acolytes would be doing the same. They'd scour the city tonight, checking every hotel within miles. But his gut told him that they lived in the area. The best way to find them would be to check the schools.

That would have to wait until Monday.

CHAPTER 7

THE LAYING ON OF HANDS

"Beware of those who wish to improve you. Too often, they have their own best interests at heart."

— Bron Jones

Late that night, Olivia watched Mike go out on his "evening rounds" of the ranch. He pampered his prize cattle as if they were children. Olivia wanted a real family, but sometimes felt as if Mike already had his own "youngsters."

Mike didn't like crowds, Olivia knew. He was so large that he'd had a hard time growing up. Kids at school had made fun of him, calling him Monster Mike. Most people were afraid of him. They couldn't see his gentle nature.

Animals seemed to recognize his goodness, though.

Olivia had never seen Mike hurt a living creature. Earlier in the spring, when a pair of barn swallows had disappeared, Mike had gotten so worried about their young that he'd searched the barn and outbuildings until he found their nest, the baby birds chirping for food. He'd spent weeks nursing them to health.

But Mike's compassion didn't extend to strangers. So Olivia went out to the barn, looking for him, hoping to put him at ease about Bron.

Olivia hated that she had to lie to him so often, hide things. She was in love with the giant, but the few times when she'd tried to tell him the truth about herself, he'd grown afraid.

The barn smelled clean, of fresh alfalfa, salt licks, and only a little of steer. She crept through it quietly.

She found Mike in the corral, beneath a hanging heat lamp, scratching the head of a pregnant cow, saying good night to his animals. His Labrador retriever, Sheila, sat quietly at his side.

The banded Galloways had a thick patch of hair on their heads, several inches long, to protect them from the cold. Their scalps looked almost human.

As Mike scratched the cow, she rolled her eyes back and laid her muzzle along his arm, then stuck out her tongue, probing for a treat. Sure enough, Mike pulled a carrot from the pocket of his jeans.

"Don't take those from my garden," Olivia said. "You promised."

Mike nearly jumped out of his shoes, surprised by her voice, made doubly afraid because he knew that he'd been caught.

"Damned store-bought carrots aren't any good," Mike said. "They've got no minerals in them. Besides, you're one to complain about waste. You want to buy that kid all new clothes? You've only known him for a couple of hours!"

Olivia had dreaded this argument. "He needed the uniforms. He can't get by without them. He's a good kid."

"He's practically grown," Mike said. "It feels like you're moving another man into our house. It's not enough that you spend all of your time with those kids at school...."

Olivia drew close to Mike, wrapped an arm around his waist, and pulled him toward her. After seven years of marriage, she didn't doubt Mike's fidelity. But their love life had grown predictable, and as he realized that all the loving in the world wouldn't give him a baby, he'd lost some interest.

"I like my kids. You like your cattle. We love each other. What's so wrong with that?"

She had imagined that Mike was half-teasing, but saw an angry curl to his lip. He stared at his cow, rubbing it on the ridge between its horns.

"I always figured that when we got a kid, we'd get a younger one—one that we could raise. This kid's almost all grown...."

"On the outside, maybe," Olivia admitted, "but on the inside he still has a lot of growing to do, and a lot of healing."

"Never figured you to be one for gathering strays," he complained. Mike turned to gaze at her. The gleam from the heat lamp just behind her back reflected in his eyes. "That boy doesn't seem to have a liking for cattle. Didn't even ask about them during dinner."

"He was just surprised to see them. He's always lived in the city. Besides, we talked about them in the car, on the way here."

Mike shook his head regretfully. "Any proper kid would be jumping out of his boots at the sight of these cattle. Little kids all want to be cowboys when they grow up."

"A lot of little kids do," Olivia agreed. "But I'm sure Bron has his own plans."

Mike bit his lip. "You've got that right. You know what boys are like at sixteen."

She gave him a questioning look, but knew where this was going.

Mike continued, "Their minds are swimming in hormones at that age. That kid up there in the house, he's lying in bed, dreaming about you. You've got him all worked up, and don't even know it. He's probably sweating all over his sheets, hotter than a bull after a heifer. It's not his fault, of course. He won't be able to stop where his mind goes. It's just nature."

"Not all boys are that way, I'm sure," Olivia said, trying to deflect Mike's jealousy. "Give him a chance."

Mike sighed, leaned against the fence, in resignation. "If you're going to get him a car, make sure that it's easy on the gas."

She looked up at him and raised a brow. She hadn't even had to ask. "A car?" Olivia had been wondering how to bring up the problem.

"Well, you work all those odd hours, and I can't imagine him wanting to stay at school till midnight. I can't always take the time to drive down and pick him up."

She was an actress, of course, so now she acted. "You're right," she said as if it had just dawned on her. "We will need a car.... It would have to be pretty cheap."

"And it has to be good in the snow," Mike enthused. "Make it a front-wheel drive. And it doesn't have to be cheap—which means 'broken down' or 'likely to fall apart' in my book. It needs to be a good investment. If we have to sell it in a couple of weeks, I don't want to take a beating on the price."

"Don't worry," Olivia said. "I'll find us a bargain."

Mike grimaced, went back to scratching the head of his cow. He took a deep breath. "I think I know why you like that boy."

"Why's that?"

"He kind of looks like you—same hair, same color of skin. He looks like he could be your own blood."

"He does look like he could be our kid, doesn't he?" Olivia agreed.

Mike grunted thoughtfully and shook his head. "Olivia, don't get your hopes up. We don't know that boy, and I've got a bad feeling about him."

"Bad feeling?" Olivia asked. She knew that it came from jealousy. Mike was uncomfortable with strangers anyway. Now she'd be spending time with this kid, spending money on him.

"Yeah, look in his eyes," Mike said. "He's a cold one."

Olivia nearly laughed. Mike didn't really believe that, did he? But she saw from his sober expression that he did, and that worried her. Mike was sensitive to the nature of other people. She'd seen that over and over again. He was a superb judge of character.

Mike went on, "Yeah, there's something wrong with that kid."

Olivia lay awake that night worrying. The car chase had her terrified, and she kept replaying events in her mind, trying to figure out whether the

Draghouls would be able to find her. Mike couldn't possibly know what kind of danger Bron presented. He was just a boy, but even if he was the best kid in the world, a Gandhi in the making, his presence posed a threat to the entire family.

The Draghouls had to suspect that she—a feral— had stolen one of their nightingales. And if they tracked her down, it would mean an end to her cozy world.

She suspected that they would leave her alive. She was too talented to simply waste. And Bron would be left alive, too. But the Draghouls would alter them, change them in ways perverse and deadly. Mike? He might get a bullet to the back of his head.

She was risking everything for a boy she'd hardly met. *Am I a fool,* she wondered, *or am I just trying to be heroic?*

The truth was though, she had been taking this risk all of her life. Every time she went to school to teach, she interfaced with others. Eventually, her luck was bound to run out.

The safest course, it seemed, was to flee. Olivia could take Bron and Mike and run away. But first she would have to tell her husband what she was, what Bron was.

How would he react if he knew? Could he give up his cattle, the ranch that his family had spent three generations building? She knew the answer.

This was all so messy.

It was complicated by the fact that Mike didn't trust Bron, and Olivia had to wonder at that. Mike was so often right.

So at 1:03 a.m., Olivia lay thinking furiously. She often found that she didn't sleep well. She was a creature of the night, after all.

Her cell phone vibrated on the table, a soft buzz. She snatched it before it could wake Mike. The caller ID identified Father Leery.

Mike was snoring gently, a sign that he was out cold.

"Hello?" Olivia whispered.

"Hi," Father Leery said jovially. "I know that it's late, but I suddenly remembered that you were supposed to bring the potato salad tomorrow, for the church picnic, and I wanted to remind you."

It had to be a code. Father Leery didn't have much of a congregation, and Olivia never went to his functions. Phones are far easier to wiretap than most people realize, so he was trying to be discreet.

"Sure, I'll be there," she said.

"Good," he said. "I'll be talking about the 'Dangers of Mortality,' for my sermon in the morning. I hear that there was a terrible auto accident this afternoon in Saint George, and a poor young teen died on the highway."

Olivia's heart sank, and she suddenly felt as if she would retch.

"Died?"

"Thrown from a car when it rolled," Father Leery said. "Let it be a warning to us all to travel safely. Better yet, just stay home."

He hung up, and Olivia lay in a panic. She'd never felt such guilt. Her skin seemed to crawl, and her heart pounded. She struggled for air, even as she fought to keep her dinner down.

She wanted to run. The Draghouls would certainly be looking for vengeance. They'd launch a full-scale hunt. But Father Leery had just warned her to "stay home." He understood the Draghouls far better than she did.

Olivia had never killed anyone before. She'd never even considered it. She felt sick. She loved children. The boy who'd died would have been high school age.

Was Riley the one who'd died? She hoped not. Then again, she remembered what Bron had said. Seeing him was like staring into the face of death.

Olivia hadn't listened to the news after dinner, hadn't checked it on the internet. Part of her had been afraid to do so, fearful of learning what she might find.

How would Bron react? It would be better if he never found out. But there would be talk at school. He was bound to hear about this.

Would Bron flip out when he heard?

She wondered what to do. Right now, there was nothing that Olivia *could* do. When Bron heard the truth, she could wipe his memory. But he was likely to hear about it over and over for months. She'd have to remove the memories again and again, and each time that he heard the news, he'd relive the shock of learning that he'd been involved in a killing.

That would be torture.

Olivia couldn't be a part of that. It would be better if Bron knew the truth, figured out how to handle it. But *could* he handle it? Did he have that kind of internal strength?

She looked over to Mike. He wouldn't wake, she knew, between now and sunrise, when he'd begin to get anxious to check on his cattle.

She stealthily climbed from bed and glanced through the dormer windows. An endless array of stars filled the sky, smoldering and burning.

She crept from her bedroom on the balls of her feet. The thick carpeting made her soundless, and she slipped down the hallway to Bron's room. When a floorboard creaked, she halted for a long moment before moving on.

She opened the door; it squeaked on its hinges. Bron lay in bed on his side.

She worried that he might wake, so she studied his eyes. They were closed, but she knew that he might be faking.

What if Bron caught her? Would he imagine that she'd come for a tryst?

He was handsome in his sleep, so serene and peaceful, like the bust that he'd carved. His face was perfect, flawless.

She crept to the side of his bed. There was no twitching or fluttering in his eyes, no catching of his breath. That reassured her that he was asleep.

The masaak brain had two major quarters, and two minor quarters. The major quarters correspond to the right and left hemispheres of the human brain, but the minor quarters, only an eighth the size of a hemisphere, were mirrored appendages on the brain stem. All of the quarters were connected by a small bundle of nerves that acted as a bridge, very similar to the corpus callosum.

Often at night, the right hemisphere of both the human and the masaak brain, the part that focuses on emotions, would wake and begin to dream. When that happened rapid eye movement indicated that the dreamer was only half-asleep.

For what Olivia was about to do, Bron needed to be totally passive, unconscious.

She almost felt that she should speak to Bron, offer some words of comfort, but she dared not even whisper.

Just as a lion hides its daggers in its paws, so Olivia kept her own weapons hidden. Now she tightened some muscles in her wrists, and *unsheathed*, as the masaaks called it. Instantly, ridges that looked like callus formed in an oval on each of her fingertips and thumbs.

She stepped to Bron, reached down, and gingerly took the right side of his head into her left hand, placing each finger carefully over the right hemisphere of the brain—the forefinger above the frontal lobe, the middle finger over the parietal lobe, the ring finger over the occipital lobe, and the pinky upon the temporal.

She sent a thought pulse through her hand and locked onto his mind. Sparks flew from her fingers. Immediately his right eye opened, and his body seized, his back arcing off the bed.

He gagged, as if he were starting to rouse. She grabbed the left hemisphere of his head with her right hand, twisting his face up toward the ceiling, and his left eye flew open, too, wide with fear.

She seized both halves of his mind.

Someone's in the room! he thought-screamed. Adrenaline coursed through his veins, urging him awake.

She drew out all of his conscious thought, discarded his fears, and just held his head for a moment until the adrenaline wasted away. She placed her thumbs up under his eyes, just beneath the supra-orbital ridge, as she gained full control of his mind.

"Don't worry," she whispered into his dreams, "I'm not here to harm you. I'm here to bring you fairy gifts. For so many years you've been asleep to your potential. Now it is time for the dreamer to awake."

She probed the surface of his dreaming thoughts—chaotic and random and emotionally charged, as they tended to be at this time of night.

She went first to the day's events. The fact that she had fired a gun at a young boy deeply disturbed Bron.

Olivia didn't like to remove another's memories. It was a type of violation. But it could also be a form of surgery, like removing a painful splinter from a hand.

Perhaps it had to be done. Perhaps with her kind it was just an instinct. Olivia simply discarded some of Bron's memories: the gun in the glove compartment? Gone. The bullet shattering the window? It never happened.

Bron would only recall that the window had broken, perhaps as Riley pounded on it and screamed.

She searched deeper into his mind, looking for damaging incidents, the kind that cause the most pain. Sights and sounds began to flash—images of Mr. Golper beating Bron on a bridge on a crisp winter's day, while Bron tightly held a burlap bag that contained his kitten. Bron had known that so long as he held out, the kitten would live.

She heard girls mocking his worn clothing at a school dance last fall, and felt the jolt as a foster mother slapped his face and bloodied a lip. Bron's body wracked with sobs as he cried himself to sleep the night after a grim Christmas when he was six, when Santa brought toys for his foster parents' real children but none for him.

Olivia found so many more harsh memories ... so many.

For her, viewing another's memories was as natural as breathing, and ripping the memories from a person's head was child's play.

She didn't dare take all of the painful memories. Such memories forced people to grow. They were like weights. Carry a little and you get strong. Carry too many, and they break you.

Besides, removing a recollection could be tricky. A memory of the kind with Mr. Golper helped shape a person's worldview. Even if Olivia removed the vile thing, Bron's habitual thoughts, his way of seeing the world, would remain for awhile.

But in time, healing might come. Eventually, he would look into his memory, and would not understand why he felt so hurt and angry, and perhaps his thoughts would be free to form new paths.

Olivia hoped for healing.

She reached for the most damaging memory that she could find—one where Bron huddled as a child while his foster father, Mr. Lewis, slapped and choked his favorite foster mother.

It was a loathsome memory. Bron remembered Helen Lewis well, her tears streaming down a bruised face.

Bron had run from the room and tried to call 911, in order to protect her. But it was Helen Lewis herself who rushed in and hung up the phone. "Don't call the police," she'd begged. "If you call them, they'll take my husband away, and they'll take you away, and I'll be all alone!"

Bron had let her disconnect the phone. Of course, within eight hours, once the paramedics were shown Mr. Lewis, huddling naked in a fetal position on the floor, he was taken to the hospital.

Without a father in the home, social services removed Bron, too. Helen was left all alone, despite her pleas. Often Bron wondered if she was happy, if she'd had a good life.

Olivia gently pulled the foul memory of the fight from Bron's head, and held it for a moment. It was as loathsome as a wriggling worm or a dead rat.

Olivia didn't want that ugliness infesting her own memory, so she simply abandoned it, tossed it away.

Bron would never recall what had happened to Mrs. Lewis when he was eight. As far as he would know, the parents would have had a happy, supportive relationship.

Then she went into his recollection of the morning after, when Bron had risen to find Mr. Lewis, naked and huddling in the kitchen, beside the refrigerator.

Moments later, his wife had called the paramedics. Mr. Lewis had died that afternoon.

Olivia wiped the memory clean.

In the future, Bron would only recall tales of Mr. Lewis dying in some hospital.

She decided to leave the memory of being chased by Draghouls. Bron needed to know that he had enemies, and she suspected that even if he learned of a teen's death, he'd be able to handle it.

Olivia considered what she'd done. She hadn't practiced like this on anyone in years.

So she cleaned away some harmful memories, then peered deeply into Bron's character. He was a humble boy. He didn't think of himself as special. He felt that he had no real talent, and so worried about what others would think about him at his new school. In the past, his art had so often been scorned or ridiculed that he'd all but abandoned it.

Olivia knew that she could change that.

But she found something odd about Bron: he was well practiced when it came to withdrawing from others. He fought any feelings of love. His life was emptier, sadder, than she had imagined.

Olivia had a code in life: give more than you take. Removing harmful memories might relieve some pain, but she wanted to give him something more. She decided to train him.

Training is harder than ripping away memories. Training requires time, concentration. She needed to recall a skill, practice it in her imagination, and transplant the knowledge into her student.

The body can be conditioned to act a certain way by repetition. For example, to run, or to sing, requires that some neural pathways to the body's extremities be trained.

Olivia studied the pathways that led from Bron's amygdala down into his brainstem, and from there to his ears and larynx, and down his arms, legs and into his wrists and fingers.

She could only "train" Bron in things she knew.

For instance, she knew how to unsheathe her sizraels. As she had suspected, Bron didn't. The muscles that he needed to access were atrophied, as were the nerves that led to them. When he'd been given up as a nightingale, someone had caused him to utterly forget those muscles, until they wasted.

She woke them, opened the neural pathway from the brain to the muscles, and let him *unleash*.

Olivia glanced down at his hands. The sizraels stood out on the ends of his fingers, nice and oval, but the ridges were small.

She didn't know what *kind* of masaak Bron might be. Most masaaks were *at-tujjaarah a'zakira*, memory merchants, of one order or another—more than eighty percent. There were rarer breeds, with different abilities, and Bron might be one of those, yet probing his mind would not tell her what talents he held. He couldn't share information he didn't know. She'd have to wait, let him experiment, and see what she could learn.

Now, she considered how best to help him.

Olivia could only share from her own store of knowledge. She'd spent most of her life learning to sing and play the guitar. She was far better in private than anyone had a right to be, better than anyone knew.

Bron yearned to play well, and she could help. She could give him some skills, but that alone wouldn't take him to the top. There was a component that he would have to bring, some innate way of communicating to the world. Lots of people have talent, she knew. She hoped that Bron had it, along with drive.

Many people with raw talent give up on music too soon, she'd learned. They don't have the heart for it. They didn't love it the way that she loved it. For her, creating music was an end in itself, not a path to adulation.

So she began to teach Bron to play. It was not simple. She had to imagine herself playing several songs in a row, envision herself fingering each note on the guitar. She had to let the notes flow through her, and retrain Bron's neural pathways so that he "naturally" held his guitar correctly, struck each note, each chord, precisely.

She had to strengthen the neural ties between the prefrontal lobes—the part of his brain that let him plan–and his medulla oblongata, the center of the brain that allowed people to perform tasks automatically.

Bron's memories showed that he tended to sing with a falsetto, trying hard to mimic his favorite pop singers. He hadn't trained his ear to hear properly, or his vocal chords to seek their full range. He didn't know how to create a vibrato, or to unlock his natural talent.

So she trained him for two hours. It was a grueling session that left sweat beaded upon her brow, while streams of it raced down her arms, down to her sizraels, so that her hands became slick.

When Olivia felt physically and emotionally exhausted, she began to pull out of Bron's mind slowly, and wondered at how much work she had left to do.

There were things that Olivia yearned to teach him. She hadn't even begun to teach Bron finger picking, or multiphonics, or a hundred other things.

But teaching that would take several sessions, and she didn't have the time or energy for it tonight. She needed sleep, like anyone else.

Tomorrow, Bron will wake, she imagined, *and he will discover that he has grown overnight, like the beans in Jack's beanstalk. He'll discover talents that he never imagined. He'll play the guitar with greater ease and precision. He'll sing like a natural-born star.*

Oh, he might not be world-class yet. That will take a few weeks....

Olivia finished and pulled her hands away. She'd left strange white pucker marks on Bron's temples, but they'd fade soon enough, when the blood returned.

CHAPTER 8

THE DREAMER AWAKES

"Ignorance lets a child sleep in peace. Wisdom is what keeps the elderly up at night."

— Olivia Hernandez

Bron dreamed a troubling dream: he rode with Olivia through red-rock country. Out the window, hoodoos of stone marched shoulder to shoulder. They reminded him of the pieces from one of his foster father's old chess sets—red knights in armor, with tall shields, looking grim as they stood ready for combat. The stones had slabs for bodies and shields, with smaller rocks forming battered faces, smashed by wind and eroded by the tides of time, until they were almost no longer recognizable as human.

Bron studied the figures. It looked as if giants must have carved them, long ago, back before people roamed the earth.

Maybe even dinosaurs carved those rocks, Bron thought, and a smile came to his face.

He held his guitar. He remembered Olivia forcing him to play, and in the dream, he recalled that he had been dreaming of playing all night, over and over.

He decided to sing about the stone warriors, so he closed his eyes and began:

"In days of yore
when dinosaurs roared,
Beside a wine-dark sea,
Guardians of stone,
Grown from earth's bones,
Swore to keep watch
For eternity..."

Bron knew it wasn't finished, but he kind of liked it. He smiled and asked Olivia, "Will you get off my back now?"

But when he glanced to his left, it wasn't Olivia driving at all. It was the old man from the electronics store—with his killer's eyes and a mouth drawn in contempt. Bron had never seen such hate in a face, and never felt so alone or frightened.

"When the serpent bites," the old man growled, "the flies shall soon gather!"

Bron sat bolt upright in bed, heart hammering so hard that his chest hurt. He gasped for breath, and glanced around.

The only radiance in the room came from a bit of starlight filtering through the open window. The air still felt stuffy, as if the room hadn't been aired in years. A sheen covered Bron's forehead and made his skin stick to the sheets.

He wiped his face, and the calluses on his fingers felt surprisingly hard, larger than normal.

Bron climbed from bed, still in his clothes, and stood for a moment, gasping.

Who is that old man? Bron wondered. *Why is Olivia hiding from him?*

The dream had felt so vivid—more like a memory than a dream.

He focused on the red sandstone cliffs. In the dream, they'd seemed ... so familiar.

Could I have been born around here? he wondered.

No one had ever claimed him. The police had made a fuss about him, and the news had plastered his face on television, with anchors pleading, "Does anyone know this child?"

Mr. Bell had told Bron that the investigators had gotten hundreds of leads, placing his parents everywhere from Austin, Texas to Ontario, Canada. But all the leads evaporated into nothing. It seemed that no one had ever known him. No mother, father, grandparent. No neighbors or friends.

No one reported him missing, and no one had ever been able to put a name to him. It was as if he'd appeared out of thin air.

He shook his head, trying to clear it of dreams that were far too lucid.

Bron went to the window, looked out. Here so far from the city lights, the stars blazed. There seemed to be a hundred thousand, twinkling and throbbing. No sooner had he glanced out the window than a shooting star barreled across the horizon. Tonight was the second night of the Perseid Meteor Shower, a moment later he saw a spray of light as three stars fell at once.

A rooster crowed in the distance. Back at the Stillmans, Bron used to like to run at dawn. He didn't have a clock, but he figured that it was close enough to morning.

He pulled on his new shoes, went outside.

The air was cooler than he thought it would be. The temperature really dropped up here in the mountains at night, but it wasn't bad for running. In fact, he'd always found a cool day to be invigorating, and he'd once heard a farmer claim that in the autumn, even the horses and dogs like to go running for no reason.

He stood gazing up into the bowl of heaven, where the River of Stars wound along, powdering the sky, and for long minutes he craned his neck and watched for shooting stars.

So high up in the mountains, he was able to spot some fast-moving satellites among the countless stars, dull reddish orbs. Things that would have been too dim to see at his old house in Alpine showed up vividly here.

There was no noise from cars. Down by the creek, perhaps a quarter of a mile out in the pasture, he heard frogs croaking, and after a few moments he heard an eerie howl up in the mountains, above the campgrounds. It was high in pitch, too high to be a wolf, he decided. Besides, there weren't supposed to be any wolves so far south in Utah. It had to be a coyote.

It had hardly begun to howl when a dozen others joined in, creating an unnerving chorus.

Bron felt wide awake now. He realized that it was full night, still at least a couple of hours before dawn. There wasn't the slightest crescent of light limning the hills to the east.

He remembered the old man, the attack—his friend Riley slamming his fist through the window to break into the car. The memory left him with jitters.

He recalled seeing how the car had rolled, and he wondered if anyone had been hurt. He hadn't listened to the news that night, but figured that nothing had happened. The wreck hadn't seemed spectacular. It almost seemed to happen in slow motion.

He thought about Mike's cool reception, and suspected that they were going to have problems.

He thought about the warm way that Olivia had spoken earlier. He could still smell the faint scent of her perfume on him. It was ... strangely intoxicating.

He tried to clear his mind, to stop thinking about her, to get her bright eyes out of his mind, and he decided that he was too wound up.

The stars lit the long driveway, reflecting off the ash-colored dirt and crushed rock, almost as if it were a river.

He decided to follow it. He hadn't had a good run in two days, and he started out at an even pace, falling into rhythm as he reached Main Street, and then picked up his pace down the long road into town. The houses were few and far apart, and half didn't seem occupied. He raced through town, and twice he had dogs bark at him—big guard dogs that woofed so loud that he worried they might waken their masters.

He reached the T-intersection leading to the highway to Saint George. There weren't any houses along that road, at least none to speak of, so he turned and ran for another mile, heading across the valley and up a sloping hill.

By the time he reached the top, he was sweating and winded, so he turned and jogged slowly, enjoying the rhythms of his breath, the way that his legs felt strong and powerful, like the pistons of an engine that worked by will alone.

The endorphin rush was on him, and he let his mind go to that place where there was no thought, only the pounding of feet on the gravel, the distant wail of coyotes, and the occasional buzz of a cicada.

It was in this place that he always found peace. *In this place*, Bron thought, *a man can touch eternity*.

He became aware that a car was coming up behind, easing down the road toward town. He got well onto the shoulder of the road. He kept up his pace until the car pulled up beside him.

It suddenly slowed, and a spotlight shot out the passenger's window. A gruff voice called, "You trying to get run over?"

Bron spotted the bubble lights on top of the car. He pulled to a stop. There were extra lights in the cab for the radio, but Bron couldn't see anything: the cop had his spotlight aimed right in Bron's eyes. Bron raised a hand.

"No, sir, I'm not trying to get hit."

"It's three o'clock in the morning!" the policeman growled. "What in hell's name do you think you're doing out here? What are you runnin' from?"

"I woke and went to watch the meteor shower," Bron explained, "and then I couldn't sleep, so I thought that maybe a run would help. I ... was on the cross-country team last year. I ... was hoping to take state this year."

Taking state was far beyond Bron's capabilities, but he hoped that it might garner some sympathy. The cop waved the light at various corners of Bron's clothing, as if a handgun might fall out of his shirt at any moment.

"You're waking people up," the cop said. "Got a call that some kid was running through town, maybe a vandal or a thief. This is a quiet neighborhood. Folks here don't run—at least they don't run in the night."

"I'm not from around here," Bron said. "I just moved in yesterday ... with Mike and Olivia Hernandez."

"You that social services kid?" the cop asked. He flipped off his light, but Bron still couldn't see much. It would take minutes for his eyes to adjust.

"You heard about me, so soon?"

"Olivia bought dinner at the restaurant. The whole town knows about you, and they got nothing better to talk about."

Bron smiled. "Wow, sounds like I'm famous." He could see the cop now—maybe fifty, with a buzz cut and glasses. His face was wide at the mouth, like a bullfrog's, but it was his eyes that bothered Bron.

The officer didn't have much use for "social service" kids, obviously.

"There's a statewide curfew, you know," the officer said, "from eleven to five. I could give you a ticket, you know."

He looked down to a little yellow pad resting on the passenger's seat, as if trying to decide whether to write out a ticket. Bron didn't think that a judge would bother fining him for taking a late-night jog, and apparently the officer reached the same conclusion.

"I'm going to give you a ride home," the officer said. "No need to set no more dogs to yappin'. Get in!"

Bron opened the door and climbed into the passenger seat. "I'm real sorry if I disturbed anyone," he said. "I used to go running before sunrise every morning up north."

"Well," the officer said gruffly as he accelerated onto the road. "You aren't up north. You're down in Little Dixie. Things are going to have to change. I don't know what kind of trouble you bring with you, but I don't want any of it around here."

Bron knew the suspicions that some folks harbored about foster kids. The truth was that he'd made the common mistakes that kids do. He'd gotten caught at the age of eight stealing a candy bar from the local 7-Eleven. He'd once cussed out a foster sister. He'd gotten in wrestling matches with his brothers.

He'd learned that the rules for foster kids were different from those of normal folks. The things that people tolerated in most children—the things that they laughed about and considered rites of passage for their own kids—were unforgivable in a foster child.

"I've never been in any trouble," Bron said.

"You got thrown out of your old house," the officer suggested, as if that were evidence of some crime. "By tomorrow I'm going to know everything about you. I don't want no trouble in these parts."

The officer fell silent, and Bron wondered what kind of trouble he might be in. Pine Valley seemed too small to have a police force. The closest thing that he'd seen earlier to a lawman was the park ranger out in his little shack. Bron glanced at the officer's uniform. He was from the Washington County Sheriff's Office. A pin on his shirt said that his last name was Walton.

They drove through town, and when they reached the driveway, the officer made a point of hitting his flashing lights. He dropped Bron off at the front door. Mike and Olivia staggered out of the house in their bathrobes, and Mike shot Bron a distrustful look.

Bron went to his room. He threw himself on the bed and waited for Mike to come yell at him or something.

Instead, Olivia came to the door. She wore a satin nightgown in a soft shade of peach that accentuated her curves, and Bron gritted his teeth, waiting for her to chew him out.

"Please," she said softly, "in the future, don't go running in the night. There are worse things than Officer Walton out there."

To tell the truth, Bron had worried about that a little. "Like cougars? Or bears?"

"Worse than that," she said as she slipped out the door.

Saturday Bron woke feeling so exhausted that he was reminded of a book that he'd once read about potato farmers in Idaho who turned unsuspecting townsfolk into zombies and made them dig potatoes from dusk till dawn. Bron's muscles ached, and his thoughts were cloudy, filled with dreams of guitars. It was the crack of dawn.

Bron got up, glanced out his open window. Morning stole quietly over Pine Valley. The wildfires in California were heating up, sending soot and ash into the heavens, so that a red haze enveloped the vale, bloodying the land. Had someone said that dragons were setting the skies afire, Bron would have believed.

He wandered to the kitchen, got a drink of water. Olivia came in from her bedroom.

"Bron," she said, "Mike's out in the barn. He's going to make his morning rounds to check on the cattle. I thought that you might like to go."

She didn't have to say more. There was a pleading tone to her voice. This was supposed to be a father-and-son outing, a chance for them to bond. Bron had been through the routine often enough.

"Sure," he said.

Mike took him out on an ATV to show him his land—eight hundred acres of grassland and forest here in the bowl of the valley, climbing up into the mountains. Mike explained that most of his cattle were still up in the hills, grazing on public lands. The government let him run his cattle in the mountains for a small fee, but Mike always kept the younger calves near the house. Tourists often came by in the summer, and Mike charged the kids $5 to feed the calves a bale of alfalfa. It offset the cost of his feed.

They drove up a dirt track into hills where gray hoodoos rose up along the hills, like ancient towers of ash.

"Wow," Bron said when he saw them, "I didn't expect to see these back here."

"Seventy-five million years ago," Mike said, "this land was all covered in dunes, three and four thousand feet high. These cliffs are all that is left of them. There are still a lot of petrified dunes around here that you can climb on. You remember the little volcano just north of the park?"

"Yeah," Bron said. It wasn't tall, but it had a perfect cone on top.

"Just across the highway is White Rock trailhead. It's just a short hike to a little natural amphitheater that climbs up a thousand feet on each side. Olivia likes to go there in the mornings sometimes, to play her songs to rabbits that live by this pool."

"If people knew that all of this cool stuff was here," Bron said, "they'd be crawling all over these rocks."

Mike shrugged. "There's so much beautiful country around here, people turn up their noses at this. Personally, I'm happy to have the tourists leave it alone. A few miles from here," Mike said, "the sand dunes dropped down into an ancient sea. At the edge of it, dinosaurs roamed. The dinosaur run at Johnson's Farm is one of the best in the world. You can see where allosaurs used to sun in the mud and swim in the lake. But there are dinosaur tracks everywhere around here. Home builders will hide them so that the building inspectors can't see, afraid that the government will turn their home lots into archaeological sites.

"There's a great place to go hiking about twenty miles outside of Washington. It's a dry creek where you can follow the dinosaur tracks for three miles, on the trail of a T-Rex that was hunting on a muddy day. *Seeing* dinosaur tracks is kind of cool. Putting your hand in one is even cooler."

Bron studied the gray hoodoos, and tried to imagine what it had looked like here seventy million years ago. He somehow felt old today, as if he were part of this land. Maybe it was the attack yesterday, but he felt wise and sad.

Mike loved his land, it was obvious. The very eastern tip of his property climbed up into the hills, into a forest of brooding pines where the shadows made it feel like dusk.

They had just started driving up a wooded hill when Mike let out a curse. High above them, on a rocky bluff, a calf lay in bloody ruin.

Mike turned off the ignition. "Let's check that out," he said, voice shaking. Mike loved his land, but he loved the cattle even more.

They climbed the steep hill for two hundred feet, circling a chimney of ash-gray stone. When they reached the top, they could see the calf clearly, its belly split.

Mike didn't get close. He stopped fifty feet away. "Looks like something got to it, a cougar maybe," he said in a soft voice. "If it was a cougar, it will usually find a little perch close by. It will want to keep an eye on its kill."

Bron looked uphill in the shadows of the pines, but couldn't see much. He spotted a few fallen trees, but nothing crouched on top of them.

"I heard coyotes last night," Bron said, "when I was running."

"Coyotes won't kill anything this big," Mike replied. He squinted at the carcass. "Let's take a seat right here."

He squatted on the ground like an Indian, and Bron sat next to him. A kid at school had once explained that there was a correct way to sit on the ground without hurting your legs. The samurai had called it "sitting seiza," or "the one true way of sitting." Bron liked the idea that something as simple as sitting required a certain type of mastery, as if, by learning to do small things well, our lives could be vastly improved. So he sat seiza, with his knees together and pointed forward, his toes pointing back, and his heels propping up his butt. It required so much dexterity that most people would never attempt it.

Mike glanced at his pose, nodded approvingly.

They still hadn't approached the dead animal. Bron could see that its belly had been split cleanly open, so that its guts were spilling out. The stroke looked almost surgical. A few flies circled, green gems in the morning sun. He could smell blood and stomach acids.

"What are we doing?" Bron asked.

"Sometimes," Mike said, "you have to look at something for a long time before you can really *see* it. Don't speak. Just look."

So Bron simply studied the calf. It was a big calf, he decided. The legs were thick, the fur clean and sleek. There were no teeth marks on the throat that he could detect, the way that he'd expect a cougar to take such a big animal.

He couldn't see where the grass around it had been beaten, as one might find if there had been a struggle. Instead, dry stalks stood up all around.

Bron studied the ground looking for a track. On television there was always a patch of clear ground where some freshly turned earth gave away the identity of a predator, but this wasn't television. The ground was rocky, and few plants rose from it.

"It wasn't dragged up here," Bron surmised after fifteen minutes. "It's almost like it walked up here."

"Or flew," Mike said.

It was such a strange comment, Bron glanced up at him.

"My grandfather used to say, 'When we imagine that we know how the world works, it closes our mind to wondrous truths.'"

"So," Bron clarified, "you think that cows can fly?"

Mike smiled, almost a laugh, as if Bron had just been suckered in by a joke.

"No. I think someone killed it," Mike said. "Sometimes kids will shoot up an animal just for fun. Or maybe a bow-hunter shot it, then cut his arrow out. It doesn't look like an animal kill."

Bron couldn't imagine a person doing something like this for sport.

"What about a skinwalker?" Bron suggested.

Mike shrugged, as if that was a possibility. But now that Bron was thinking about creepy humans, he couldn't help but think of others.

Could it be that old man, Bron wondered, *the one who chased us? Is this some kind of a sick warning?*

Mike sat for another twenty minutes, shoulders sagging, face dejected.

140

Bron realized something. "You loved that calf. He was a nice one."

"You got that right."

They were spending a lot of time just looking. "How much is a calf like that worth?" Bron asked.

"Hard to say," Mike admitted. "Some people, they'd have turned him into a steer and put him in a feeder lot. Let him grow a little, and he'd be worth maybe $800. They're the kind of ranchers who slaughter ten thousand head a year, and they don't see what kind of calf they're looking at. It's all just meat to them.

"But when I look at a calf, I look at it as a breeder. That calf had a pedigree that goes back four hundred years. I was raising him to be a prize bull. I don't raise my animals for meat. I don't want to kill ten thousand a year. I just want one calf, one calf, that's perfect."

"So he was worth like what, a million dollars?"

"Probably," Mike said. "The right calf, with good breeding fees, can bring in three or four million dollars over its lifetime. Maybe more."

The air went out of Bron's lungs. He hadn't imagined that he was looking at millions of dollars of dead meat.

"I'm so sorry, Mike," Bron said. "I had no idea."

Mike shrugged. "It's all just speculation. That calf might not have turned out. It happens to ranchers. Calves die."

They'd been sitting now for forty minutes, and suddenly Mike turned and peered at Bron, stared at him thoughtfully for a minute.

Down in the valley below, Bron heard a calf moo plaintively.

"Okay," Mike said. "I'm ready to go."

"Leave?" Bron asked. "Don't you want to search the ground for clues or something? Or should we call the police?"

Mike shrugged. "I don't see any clues, but I think I learned what I was supposed to."

"What's that?" Bron asked.

Mike fought to explain. "When other people look at calves, they just see meat. When I look at them, I see potential. Some ranchers, you can put a prize baby bull in front of them, and they think steaks. But I make my living by seeing a calf for what it will become...."

Bron nodded.

"Olivia, on the other hand, sees kids the same way. She spots *human* potential.

"When school starts, she's in heaven, checking out the new students. She'll come home on Wednesday after the auditions are over, and I'll ask her, 'Did you find any new stars?' And she *knows,* man, *she just knows.*"

"So you two are a lot alike?" Bron asked.

"I guess so," Mike said. "Except I'm a giant, and she's more like a pixie." He laughed, then gave Bron an appraising look. "She likes you. She says you're a keeper, and she's desperate to have you. She wants to adopt. So I'm thinking, I'm going to trust her on this. Is that all right with you?"

Bron had never had two people who wanted to adopt him before, at least not that he could remember. On the one occasion that it had happened, social services had immediately taken him from the home. After all these years, he couldn't believe that this would happen, and he couldn't really even hope that it would happen. He didn't feel ready for this.

"I guess," Bron replied.

Mike said, "The way I see it, the calf I prized the most just died up here last night, on this altar. God took it away from me, and gave me something else in return."

Down in the valley, a calf mooed again, and Mike raised his hand to his mouth and mooed in return. All through the forest below, calves suddenly began to bawl, from every corner of the woods.

Mike smiled.

"Got to say 'hi' to my calves. Excuse me."

Mike trundled downhill, and Bron crept near the dead calf. He really couldn't see any bite wounds or bullet holes. He carefully kept searching the ground for tracks, but there was absolutely nothing.

When he looked downhill a few minutes later, Mike was there with his Oreo Cookie Cattle. Two dozen calves surrounded him, licking him, just wanting to get petted, and more were walking in from the woods in every direction.

Bron went down to him, and the calves shied away.

"You drive the ATV for me, little brother," Mike said. "I'll lead the calves."

"Little brother?" Bron asked.

"Hey, I'm only thirty," Mike explained. "I wasn't fathering no kids when I was thirteen. Besides, I always wanted a little brother."

So Bron figured out how to drive the ATV as Mike led the calves, like the Pied Piper of cattle. When they reached the upper pasture, Mike urged the calves out into the fields, then watched.

He came and crouched beside the ATV. In the mountains, a gun fired once, twice.

"You about ready for breakfast?" Bron asked.

"Shhhh..." Mike urged, tilting his ear. There was only silence. After fifteen seconds, he said, "I was listening for a third shot. If a hunter or hiker gets lost or injured, they call for help by firing three times, slowly."

When it became clear that no more shots would be fired, Mike squeezed Bron's shoulder. "It's got to be eight by now. Olivia will have breakfast."

CHAPTER 9

MUSIC LESSONS

"The oldest tales say that the gods sang rather than spoke. Such things are forgotten now, but it was once said that 'In the beginning, God sang, Let there be light!'"

– Olivia Hernandez

While Mike and Bron had made their rounds, Olivia took her plates from the CRV. She scraped her registration tags off and glued them onto her spare set of stolen plates, and attached them to the Honda.

She hadn't been stopped by a policeman in years, so she hoped that her luck would hold.

Mike hadn't had time to fix the window, but he'd get to it soon. He was handy that way, able to repair anything that broke. It came from growing up in poverty, living with parents who knew how to "make do."

While Mike and Bron were gone, she went online and ordered a computer and an iPhone. The phone she had overnighted, so Bron would get it in time for school. She realized that if she worked things right, she wouldn't have to go into town for weeks. She could buy her produce at the market in Santa Clara, eat meat out of their freezer.

She'd keep a low profile.

So she plotted and worried about what the Drag-houls might do. One of them was dead. That might actually be a good thing—having one less Draghoul in the world. She wanted them all dead.

If I had any guts at all, she thought, *I'd go confront them. I'd put a bullet in each and every one of them. Finding them wouldn't be too hard. They'll be holed up in the nicest hotel in town.*

But she could never confront them.

There were some things her mind just couldn't wrap around, and killing was one.

Dying was the other. Logically, she knew that she had made some dangerous choices—falling in love with Mike, teaching at a school. She'd always feared that the enemy might catch her.

But just as a smoker always imagines that it will be the other guy who gets cancer, Olivia had never really confronted the truth: that she was living too close to the edge.

Right now, she felt as if she were walking in a canyon, and an avalanche was poised to slide on top of her—rocks and dirt by the ton.

She fought back her fear until it felt manageable, then went in the house and made breakfast for "the boys."

Neither spoke for a bit. She knew that Mike was anxious. He had a breeder coming in from Australia at nine, and a lot was riding on this visit. Anyone who flew eight thousand miles to look at Mike's cattle was nearly sold already. The question was, what would he want to buy, and could Mike part with it?

They were halfway through breakfast when Mike said, "You should probably take the truck into town, pick out a car."

By that, she surmised that their talk had gone well.

"You sure?" she asked. He knew that her savings were running low. "You don't want to come?"

"I trust you," he said.

She looked to Bron. He seemed anxious. "Okay."

A few moments later, the Australian knocked on the door, and Mike went to talk with him, both as excited as boys out catching lizards.

Olivia took Bron to Saint George, and there picked out a used Toyota Corolla with tinted glass, a sunroof, and an upgraded sound system.

Olivia paid a couple thousand down, and financed another fourteen.

When she threw the keys to Bron, he stared in surprise.

"Follow me home?" she asked.

"But, don't you want this one?" Bron asked.

Olivia smiled. "You're old enough for your own car. Just take good care of it. It's the only ride you've got. But it's a Toyota. It ought to last you for the next twenty years."

Bron's hands tightened on the keys, and he just stared into Olivia's eyes. She knew that he wasn't used to people giving him things—anything—much less a car.

"What about gas?" Bron asked. "I'll have to get a job."

"Your job is to go to school and prepare well for the rest of your life. Let me worry about the gas."

She figured with the extra money that they got for taking care of Bron, she could make the car payments—and more.

Bron stood staring at her for a long moment, and then asked, as if the question were being painfully extruded from him, "Olivia, are you my real mother?"

She knew what he was asking. Did you give birth to me? Did you give me up? What the hell is going on?

"I'm not your birth mother," Olivia said. "But that won't matter. You'll see."

Mist filled her eyes, and she drove home in tears, watching every few seconds to make sure that Bron was still following her.

That afternoon when they got home, Mike was still dickering with the Australian out by the back fence.

Probably talking about feed mixes or some such nonsense. She wondered what the Australian wanted—a bull, breeder cows, bull semen, calves?

He might want to buy the whole darned ranch, she thought hopefully. She'd heard once that Australia had more millionaires per capita than any other country in the world. The breeder had never even given Mike a hint about what he was after.

She made a stir-fry with mixed vegetables, pine nuts, and chicken breast, then added a little glaze from a sweet Asian sauce. It took less than thirty minutes to prepare, and it went well with a little imported Japanese rice.

She set the table, went into the living room, and found Bron watching television. The news would be coming on in three minutes.

"Time to eat," she told Bron, flipping off the tube.

Just as they sat down, Mike came in, having said his goodbyes to the breeder, who was driving off.

"So?" Olivia asked for his report.

"I made a quarter of a million today on stud fees," he said, smiling weakly

Olivia breathed a sigh of relief. She'd spent a lot of money in the last couple of days. The stud fees would almost give them enough to keep the ranch running for the year. "Haven't the Australians heard that there's a recession on?"

Mike shrugged. "That *was* with recession prices. I should have made half a million, but I gave him a good deal."

She studied him, to see how he felt about that. Relieved, she decided, and secretly happy.

"You are my wise giant," she said, "and a masterful rancher."

"And you are my Fairy Queen!" he replied, "bold and majestic."

Olivia looked to Bron, whose face was red with embarrassment.

"You can say it, Bron," Mike told him.

"Gross!" he exclaimed.

Mike laughed. "You'd better get used to it, Little Brother. You're going to hear that kind of fluff all the time."

B ron hadn't failed to notice that Olivia had turned off the news. He wanted to learn what he could about their attackers. But Olivia didn't *want* to know.

So they sat down for dinner, and when Bron was nearly finished, he kept the conversation on a safe subject. He asked Olivia, "So those clubs that I have to audition for next week. Can you help me get ready?"

Olivia glanced to Mike. He threw his hands in the air and shrugged. "I guess I can fix dinner for a couple of days."

She kissed his cheek, turned to Bron. "Get your guitar."

Bron went to his room, pulled it from its case, and found that it somehow felt more familiar than ever before. He'd dreamt last night that Olivia was making him play, hour after hour. He'd grown more comfortable with it in his sleep.

For the rest of the evening, they worked on the guitar. He'd never had a formal lesson. His scant knowledge came from watching kids on YouTube, and downloading chords off the internet.

He was amazed at how much he'd learned from Olivia's one lesson. As he put his fingers to the strings, everything clicked, and music flowed from him.

Olivia smiled. "Wow, you *are* a fast learner!"

Bron felt his chest swell, and a fierce dream was suddenly born in him: the hope of playing like this all the time—perhaps even becoming a professional.

So Olivia began grounding him in music theory, telling how musicians create resonance in their listener's minds, and then do changeups to create interesting variations.

He spent a lot of time biting his lip and clutching the neck of the guitar too tightly.

Olivia taught him "House of the Rising Sun," an old song that he'd never heard before. The basic melody was simple, but it had a guitar solo in the middle that begged for wicked interpretations.

She tried to get him to sing along, but his voice shook so badly that he wanted to give up.

Olivia encouraged him to keep working until after midnight, and then called for a rest.

"Well," Bron asked when they were done. "Do you think I'll have a shot?"

"You've still got a few bad playing habits, but work with me. Passion and practice, those are the ingredients for artistic success."

"What about talent?" Bron always wondered if he had that elusive quality that everyone said was so necessary. *Sure,* he thought, *talent is easy to see in a pro, but what about someone who's only starting?*

"All great art comes from the same place," Olivia said, "the human heart. A painting, a song, a dance. It's as if the heart longs to communicate so clearly, so perfectly, that words and expressions won't do. So the artist's feelings force themselves out through some other medium. That's the kind of passion I'm talking about. And when you practice any art, it's that passion that drives you toward perfection. It makes you stay up an hour later to work on your voice, or rise an hour earlier to play an instrument. When people witness that combination of practice and passion, too often they confuse it for 'talent.'

Some things you'll find that you do a little easier than others, but the truth is, talent is mainly just sweat."

"I only have a couple of days till the auditions," Bron said. "Most of these students that I'll be up against have studied for years."

"It will be all right," Olivia said. "There's a reason why I got hired at Tuacahn. For each department, they get hundreds of applications every year, and they take only the best. Give me a couple days. Together we'll work miracles...."

The house had grown quiet. Mike was already in his bedroom. Bron said softly, "Have you heard any more about those guys that were chasing us?"

Olivia smiled secretively. "Let's not talk about it. Tonight we sleep." She kissed his forehead and sent him to his room.

In bed, Mike was lying awake, smiling. Olivia lay down beside him. Mike whispered, "That kid sucks, compared to you."

"Give him time," Olivia said. "I can teach him."

"You're good," Mike argued, "but face it, he's not like you. He doesn't see sounds as colors, or imagine songs to have three-dimensional shapes, or write papers on how Beethoven's Fifth is a perfect musical conversion of a fractal equation."

Olivia sighed. "Maybe not, but not everyone has to see music in order to make it. There's music inside him, wanting to get out. He can't sight-read yet, but that will come. Even when he strums, though, he has perfect rhythm."

"So buy him some drums," Mike suggested.

"When he sings, his pitch isn't bad," Olivia argued. "He just needs to learn to really listen to his own voice, and then correct, until he learns how to shape pure notes."

Mike looked at her, bemused. "You really think you can teach this kid?"

"I know I can."

Mike suggested, "Maybe it would help if he made a pact with the devil."

CHAPTER 10

A BREED APART

"Bron was never deceived by beauty. That is hard to remember, considering how close he became to his father. How could one love a killer? How could an entire nation bow down to Hitler? Some have sought to excuse Bron because he was young and gullible, but the truth is far more complex. Bron was never deceived by appearances."

— Olivia Hernandez

Bron woke that morning feeling refreshed and relaxed. Apparently there was some sort of tradition of having big Sunday breakfasts, so Olivia got up and made waffles with bacon in them, smothered in fresh blueberries, with whipped cream on top.

The concoction tasted better than it sounded, and apparently it was one of Mike's favorites, so he ate a mountain of them. Bron planned to go to his room and practice his music, but just as soon as breakfast was done, the doorbell rang.

Mike looked at Olivia, and she peered back at Mike. Apparently they didn't get many visitors. "Sunday tourists," Mike suggested, "come to feed the cows?"

He went to the door, but it wasn't tourists. He shouted, "Hey, Olivia, the Mercers are here."

A small family piled in, a stunningly beautiful blonde woman with a perfect figure and a huge basket of fruit that included bright peaches, kiwis, and red apples. She introduced herself as Marie, and her daughter—even more stunning—as Galadriel.

The daughter, whom Olivia had warned was an "idiot," had a gymnast's lithe body and hair like her mother's. She was even prettier close up than Bron had thought when he saw her in her swimsuit. She had a heart-shaped face, with a broad forehead and penetrating eyes so dark blue that Bron could never remember having seen the like. Her petite nose, he decided, was elfin in size and shape.

She wasn't the kind of girl that he would normally introduce himself to. In fact, one look at her, and he couldn't even speak.

Olivia took the fruit basket from Marie, who apologized that her husband Doug was on a business trip in Alaska, fishing at a lodge with some senators and a general.

The women went into the kitchen and sat down at the table to "catch up." Olivia watched Bron just stand there like a moron, and suggested, "Why don't you go show Galadriel the cows?"

"Good idea," Mike encouraged, and shoved Bron toward the door.

Bron felt like a buffoon. Mike and even Marie acted like they were trying to get him and this girl off alone. Mike thought it was funny. Bron didn't know much about cattle, except that they could be eaten as hamburger—or killed by mysterious animals up in the woods.

Galadriel strolled at his side, and Bron tried not to stare too much. He led her down to the fence, just beside the barn. A cow was standing nearby, and others grazed off in the distance.

He waved with a flourish and said, "Cows."

Galadriel smiled, laughing more *at* him than with him, he decided.

He wanted to say something informative. "They're called Oreo Cookie cattle. They're from Scotland, so they all moo with a brogue."

"Is that right?" Galadriel asked.

"Yeah, and they play the bagpipes at all hours of the night, and they can all dance the Highland Fling. Some of the more talented ones are hoping to audition for Riverdance."

Galadriel grinned like a cat that had just eaten a mouse. "Riverdance is Irish, I'm pretty sure."

"Yeah, but what's an Irishman but a wannabe Scot?"

She laughed outright. Her teeth were dainty, white, and perfect, and her eyes smiled as much as her mouth.

She was beautiful.

Galadriel leaned against the fence, peered at the animals in the field. "Your cattle are called Scottish Galloways," she said. "And the cow you just waved at, he's a bull. He wouldn't like you calling him a 'cow.' His name is Lazarus Wisdom, and his stud fee is $100,000. Mike has been perfecting his line for years. Lazarus is one of the best breeders in the world."

"Oh," was all that Bron could think to say. He kept trying to figure out just how much money Mike and Olivia really had. He decided that they were cow rich, cash poor.

"So what do you guys do for fun around here?" he asked.

"There isn't much to do in town," Galadriel admitted. "You can go fishing up at the reservoir, or hang around one of the parks. If you've got satellite TV, you can watch it, or you can play on the internet. But I'm grounded from both, right now. My mom keeps telling me to go outside and play, enjoy the summer while it lasts."

"It's pretty here," Bron admitted. "But you can't go running at night."

"You guys have a pond on your property, just up the creek," Galadriel suggested. "You want to go swimming sometime?"

Bron's breath went out of him. The prettiest girl he'd ever seen had just asked him to go swimming. "I ... would, but I don't have a swimsuit."

She smiled broadly. "You wouldn't need it with me," she suggested. "Swimsuits are optional—for both of us." She gazed into his eyes, studying his reaction.

If I fall for the bait, he thought, *she'll laugh at me, claim that I misunderstood her, and that I'm a dope.*

"We could just swim in our clothes," he admitted.

She stifled a laugh. "Bron, I'm a naughty girl. That's why I keep getting grounded. You and I are going to go swimming, *tonight,* without any clothes on. I'll meet you at midnight."

Bron's mouth slowly fell open. He'd lived in half a dozen homes, and in each one of them the rules were different. He'd lived with a Mormon family that studied from the scriptures every morning, and he'd lived with an atheist family where the mother had pierced his nose when he was only eight, and talked to him fondly of the day when he'd get his first tattoo.

In none of the families that he'd been with, though, had he been propositioned by the neighbor girls.

She's heard that I've been placed here by social services, he realized, *and she thinks I'm trouble.* He'd met that kind of girl before. He corrected himself: *no, she* hopes *I'm trouble.*

Of course a girl like that would only make life impossible for him. She might try to lure him into doing something exciting—like taking her dad's car for a joyride, or hopping into bed.

But when it came time to face the consequences, Bron would be left to deal with them on his own. Galadriel's family had wealth and prestige. If they stole a car together, he'd go into juvenile detention while she got grounded. That's the way it worked with rich kids.

Bron hadn't realized it, but he was clenching his fists. Suddenly he noticed something odd, strange calluses around the rims of his fingers, and there was something creepy going on with his hands, too—it felt like there was lightning in them, just waiting to escape.

He broke out in a sweat, caused by nervousness around Galadriel, and fear. He glanced down at his fingers and saw the weirdest thing: a ring on the tip of each finger, like the suction cups on an octopus.

It's like some weird disease maybe, he thought. *Can you catch something like this from cows?*

His heart hammered, and he worried that Galadriel would see. He could feel his hands throbbing, those calluses pressing hard, as if to make themselves permanent.

He wiped sweat from his forehead, turned away nervously, and clenched his fists in order to hide.

"Are you all right?" Galadriel asked.

He was scared nearly to death, and angry. He really just wanted her to leave, but he didn't want to be impolite, so he tried to change the subject. "So, Galadriel, your parents were Tolkien fans, I'm guessing."

He stuck his hands in his pockets, turned to Galadriel.

A pained look crossed her face. She'd probably been teased often enough. "Cate Blanchett has nothing on me," she said. "She never looked this good on the best day of her life." She stood straight, then turned to the side, as if posing for a photo shoot.

Sweat dribbled down Bron's face, and he breathed heavily. If anything, her seductive looks only made the tingling and throbbing in his hands worse.

"Yeah, you're right," Bron said. He decided that this girl was all kinds of trouble. He growled, "Look, you can go skinny-dipping out back all you want, but I won't be joining you in the moonlight. I'm ... not interested in sleeping around. I've decided that I'll probably only ever fall in love once in my life, and I'm going to save myself for my wife."

"Ugh," Galadriel said. "Are you a Mormon?"

Bron had been baptized at the age of ten, and the truth was, he'd burned with righteous desires, but had moved out of that home a year later and had seldom ever gone back to church. Like a coal taken from the forge, the fire in him had cooled long ago. But he still held to certain ideals. "Yeah, true blue, through and through." He hoped that would appease her.

"You're so boring," she said. "I was hoping for better from you. This whole town is boring!" She screamed, like a little girl having a tantrum, and pretended to pull her hair. "I want to get out of this place so bad. Do you ever think about running away?"

His hands were still throbbing, and he felt odd—as if the energy was coming from outside of him, shooting through the air, and gathering into his hands. His whole body seemed to respond to it, humming like a crystal glass when exposed to song.

I'm really sick, he decided, in a panic.

He looked around Pine Valley, at the decorative homes and the idealistic atmosphere. Couldn't she see: this was practically paradise? "No," he said.

But the truth was that he'd thought about running away often, when he was with the Stillmans.

"If you ever decide to go," Galadriel said, "let me know. I want out of here sooo bad!"

The initial fear was past, and Bron relaxed just a little. In fact, it seemed as if the ridges on his fingers were vanishing. He could feel something odd in his wrists, as if a muscle that he never had known even existed had been cramping. He let it relax.

"Where would you go?" he asked.

"Vegas ... or Hollywood."

Bron could understand that—people having dreams. "So, are you an actress, or a dancer?"

"Neither," she admitted. "I don't want to do anything there, I just want to *go* there."

Oh, a tourist, he thought, disappointed. Galadriel had zero ambition. She had a great body, and stunning looks, and with her parents' money, she had every opportunity in the world. But there was nothing of value inside her. A moment ago, she'd practically been driving him crazy. Now she repulsed him.

"If I was going to Hollywood," he said, "I think I'd want to be an actor first. It would take years of study and preparation."

"Ugh," Galadriel said. "You sound like Olivia. She tried to get me to go to that school of hers, but I don't want any part of it."

Now Bron saw why Olivia had tried to steer him away from Galadriel. The girl was a total loss.

He understood something else: Olivia was offering him an opportunity, perhaps the greatest one of his life. She could teach him to be something, gain a skill that he'd never really hoped to master. At that moment he decided to make the most of it.

"I think I'm going to go in now," Bron suggested. "The mosquitoes are coming out."

Galadriel smiled coyly. "I'll be here at midnight, if you change your mind. You're staying in the back room? I'll meet you by your door...."

He hoped that she wouldn't come. He could imagine her there in the dark, at his back door, less than twenty feet from his bed. The girl was beautiful, so beautiful that it messed with his mind. He couldn't give in to her. So he wished that she would change, that she'd just give up on all of her stupid, irresponsible plans.

Suddenly the suction cups sprang upright on his fingers again, and a wave of dizziness struck. He had a powerful urge to grab Galadriel by the head, try to shake some sense into her.

He fought the urge.

Galadriel watched in shock as Bron turned and headed back into the house. Bron felt sure that no one had ever abandoned her like that before.

CHAPTER 11

LIES AND ACCUSATIONS

"When a man is accused of assaulting a beautiful girl, people are predisposed to believe the accuser. Human nature demands that we protect women and children. Even if he is innocent, the man's best friends won't believe him."

— Mike Hernandez

Sunday afternoon was lazy, with Mike watching football in the living room, snoring through a boring game, while Olivia fretted in the kitchen and Bron worked on his music.

There was plenty for Olivia to fret about. It had been two days since she'd encountered the enemy, and she worried that she felt that sense of false security that comes after a little time has elapsed. She resolved not to go anywhere today, so there would be no risk of exposing herself.

But even as she lay low, they might hunt her down. Yet she suspected that if that was going to happen, the Draghouls would have located her by now.

She finally realized that she wasn't just afraid. Her jangled nerves, her beating heart, were signs of something else. She was excited. School started tomorrow.

She always felt enthused with the return of school, and she'd begun rehearsing her class introductions, imagining the little jokes that she could toss out in order to put her students at ease.

She worked with Bron a bit, impressed at how he devoted himself to practice. He was improving dramatically. Even with time off for dinner, he put in eight hours of singing and playing during the afternoon. Mike even joined him, sang a couple of songs while Bron played.

So when Bron went to bed just after midnight, she decided to reward him.

Bron went and lay on his bed, sweating. It was just past midnight when he went to bed. He hoped that Galadriel would leave him alone, or that she'd come and gone.

But at 12:13 a.m., Bron heard a scratching at his back door, like a puppy trying to get in.

It's Mike's dog, he thought hopefully. Mike kept his dog outside at night.

"Bron?" Galadriel whispered softly, then laughed. "You in there? Come out, come out, wherever you are?"

Bron's heart pounded. He resisted the urge to go to her. She shoved gently against the back door. The deadbolt was still locked.

"Open up!" Galadriel called.

Bron imagined opening the door. He wondered if she was wearing anything at all. What would happen if he did open the door?

I'd kiss her, he thought, *and fall into her arms.*

He decided that it was safer to pretend to be asleep.

He felt those ridges on his fingers harden, and looked down at his hands. Purple lights exploded from them, sizzled.

He looked up to the window. He'd left it open, to let in the fresh air. He was afraid that Galadriel might come and climb in.

The pounding came harder at the back door.

"Are you asleep in there?" Galadriel demanded.

She waited for a count of three, then he heard dry grass crunching as she walked off.

He lay there, for a long moment, sweat rolling down his forehead, wondering what he'd missed out on, glad he'd had the strength to resist.

Olivia waited until she thought Bron would be asleep, then crept into his room.

He was lying on his back, and at first she thought that his eyes were open. But he was breathing deeply, evenly, in sleep. She knelt beside his bed and placed her hands upon him, seizing his mind.

She peeked into the day's memories, surprised to see how agitated he'd become with Galadriel. He'd unsheathed his sizraels, and had been embarrassed and frightened.

There was nothing that he could have done, of course. He was too young to control such a visceral response. Unsheathing was a defense mechanism, a natural response to danger.

But Bron was worried sick about it, wondering if he had some strange cow disease. Olivia smiled at that. It was charming and silly and endearing all at once.

She hadn't even noticed Bron's mood. She'd thought that he was being quiet all afternoon because he was studying, not because he was worried.

I'll have to explain what is going on to the poor boy soon, she realized. *He can't wait much longer.*

She was shocked to find that Galadriel had come to his door, tried to enter.

Just when you think you know all of the problems your teen might face, she thought, *something like this comes up.*

Bron had fought the impulse to go to Galadriel, to even touch her, and that was good.

Not everyone could have fought such a powerful craving. If the danger had been greater, he might have taken her—and what? Sucked the memories from her, leaving her a clean slate? Or would he have taken even her memories of how to breathe, so that she would suffocate?

Olivia was grateful that he hadn't gone so far. He'd have had a lot to explain to Officer Walton.

As of yet, Bron hadn't heard about the accident, about the death. She wanted to keep it that way. She worried what would happen when he heard, on his first day of school.

She'd have to prepare him for bad news.

It was late. Olivia wondered if Galadriel might be outside, if she might even be curled up asleep at the back door. She went and opened it for a moment, peered out in the starlight. The backyard was empty, no one lying in the shadows.

Galadriel had apparently given up and gone home.

So Olivia returned to Bron and began a new lesson, training his fingers to respond to the urge to play, unlocking his resistance, so that music would flow to him in a continuous stream of sound and joy....

At six o'clock on Monday morning, Bron woke to someone pounding on the front door. He got up groggily, looking for his pants, mind swimming.

He remembered the lessons he'd dreamt about at night, playing songs over and over. The dreams had left him exhausted. He lay back down.

Mike came to the bedroom, whispered urgently.

"What?" Bron asked, unable to focus.

"The police are outside," Mike repeated, nearly a shout. "They want to talk to you."

"What about?" Bron asked, baffled. He wasn't thinking straight. He wondered if Melvina was pressing charges over the stolen peaches, or if perhaps after all of these years, one of his relatives had come forward.

Then he remembered the car chase, and sprang wide awake.

When Bron got to the door, Deputy Sheriff Walton stood on the porch with his hands on his hips. A second officer stood at Walton's back, down closer to the car. True to form, the car's lights strobed red, white, and blue in the pre-dawn.

"Here he is," Mike told the officers. "What can he do you for?" Bron simply nodded, determined not to say anything that might get him in trouble.

Olivia came in from her bedroom, put an arm on his back. Bron glanced at her, in her long nightgown, and felt reassured.

Officer Walton came straight to the point. "Bron, do you know where Galadriel Mercer is?"

"What?" Bron asked. The question caught him by total surprise.

"Did you see her yesterday?"

He didn't dare tell about last night.

"Uh," Bron said, "sure. She came over with her mom and brought a fruit basket."

"I'm talking about afterward, smart ass," Walton said.

Bron shrugged and looked back to Mike. "No, I was here all night." Bron still wasn't awake. He blinked his eyes and shook his head, trying to snap out of it.

"Do you have anyone who can corroborate that?" Walton asked.

"Um, I was up until midnight, practicing the guitar with Olivia." He looked back to Olivia hopefully. She nodded.

"What about after that?"

"I was in my room all night," Bron said, "asleep."

Officer Walton looked to Mike, who just shrugged. "As far as I know, he was in his room."

Olivia chimed in. "I woke up in the night and went to the restroom. I heard Bron singing at about 1:00 a.m., and peeked in his room. He was singing in his sleep."

Officer Walton turned away angrily, as if to cuss, then whirled and glared at Bron. "You were the last one to talk to that girl. What did you two talk about?"

Bron's heart pounded.

Had the silly girl gone skinny dipping and drowned—or been attacked by a wild animal?

Bron held silent. He couldn't tell them that Galadriel had suggested a tryst. In part he didn't want to ruin her reputation, but mostly he didn't think Walton would believe that he had turned her down.

But Bron *did* want the Mercers to find Galadriel, no matter what stupid thing she might have done.

Olivia touched Bron on the shoulder reassuringly, as if urging him to speak up.

"She told me that there was a pond out on our property," he suggested. "She said that she was thinking of going swimming out there, in the dark."

Officer Walton squinted suspiciously as his face darkened with rage. "For such a short conversation," he said in a voice as hard as gravel, "it sounds like you sure led that girl down an awful dark path. What else did you two talk about?"

Bron bit his lip. He didn't dare say anything more, not when Officer Walton would twist his words against him.

"Sheriff," Olivia said, "you can fish for confessions all day long, but that won't help. Maybe we should look down by the pond?"

Mike told the sheriff, "I'll unlock the gate for you."

Walton's eyes were like magnifying glasses on a hot day, and Bron was a small creature, burning beneath their cruel attention.

•

Mike trundled in that hunched way of his back to the gate and unlocked it while Deputy Walton grimaced and stalked to his car. When the police officers got through the gate, Mike ducked his head and folded himself into the passenger seat. They drove down an old trail that probably only saw a tractor three times per year.

Bron wondered if he should have gone with them. He wanted to help them find the girl, if only to clear his name.

"Don't you worry about them," Olivia suggested. "You come in the house, and help me make breakfast."

Bron followed her into the kitchen, where she fired up a griddle. He molded sausage patties and sliced cheese while she toasted some muffins, then fried the sausage to make sausage-egg muffins.

Work helped a little. Bron kept imagining the worst—Galadriel floating naked in the pond, with Officer Walton certain that she had been murdered. Or maybe someone had cut her open, flayed her like that calf, and her guts would be lying out in a steaming pile.

Walton would accuse Bron of course, but there wouldn't be enough evidence to convict. *After all,* Bron told himself, *how could they convict me when I haven't done anything wrong?*

So Bron focused on putting together the sausage-and-egg muffins, and the room began to fill with heavenly aromas.

Back at the Stillmans', Bron had been ordered to make pancakes just about every day. Bron hated pancakes, especially ones made from mixes. The ones he'd eaten in that house had tasted as bland as cardboard, and probably were just about as nutritious.

But breakfast here at the Hernandez house was special.

When the table was all set and the food steaming hot, Bron looked around nervously. It had been half an hour. The sun would be up soon, and Bron needed to get ready for school.

"They should have been back by now," Olivia said. "That pond isn't more than five feet deep at this time of year, and not a hundred feet across. It wouldn't take five minutes to search it."

Bron shrugged, and she gave him a piercing look, as if to draw him out. When she saw that he would hold silent, she shrugged and said, "Let's eat."

Bron felt guilty about eating without Mike, but they really had no clue when he might return.

Something is going on, he reasoned. *Either they've found Galadriel dead, or they're searching around the pond. Otherwise, they would have come straight back.*

He worried about Riley and that creepy old man. Had they come to the house in the night, found the girl, and killed her for sport? Were they trying to terrorize him and Olivia?

Maybe the police had found her corpse, and were trying to put together the clues.

The two ate in silence for several minutes, and Olivia said, "There's something that you didn't tell Officer Walton. I could see it in your face, and I'm sure that he saw it, too. Is there something more that you wanted to say?"

"Not to him," Bron said. "He already thinks I'm a creep. Anything that Galadriel told me, he'd twist it around in his head."

"So this Mercer girl, she told you something that bothers you?"

Bron ducked his head a little, swallowed a bite of muffin. "She told me that she was bored," Bron admitted, "and she asked if I've ever thought of running away. She said that she was thinking of going to Las Vegas, or maybe Hollywood."

"So she might have run away?"

"Maybe," Bron admitted.

"Did she want you to go to the pond with her and go swimming last night?"

"Yes."

"Did you go?"

"Of course not," Bron said vehemently. "I didn't touch her. I wouldn't. I just wish that I hadn't even talked to her. I wished that she'd—I don't know—I just wanted her to ... quit wanting the things she wants."

Olivia nodded. "She's a dangerous girl, especially for someone with your past."

Outside, a bird flew into the window. Bron looked up. Two male hummingbirds, scintillating creatures of emerald, blurred about the feeder.

"I don't have a past," Bron said.

Olivia frowned in concern. "What do you mean by that?"

"I don't have the kind of 'past' that people think I do. People always think I'm crazy, or a liar, or a criminal or something just because I come from social services. If you look into my file, you'll see plenty of weird accusations. When I was little, people thought that I was schizophrenic. One doctor said I was autistic when I was four. Another thought that maybe I had split personalities."

Bron's voice quavered. "To tell the truth, I've always thought that something was wrong with me, but I can't figure out what it is!"

Olivia reached up and smoothed his hair. "There's nothing wrong with you. You're right not to tell the sheriff that Galadriel asked you to run away. He suspects that you tried to seduce her. He can't see the truth. So keep quiet."

"Okay," Bron said.

"If he presses you, tell him that you talked about the cows and the weather. Just make up something."

No adult had ever told Bron to be so evasive before. It was refreshing to see that sometimes even adults could admit that being completely honest was foolish.

"But what if she did run away?" Bron asked. "Shouldn't we tell them where she went?"

"I could tell them for you, if you want?"

"She was thinking of going to Vegas or Hollywood."

"The usual places," Olivia sighed. "They're magnets for the young, vapid and pretty."

Bron was just finishing up his breakfast when he heard the police siren blurt out by the gate. He raced for the side door, to see what was going on, and Olivia came up to his back.

Mike was opening the gate to the pasture, while the car waited, lights flashing. His dog was leaping about at Mike's side. The siren began to scream, and Mike shouted, "We found her!"

He swung the gate open, and the car sped out, spitting gravel, siren wailing. Bron tried to see inside, and could only glimpse Galadriel in the backseat, her face pale and dotted with cold sweat. Her hair was stringy, and she appeared to be shaking violently, her lower jaw trembling.

"Oh, my god!" Olivia whispered as the car neared, and she gripped hard onto Bron's bicep, as if to keep from falling.

Bron wondered if Galadriel really had been attacked.

Officer Walton glared up at Bron and looked as if he would pass, then he stomped on his brakes and rolled down his window. In the back of the car, Galadriel was weeping and growling like an animal.

"You're involved in this, boy," Officer Walton said. "I don't know what part you played, but this is your fault, and I'm going to get you."

Bron shook his head. "I didn't do anything."

"I've lived up here for eighteen years," Walton said, "and we've never had no kind of trouble. You're here one day, and now we got this...."

From the back of the car, Galadriel shrieked, "Let me die! I just wanna die! Let me out of here!" she thrashed about, and the emergency blanket that was wrapped over her came off. Her clothes were soaked and muddy. Her hands had been cuffed.

She looks like a crazed animal, Bron thought.

As the other officer pulled the space blanket back in place, Officer Walton hit the gas and the car surged down the road, turned on Main Street, and sped through town.

Mike came jogging up to the house, panting. Olivia asked, "What happened? Where did you find her?"

Mike shook his head. "Down by the pond. We found her clothes first, all stripped off, like she went swimming. But there wasn't any sign of her, so we had to search that marshy area. We found her about a quarter of a mile away, naked, just huddling up with her arms wrapped around her legs."

"Was she okay?" Bron asked. He added, "She didn't get, like, attacked by an animal or something?"

Mike shook his head. "Nothing like that, no bruises or nothing that I could see. She's just...." He shrugged, unable to explain what was wrong. "Walton's going to take her down to the hospital in Saint George, get a rape kit done on her, have her checked out."

"Rape?" Olivia asked. "They think she was raped?"

Mike glanced at him. Bron wondered if Officer Walton really thought that Galadriel had been raped, or if the test was just a ruse to determine if Bron had slept with her.

"Just a precaution," Mike said. "I don't know what's wrong with her. Maybe it's drugs or something. She was just curled up in a little ball, and wouldn't talk, and when we tried to take care of her, she said that she wanted to die. I don't know, maybe she had a mental breakdown."

Olivia bit her lower lip, looked back and forth between Mike and Bron. Her eyes widened, and Bron realized that she knew something, that she wanted to talk privately with him.

"Hey," Mike said, as if trying to ease the tension, "is that breakfast I smell?"

"Better go in and get some," Olivia urged, "before it gets any colder."

Mike lunged through the door. Olivia closed it so that Mike wouldn't hear.

She peered deeply into Bron's eyes. "Have you ever seen anyone act like that before, like Galadriel did just now?"

"What?" Bron asked.

"Someone who no longer wanted to live?" Olivia clarified. "Someone who begged for others to just let them die?"

Bron looked at her blankly, shook his head "No."

"What about Mr. Lewis, in the third family you stayed with. He had a mental breakdown. Do you remember?"

Bron shook his head. "I was just a little kid back then," he said. "All I know is that he died in the hospital."

Olivia stammered, "You and I need to have a talk!"

Bron shifted uneasily. "About what?"

"About the people who chased us in town—about what they are. About what *you* are."

CHAPTER 12

LEARNING THE HARD WAY

"Life's most profound lessons are often learned on the streets, when someone pounds them into you."
— Mike Hernandez

Bron grabbed his pack and dressed for school by 7:30, feeling jarred and rattled. He'd been troubled by dreams all night, dreams in which Olivia forced him to play the guitar while suction cups formed on his fingers, and now the accusations about Galadriel only muddled his mind more. He worried about the people who had tried to attack him, and about the cow that had died in the woods.

All of these things circled like wolves, and he didn't know which to fear most.

Olivia knows something about what is going on, but how much does she really know? he wondered. A worry hit him. *Does she know about the suction cups on my fingers?*

Those scared him most of all. He dared not talk about it.

If it was a disease, he didn't want to have to deal with it. If it was something else.... He felt overwhelmed by the possibilities.

As he prepared for school, Olivia rapped on his bedroom door. "Do you want to drive with me," she called, "or do you think that you can find your own way?"

"I'll come with you," Bron said. His thoughts were too jangled to let him drive. There was no sense getting lost on his first day. He already felt like enough of an idiot.

Olivia drove his Corolla that day, wearing big sunglasses, hidden by the tinted glass in every window. Bron suspected that he understood now why she'd purchased this particular model. The dark interior let her hide.

Bron waited for her to broach the topic of the strangers, sure that she would talk about his problems, but she never did, and he angrily tried to force it from his mind. If she could be patient, Bron decided, he could be more patient.

So as Olivia drove that morning, he silently paid attention to the route, trying to take refuge in a simple task. Getting to the highway was easy enough, and once there, all he had to do was turn left and drive for fifteen miles until he reached the first stoplight. After that, signs along the road would lead him straight to Tuacahn.

The morning sun shining upon the red cliffs above the school stained them like copper. His heart thrilled. They went to the school and waited for nearly an hour before classes started at 8:30.

He sat out by the concession stands as the sun rose, a dry morning wind rising from the valley floor. For a long time, no one came. There was no reason to be early.

Then cars began winding up through the canyon, while parents dropped off students in their uniforms. There were a lot of girls, Bron decided, a sea of girls. Most of them were pretty, many downright beautiful.

The guys, Bron didn't care for so much.

Most of the new students lounged around the concession stands or the green theater or the Indian statue, and just talked. They didn't separate into the normal cliques, with jocks, social snobs, geeks and dopers.

Oh, they had cliques, he just couldn't quite tell what united most of them. The dancers he spotted easily enough, and a couple of kids sat down with sketch pads and began to draw, forming another small group.

A young man came and asked, "What's your name?"

"Bron Jones," he replied.

"Are you the one living with Olivia Hernandez?" he asked.

"Yeah," Bron said. He thought the young man would sit and talk. Instead the kid turned and went to a large group. He whispered to a girl, who picked up her cell and texted furiously. A dozen phones around the school rang at once.

There were a lot of kids peeking at him for the next thirty seconds. News of Bron's identity spread as if a rock had dropped in a pool. He heard muttered whispers and tittering laughter.

I've been through this all before, he told himself.

But he'd never been dressed this well. He'd never had his hair cut and dyed. He'd never looked cool.

He sensed that it was making an impression. He remembered Olivia's suggestion, that he act as if he were king of the school, and so he sat alone, threw his shoulders back casually, and smiled with genuine affection at his beloved subjects.

It had an effect. The kids at school all greeted one another with hugs and squeals, but he saw a lot of questioning glances thrown his way, heard bits of whispered conversations. One pretty blonde ventured that he was "Cute." A Mexican girl just stared at him with wanton eyes. He tried not to get his hopes up, and when the doors opened, he hurried inside, grateful that he didn't have to be on display.

The first day at Tuacahn was like the first day at just about any other school. Aside from the freshmen, there were maybe a dozen other new students, all dressed alike. Though Bron wore the uniform, he felt like a stranger.

His first period, mythology class, was full of freshmen, mainly, with a surprising ratio of good-looking people to the plain folks, and more girls than he'd even been led to expect. He sat next to a brunette who chewed bubble gum in secret, and did a great job of texting under her desk.

The class was all introductory stuff: here's the book. I'm the teacher, Mrs. McConkie. This is our schedule. I hope that you're excited to learn! The teacher seemed devoted to her subject, not your average cheerleader for education.

Sometimes, Bron thought, *teachers get the idea that the best they can hope for is to prepare you for a life of drudgery.*

"We'll be learning about gods in this class," Mrs. McConkie said, "but in learning about them, we'll learn about entire cultures as well, about their hopes and aspirations. Maybe by learning about them, we'll even raise our own sights, and learn to dream greater dreams."

She looked so cheerful when she spoke. She finished her intro early and started talking about her Star Wars club, where she'd be showing movies at lunch. They couldn't watch a movie in just an hour, of course, so sometimes they had to spread it out over days. She made sure to let the kids know that everyone was invited.

Bron thought that the Star Wars club sounded entirely too weird for him. He wasn't that into science fiction, and he didn't want to embarrass himself.

Class was half over when two guys and a girl came in to deliver a "one-minute musical" to the students. One boy carried a lute and was dressed as a troubadour, while the other two were dressed in medieval garb—the boy in tights, the voluptuous girl in an archaic dress.

They presented a play called "Lassiter's Lament." The troubadour, a tenor with red hair and freckles, played the lute expertly and sang of how "In ages past, our semester last," Sam Lassiter sought to impress the fair Ophelia Bascom by leaping from the landing of the stairwell to the bottom of the atrium here at Tuacahn High School. The boy and girl danced their parts as the tenor sang:

"But the maid was not impressed,
and indeed was quite distressed,
at the fateful leap that did occur.

For John fractured many bones,
And in traction stayed at home,
For the rest of the se-mes-ter!"

The song ended with Sam Lassiter lying on the ground in pain, while the troubadour sang a dire warning:

"So obey the safety rules,
Don't get hurt like some darned fool!
Don't end up like Sam Lassiter."

At the end of the song, the troubadour took the arm of the girl and escorted her away, while her injured Romeo looked on helplessly.

Cheers erupted from the class, and the three stood together, took a bow, then sang in harmony, "Remember: Hyperion Club Auditions begin tomorrow!"

They left amid applause, and Bron asked the gum-chewing girl, "What is the Hyperion Club?"

"It's a club for musical theater," she said. "You have to be a triple threat: singer, dancer, actor. Only the coolest of the cool make it in."

Bron frowned. He was just getting ready to take beginning dance. He'd never sung in public, and his acting experience consisted of playing The Great Pumpkin in a Charlie Brown play in third grade—if you can call rising from a pumpkin patch acting.

I'll never make it, he thought. *At least not this year.*

His second class was mathematics, and Mr. Hayward, a bespectacled old gentleman, explained that, "I know that you all think that you're artists, and you'll never need math, but as artists of course you'll need to learn to invest your money wisely. So this semester, I'll be adding a lot of interesting story problems to the curriculum. You will learn, for example, how movie studios use legal loopholes to steal money from both their actors, directors, and their investors."

That led to a lively discussion and demands from students for examples, so the entire class became a blur of story problems based upon things like, "How Arnold Schwarzenegger landed a cool deal on Terminator 3," and "How Peter Jackson learned, after he directed Lord of the Rings, never to take money on the back end."

The teacher had students nearly in tears as they begged for "story problems," which taught as much about cutthroat entertainment practices as they did about math.

Bron decided that the class he had expected to be the one most likely to put him to sleep would now be his favorite.

In the midst of a story problem, three teenage girls entered the room dressed as witches in black, with very dramatic green makeup, and presented a "musical memo."

The girls sang *a cappella*. In a mock-operatic tone, one witch warned, "There are scorpions in the lockers!" while the next young lady chimed in during mid-sentence, "And rattlesnakes in the halls!"

The first shrieked her lines as soon as she was done, so that the warnings came in French Rounds, growing louder and more frantic.

Then the third girl sang "Don't get bitten! Don't get stung!"

As they kept up the rhythm, the girl's lines began to change to warnings about how tarantulas and gila monsters seek shelter from the cold in the fall, and then the trio ended up singing an admonition:

"If you get hurt,
don't be shy:
run to the nurse
before you *Die*!"

When they finished, they urged the class to come to madrigal tryouts on Wednesday, then departed amid fervent clapping.

As class finished, Olivia came down and delivered Bron's new iPhone, along with $10.

He was delighted by the phone, and lunch money. Other kids came to admire it as he opened the box. All of the kids seemed to know Olivia, so it wasn't too weird to have your "mom" handing out presents at school. But he was hungry, so he went outside to the concession stands to buy lunch.

Whitney Shakespeare had never believed in love at first sight, but her mother had warned her that it could happen.

It happened that Monday. At the Green Show Theater, during lunch, she was singing with her band.

She had a drummer, a base guitarist who wanted to play lead, a keyboardist who only hit the right notes about ninety-eight percent of the time. She hoped to recruit some better musicians with a tune that she had written three weeks earlier.

"I see you coming, babe, and panic creeps—
　　why can't I breathe?
You say 'hello' and walk right past me—
　　why can't I speak?
This happens every day, five times a day—
　　what's wrong with me?
And on the weekend I'm alone at home,
　　and I dream ...

The song had a country pop beat, and Whitney sang with a youthful innocence. She drew from several inspirations—Taylor Swift, Katy Perry, maybe even a hint of Adele. The song required a lot of emotional range—longing one instant, hurt and pleading the next.

Choreographing the song to dance required Whitney's total concentration. She was lost in the music when she saw Bron.

Suddenly her heart began thumping to a whole new beat, and she remembered something her mother had once said: "When you see a boy and fall in love, don't hide your feelings. Just try to claim him as a friend. That way, even if the feelings don't stick, you might still have a bud."

She instantly recognized Bron. All morning, she'd heard how Mrs. Hernandez had adopted a hunk, and rumors were flying. Some said she was adopting him because he was a fantastic sculptor, others said it was because he was a tortured soul. Whitney's old boyfriend, Justin, had warned that Bron was a loser, already in deep trouble with the law.

Whitney took one look, and saw something amazing: Bron was handsome, heartbreakingly so, yet he had a timid smile. There was no sign of the conceit that had ruined her relationship with Justin. More than anything, Bron looked a little lost and frightened.

But there was something more. Bron watched her sing, but he wasn't just looking *at* her. He was connecting to her song in a way that few people did. He was nodding in rhythm to the music, as if he'd captured the beat of her heart, and when he looked at her, his eyes focused off in the distance, as if he could see through her.

Whitney sang her second chorus, then stepped backward while her guitarist, Damien, took the lead.

Damien couldn't quite keep up. He normally just played base. The whole reason for playing on the green today was to try to attract a new lead guitarist, and maybe someone for keyboards. Damien had the rhythm down, but he tried a couple of flourishes in his solo and tripped over his own fingers.

Bron was deep in the music, too, zoned out, and suddenly Whitney saw a gleam in his eyes, and he smiled.

He sees how to make this better, Whitney realized.

It wasn't a great song, she knew. It was what the Germans called an *ohrwurm—an earworm*—a piece of music whose rhythm gets stuck in your head. Most musical hits aren't masterpieces of composition, but simple earworms.

Whitney launched into the third verse, and when she reached the chorus she did something bold. She danced up to Bron and sang to him:

"I'll text you when I'm ready inside.
To climb out the window
down the old drain pipe.
We'll paint the town red in my daddy's blue beat up Ford.
And long after we should
we'll race the dawn back home.
And everyone now knows.

As she sang, she put her hand up and made the phone signal, and got in his face.

Whitney was pretty, she knew: with cinnamon-colored hair, a dazzling smile, and a lithe body. As president of the Madrigals, she had to be a triple threat. She'd worked hard to reach her position.

But she wasn't wealthy, not since her father's suspicious death. In fact, she was so poor, sometimes it hurt, and she was afraid that Bron would look into her eyes and see right through her.

It took him a minute to realize what she was asking, but his eyes widened and he pulled a new cell phone from his pocket and handed it to her. She quickly pulled up his contact list, and was glad to see that it was empty.

She typed in her name and number, put herself on speed dial, handed it to him, and sat next to Bron.

"Wow," she said, "a brand new phone, and only one person to call. That should make life easy."

Bron grinned shyly, as if girls never threw themselves at him.

"Just a minute ago," Whitney said. "I saw light bulbs going off over your head."

He was at a loss for words, so he just said, "What?"

"There were great big ones!" she went on. "Like the flash on a camera. There were beams of light shooting out your eyes, too, and rainbows flowing from your ears. So what were you thinking about?"

"I ..." Bron had a hard time responding. "I was thinking about the song, the guitar riff. I might have a way to make it better." He went on with guitar-geek speak. "The problem is, the guitar is punching out the words with strong beats when it should be flowing into the phrase. The focus is all wrong. It should be a pickup, not the destination, you know?"

Whitney nodded, interested.

"The guitar needs to keep moving, keep telling the story. You lose momentum during the solo and the song never really recovers. It can be done, but the guitarist has to choose his notes more carefully, make them count."

Whitney smiled, "I can see that."

"Yeah," Bron continued. "So you over-compensate vocally to try to regain the magic. You start pushing, but it's already gone at that point."

"So what should I do?"

"You need a better bridge into the solo, one that builds momentum and launches the solo like a rocket. Then the solo needs to keep the groove going while soloing in the margins. Then the guitar has to stop once it's had its say and give it back to you."

Whitney stared at Bron, measuring him up.

"Most importantly, the guitarist has to keep his focus on the story and the vibe and connect with the audience without losing the connection. He's too ... self-conscious. The song isn't about him and his guitar solo. The song is the story."

"I'd like to hear what you've got in mind," she said, wondering if she'd just found a new lead guitarist, or maybe a composer. "Where's your ax?"

"At home," Bron apologized. "It's just an acoustic."

"Tomorrow then," she said. "Play it for me at lunch." She smiled wide, leaned in close, and as he glanced down at her chest, she had a revelation.

"You're not gay!" she said.

"What?"

"Some guys were having a debate in the hall," she said. "They thought you must be gay, because your hair is too cool for a straight, and you're too buff. Without much in the way of athletics in this school, we don't have many hunks. Still, we couldn't be sure. But just now, you were checking me out."

Bron looked as if he was going to deny it, but admitted, "Right on all counts, I guess. I'm straight, and you ... definitely check out."

"I'm Whitney," she said. "Whitney Shakespeare." She stuck out a hand to shake. He had a firm grip, callused hands. She held his for a bit longer than was necessary.

"Bron," he said.

"Bron Jones," she corrected. "You're living with Mrs. Hernandez." She smiled secretively. "You're going to love her. She's my favorite teacher." She leaned in, gave him a bump with her shoulder.

"Yeah, she's great," Bron said, and as the band packed up, they got lost in conversation. Bron's face, his voice, were dizzying. Whitney told him about her old home, down in L.A., and her father's business as a film financier, before he'd died. They talked about their favorite pizza, and she found herself taking his hand and leading him like a puppy as she strolled back into school, down the hall to Room 205.

She clung to his hand self-consciously. There were a lot of pretty girls in the school, heavy competition, and she wanted to signal that "this one is mine."

Whitney's stomach rumbled from hunger, but she decided to skip lunch in order to be with Bron.

As they began to enter the classroom, Bron suddenly looked up with a start. The little room was nearly full of students, some sitting along the back walls.

"What's this?" Bron asked.

"The Star Wars Club," she said. "You should join." She pulled him into the room, and they took a place against the back wall, since all of the seats were full.

The teacher, Mrs. McConkie, stood at the front, next to a television with a built-in Blu-Ray. "We're going to start the semester with Star Trek, the J.J. Abrams version. Notice how it starts with the birth of a hero, who is also the son of a hero, in the very oldest of Greek tradition. Yet in reinventing the Star Trek universe, J.J. Abrams is doing what mythmakers have always done, adapting the tropes of the past to our day...."

She flipped on the television, and within moments Whitney felt lost in the story. From time to time, the teacher would make some comment: "Here's where

Kirk proves that he's a hero. He gives his life in order to save his crew. Note also that in losing his life, it ensures that his son will have to come back and face the villain that destroyed him." Or, "Notice how Young Kirk is lost, impulsive, and self-destructive in this scene. All young heroes are shown this way, almost always with these same flaws. These aren't flaws in character so much as the foibles of youth...."

This wasn't just vapid entertainment. The teacher was explaining how this silly story connected with a wider world, and as she watched it, Whitney glanced over at Bron and wondered, *Could he be the son of a hero?*

He looked the part. He had a strong chin, a noble brow.

Bron glanced to the side, saw Whitney studying him. She smiled as if to say, "Ah, you caught me."

"Were you just checking me out?" Bron asked.

She grinned.

"Well?"

"No, we're way past that," she admitted. "I was more ... *admiring*."

Bron couldn't wipe the grin from his face after that. Upon seeing Whitney, hearing her sing, it had seemed that joy just gushed out from her, like clear water from a mountain spring. He imagined instantly that she would be the most popular girl in the school.

There were a lot of pretty girls at Tuacahn, and he was definitely standing next to one of the hottest in the school. Whitney, with her cinnamon-colored hair, sea-green eyes, and dancer's physique was awesome, and she was holding his hand.

He'd never held hands with a girl before.

But there was more. When she'd sung, he felt that he connected on some deeper level. They were both the same inside—hurt, longing, alone, in need.

Life seemed good.

The movie had to be halted partway through, and Bron said goodbye to Whitney. She walked a few steps, turned back and caught him staring. She made the "call me" sign, and turned away.

He put it on his to-do list, promised himself that he'd call her tonight, after school.

After that, third period was a blur. Something about a Spanish class? He was so mesmerized by Whitney, he didn't remember much. She had such an astonishing effect on him that it drove out all of his concerns from the weekend, all of his worries.

The teacher was explaining how to conjugate the verb *ser,* to be, when the door burst open and a young man came into the room, dancing and spinning with a boom box on his shoulder, playing Owl City's "Fireflies." The teacher looked stunned and shouted for him to leave as he danced around, seemingly oblivious to her shaking fist.

Seconds later, a young man came tumbling into the room and began to break-dance, spinning on his head on the floor, followed by a ballerina.

The teacher kept shouting for them to get out, and they all ignored her, until Bron realized that it was all an act, and the teacher was in on it. A fourth girl danced into the room bearing a sign, "Dance Club Auditions: Thursday!"

The room erupted into enthusiastic applause and whistling, and the dancers whirled from the room, taking their show on the road.

Bron's last class of the day was beginning dance, his first and only real "arts" class for the semester. Most of the classes had already been full when he registered, and Bron felt silly in this class. Though it was a beginning class, Bron was less than a beginner. He'd hardly danced before. One bad experience had left him never wanting to dance again.

If he thought that this might be like any of the dance classes he'd seen at other schools, the teacher, Mr. Petrowski, quickly dispelled all illusions. One girl whispered, "He danced with the National Ballet in Moscow."

When Mr. Petrowski entered the room, he came in black tights. The man had thighs like a weightlifter's but managed to walk with the grace of a doe. In a thick accent he said, "This dance class will be toughest in your life, both on emotional level, and on physical realm. We have musical events to prepare for. The first one comes with the Renaissance Feaste, on October first, six weeks from now. We need dancers to perform in medieval costume. The Christmas Dance Recital comes in December, fourteen weeks from now. Auditions for performances start Wednesday."

This caused a stir in class. Many girls had a hopeful gleam in their eyes, and Bron realized that this was one of the big events at the school.

A young lady at his side whispered, "Don't worry. You've got a good shot, so long as you don't trip over your own feet. They always need guys."

"Yeah, but this is a beginning dance class. We won't have a chance, will we?"

She smiled up at him. "Petrowski is always looking for beginners to put in the show. He wants the upperclassmen to know that there is always someone younger nipping at their heels."

Bron nodded.

Petrowski introduced four older students who would be working as teacher's aides, two guys and two girls. Bron recognized one of the boys—tall, broad-chested. He'd been talking with Whitney in the hall, earlier in the day.

"You any good?" the girl at his side asked. She was studying his arms, his abs. Bron knew that he was pretty ripped. Most days this summer, he started the morning with a hundred crunches and ended the day with two.

"I've never even tried dance," he admitted. "Sorry."

"You're an athlete, though?"

"Wrestling and cross-country. I wasn't that good."

"Wrestling is a lot like dancing," she whispered. "If you can learn how to do a takedown, a dip will be easy. If you're used to running, you should have good wind. All we really need to find out is if you've got rhythm and attitude."

The girl wasn't pretty so much as seductive. She was shorter than a dancer should be, with exaggerated curves. There was intelligence in her brown eyes, a quick wit.

She smiled up at him provocatively. "Tell you what, I've had a year of ballet when I was a kid, along with a little Jazz. I'll give you private dance lessons, if you teach me how to wrestle."

Bron smiled self-consciously. "Are all the girls in this town so forward?"

She grinned mischievously. "Do the math: we have 274 students. Of those, only 87 are guys. Of them, 12 are gay. That leaves 75 guys. Only nine of them are really cute. Eight of the nine have girlfriends. That leaves only one. You."

At his last school, Bron hadn't been popular. Part of it had to be the clothes. Back in Alpine, his hand-me-downs advertised his poverty. Here, the uniforms made everyone look the same. The only thing beyond that was his haircut and style. It definitely made him stand out.

He knew that he wasn't bad looking, but everyone here treated him ... special.

Suddenly he almost felt as if there was something more, as if he was suddenly leading a charmed life. Things were really turning around for him.

"I'll have to think about the wrestling lessons," he said. "I have a feeling that you're more dangerous than you look."

Down on the floor, Mr. Petrowski called, "Pair up! Pair up!"

The girl smiled miserably. "Will you dance with me? I don't want to get stuck with another girl as my partner."

"Sure," Bron said. He got up, pulled her to her feet, laid one hand on her shoulder and another on her hip. "My name is Bron, by the way."

"River," she said. "River Hendricks."

One of the teacher's aides came over and suggested, "Move in a little closer." It was the tall young man who had been speaking with Whitney. He pushed

Bron gently, so that the two were pressed together intimately.

"There you go," he said to both. He added, "Sorry to hear about that neighbor girl of yours, Bron."

Bron shrugged, but River asked, "What girl? What happened?"

"Bron's neighbor was attacked and raped last night," the boy said. "Bron's the main suspect!"

How does he even know about that? Bron wondered.

River suddenly froze in Bron's grip. She gasped and stepped back involuntarily. Suddenly everyone was staring at Bron.

Bron looked up at the aide and saw that the young man had mocking eyes, a scornful grin. He'd spoken loudly enough so that everyone in the room had heard.

"I never touched her," Bron said. He realized that he'd spoken too loudly, that he sounded scared and defensive.

The young man glared at him angrily, then nodded. "Maybe not," he admitted as if he could be wrong, but his next words twisted into Bron's gut like a dagger. "Even you have to know, you weren't good enough for a *fine* woman like that. On the other hand, that probably made her that much more of a temptation."

Bron felt something odd, a tingling in his hands, as if an electric current were washing through them. The tips of his fingers went hard, and he knew that if he dared look, he'd see little rings of callus protruding around the tip of each finger.

What kind of freak am I? he wondered. He clenched his fists in order to hide what was happening, and considered punching the teacher's aide, but knew that a fight would just draw more attention. Besides, he wasn't sure that he could win. This guy was a good three inches taller than him, and all muscle.

He whirled, face burning, and began to stalk from the room.

"Wait!" River called. She rushed up to his back.

The aide laughed and called out, "You two make a good couple. Did River tell you that her dad's in prison? Did she tell you that he's a burglar who goes into empty houses and rips the copper wires out of the walls? What a low-life! You two are perfect for each other."

The room was noisy, with people chattering as they selected dancing partners. Bron looked to Mr. Petrowski to see if he had heard this outburst, but the teacher was talking to a group of students on the far side of the room. Bron decided that the teacher had pretended not to hear. He'd be no help.

River had grabbed his hand, and now she whirled as if to hurl insults at the teacher's aide. Bron hit the door and kept walking out into the hall. To his surprise, River followed.

He turned on her. "Who is that creep?"

River's jaw was set, angry, and her eyes flashed with indignation. "His name is Justin Walton. He was Whitney's boyfriend last year, until she dumped him."

It all fell into place, except, "Walton? Like Sheriff Walton?"

"Yes," she said. "His dad's a sheriff. Justin's family has lived here since the 1850s. They act like they own the place."

Bron stormed through the halls. He didn't know where to go, what to do. The corridors were nearly empty, and he didn't want to be caught out of class, so he decided to go to the men's room.

On the way he passed two girls near the theater. One casually asked the other, "Hey, did you hear about the kid that got killed in Saint George on Friday?"

Bron froze. His heart began to hammer.

"You mean that car that rolled?" the other girl said. "Freaky, huh?"

"Yeah," the other said. "My neighbor has a white Honda, and the police are stopping all of them."

Bron felt his stomach churn, and a wave of nausea rushed over him. He went into the restroom, wondering which of the teens had been killed. Could it have been Riley?

He would have to tell Olivia—but first, he had to be sick.

Chapter 13

The Hunt Widens

"For well over a thousand years we have hunted our enemies. The search cannot end until the last one is brought down."

— Lucius Chenzhenko

At the end of a hot day, Riley O'Hare drove his rental, a white Chevy van, into the parking lot at Tuacahn.

The view was stunning: red rock cliffs rising above the school and theater complex, vivid green lawns, a picturesque stream running through the complex to cascade into a large pool.

Something inside him thrilled. He'd checked dozens of hotels over the weekend, and struck out on that front, but he was a hunter by nature, and he felt energized by this virgin territory.

School was still in progress. That would make it hard to interview students. A sign out front said that this was the first day of class. Even if the prey was here, Riley suspected he might be a new student, and so other classmates might not recognize him.

So Riley opted for the most direct approach to the task. He strolled up to the school, opened the glass door, plastered with posters for upcoming plays, and viewed the foyer. Trophies adorned the wall. Most schools would have celebrated their sporting achievements, but these were for dance, theater, music, and art.

Beyond the foyer, he found offices. A secretary sat at a desk, a middle-aged woman with a plump figure. A sign gave her name: Allison Holmes.

Riley glanced around. Allison was alone. He could have taken her head in his hands, read her memories, but the site was too exposed. The glass walls left an open view to the hall. The principal's office loomed at his left. The principal glanced up from his desk curiously.

Riley said, "I'm looking for a student here, Bron Jones."

The secretary looked up from some paperwork, smiled, went to her keyboard and typed in the name.

"What would you like with him?" she asked.

"Mom asked me to stop by and give him a message," Riley said. It seemed like a casual enough lie, likely to produce good results.

The secretary's brow scrunched as if she detected the deception. She peered at the screen for a long moment, and said, "How is that first name spelled?"

"Bron—B.R.O.N."

Riley looked forward to seeing Bron again. It was more than just the thrill of the hunt. He'd liked Bron as a kid. Soon, he hoped to welcome him as a brother, and a colleague.

She shook her head. "We don't have anyone by that name here. Our only Jones is a girl, Sidney. Are you certain you have the right school? Did you try Snow Canyon?"

"I'm sure that he was registered here," Riley said. He leaned to the side, tried to catch a view of the screen, but the secretary hit a button and blanked it.

"I'm sorry, we don't have anyone by that name," the secretary said. "In fact, we don't have many young men here at all."

Riley felt his sizraels surface, the tips of his fingers growing hard and taut. He ached to grab this woman's cranium, draw out her secrets, but the principal stood up in his office, about to stick his head out the door.

"Thank you," Riley said.

He exited, but instead of heading out the way he'd come, he stalked deeper into the school, to a wide atrium. He found some classrooms, but there were no windows to let him peer in.

A student came down the hallway, a young man with long arms and curly hair. His slouching look suggested something criminal, and if Riley had been looking to score, he would have figured that this kid was the go-to dealer at the school.

"Hey," Riley said. "I'm looking for a kid. You know this guy?" Riley held out his cell phone, showed the picture of Bron getting into his car.

The young man reached out for the phone. Riley looked left, right, and then struck. He unsheathed his sizraels, grabbed the boy's skull in one hand, and lightning arced with an audible snap. The young man fell backward, but Riley shoved him against the wall, holding him upright.

The boy's name was Kendall McTiernan. He'd started school here near mid-semester a year ago, and his whole life centered on a pathetic little rock band that he managed. His mind was a mess, filled with terrible longings and remorse. He knew every boy in the school by sight, but had never seen Bron Jones before, had never heard his name.

There was a slim chance that the object of Riley's hunt was a new student, someone that Kendall had never met, but it was a very slim chance.

Riley ripped all memories of the encounter from Kendall's mind, and left him slumping to the floor. He glanced up, peered around. No one had seen.

Riley felt a surge of adrenaline, fought the urge to go find another student. Instead, he strode out the side exit to the school. He stood for a moment in the bright sun, inhaled the clean air, and studied the high cliffs.

A golden eagle screamed and leapt from a precipice, went hunting on steady wings, swooping to the south.

It seemed like a good omen, as if nature encouraged Riley to widen the hunt.

CHAPTER 14

CREATURES OF THE NIGHT

"To define yourself is to enter a sort of prison. By telling yourself what you are, you limit what you may become."

— Bron Jones

On the first day of school, Olivia decided to leave early. Club auditions wouldn't begin until tomorrow, so she decided to cut out earlier than she normally would.

As Olivia stopped by the office to check her mailbox, the secretary stopped her.

"A young man came by just a few minutes ago," Allison said, "looking for Bron."

Olivia's heart slammed to a halt. Her hand froze at the mailbox. "What did you tell him? Where is he?" Olivia imagined the worst.

"I sent him away," Allison said. "He told me that his mom said to give Bron a message. I knew he was lying, so I told him that he had the wrong school, and sent him packing."

Olivia nodded her head, grateful for small favors.

"What's going on?" Allison asked.

Olivia scrambled to come up with a cover story. "Bron had a girlfriend at his last school. Her old boyfriend was jealous. I think that the young man you met may have been looking for a fight. Do you have him on the security cameras?"

Allison swiveled in her chair, flipped on a monitor, behind her, and then went to channel three. She backed up the camera by fifteen minutes, until it showed Riley entering the school, pausing momentarily to look at the trophy case. The camera got a good side view of his face.

"Do me a favor," Olivia said. "If this boy comes back—or any of his friends—just do what you did today. Send them packing."

"Okay," Allison said. "Do you think we should call the police?"

"I doubt that they'd be any help," Olivia said. "No crime has been committed." Allison nodded. "Now do me another favor. Show me the parking lot view."

Allison went to work on the cameras, showed Riley arriving in a white van, then leaving not three minutes ago. As Olivia watched, her stomach cramped with nervousness.

Things were getting messy. Olivia wasn't supposed to tell a nightingale what was going on, but between the Draghouls hunting him, and Galadriel's strange illness, Bron needed to know more, and now!

B ron spent most of his last period in the bathroom, locked in a stall, panicking. When the last bell rang, he fought down his nervousness and strode down the hall.

Whitney waved at him and flashed a smile. He smiled back, turned to say "Hi."

A hand clapped his shoulder, and he jumped. Somehow, he knew that it would be one of those freaks from Best Buy. He turned to see Olivia.

"Bron," she whispered discretely, "we need to get out of here. Now!"

"What's going on?" he asked. The halls were crowded with kids, giving him a sense of anonymity.

"Just come to the car," she whispered.

Whitney came down the hall. "Hi, Mrs. Hernandez," she said. She looked as eager as a puppy.

"Nice to see you, Whitney," Olivia offered. "We've got to run to an appointment. See you tomorrow."

She steered Bron toward the door, hurried to beat the crowds. Bron waved to Whitney, who made the phone signal and said, "Call me!"

Then they rushed outside.

"You heard?" he asked softly. "About that boy?"

"I heard," Olivia answered.

"It was an accident!" Bron apologized.

"Keep quiet," she said. "We'll talk in the car."

Immediately, he realized from her tone that this wasn't going to be just any talk. This was going to be *the talk.* Olivia smiled as she passed another teacher. They crept out of the school in the midst of a crowd.

As they exited Olivia halted in the shadows and stood peering over the parking lot. Bron felt acutely aware that she was searching for something, someone—some sign of the enemy. The sun was so bright that every shadow became impenetrable. Any of them could have held a lurking figure.

She pulled Bron out into the sun and hurried downhill to the parking lot. When they reached the car, Bron felt a sense of relief wash over him. Tuacahn was far from the main drag down in Saint George, and though it was only ten miles outside the city, the setting was remote, off the beaten track.

They climbed in the car, and Bron asked, "Are we ready for that talk?"

Olivia opened her mouth as if to speak, closed it. She started the car, put it in drive, and joined the caravan of students heading down from the hills for the day. When she reached the main road, she drove past some homes, and finally pulled off onto a gravel road that led to a stalled housing development.

She turned off the engine, and sat.

There were no houses here, no plants. Everything had been bulldozed. The world was pared to the basics—stone, sky, sun, shadow.

Bron studied Olivia's face. He could see worry lines in her brow, and stress in her lips. She seemed to be looking inside herself more than at him. She finally let out a deep breath, and prepared to speak. "You understand what man is, *homo sapiens sapiens*?"

"Yeah," he said.

"You know that ... creatures evolve. You know that there were once *homo sapiens neanderthalensis*, a humanlike species that lived beside early man for hundreds of thousands of years? Fossil records show that they lived in caves together, hunted together, and lived as friends. They stalked woolly rhinos, traded beads made from shells, buried their dead beneath blankets of flowers. But they were different from each other, two different species. They couldn't inter-breed."

Bron wondered where she could possibly be going with this. What did it have to do with the boy who was killed?

"Recently, a new species has been discovered, which lived at the same time as them, in the same area of Asia, near Kazakhstan. Did you know that? There were three distinct species of early humans in Eurasia, and there was another in Indonesia."

Bron felt confused. "What are you trying to say?"

She said bluntly, "Bron, I'm not human. Neither are you."

Bron studied her face for a long moment. He broke out in a long laugh. "That has got to be the greatest joke ever!"

Olivia's face betrayed no hint of mirth. Her mouth was straight, and worry lines creased her eyes. He wondered if she might be crazy, or on drugs.

"I know that this sounds hard to believe. Let me show you something." She held out both hands. "Look at my fingers."

She had dainty hands, a musician's fingers, toughened and wizened. He'd seen her guitar calluses before.

"Watch carefully...." she warned as she raised her palms toward him. He saw muscles flex inside her wrists. Suddenly on each thumb and fingertip, a single oval suction-cup sprang up.

"Ah!" Bron shouted, and instinctively leapt away from Olivia. He grasped blindly for the door handle, and nearly fell from the car before he realized that she had suction cups on her fingers. *Just like his.*

He demanded, "What are those?"

Olivia held her hands up so that he could see. "I won't hurt you, Bron. I'll never hurt you, but I had to show you this. These are called *sizraels.* They're ... a mutation, an advantage that our species has over normal humans. You have them, too. There is no sense in pretending otherwise."

He stopped, stared at his own hands for a long moment, trying to let this sink in. He couldn't deny it, so he asked guiltily, "What ... what are we supposed to do with them? Do you use them to, like, climb walls?"

She grinned. "We're not flies, Bron. We can't climb walls, or crawl around on the ceiling like Spider Man. Our sizraels are far more ... dangerous than that."

She relaxed her wrist, and the sizraels vanished. "You see?" she said. "They're like the claws on a cat. We can make them appear, and disappear. Mostly, we keep them sheathed."

Bron began breathing hard, taking great gulps of air. It felt as if the hair began to stand up on his head. He shivered.

"Take it easy," Olivia said. "I won't hurt you."

"Yeah, but—"

"I won't hurt you." Her tone was convincing enough, and he calmed a bit, but he was still scrunched against the far door.

"Just my luck," he whispered. "I finally get a cool mom, and you're not even human." Olivia didn't smile at the compliment. This wasn't an occasion for humor.

210

"So what do you do with them?" he asked.

"That's kind of hard to explain," Olivia said. "You're familiar with mythology, right?"

"I'm taking a class this semester," he admitted.

She struggled to elucidate. "You've heard about creatures like me," she suggested. "For thousands of years, humans have been aware of us. We call ourselves masaaks, to differentiate ourselves from humans. I use my sizraels to ... help draw memories from other people, or to insert new memories into them."

Bron didn't know what to say to that. The situation sounded more and more insane, but she went on. "Bron, among my people, I'm what you would call an *at-tujjaarah a'zakira*, a *memory merchant*. I can borrow memories from others, or steal them completely, but I can also give you memories. Would you like to see how it works?"

Bron nodded slightly, yet shrank away. He didn't really want to see how it worked. The very notion that it could work terrified him, but he didn't want her to know how frightened he was.

"Come closer," she said. "I need to touch you, on the head."

Bron drew closer, and Olivia leaned forward and grasped him by the forehead, her sizraels locking onto him. She placed her thumbs on his supra-orbital ridges, just above each eye. Then her fingers splayed out, her forefingers on his brow, and her little fingers resting on the very back of his skull. Her fingers felt cool, and suddenly there was a tingling sensation as electricity arced between them.

Olivia held him for a moment, but nothing had changed. The cab of the Corolla was just as bright as it had been. The air carried that slightly new car scent.

"So what is my name?" she asked.

"Olivia. Olivia Hernandez."

"And what is your name?"

Bron opened his mouth to answer, but nothing came out. He felt as if it was just on the tip of his tongue, but he couldn't quite get it. "I ... I can't—"

"I'm sure you can remember your own name," Olivia said. "You've heard it a hundred times per day, for your whole life. What was it again? Carl? Sanjay? Bron? Miguel?"

He shook his head. None of those names sounded familiar to him, or at least none sounded right. His mouth opened in astonishment, and he peered about, as if he might find a clue just floating in the air. "Give me a minute," he said. "I'll remember."

"A minute?" Olivia said. "A minute wouldn't help. A year wouldn't help. You see, it's not up there anymore. I have it now. I own your name. I'm storing it right here." Olivia grasped his hands and raised them up, put them on her skull, way back up about four inches past her jaw.

"Can you feel this bump here, on the back of my skull?" She held his hands there. "Those are called the secondary lobes," she said. "Humans have only two lobes to their brains, masaaks have four. Ages ago, when humans first evolved, that new brain of theirs, with its two lobes, was a huge evolutionary leap. It doubled their capacity to learn. Our brains, with their four lobes, are the next step.

212

"You must never let a doctor give you a brain scan. They'd be baffled by what they'd find."

He touched her lobes gingerly, but there wasn't much to feel. He had the same odd bumps, he knew. He might have thought that Olivia only imagined a physical difference, but he couldn't remember his own name, and he felt bewildered by that, shocked and confused.

"Is this ... some hypnotist's trick?" he wondered.

He squinted and struggled to remember. Nothing would come.

"Now," Olivia said, "I'm going to remind you of your name."

She touched his head again in her way, and held him for an instant. Though her mouth did not move, she whispered his name into his mind, so that it exploded as if spoken by ten thousand voices. His name roared in his ears, and even his bones shivered.

"Bron!" he shouted.

Olivia smiled.

A moment ago, he'd been struggling. Now the memory burst upon him so clearly, so naturally and profoundly that Bron felt elation. Tears came to his eyes. He sat blinking stupidly, mouth open, at the revelation of his own name.

"You see," Olivia said. "I can take your memories from you, and I can return them. Or I can just sit and sort through them if I like, looking for information— even your deepest, darkest secrets. That's how I know what is happening to you. I know how your sizraels unsheathed yesterday, when you were talking to Galadriel. Anything that you know, any skill that you have, I can take it away from you. Anything that I know, I can share with you—within some limits."

Bron's mouth had gone dry, and he licked his lips, took a deep breath. "What limits?"

"Those lobes that you felt, they're very small. I can't hold all of the memories of even one person. So I have to specialize, pick and choose. I try to take only certain kinds of information, the kind that I love best."

"I don't follow," Bron said. Outside, a hawk shrieked as it floated just above the field, trying to startle mice from hiding. Bron shivered.

"The memories that I love best," she said, "are all about music. I've learned all that I can. I've borrowed knowledge from so many great minds.... I've even traded for it. There are others like me, you see, other memory merchants around the world. We form something of a 'living library' of knowledge and experiences. Would you like to know what Beethoven knew? Or Caruso? Or Michael Jackson? I can share that with you. Let me know a favorite composer, and I might be able to call a friend, get some of the memories that you're after."

Nothing in his life had prepared Bron for this. "You, you said something about mythology," Bron said. "What are you *really*?"

"Can't you guess?"

Bron shook his head.

"In the Mediterranean, we were called the 'Ael,' the speakers for the gods. We have been called many things—and most of the names have been lost in time—the shazaal, the massa, m'kithra—but you'll recognize some of the more-familiar names—'witches,' 'demons,' 'angels.'"

"How can you be both angels and demons?" Bron asked.

"Some of us are evil," Olivia replied. "Some of us feel nothing for humans, and use them mercilessly."

"Like those guys that chased us?"

"Yes," Olivia said. "Like them. Bron, the information that my people hold is very precious. There are tens of thousands of us hiding around the world. We're like ... a vast storehouse of information that you can't even imagine—math, history, philosophy. There are secrets we know, hidden from mankind for thousands of years. We're trying to save the world, make it a better place. But our enemies would destroy much of that, take what we know, and throw it away."

"Why would they do that?" Bron asked.

Olivia grew quiet. "That's not for me to answer, not now. You'll find out soon enough."

She fell silent for a moment, then said, "In ancient Greece, they would have called me a *muse*, a goddess who comes to bestow the gift of music and inspiration."

"Oh," Bron said. He felt dumbfounded, as if he might explode with this revelation. She knew what was going on in his mind. He remembered his training sessions in his dreams, and now he understood why he was suddenly ... talented.

"So," he wondered, "what do you want with me? Why are you telling me all of this? I mean, I could have lived here for years, and I never would have imagined something like this."

"You're wondering why a muse would give her gifts to you?" Bron nodded. "I'm a teacher. That's what I do—spread knowledge, and hopefully help bring a little light, and joy, and beauty into the world."

A white sedan pulled into the empty development and sat for a moment, blocking the exit. Olivia put her hand on the key, peered at the sedan through the rearview mirror.

Bron feared that they'd been found. He studied the driver, a middle-aged woman with bad hair and pale skin. She peered about, as if lost, then backed out and drove away.

Olivia let out a breath. Bron decided that there was nothing to worry about.

Bron asked, "Does Mike know what we are?"

Olivia shook her head. "No, and you must never tell him. He knows that he and I can't bear children, but he hasn't guessed at the reason, and I won't tell him. He ... did find out a couple of times. Before we got married, I made the mistake of trying to tell him. He became very frightened and upset, every time, and so I had to sneak into his room as he slept and take the knowledge."

Now Olivia reached out, took Bron's hand gently, and gazed into his eyes.

"That's another gift that I can bring you, if you want: forgetfulness. Are there any memories that trouble you, any dreams that wake you in the night?"

"No," he said. Bron had more than his share of painful memories, but he wouldn't want Olivia fooling around in his head.

She smiled benevolently. "If you understood my powers, you might think better of that. The offer will

216

always be open. If dark thoughts trouble you, I can offer relief."

"I don't want anything from you," he said. "I don't need anything."

Olivia recoiled just a bit, as if offended, and Bron regretted his words. "There's something that you need," she said. "You need to understand who you are, what you are."

"How did you know that I was one of you?" Bron asked. "I mean, even *I* didn't know!"

"There are signs. There aren't many of us, but I spot others from time to time. You've got an odd shape to your skull, rather boxlike. That was the first clue. But then I smelled you, and I knew. Male masaaks your age give off ... a scent, pheromones that draw women. When you go into musth, it will attract every female who is ready to breed within miles."

Bron had no idea what to think about that. "What do you mean, when I go into musth?"

"In a year or so you'll be old enough for your first musth," she said. "Your scent right now, it's very ... uneven. But when it comes, it will be powerful ... and dangerous. We call it *flourishing.* Just as a flower puts out its scent, so will you. I won't be able to be near you then. When I smell it beginning, I'll leave."

"I don't understand," Bron said, though he suspected that he understood her all too well. "What will happen?"

"You will begin to flourish, and any of our kind who taste your scent, any women who are fertile, will come to you. They'll smell it from miles and miles away. Do I need to make it any clearer?"

"What if I go away, into the mountains or something?"

"Then no one will find you. But the musth will come upon you again, and again, every six years or so. You mustn't fight it. If we're to survive as a species, you mustn't fight it."

Bron grew thoughtful, and for a long time he didn't say anything. "If I'm a masaak," he asked, "then why haven't my sizraels ever come out before this? I mean, until a couple of days ago...."

"Isn't that obvious?" Olivia said. "Someone erased some of your memories, the ones that let you know how to extend them. I suspect that it was your mother. She didn't have to take much, since you were only a child. Someone wanted you to live among the humans, learn to pass yourself off as one of them. We're different from them, you and me. If you had grown up with a masaak, it would only accentuate the difference in your mind. Some of our children learn to see themselves as superior to others. They grow up cold and cunning, without compassion. They see humans as animals to be herded and used."

Bron felt confused, betrayed. "I can't believe that a mother would abandon her own child that way. I mean, I don't know how different a masaak is from a human, but even a crocodile loves her young."

Olivia shook her head. "I can't guarantee that your mother loved you. Those people we saw Friday, they are masaaks, too. They're more than just a cult. They're more evil than you can imagine. They're bred to be cold, dispassionate. The old man, he was training the young. Very often, their women mate in a frenzy, and then don't want to keep their young. So they give them to humans to raise.

"It's called 'brood parasitism.' Just as some birds lay their eggs in other's nests, so do some masaaks. That boy that you saw at the store, Riley? He was one of them, a child left to be raised by humans. But such children are still precious to our enemies, and in time they will be gathered up by their masters."

Bron wondered at this. He was cold and dispassionate, he knew. Or at least he could be that way. He'd learned to turn off any affection that he felt for most of the adults in his life. He'd loved the Stillman children, but in the end, he was able to turn even that off.

"So," Bron said. "I come from some kind of a breeding program?"

"Probably," Olivia said. "For thousands of years, your people have selectively bred for strength, speed, intelligence, and beauty. How well did you do in wrestling?"

Bron shrugged. He didn't want to brag. "Fourth in state, for my weight division."

"That's a relief," Olivia said. "If you were a purebred, there's no way that you would have placed only fourth."

"Why is that a relief?"

"Because it means that you're not completely evil. The evil masaaks ... think of their bodies as being like the hardware to a computer. They're bred to be cold, cunning, indifferent. If you were one of them, you would be ... easily corrupted."

Bron worried about that. He sometimes felt so distant from others, so ... broken. Now Olivia was suggesting that someone might have made him that way, left him broken on purpose.

"But what about training," Bron said. "Some people say that nurture is more important than nature."

"Imagine that I could take out your memories, your 'software,' and put in new ideas and attitudes— anything that I want. If I inserted the right propaganda, the right mix of hatred and cynicism and superiority, I could create something ... completely evil, both on the genetic level, and on the nurturing side. Your friend Riley had that happen to him. That's what our enemies do."

"So you think they'll come for me?" Bron asked. He was frightened by the thought, but Olivia was pale and shaking, and he wondered if he should be even more scared.

"I think they should have come a year or so ago. You're growing quickly, and just as your body matures, so do your powers...."

Bron felt intrigued by the possibilities. "I read a story about changelings once," Bron said. "The fey, the dark elves, put their beautiful babies in human cribs, and let the humans raise them."

"Some fairytales come close to the truth," Olivia said. "That is but one name that we have been called, 'the fey.'"

Bron had to ponder that. The word 'fey,' had so many undertones—powerful, dangerous, beautiful, and deadly.

"The changeling grew up," Bron said, "and went to war with the fey."

Olivia didn't say anything, but there was a hopeful look in her eyes. *That's what she wants* me *to do,* he thought, *go to war with her enemies.*

"Bron," Olivia said. "That boy Riley came to school today, hunting for you. The secretary caught him in a lie, and told him that there was no one at Tuacahn with your name. Maybe she threw them off our trail, but you need to know, our enemies are looking for us now. We'll need to keep a low profile. Don't go into town. Try not to attract any more attention."

"Okay."

"And you need to know that the boy who was killed, it wasn't our fault. They hunted us. I threw the caltrops out of the car hoping only to disable their vehicle. If they hadn't been speeding, no one would have gotten hurt. If they had caught us, you can't imagine what they would have done."

Bron considered that for a moment, nodded. But a thousand questions warred in his head. "So, do you think I can take people's memories, too?" It seemed like a tremendous power, greater than anything that he had ever conceived.

It also seemed absurd. Everything that Olivia had said was warring in Bron's mind. He couldn't process it fast enough, and yet, he had to believe her.

"Not all of us can take memories, or grant new ones," Olivia replied. "We will have to perform some tests with you, begin training. But I think that you're not a memory merchant, like me. I think you're something far rarer. Mrs. Stillman said that you sucked the energy from her at your last home. Your social worker was quite amused by that accusation. It could be madness talking, or she could be right, in a way.

Yesterday, you rejected Galadriel, and she just curled up in a ball and quit breathing and all but died. And Mr. Lewis, back when you were a child, he curled up and died, too."

"I've never heard that," Bron said.

Olivia paused. "It's in the state's records. I think that you're a danger to those that threaten you. You're what we call an *asufaak arru'yah,* a *dream assassin.*"

"A what?" Bron demanded.

"A dream assassin. It's a rare kind of masaak, the very rarest. With my powers, I can access many parts of the brain, but not all. I pull memories out of the cerebral cortex. I can even train neural pathways. But a dream assassin can go into a place that I never see, deep into the amygdala. He can draw out ... hopes, desires, and ambitions from those around him. He can use them as fuel to shape his own goals."

"I couldn't have done that," Bron said. "I never touched any of those people!"

"A very powerful dream assassin wouldn't *need* to touch them," Olivia said. "Your will alone could have sapped them, even from a distance. Among every breed of masaak, there are some who can sap others from afar. We call them *leeches.* I think that you're not only a dream assassin, you're a powerful leech."

"Wow," Bron said sarcastically, "an assassin *and* a leech. Can you think of anything *else* to call me?"

Olivia smiled through tight lips. "We've been using these appellations for thousands of years. Among our people, they don't have negative connotations. Far from it. Leeches are revered, and dream assassins ..."

She changed the subject. "Think about this, Bron: each one of these people gave you reason to fear or dislike them. You saw Mr. Lewis as a threat to your mother, and how did he die? He lost the will to live. He simply curled up in a ball and quit breathing—just as Galadriel will, unless you learn how to control your powers!"

Bron took a deep breath in surprise. "I wasn't trying to hurt her! I never wanted to hurt anyone!"

"I know," Olivia said. "Don't blame yourself. It's a natural defense mechanism, like an adder striking by instinct when surprised. We're going to have to go to Galadriel. You'll need to return what you took—by accident. You're going to have to give her the will to live."

Bron considered. "What if I give Galadriel too much ... ambition? I might end up like her, without the desire to do anything at all."

"No, you wouldn't," Olivia said. "You would simply save yourself. You'd leech the will from others around you."

He considered this for a long moment, then said, "Why should we bother with her? Why not let her die?"

Olivia shuddered and took a deep breath. "How could you even think such a thing?"

Bron shrugged. "People die every day. She's trouble just waiting to happen. She's the kind of person that when she trips, someone else gets to take the fall. When she gets cut, the rest of the world bleeds."

"What do you mean?" Olivia asked.

Bron tried to explain. "She's rich, beautiful, spoiled. She begged me to run away with her, but if I had, what do you think would have happened when we got caught?" He waited for Olivia to answer, and explained, "*I* would have gone to juvie. *She* would have gotten grounded. *I* would have gone up on charges—runaway, rape, theft, kidnapping. *She* would have lost her cell phone privileges. That's the way that it works when you're a kid from social services. You saw Officer Walton. He can tell you. If a window gets broken, must be one of us who did it— not some kid from a 'good' family. As soon as Galadriel went missing, he came knocking on my door. How fair is that?"

"It wasn't fair," Olivia said.

"Damned right it wasn't fair. That girl is a danger to everyone around her!"

"You can't be that cold!" Olivia said.

Bron gave her a knowing smile. "Oh, yeah? Watch me."

Olivia didn't know him at all. He'd been pulled from one home after another, abandoned by his mother. Everyone he had ever loved had been stripped from him. No one had ever cared for him. Why should he care for someone else?

Or is there something even more wrong with me? Bron wondered. Had he been bred to be cold and callus? Did that lie at the root of his problem?

Or maybe he was just scared to try to fix Galadriel, afraid that he wouldn't be able to do it.

"Bron," she said. "You have been hurt so much, it's going to be hard for you to reach out. You've got to overcome that!"

Bron had never actually wanted to kill anyone. He might have been angry and hurt, but he'd never acted on that anger. He'd never lashed out at someone.

"You're right," Olivia said, trying another tactic. "She's a danger to others. Maybe it would be just to let her die. But have you wondered why Galadriel's such a danger? It's because she just doesn't give a damn about anything—you, herself, her future. The thing that she lacks, the thing that nobody else in the world can give her, is yours to give. You can do more than just help her survive. You've never felt what she's feeling right now, so you don't understand her, but you could *make her whole.*"

Bron studied the red-rock cliffs to the north for a moment, and his dark eyes flicked up with interest. Olivia felt small for using this tactic. Men have a powerful instinct to save others, to risk their lives. That's why from time immemorial, men have gone to war. She was using Bron's instinct against him, but she told herself: *it's not just to save Galadriel. It's to save Bron, too.*

Bron asked, "How do you do it?"

"I usually sneak up on them at night," Olivia said. "It can take a long time to reorganize memories—"

"No, I mean how do *I* do it? How am I supposed to fix her?"

"Look, ducks are born knowing how to fly south for the winter," Olivia said. "Just touch her forehead. Instinct will take over."

Olivia bit her lip, then fell silent. She started the car and drove slowly back onto the highway. The new white Corolla was as much as one could hope for in the way of camouflage. With the overbearing summer heat, white was the color of choice for cars in Saint George, and with the tinted windows, she and Bron were about as anonymous as one could be.

Yet as she peered up the road at a sedan approaching in the distance, she could not help but feel that a noose was tightening around them.

The Draghouls are coming, she thought. *We can't see them, but I know they're here. I can almost feel them....*

A phone call to the hospital that afternoon confirmed that Galadriel was in the Intermountain Regional Medical Center, undergoing treatment.

Mike had left a note at the house. He was up in the hills, checking on the cattle that were out in the open range. He wanted to get them back out of the hills before the muzzle-loader hunters descended on the area.

So Olivia offered to drive Bron to the hospital. Reluctantly, he agreed to go. He didn't want dinner. He paced around the house, nerves on edge. While Olivia got ready, Bron went outside. Clouds were scudding in from the south, big thunderheads streaming up from the Pacific.

Bron stood by the Corolla and watched some birds flitting by the rail fence—bee eaters that seemed to dance in the air, hover and dive, snatching up flies and mosquitoes and honeybees. He tried to capture the rhythms in his mind, put their dance to music.

The air smelled of dust and a rising storm.

Bron went to a rose bush by the hummingbird feeders. From a distance the white roses looked tawdry. Their petals were aging, burning brown on the edges. Bron picked the nicest blossom and peeled away the older petals.

"Ready?" Olivia asked as she came out of the house

"As I'll ever be," he mumbled.

Olivia eyed the white rose. "Nice touch," she said. "I thought you didn't care if Galadriel lives or dies?"

"Aren't you supposed to take gifts when you visit the sick?"

They piled into the car and headed through town, past the juniper forest and then out of the valley altogether, where the sagebrush poked up through rocks. Once the scenery turned bland, Bron's thoughts focused inward. He sat staring out the window, clenching and unclenching his fist.

"You all right?" Olivia asked, just to fend off the silence.

"I feel like I'm being asked to take a test," Bron said, "in a subject that I've never studied before—never even heard of."

"Relax," Olivia urged. "You'll do fine." He wasn't sure she believed it. "Now that you recognize what's going on, I think that these incidents will become fewer and further between. I know that you didn't really want to hurt Galadriel. Once you wish her well, if you wish her well strongly enough, I think that she will heal."

"What about Melvina?" Bron asked. "I might have accidentally taken something from her, too. I ... didn't like her."

"She lives so far from here, you can't do anything for her today. She'll stay the same cramped, miserable person that she is now—until you return the ambition you've taken."

Bron considered. He didn't want to see Melvina again, but his reluctance shamed him. Olivia talked about it as if it were a done deal. "When would we go?"

"Maybe next Saturday?" Olivia suggested. "You're going to have to learn how to use your powers anyway. We could make a day of it, maybe find something fun to do up in Salt Lake? When was the last time you went to the water park, or took in the rides at Lagoon?" Lagoon was a large theme park in the northern part of the state.

"I went to the water park last year, but I haven't been to Lagoon since ... I was eleven."

Olivia smiled. "We should go to Lagoon, unless there's something you'd like better? 'Lion King' is coming to Salt Lake—the musical."

"That would be fun," Bron said, but there was an edge to his voice, a lack of enthusiasm. He didn't really want to go. She was the one who loved musical theater.

"No, wait a minute," she suggested. "Why choose between the two? We can do both!"

She talked excitedly as she made plans—suggesting that they go to one of the better places for dinner: Zinn Bistro.

Bron broke in, "If I give these people ... ambition, what happens to me? I mean, I don't have much myself, or at least not so much that I want to get rid of any."

"As I understand it," Olivia said, "you were the one who was cleaning the Stillman's house, doing the dishes, fixing the meals, taking care of the children—all on top of going to school?"

"Yeah," Bron admitted.

"You've got more ambition than is good for a kid your age."

"Yeah, but what if I give too much away?"

Olivia glanced out of the corner of her eye, kept her attention on the road. "I don't know much about dream assassins," she admitted. "No one does. There hasn't been one for a long time...."

"Why's that?" Bron asked.

Olivia chose her words carefully. "Too few are born."

"My parents were dream assassins, right?"

Olivia shook her head. "No." She sounded a little bewildered. She finally said, "I told you that masaaks don't have a lot of offspring. That's part of the reason that there aren't many of us. But you should know that our talents are ... like hair color. Most people in the world—throughout Asia and Africa—have black hair, more than seventy percent. Us memory merchants, we're like people with black hair. Most masaaks have my gift, though few have it so powerfully. You're ... like an albino, which is a very rare thing, even for a masaak. Your parents could have been ... anything."

"So there are other kinds of masaaks," Bron asked, "with different talents?"

"Let's not worry about that right now."

"You said that we don't have a lot of children," Bron said. "But there are other reasons why we're so few, aren't there?"

Olivia smiled. "In the old days, the humans sometimes killed us. They called us witches or warlocks...."

"Cool," Bron said.

"Why is it cool?"

Bron struggled for words. "I guess, everyone wants to be an oppressed minority."

Olivia grinned. "Everyone wants to feel special. I'm not sure that they want to be oppressed." She tried to sound casual. "I told you that I'm not supposed to answer your questions. Someone else will: the Weigher of Lost Souls. She'll tell you everything that you need to know."

Bron grew quiet. At last he said, "I don't know. Would she have to ... touch me? I mean, isn't it kind of dangerous, what she does?"

Olivia suggested, "She doesn't have to 'teach' you. She can just show you some things. It would be like watching a movie, except that you would smell and touch things, and you'd feel the world, and think remembered thoughts. It's better than 3D."

There was something that she wasn't telling him, Bron knew.

"All right," Bron said, "as long as she doesn't do anything wonky to me."

"She won't," Olivia assured him. "This woman and I, we're more than just friends. We're more like ... allies. There are a lot of muses like us—math, science, athletics. You'd be surprised at what you could learn."

Bron cast a sideways glance. "Allies against what?"

She smiled nervously, kept her eyes fixed to the road. He was fishing for information that she wasn't supposed to reveal. They were coming past some scenery now, three volcanoes up ahead. With the thunderheads coming in from the south, the black volcanoes looked as if they were lowering beneath clouds of ash. Her answer seemed evasive. "Against the rising tide of ignorance."

Olivia shifted her hands on the steering wheel. She had been clutching it so tightly that her knuckles had gone white.

"I've been thinking," Bron said, "about what kind of damage a memory merchant might do. I mean, they could steal secrets from corporate executives, or government leaders! Right?"

"Yes," Olivia admitted. "I would even go so far as to admit that such things have been done—though not by me."

"They could, like, wipe out memories from their enemies. They might make great spies—sort of like James Bond, except with super powers."

"Yes, they could be like that," Olivia said.

"So if we're on the good side, who's on the bad?"

"You're not ready for the whole truth," Olivia said. "And I'm not the one to tell you, even though I really want you to know."

CHAPTER 15

HEALER

"Nearly all masaaks are left-handed. Anciently, being left-handed, being sinister, *as the Romans called it, could be counted as proof that a person practiced sorcery, was in league with the devil. Today such things are considered foolish, but modern men don't understand how close to being right the ancients were."*

— Olivia Hernandez

B ron waited for Olivia to answer his question, but she never did. *That's all right,* he told himself. *I can be more patient than you.*

Yet he worried about the consequences of her silence. They'd been attacked once already, and it was obvious that their enemies terrified Olivia. Couldn't she see that he needed to know more?

She drove them in silence as they passed the trailhead at White Rock. Olivia nodded off to the side. "That's where I go to practice the guitar sometimes," she said casually, jutting her chin toward some cliffs the color of eggshell. The valley between was spotted with sagebrush, yucca plants, and juniper trees, with a ridge from an old lava flow running down the valley.

She indicated a small warning sign. "All of this land is on the desert tortoise refuge. If you see one by the side of the road, don't pick them up. You'll get a fine."

"Have you ever seen one?"

"Oh, they're all over the place," she said. "They hibernate in the winter. Otherwise they come out to eat in the morning, before the heat of the day."

At that, Bron smiled. It meant that he'd have a good chance of spotting a tortoise.

"But if you pick one up," Olivia warned, "it will get scared and pee, and if it loses too much moisture ... well, we live in the desert. Life here is fragile."

She fixed him a warning glance, and he fell silent. He knew that she was talking about more than tortoises.

Soon they reached the Intermountain Medical Facility. The hospital in Saint George was a new affair, backed by cliffs on the east side of the city. It was made of sand-colored rock to blend in with its background.

Galadriel was in Room 411, and when Bron and Olivia reached the room, Bron felt astonished to see how poorly the girl was doing.

She was strapped to her bed, her face contorted and staring blankly at the wall. A heart monitor beeped steadily, while a pair of catheters dripped fluids into her wrist. Her face was pale with shock, and her blue eyes seemed empty of life.

Galadriel's mother sat in a chair at her side. Mascara tracks showed that she'd been crying. She sobbed when she spotted Bron, then broke into fresh tears at the sight of Bron's white rose.

"You shouldn't have come," Marie Mercer said. There was just a hint of blame in her tone, as if this was Bron's fault.

Olivia gave her a hug. "We had to come, sweetie. We had to give you a break." She squeezed hard and asked, "How has Galadriel been?"

Bron held his white rose. He didn't see a vase to put it in.

Galadriel just stared at the wall, completely unblinking. Her chest didn't even move when she breathed. She looked like someone who has witnessed a tragic accident, and then given up on life.

Marie broke into tears. "There's no change. I don't know what could have done this to her. The hospital checked her with a rape kit. She came back clean. There are no marks, no bruises. It's like, like she's looking into the depths of hell. She quit babbling once we got here."

"So do you have any idea what could have caused this?" Olivia asked. Of course she wouldn't have a clue.

Marie pointedly looked away from Bron. Obviously, she suspected that he had something to do with it. In a momentary silence, the beep, beep, beep of the heart monitor seemed unnaturally loud. The smell of antiseptics couldn't hide a peculiar musty odor in the room, as if Galadriel had been lying here, rotting away for days. Bron suspected that the scent came from the muck at the pond.

"We don't know what's wrong exactly yet. The doctors think she's had some sort of psychic break, one that has thrown her into deep depression. She won't eat, won't drink. They've got her on fluids, and they've started her on painkillers and some other pills, serotonin reuptake inhibitors, but it might take days before they begin to have any effect."

Olivia smiled sympathetically, offered some comforting platitudes.

Marie had no idea what she was up against, Bron realized. If Olivia was right, modern medicine was powerless to help the girl.

For a moment, Olivia held Marie's hand reassuringly.

Marie nodded to Bron. "White," she said, nodding toward the rose. "It's the symbol of pure love, wholesome and unselfish."

Bron nodded, but he hadn't known that. Obviously Marie thought that he was being gallant, and he wondered what she would have thought if he'd brought another color—say the peach-colored roses by the back door. What meaning was attached to those? Would they say something crude, like "I want to hook up?"

"Thank you for bringing it," Marie said, as if she might burst into tears. "It's nice to know that she's loved—I mean, that someone else loves her besides me. I don't think she has gotten that through her thick head—just how much she's loved."

Bron smiled sheepishly just as a nurse came in, making her rounds. She checked the fluid levels in the I.V.s, and then jotted some notes on the chart at the foot of Galadriel's bed.

Even now, Galadriel looked beautiful. Not beautiful and seductive, as she had yesterday. Beautiful and tragic, Bron decided, like a victim of the Holocaust.

Marie was talking ... "move her up to the psych ward" ... but her voice came from far away.

The suction cups suddenly manifested at the ends of Bron's fingers. He was eager to get this over, and somehow the sight of Galadriel looking so helpless called to him.

The nurse was so busy, she didn't even notice, just left the room in a hurry. Marie Mercer was distracted, talking to Olivia. Down the hall, an old woman cried out in pain, while a nurse's call bell dinged.

Bron looked into Olivia's eyes. She'd noticed his sizraels. Olivia shook her head, just the tiniest movement, warning him to take control of himself.

She spoke to Marie Mercer, "Sweetie, why don't you go home and rest. You look positively worn out." She reached up as if to smooth a stray strand of Marie's long blond hair, and suddenly her sizraels popped out like claws. Olivia touched Marie's temple, and Marie said, "Oh, my gosh, I forgot to feed the horses this morning, and they didn't get fed last night at all. I have to go!"

With that, she grabbed her purse and pleaded, "Can you stay with Galadriel—just until I get back?"

"Of course," Olivia offered.

When she was gone, Bron accused, "You made her forget feeding the horses, didn't you?"

"Yes."

"Is it always that quick?" he asked.

"Pulling a simple memory? Yes, it can be done easily. She was just holding the memory short term. But training someone can take a long time, especially when you have to lay down a whole new skill. For those who can do it at all, it takes hours." She came

237

around Bron and closed the door to the room, for greater privacy, then turned off the lights. "Go ahead," Olivia urged, "do it."

Bron winced at the unfortunate choice of words, yet he yearned to see if he really did have this power. The suction cups on his fingertips hardened into little ridges. He cautiously laid the white rose on Galadriel's med tray, and he reached out to take her face in his hands.

Her skin looked smooth and as luminous as porcelain. He pulled her head so that she was staring up into his eyes, but Bron could see no change in her expression, no sign of recognition. Her pupils were pinpricks, gazing off into eternity, as if she could see beyond him, beyond the room, beyond the atmosphere into space where galaxies whirled like pinwheels and universes grew ancient.

Instinct took over. Bron fumbled for an instant, trying to figure out where to place his fingers, but then he reached under her eyebrows with each thumb, careful not to touch her eyeballs. His fingers fanned out around her skull, moistened by the thin glaze of Galadriel's sweat, until his pinkie touched just below her ear.

Galadriel let out a low moan, as if in pain.

Then Bron just stood, holding her cranium in his hands as if he might crush it, or perhaps carry it away for safe keeping. He studied the helpless girl and didn't know what to do.

"Is something supposed to happen?" Bron asked.

"Give her your gift," Olivia said. She studied his face. He didn't understand. She shook her head impatiently. "You have to *will* it into her."

"I don't feel anything," Bron admitted. "I don't think that it's working."

Olivia came and stood beside him, observing. "What are you thinking about right now?"

"Nothing."

"Nothing?" Olivia peered into his eyes. "Nothing at all?"

"Not really. I guess I'm just curious to see what happens."

"Nothing *just* happens," Olivia explained. "You have to make it happen."

Bron glanced up to the clock on the wall. It read 5:23. He'd been standing there for two minutes.

"What are you feeling right now?" Olivia asked.

Bron shook his head, moistened his lips with his tongue. "Empty," he admitted.

"Don't you feel anything for her?" Olivia asked. "Warmth? Compassion? Lust? Even the tiniest bit? This isn't just a body that you're holding—it's a life. You're holding her life in your hands...."

Bron considered. "I feel ... relieved," he admitted. "If she was aware and knew what was happening, she'd be screaming. Right now, it's like she's asleep."

"That's the opiates keeping her dazed," Olivia whispered. "Don't you want her to get better?"

"To tell the truth," he said solemnly, "I'm not sure."

At that instant, he saw a purple flash beneath his hands, and the heart monitor began to beep violently. Galadriel's back arched off the bed and she opened her mouth in a wordless scream.

Olivia launched herself across the table and shoved Bron backward, so that he fell against the door to the room's restroom. She shouted, "Stop it!"

"What?" Bron asked defensively.

"You were killing her!" Olivia whispered vehemently. "You can't do that: you can't put your fingers to someone's head and wish them harm, not unless you really want to do them harm!"

Bron stared in disbelief, shocked at the accusation. He felt confused, afraid that he'd fail. He felt guilty.

He hadn't meant to harm Galadriel. He'd just thought, *I wish she had died.*

Now that the damage was done, he didn't know how to undo it.

Everyone was always pushing him around. In the past few days, he'd been pulled a dozen directions at once. He snapped.

"I give up," he said. "I'm out of here!" He headed out the door, and Olivia was left standing in shock.

She rushed into the hall, grabbed his arm, and spun him around.

"What's going on?" she asked.

"I ... can't do it," Bron said. "You want me to heal her, to wish her well, and I can't do that. It's a lie."

"We can't leave," Olivia said. "I promised her mother."

"That's right," Bron said, "*you* promised her mother!"

He turned to walk away. He wasn't sure where he would go. Certainly he wouldn't return to Olivia's house. He imagined walking to the freeway, standing on the on-ramp, and sticking out a thumb.

"Bron," she begged, "this is important!"

He knew that he couldn't do it. He'd never had a close relationship with anyone. He loved no one, least of all Galadriel.

He stood with his head tilted, jaw set, unwilling to move.

"Please," Olivia said. "When you look at Galadriel, you see a stupid teenager. When her mother looks at her, she's her only child. You want to play the guitar, have people think that you're great. But if you miss this chance, nothing else that you do in life will ever matter. You'll *never. Be. Great.*"

He thought for a long minute. He was afraid of failing. He was afraid of Galadriel.

Deep in his heart, though, he realized that what worried him most was that Olivia might be right about him. What if he had been bred to be cold and cruel? What if his emptiness, his lack of compassion, was like ... having an amputated leg, a missing limb?

Shouldn't I fight against it? he wondered. *If someone tried to make me into a merciless killer, shouldn't I prove them wrong?*

That bothered him more than anything.

He returned to Galadriel's bedside.

"Let me help," Olivia suggested.

Olivia stood at his back. Galadriel kept gasping, and now she trembled over the length of her body. At any moment, Bron expected a handful of doctors to rush in with a crash cart. He worried that Galadriel was having a heart attack, but when he looked up at the monitor, Galadriel's heart seemed to be beating evenly.

"Try it again," Olivia said. She tried to hide some of the disappointment in her voice, and even some of the fear. "Try it again, but think only warm feelings for her. You have to love her, wish her well, with your whole soul. It's like, it's like you have this fire in your chest, a burning ember, and you have to will it out of you, will it into her, so that she can feel its warmth. Do you think you can do that?"

"I'll try," Bron said. He calmed himself, drew a deep breath, reached down, and took Galadriel's face in his hands.

He shook his head, gritted his teeth. Her skin felt surprisingly cold and moist, reptilian. He recalled a snake that he'd found under a board when he was a kid—a big king snake the color of a rattler, as cold as rubber on a cool day.

"What are you thinking?" Olivia asked.

"I was thinking that she feels cold," Bron said. "Like a snake, when you pick it up in the winter. It's barely alive."

"What do you feel for her? Compassion?"

"Nothing," Bron admitted. "I don't like her."

"You don't know her well enough to make that decision," Olivia suggested. "You're afraid of her, and we tend to try to destroy people we fear. But what if there is a side to her that you haven't seen? She was trying to impress you by showing how wild and reckless she could be, but there's more to her than that. You could help her become a better person. If only she had a little more ambition, if only she could dream. It's our dreams that shape us, all of our hopes and desires...."

Bron closed his eyes, shut out the lights of the room, the sound.

"Dreams shape us," Olivia whispered. "We come into the world as infants, empty of purpose and thought, and someday a dream comes along and gives our life a direction, a purpose. Everyone's dream is different. Some dream of loving, or being loved. Some dream of fame or glory. Others dream only of being of service to the world.

"Could you love this girl," Olivia asked, "if she found a purpose for life?"

He wondered at that. Right now, Galadriel's life was a waste, a bore. He wondered if he really could change that.

I don't have that kind of power, Bron thought.

"I feel like I'm just standing here," Bron whispered. "Nothing is happening."

Olivia sighed. "Here," she said. "Maybe I can help." She walked behind him and put her arms up over his shoulders, so that her hands touched his face. He felt her warmth as her body leaned into his back.

A memory flared.

Suddenly he was transported back in time. Bron found himself as a child, standing upon a bridge over a roaring river. He was cold, and shivering. His butt stung from the spanking that Mr. Golper had given him. A kitten meowed plaintively in its bag, floating in the river, as the current carried it downstream.

Mr. Golper pulled at Bron's hand, dragging him toward the car, but Bron fought and turned to see if his kitten was still alive.

Something changed. His memory of events seemed to twist.

Suddenly the bag sprang open, and the kitten's head popped up in the water. It meowed plaintively as it tried to swim to shore, the fur of its head looking slick and black. Its tiny white paws lashed at the waves.

Swim! Bron cried in his memory. *You can do it!*

Bron tried to stay for a moment, hoping that the kitten would escape.

Mr. Golper whirled in anger, lashing out at a willful child. "Come on!" he said. "Let's go. Live or die, that kitten is none of our affair."

But Bron wanted it to live. With his whole soul he cried out, "Boots! Come on!"

Mr. Golper jerked Bron's arm, pulled him away.

In his imagination, the kitten was swimming blindly against the current, borne downstream toward rocks and white rooster-tails of foam.

Something inside Bron broke.

A stone seemed to erupt from Bron's chest, as if it tore free. Bron staggered backward, winded, and stared at his chest, as if perhaps the Alien had burst out. He was in the hospital room, blinking.

Purple sparks lashed out of his hands, flashed and popped around Galadriel's head. She gasped, and her eyes flew wide. She let out a strangled cry and rose up for an instant, clutching at Bron. She grabbed his shirt, and then fainted.

Bron waited to make sure that she really was out, then Olivia invited, "Come, sit down."

He sat on the couch with her beside the bed, so exhausted he wasn't sure he could stand any longer. He bit his lip, brooding. For a long moment, he said nothing, then at last blurted, "You screwed with my memories!"

"Only a little," Olivia said.

"Could you have been any more obvious in your manipulation?"

"Not if I tried," Olivia said. "You still remember what really happened that day. I didn't take that away from you. I didn't try to insert new memories in your sleep. I only showed you a possibility, one that you had never imagined."

"What do you mean?"

"When you left the bridge," she tried to explain, "the bag was floating away. You've always believed that the kitten drowned, and perhaps it did. Probably, it did. But maybe it escaped. It could have fought its way free and climbed ashore downstream. It happens every day. Cats are surprisingly resilient. Even now it might be living with some family who loves it."

Bron fell silent, considering the possibility, and he remained quiet even after Marie Mercer returned.

They said goodbye, with Galadriel sleeping peacefully, her face pale and breathing slowed from sedatives.

Bron remained subdued as they drove toward home, with clouds growing black over the red mountains. He closed his eyes, weary to the bone.

He felt like that kitten, tossed into dangerous currents, bound by conventions and responsibilities. There was no solid earth beneath his feet, and he was beginning to feel desperate.

Perhaps he too could get free.

CHAPTER 16

NUMEROUS PLANS

"When you're a child, it seems that everyone has plans for your life but you. There comes a time when you must take control of your own destiny."

– Bron Jones

Olivia drove home from the hospital as Bron nodded off. By the time they had gone five miles, he was sound asleep. When they reached the house she roused him and offered to make him dinner, but Bron staggered from the car.

"That wore me out," he explained groggily.

Olivia fixed him with a measuring gaze. She'd never seen him like this. "It can be tiring," she admitted, though it had never made her *that* tired. "Go lie down. I'll bring you some dinner in an hour."

Bron went to his room. It was late enough so that Mike would be out taking his evening rounds. Olivia made hamburgers and fries. Outside, with the coming of the storm, the wind raged and the cottonwoods beside the house swayed. Here in the mountains, the clouds swept in low over the valley floor, and when lightning began to strike, it seemed to be right on top of her. In the clear mountain air, the thunder snarled and boomed as if it were meting out the judgments of god.

Mike went out to secure the barn. The cattle often went mad with fright in such storms and would huddle under the cottonwoods down by the creek. One bolt of lightning, a few years earlier, had killed nine head of cattle at once. It was a terrible loss, of course, but Olivia had learned something from it: all nine of those cattle were surprisingly tender.

Later she had heard from another farmer that electrocution caused the muscles to relax, and at some slaughterhouses, cattle were electrocuted in order to tenderize the meat.

Today, though, they didn't want a herd of tenderized calves, so Mike stood out back and called them into the barn.

She fixed dinner and let Bron sleep. Mike came from the fields and announced, "The calves are all in. Wisdom's Promise had her calf this afternoon—a sweet little heifer."

"Everything look okay?"

"The mother and calf are fine. They're in the birthing stall, under a heat lamp."

Suddenly blinding light flashed outside, followed by a boom that nearly took Olivia off her feet.

"Zeus is pissed," Mike said. He looked out the window, just as a web of light tore through the clouds. "What's Bron up to?"

"Napping," Olivia said. "He spent the night worrying about his first day at school—didn't get a lick of sleep."

Mike grumbled thoughtfully, stalked around the house, peering outside. "So how was Galadriel?"

"She was resting peacefully when we left," Olivia replied.

"Humph," Mike said. He mused for a moment, wondering what could have happened to the girl, but when he didn't come up with any new insights, he went into the living room and turned on a DVD of Braveheart. The storm raged outside.

Olivia finished dinner, then peeked into Bron's room.

He was lying in bed, face to the wall. It was the same pose that Galadriel had in the hospital. Olivia tried to chalk it up to coincidence, but she worried: Was this normal for a dream assassin? Would he get weary each time he used his powers, or had he given the girl too much?

And what was with the violet lights when he transferred? Other masaak gave off lights—pale blue, yellow, citrine, or even scarlet flames—but she'd never heard of anyone giving off violet flashes. It had been centuries since the world had seen a dream assassin, and she wondered if those colors only came to people like Bron.

She went back to the kitchen and puttered about the house until she realized that she was too worried about Bron to let him sleep anymore.

She cooked the fries and made up a hamburger, adding tomatoes and relish, ketchup and lettuce. She wondered if Bron would like it. Would he have preferred vegetable soup to fries? Would he have rather had peanut butter sandwiches than a hamburger?

I hardly know this boy, she realized. She loaded the plate, grabbed a cup of milk, and took it to his room.

Bron hadn't moved.

She went to his bed, sat on the edge, and poked him awake.

He rubbed his eyes and looked up. "What's going on?" he asked. He sounded concerned.

"It's time for dinner."

Bleary-eyed, he gazed at the food blankly. "Not hungry." He turned over to go back to sleep.

She grabbed his shoulder and pulled his face so that he looked toward her. "Bron, this is important: do you *like* hamburgers?"

He raised a brow, as if that was the strangest question in the world. "Yeah."

"Then," she begged, "eat this before it gets cold."

Bron sat up sleepily and began to eat.

"Are you really that tired?" she demanded.

"I'm sorry. I'll wake up in a bit."

She mussed his hair, went into the kitchen, and peered out the window. Summer storms in Utah usually didn't last long, dropping half an inch of rain in an hour or two, then passing on. This one looked as if it would hang around for a bit. There were nice puddles out in the driveway, and scattered droplets ruffled the puddles' surfaces. Gray skies loomed, and though the thunder had quieted, it grumbled in far places.

Olivia went to her cell phone, pulled Marie Mercer's number from her contact list, and punched in a call. Marie answered.

"Hi," Olivia said. "Sorry to disturb you. I was just worrying about Galadriel?"

"She's doing *spectacular!*" There were smiles in Marie's voice, but Marie was the kind of person who liked to hide bad news. Her family was always doing "wonderfully." She could have been standing in the driveway with a bear trap on her leg, and she'd have said that she felt wonderful.

"So she's awake now, and talking?" Olivia prodded.

"Oh, it's a miracle!" Marie exclaimed. "I've never seen her so *effusive!* She really wanted to thank Bron for that rose; it's so beautiful. The doctor was just here. He said he's never seen anything like it. He's thinking about releasing her."

There was such excitement in Marie's voice that Olivia was tempted to just hang up on her. After the day that Olivia had just had, no one deserved to be so happy. She asked, "So what's Galadriel talking about?"

"Oh, you know, the usual—her plans for school this year, and for college, that kind of thing. We were just discussing the kind of man that she wanted to marry," Marie said, then added to Galadriel, "weren't we dear?"

Olivia graciously said goodbye and then clicked the phone off with unaccustomed zeal.

Damn that Galadriel, she thought, *planning out her life like that.*

Olivia peered into the living room. Mike was asleep in his La-Z-Boy, arms hanging over the edge like a gorilla's.

Olivia worried. She went to Bron's room, found him lying in bed, blinking stupidly. The half-eaten burger was languishing on its plate. A couple of fries were gone. He'd taken less than a swallow of milk.

"Get out of bed," she warned.

"I'm up now," he apologized. He climbed to the edge of the bed and sat.

She knelt in front of him, took his hands and stared into his eyes. "I just spoke to Galadriel's mother. She's planning for college, and dreaming of the kind of man she hopes to marry."

"Really?" Bron asked.

"That girl has never planned anything in her life," Olivia said. "A rabbit plans its day better—eat, poop, sleep!"

"So you're saying it worked?"

"I'm saying ..." Olivia gripped his hands tighter, "I'm worried that you gave her more than you took. She's in the hospital setting her life goals, and you can't get out of bed. If you don't wake up soon, I'm going to take you back and have you drain a little of the foam off the top."

Bron frowned. "I couldn't do that...."

Olivia studied his eyes. He was serious. He didn't want to have to deal with his powers. She felt relieved by that. He wasn't likely to use them against others, if that was how he felt.

"Sure you could. Just to even things out."

Bron furrowed his brow. Olivia breathed a little easier. Bron's powers were dangerous. If he ever got angry enough, he could drain her without a thought.

"I'll be all right," Bron assured her, and got up.

Olivia watched. It seemed he was moving a little easier, but he was strained. She let it go.

By 8:30 p.m. the clouds were fleeing. Sunset brought red and purple ribbons of light above the bowl of the shadowed vale.

Olivia got a call on her cell.

"Olivia, this is Monique," the speaker said. "Fill me in."

This was the call that Olivia had been waiting for. Monique was the Weigher of Lost Souls. Olivia had known her in college. Monique had taught Olivia to speak a couple of foreign tongues. Olivia slipped into French, using a dialect that had been popular during the Third Crusade. *"J'ai un problème."* I have a problem.

"What kind of problem?" Monique asked guardedly. Neither of them liked talking over the phones.

"I took in a young man from social services. He's a dream assassin."

There was a silence on the end of the phone, probably while Monique tried to pick her jaw up off the floor. "Are you certain?"

"Oh, yeah."

"It's been six hundred years since we've seen one," Monique said. "Does the enemy know that you have him?"

"This kid has never even heard of the enemy."

"Don't tell him," Monique said. "It could be dangerous. If he was born one of them, with a little shove ... If he knew what they offer, he might be tempted." Monique held silent as she considered what to do next. "The best thing might be to kill him in his sleep. That's what our ancestors did to the last one."

"He's just a kid," Olivia said. "We may both be soldiers in an eternal war, but neither of us has ever shed a drop of blood."

"There is wisdom in the old ways. I could send someone to do it for you. A real dream assassin, in today's world? I thought that there would never be another." Monique considered, and offered, "Every minute that you're around him, you're in danger. Even if you're not in danger from him, the danger grows. The enemy will come. It is only a matter of time."

"I know," Olivia agreed. "We had contact with five over the weekend. I'm afraid. I only hope to prepare Bron for our next encounter, before it is too late."

"Don't tell anyone about his powers," Monique ordered. "We can't afford to let this slip out. I'll arrange to meet him—soon."

"Are you close by?"

"Ireland, at Geata Na Chruinn."

Olivia had a brief image of the old castle brooding over the downs, and to the west was a sea of silver. She had never been there, but she knew the castle intimately. She'd seen it once, in Monique's memory, when they were girls, still just playing with their powers. The image conjured wistful feelings, and Olivia yearned to see Monique soon.

"Come quickly," Olivia begged.

"Do you have a gun?" Monique asked.

"Yes."

"Keep it handy."

After the phone call, Olivia wondered how she might create some kind of link to Bron, enlarge his compassion.

There is a reason why muses had been worshipped as gods. In ancient villages, as people sang and danced around the campfire, there were times when a dancer would leap in the air and twirl, and all who saw how high she leapt would declare in wonder, "Allah!" God, "I see god in you!"

Art was considered divine, and those who had great skill were thought to have been touched by the gods.

In time, the saying got shortened and corrupted to "Olé!" So that still today, in parts of the world, when someone does something magnificent and worthy of praise, the audience shouts god's name.

Olivia could not easily give Bron memories of love. Oh, she could manufacture such memories, but she had qualms about becoming that invasive. Still, she could give him something that he craved. She could give him the gift of music.

So late that night she went into his room, and lightly touched him. For a moment, she peered into his memories, looking for moments when he felt loved, and when he had given love in return.

She found very little. Bron was so alone inside. The harder that she tried to reach him, the more he would build up walls to protect himself. She wasn't even sure if he *could* love anymore. It was as if part of his brain were stunted, as if it had atrophied from lack of use, and had died.

She might be able to cure him over time, but that would be a call for the Weigher of Lost Souls.

Oh, he'd never hurt anyone on purpose. He wasn't intentionally cruel.

In searching his memories, she found a song that he was composing—a guitar solo, as beautiful and as dark as a summer's night. She listened to the imagined riff, and her heart broke—a nightingale's song that had never been sung.

Bending her head in thought, she reached into Bron's mind and began to teach him, to prepare him for the moment when he would have to play....

CHAPTER 17

BEAUTIFUL CREATURES

"History shows that the meek can never inherit the earth. The meek inherit only what the powerful abandon."

– Lucius Chenzhenko

Blair Kardashian felt humiliated. He was a good agent, and his acolytes had worked hard, but they had not been able to generate any leads on the pair of masaaks.

Perhaps that justified sending reinforcements, but did they have to be dread knights?

The agents who appeared at the hotel—three men, one woman, were all brutally handsome, and all dressed in black leathers, with silver bling. It wasn't a fashion statement; it was a uniform. The leather jackets and pants were equipped with a padding made of spun selenium crystals, far stronger than Kevlar.

But it was not the clothing that dismayed him: it was the demeanor of these people. They glided across the floor as smoothly as if they were skating on ice, while their eyes roved the room, like those of mountain lions, hunting with a cool regard. There was a deadly grace in the way their hips rolled. It came from decades of practicing martial arts, of being exquisitely aware of their centers of balance, of always being prepared to instantly attack or defend.

The woman threw a suitcase on his bed, opened it to reveal black helmets and night goggles.

The lead hunter, a man with spiked hair bleached white, asked, "So you have pictures of the targets?"

"Just the boy," Blair admitted. He held out his cell phone, showed the image of Bron, climbing into his car.

The dread knight dismissed the picture with a sneer. "Show me the woman," he said, and reached up to grasp Blair's cranium before he could object.

CHAPTER 18

A TRIBUTE TO A HUNTRESS

"We are more wondrous than we know."

– Monique

Bron woke amid dreams of Whitney. He'd seen her soulful green eyes peering up at him from behind a living curtain of honeysuckle that parted like hair. White and golden flowers trailed down her bare arms.

In the dream, she was more than human, something wild, like a fawn, quick and playful and dangerous.

She had been singing in the trees, and he realized now that he'd dreamt that she'd been a creature of legend, a wood nymph perhaps, singing in a deep forest, secreted by vines and secluded within the shadows of weeping willows. She sang, but her song was incomplete.

His guitar needed to accompany her.

Bron's eyes flew open. He'd dreamt of that guitar riff, and in the dream it had been perfect. He went to his guitar.

He heard a creak in another room that might have come from the weight of a footfall. He froze. He wanted privacy.

A little voice inside reminded, "You're going to a high school for the *performing* arts."

He felt stupid trying to hide from Mike and Olivia, but it was the crack of dawn and he didn't want to wake them.

He took his guitar and crept out the back door, where he stood in the mist and gazed into the fields. Not a hundred feet from the house was a herd of elk—a bull, five cows, and six calves. The huge bull had six tines on each antler, which were still in velvet, so that they were covered with wheat-colored fuzz.

The bull fed contentedly. Two cows lay under under an apple tree, while at the edge of the yard, the other animals grazed, legs straddled and heads lowered as they cropped the grass.

The sun wasn't yet peeking over the mountains to the east, though the sky was colored in ribbons of violet and plum, ruddy orange and gold. The air smelled of a drenching fog.

Bron did not want to disturb the animals, so he struck south, hoping to circle the herd, but had not gone ten yards when the bull raised its massive head, gave a whistle of warning, and loped away. The herd followed, and the bull slowed, letting the cows and calves take the lead while he guarded them from danger.

The bull gazed back over its shoulder. It hesitated, as if it might continue its watch, but at last strode away.

Humbled by the majesty of the animal, Bron crept to the barn. He climbed into the hayloft, looked out over the valley, and saw several deer down among the

Oreo Cookie cattle. The animals would be his audience.

He sat for a moment, relishing the touch of his
Yamaha guitar. It didn't have a single scratch or
scuff. The back was made from rosewood, while the
surface was all of spruce. He caressed the wood, laid
his cheek along the neck and just enjoyed the scent.

He closed his eyes, touched the strings, positioned
his grip, and strummed once.

He was gone. For a solid hour Bron began to pick,
thrilled at the way the guitar strings responded to his
touch. The nylon strings were easy on the fingers of a
beginner, and the music came mellow. But he found
himself hungering for steel strings. They gave a pithi-
er sound, greater volume. Mastering them would be
hell on the hands.

He began to strum the song that Whitney had
sung, playing from memory. When he reached the
guitar solo, he re-cast the bridge and captured that
wild, sultry undertone of Whitney's, borrowing from
the storm the night before—the grumble of distant
thunder, the hiss of the wind and rain. Then he
brought in his own harmony to answer and draw out
her melody.

It was not until he had practiced the piece several
times that he stopped and recognized that something
was wrong.

He'd begun playing the song from memory, and
he'd been able to finger the piece even though he
hadn't seen the written music. He'd never done that
before. Nor had he ever felt the music spring to his
hands so willingly.

It couldn't have come from practice. He'd been so exhausted on Monday that he hadn't touched the guitar. There was only one answer: Olivia had wormed her way inside his head.

Bron flushed with anger. He wondered what memories she might have pried, what secrets she might have learned from him.

Had she taken anything? She'd asked if there were painful memories that he might want removed. Sometimes memories fester. Sometimes the infection spreads, until the whole body is wracked with fevers. Had she tried to do him any favors?

And what about new memories? Had she added anything pleasant?

No, he decided. If she had wanted to play with his mind, she would have erased his memories of their talk. She would have left him ignorant, never knowing her powers, or his.

After consideration, he suspected that she had left him only with this gift: the ability to play the guitar.

He experimented, fingering riffs that he'd never tried. Whole new songs sprang to mind, songs that he knew how to play in theory but had never mastered.

He experimented, put the guitar behind his back and played "God Bless America," as Jimi Hendrix had once done. He fumbled a few notes, but it was passable.

Then he brought his instrument around front and moved smoothly into Eddie Van Halen's "Eruption," struggling to adapt it to the acoustic guitar. He was surprised at how good it sounded.

Without amplifiers and the distortion common to an electric guitar, the music felt classical in texture, and he thrilled to the sense of reckless abandon in Van Halen's style warring with the need for precision and beauty.

He didn't have Van Halen's control, but he could feel it coming, just out of reach. It was like trying to pick an apple from a high limb. He could touch it, juggle it on the tips of his fingers, but not quite grasp it.

What had Olivia said? "Deep teaching takes days." Yet she'd only offered to teach him the guitar yesterday.

She must have come to his room more than once. He'd been here only since Friday; he had learned more about technique in that time than he could have learned in five years on his own.

Yet there was something more. He could feel that imaginary apple, the rough texture of its surface. He could thump it and almost taste the crispness of its interior. He was only hours or perhaps days from being able to take it, make it his own.

He yearned for it.

He was angry at Olivia for having violated his privacy, delving into his mind, and yet he was more grateful than words could express. *What price would I be willing to pay to be touched by the gods?* he wondered.

He knew.

He returned to the house and found Olivia making breakfast, dropping whole wheat bread into the toaster. Bron could hear Mike in the shower, singing a country song accompanied by a hiss like warm rain.

Olivia glanced up, saw Bron with his guitar, and froze. "Everything all right?" She looked pointedly at the guitar.

"Yeah."

"Do you want more lessons?"

He knew what she was asking. "How many more do I need?"

"Three, maybe four."

"To be as good as Hendrix?"

"A few lessons, yes, and a lot of practice," Olivia said. "I heard that song in your head. You have a gift, Bron, one that I didn't give you, one that you were born with. You could be great."

He could see now that Olivia was tired. She had dark bags, like bruises, forming beneath her eyes. She must have been up half the night, and the workload was costing her. "Do I ever wake up when you're doing it?"

"Part of your mind does," she says. "That's why all of your dreams lately have been about playing guitar."

Bron nodded. "You're exhausted. You should take tonight off."

"I can handle my part. I can teach your neural pathways, train your fingers and brain to work in harmony, but even Beethoven lost his skills if he didn't practice every day."

"So will I learn faster if I practice more?"

Mike's shower turned off and the singing abruptly stopped. Olivia nodded, then whispered, "Don't show people what you can do yet. It would frighten them."

Bron guffawed. He couldn't imagine it frightening anyone.

"I'm serious," Olivia said softly. "The things I can teach you.... They'll say that you're in league with the devil, just like Poe and Paganini and Mozart." She was so serious, Bron stifled a laugh. "More than that, you could attract unwanted attention."

"Okay," he said. Bron went to his room. He imagined fingering a song, a more-complex version of the piece that he wanted to do for Whitney. He grinned.

Me, touched by the gods, he thought, *and in league with the devil!*

School buzzed that morning with news of upcoming auditions. Tryouts began for the Hyperion Club—the most prestigious of all. Everywhere Bron went, people were prepping. Thespians wandered about the grounds delivering lines, talking to the empty air as if they were schizophrenics. Out on the plaza by the Green Open Theater, kids were doing voice exercises. Down in the dance studio, everyone was leaping about.

Amid all the excitement, Bron felt alone, like a wolf on the prowl. He wasn't into musical theater, and because he had nothing else to do, he took his backpack and guitar up to the plaza and sat at a table.

He pulled out his guitar and began to tune.

Suddenly Whitney appeared, sneaking up from behind, took a seat next to him, and sat smiling.

Bron bumped shoulders, drank in her eyes.

"You ready to show us what you've got?" Whitney asked.

Bron froze, looked up at the crowd. Already heads were turning. Whitney had a couple of friends at her back, including Sheriff Walton's son.

Bron had never felt quite so embarrassed.

Whitney said, "Don't worry. We're all performers, and we support each other. We all need applause, so we give it freely."

Bron felt blood rush to his face. He wanted so badly to impress Whitney.

He'd once heard that if you were shy about speaking in public, all you had to do was imagine the audience naked. One glance at Whitney, and his blush deepened.

So he imagined that he was in the barn, playing to the open fields, and to the elk and the cattle.

He swept into the intro, and let instinct take over. With eyes closed, he played by touch, never looking at his fingers or the strings. Whitney fell in, and she took his lead on the rhythm, singing:

"I see you coming, babe, and panic creeps—
why can't I breathe?
You say 'hello' and walk right past me—
why can't I speak?
This happens every day, five times a day—
what's wrong with me?
And on the weekend I'm alone at home,
and I dream...."

At first, Whitney was hesitant, and she listened as much as she sang, as if they were a duet, her voice with his guitar. Most listeners wouldn't have heard the clumsiness or recognized that the timing was off by milliseconds, but when Whitney's voice merged with the guitar, they gathered power, creating an overtone.

It was as if an electric arc shot through Bron and into the crowd. The audience responded with gasps of surprise, sighs of relaxation, feet tapping in time, a shuffling and swishing as people began to sway. Someone near the back of the crowd called excitedly, "Hey, you guys, come here!"

This is the way Stevie Wonder experiences music, Bron realized. *He can hear when the audience captures the joy, can feel how he moves them.*

They blended seamlessly on the chorus:

> "You'll text me when you're waiting outside.
> I'll climb out the window,
> > down that old drainpipe.
> We'll paint the town red in my daddy's
> > Blue, beat-up Ford.
> And long after we should,
> > we'll race the dawn back home.
> And no one will ever know."

Bron gave himself to the music then, as Whitney cycled through the verses. When she finished with the bridge, he hit the guitar solo and didn't even think about fingering, just capturing the joy of the tune, enhancing it. It was a complex piece, worthy of Slash or Keith Richards.

In it, he stripped Whitney's song down to its bare essence, like a humble cottage stripped to its foundation, and then he rebuilt it stone by stone, turning it into a castle bold and majestic, towering above the hills.

267

It was perhaps more complex and intricate a piece than he had first imagined, but he purposely embellished it, hoping to impress Whitney.

Yet he didn't push it too far, only let the music surge through him and surround him, entrance him, as if a spring rain now fell upon his castle, nourishing the fields of the villagers across the land.

Each note became liquid and round, a raindrop plunking upon water, driven by the wind, until he felt as if he too had fallen into the rising pools.

He finished the solo and nodded, letting Whitney know to join back in, and she finished up with

"I'll text you when I'm ready inside
            to climb out the window,
            down that old drain pipe,
      to paint the town red in my daddy's
            blue beat-up Ford.
      And long after we should
            we'll race the dawn back home,
      And everyone now knows."

He stopped playing as Whitney sang the last note, riffling up and down the scales, letting her voice fade off into silence.

Only then did he notice that the swishing movement of clothes had stopped, along with the tapping.

He opened his eyes and saw that a crowd had gathered around their table, perhaps sixty people in all, a fifth of the school. Students and teachers alike were gaping at him, open-mouthed.

He saw astonishment, but there was something more, something bordering on fear.

As Olivia had warned, he had just been too good.

In the silence, one young man whispered in awe, "Damn, you can grind that ax!"

Then the applause began, people hooting and clapping. Whitney grabbed him and kissed his cheek, and said a heartfelt "Thank you," with tears in her eyes. He gave her a brief hug, but she kept clutching him, as if she never wanted to let go.

Students surged forward to slap him on the back and tell him, "That was sooo great!" and he heard one girl tell a friend, "No wonder Mrs. Hernandez wants to adopt!"

Her friend answered, as if he were a puppy, "Oooh, I want him, too!"

Amid the congratulations and fist bumping a young man asked, "Can I get your autograph?"

Bron was so startled he said, "No one has ever asked me for that before."

The young man shoved a pen and paper his way. "Can you write on it, 'To Joel, my first autograph'? Then put the date on it?"

Bron signed the paper, glanced up at the crowd, wondering how Justin Walton might have reacted to the song, but he was gone. Bron imagined that he had just sulked off in anger.

A boy who looked too young to be even a freshman asked, "Where did you learn to play like that?"

"Uh, Guitar Hero," Bron lied. Other kids began to ask for autographs. The bell for first period rang, and people hurried off to class.

A young man with curly hair, beefy in stature, got Bron's guitar case and opened it, and then laid Bron's guitar in reverently. "Wow," he said as everyone else was leaving. "I think you're going to be the most popular guy in school."

Whitney smiled at that. "I think he will."

The young man stuck out his hand to shake. "I'm Kendall. I've got a band. Want to join?"

Kendall stood shyly, almost as if he were overwhelmed to be in Bron's presence, and Bron couldn't just say no. It would have broken Kendall's heart.

"Your band any good?" Bron asked.

Kendall shrugged. "With you in it, it could be great."

Bron nodded. "I'll give it a try." He glanced at Whitney, expecting a smile, but saw panic instead. He realized his mistake. "So long as it doesn't conflict with playing for Whitney."

Kendall nodded thoughtfully. "I think we can reach an amicable agreement."

Whitney clutched Bron all the harder, and her smile spread across her face, encompassing her entire body—eyes, skin, soul.

Bron reached for his guitar case, but Kendall swooped it from the table. "Allow me, sir." He took the guitar gingerly, as if it were a treasure. "I liked your playing," he said. "It was as if you ... took the essence of her song and stripped it bare. At first, I thought that you would hold it up for ridicule, something so weak and so pop, but instead you clothed it again, more majestically than I could have imagined, and then you just gave it back to her! Damn, that was righteous!"

Bron smiled. He appreciated the criticism, but he had to wonder: Is that what I was doing? He realized that in part, the young man was right.

"So what's the band called," Bron asked.

"Wasteland," Kendall said. "When we play, we all act like we're wasted. It's not a cultural statement or anything, just theater."

Bron peered at the guy curiously. Kendall was beefy, like a lineman on a football team, with dark curly hair and a killer's pale blue eyes.

I don't just have a band, Bron realized. *I have a fan and a valet.*

Kendall walked with a dangerous swagger, as if he might beat up anyone who imposed on Bron's time. The kid seemed like a follower, one of those clingy ones who latch onto rockers and movie stars.

What am I getting myself into? Bron wondered.

CHAPTER 19

WARNING SIGNALS

"Once we give into weakness, others will define us by our weakness."

— Lucius Chenzhenko

Olivia and Bron took separate cars that day. To avoid recognition, she drove Mike's pickup, and wore sunglasses, arriving at school later than usual. She checked the parking lot for any sign of strangers before she got out of the truck and hurried in. The broad walkway was set beside a creek, and every hundred feet or so, she had to leap up some shallow steps.

She had just reached the plaza when she met Mr. Petrowski, the dance instructor. He was eyeing students as they practiced their dance routines.

He jutted his chin toward Bron, who was just walking into the building, while Kendall McTiernan lugged his guitar. In a mild Russian accent Petrowski said, "You just missed a wonderful performance. Your foster son astonished the school, and he won the admiration of ... Mr. McTiernan."

A chill crept over Olivia. Kendall McTiernan had been the subject of more than one faculty meeting this summer. Not everyone at Tuacahn was a devoted artist. Some teens were special cases. Tuacahn was so new, it hadn't quite maxed out its attendance, and the administration had been pressured into taking a couple of students who didn't quite fit in elsewhere. The hope was that these students would thrive at Tuacahn. Kendall was one of these test subjects.

Kendall was trouble. Several teachers were trying to figure out how to save him. Others just hoped that his explosive temper wouldn't go off at school. Some said that Kendall was just another Columbine, waiting to happen.

"Are you going to warn your son to stay away?" Mr. Petrowski asked.

Olivia wondered. Kendall had his good points. He'd transferred from a rough neighborhood in Dallas, one where he'd watched his older brother get stabbed to death in a senseless gang battle. Ever since then, he'd been toughening up.

He was brilliant, ruthless, devoted. Mostly devoted. It came from watching his brother die. He'd never gotten into a fight where he wasn't protecting someone else.

His guitar skills were almost non-existent. Olivia had him pegged to become a roadie for a couple of years, then graduate to becoming a band manager, maybe even a record producer.

Kendall has a mobster's mentality, Olivia thought. *He should do well as a record producer.*

"I'll have a talk with Bron," Olivia promised.

Olivia didn't see Bron for the rest of the morning, didn't even really have much time to think about him—aside from the fact that half the school was talking about his "awesome guitar skills." The air was electric in the hallways. Tryouts were going to begin for the Hyperion Club. A bevy of students ran the club, but as the faculty advisor, Olivia's opinion carried tremendous weight.

At the auditions this afternoon, Olivia could just about guarantee a student's acceptance into the club with the slightest nod of the head, or send them packing with even a bit of a frown.

She didn't take such power lightly. These kids worked and prayed and dreamed for this. Entrance into the club got them extra training for their careers. It helped seal them spots in plays, and since so many of her students ended up going to work on Broadway, she'd need to take special care today.

She stood outside on the plaza and listened to the students reciting lines in their own private worlds, singing openly, or practicing dance steps. She knew that timid students often did not perform at their best when put under pressure. So she studied them as they practiced, when they thought no one was watching.

She felt it important to begin developing her opinions on each student now—before the actual audition. If she found someone who needed a confidence boost, she could give that later. What she wanted today was to gauge their real talent.

So she spent time on the plaza, and patrolling the halls, and peering into the various darkened theaters and onto the dance floors to find the students lurking in the shadows.

She had made her way upstairs, when she halted abruptly: Marie Mercer stood in the office, Galadriel in tow.

Galadriel waited at the principal's desk, lithe and blonde and beautiful, and it seemed that the air went out of the hall. Kids were whispering to one another, "Who's that?"

Galadriel had transformed. She stood taller, and had a more commanding presence, as if she owned the school. Even her expression had altered: there was a fierceness to her eyes, determination, as if someone else had taken over Galadriel's body.

She was easily the prettiest girl in the school. It was as if a handsome caterpillar had just burst from its chrysalis, and sat in the morning sun stretching its wings, scintillating and sparkling in the sunlight. What she had been was forgotten. What she could become was heartbreakingly beautiful.

She spotted Olivia, rushed up, and with boundless enthusiasm she asked, "Where's Bron?"

As Galadriel said it, she actually leapt into the air a little. In anthropological circles the move was known as "the bounce." Females around the world did it. It was a subconscious display, one that drew attention to one's breasts, and it signified her willingness to mate.

Instantly Olivia knew: Galadriel had come to this school just to be with Bron.

"I'm sure that he's around somewhere," Olivia said. "Are you ... transferring schools?"

Galadriel beamed. "My mother always said I should be a movie star. So I thought I'd give it a try. It's not the kind of thing that you can learn just anywhere. This is the place to do it."

"Well, good luck," Olivia said. She wondered how long Galadriel might last here.

"I thought maybe you could help," Galadriel said. "I read online that there's this audition today, for this thing called the Hyperion Club? So I need to try out. But I've never had an acting lesson or a singing lesson, and I want to be great!"

Olivia opened her mouth, trying to fill it with something intelligent, but nothing would come. This girl wanted her to stop everything and teach her to be a Lea Michelle. "I, it takes a lot of work, Galadriel." She decided to be honest. "Most of our students study for years before they make it into the Hyperion Club. There's not much that I can—"

The bell rang. "Oh, sorry," Olivia said. "We'd better get to class." She smiled graciously, relieved to make her escape.

News of Galadriel Mercer's arrival at Tuacahn surged through the school like a tsunami.

Whitney Shakespeare heard bits and pieces of it in the hall as she walked between classes. Girls were whispering, "Have you seen the new girl?" and despairing whimpers of "She's so beautiful!" and "Who is she?"

It was Dia Sosa who supplied the answer in a ghetto accent. "She live next to Mrs. Hernandez.

Funny thing, she's never wanted to come to this school befo'."

Whitney stopped in her tracks. Dia hung with a crowd of girls, talking to them, but her gaze was fixed on Whitney.

A chill ran down her spine. Whitney understood instantly. This girl, Galadriel, hadn't come to the school looking for an education.

"That's right, sista'," Dia joked. "You got the fight of *your life* on your hands. Want I should borrow you a razor, or something, to cut her face up?"

Just then, Dia nodded, jutted her chin toward the stairwell. Whitney followed her gaze.

A gorgeous blonde in a stylish pink shift came down the steps, seeming almost to float. She reminded Whitney of a water lily, resting on a glassy pool, so perfectly vibrant and wholesome.

For a moment Whitney forgot to breathe.

With everyone else wearing their school uniforms, the girl's outfit was completely out of place. The teachers were letting it slide for her first day.

Whitney felt a pain in her palms, glanced down. Her fists were clenched. She'd pressed her fingernails into her skin so hard, she'd nearly drawn blood.

In second period that day, just before lunch, Olivia found that Kendall McTiernan had unexpectedly transferred into her class.

He was a singularly odd young man, with broad shoulders and arms so long that he should have been able to walk on his knuckles. She wasn't sure if he gelled his curly hair, or if it was just oily. He had a brooding expression, as if he was sad and angry, but Olivia studied him all through class and realized that his heavy brows just cast deep shadows. His brown eyes were really quite gentle and inquisitive.

When class finished and the kids were grabbing their backpacks, she called, "Kendall?"

He looked up in alarm, as if he expected her to yell at him. "Yo, Mrs. Hernandez."

"Could I speak to you in private, please?"

He shrugged, as if to say "fair enough," and waited for the other students to leave. Not wanting to cut into his lunch time, she got right to the point. "I saw you with Bron this morning. You plan to hang with him this year?"

"The guy's a freakin' genius," Kendall said. He shrugged apologetically. "I thought maybe some of it might rub off. With a little luck, I'll pick up a bouncer."

"A bouncer?"

"You know," Kendall explained. "Pretty girls throw themselves at him, one bounces off, and maybe I pick her up."

Olivia nodded her head wisely. "Ooooh. Good plan."

"That all?" he asked, seeking permission to go.

Olivia licked her lips. "I wanted to talk to you about Bron. You see, he got in trouble at his last school...." she figured that Kendall could relate. "I don't know all of the details, but there are some young people who have been looking for him, and they might come here." Kendall immediately stiffened,

279

and his right hand strayed toward his back pocket. She didn't want to know what he kept there.

"In any case," Olivia said, "if anyone comes around asking questions—"

"I'll handle them, Mrs. Hernandez."

That was the problem. This boy might be good in a fight, but he wouldn't stand a chance against a Draghoul. "No," Olivia said, "I don't want violence. Just make sure that you warn me. If any strange people come onto the campus, I want to know about it immediately. You run straight to my class, or to my office—whatever it takes."

"Sure thing, Mrs. Hernandez," he offered. "I'll tell the boys in the band to keep their eyes out."

She'd seen the boys in his band—a ragtag team of losers and dreamers who could somehow seem frightening when they got together.

"Thank you," she said. "That's all that I was hoping for—a few more pairs of eyes on the lookout."

CHAPTER 20

IN ENEMY HANDS

"A wise person recognizes that sometimes there is no difference between a friend and an enemy. Both can destroy you with equal delight."

– Olivia Hernandez

The day at school had started out so well for Bron, but all too soon he felt as if he wanted to hide. All through his first class people had asked if he would play again at lunch. He couldn't really keep a low profile.

Since he didn't have a locker at the school—those were reserved only for freshmen, and came with the fear of scorpions creeping into your gym shoes at night—Bron had to carry his guitar from class to class.

Within an hour he was so famous that at the beginning of second period, social sciences, his teacher announced, "I've had several requests for Bron to play for us today, and so if you're all quiet and attentive for the first hour, I will ask our guitar virtuoso to play."

The entire class was angelic, so Bron played.

He felt conflicted. Olivia had warned against attracting attention. She wanted him to keep a low profile, but he'd never felt popular before.

He wondered if he should come up with a cover for his new-found skill. After all, it had come out of nowhere. But no one here knew him. Back in Alpine, at the Stillman's, he'd played only in secret. As far as anyone knew, he'd always been talented.

So he made sure to hit a wrong note in class, just so that folks didn't get too excited.

At lunch, he wanted a little anonymity, so he hid his guitar in the car and huddled in a corner beneath the stairs at the atrium and ate a sandwich from a sack lunch.

A couple of the guitar geeks in the school sought him out—a pair of undersized kids who apparently felt that he might spout some wisdom that would multiply their own talents. They squatted on the floor next to him and talked softly about their World of Warcraft exploits while munching on carrot sticks and bologna sandwiches.

As Bron ate, he closed his eyes and listened to songs on his iPhone. Someone kicked his feet. He peered up at Justin Walton, the teacher's aide for his dance class, who was all glaring eyes and square jaw.

A couple of Justin's friends hovered at his back, thugs eager for some entertainment. Bron pulled off his headphones and said, "Hey, looks like you found Crabbe and Goyle!"

"You've played your last song with Whitney," Justin growled, nostrils flaring. His face was red, and his curly hair looked like the mane of a wild animal. His sculpted body was all sinew and muscle, without an ounce of fat. He breathed heavily, as if he'd just gotten out of dance practice. "I know all about you. You're just welfare scum."

Bron thought of a couple of comebacks, all having to do with piglets, but decided to take it easy.

He'd often found that the best way to avoid a fight was to simply ignore the aggressor, and he suspected that any match between him and Justin wouldn't be even.

"Whitney can hang out with anyone she wants," Bron said, and slipped his earphones back in, as if he was disinterested. But he just couldn't let it go at that. "Besides, I don't take orders from ballerinas."

Justin kicked Bron's feet again, hard, and made a face that was half snarl. This fool didn't know who he was dealing with. Sure Justin was bigger and more muscular, but Bron figured that he could teach the cop's son a few wrestling moves.

As quickly as he considered how to go about a takedown, Kendall McTiernan stepped around the corner, appearing at the edge of the stairs, as if he'd been standing guard duty.

"Is there a problem here, Walton?" Kendall asked. He stepped in front of Justin, and glared, the muscles bunching in his broad shoulders. The two kids who had been sitting next to Bron also rose to their feet, backing Kendall.

Suddenly Bron realized that his newfound friends *had* all been standing guard duty.

"I was just ... advising Bron here to stick with his own kind." Justin retreated a pace, as if unsure whether he could win this fight.

"Oh," Kendall said easily. "His own kind? You must mean the really *cool* people? Whitney's crazy about him, in case you haven't noticed, and he's crazy about her. I really think that they should hook up, don't you?" Justin's face fell at the sexual innuendo. "That's okay with you isn't it? There's no law against it."

Bron's fingers began itching, his sizraels extending. He closed his fists, even as his palms began to tingle.

For an instant, Justin's nostrils flared as his frustration turned to wrath, and then just as suddenly his face paled in dismay. Bron felt energy flow into him, like living water.

Justin's pupils shrank to pinpricks of fear. His nostrils flared and his face went white.

Bron had begun draining Justin of will. The effect was palpable, instantaneous.

At that moment, Kendall's hand strayed to the back pocket of his slacks. Bron expected Kendall to pull a knife, but instead he pulled out a comb. "Get out of here," Kendall told Walton, "unless you want to party?"

At that moment, Justin's resolve crumbled. He turned and strode away, his entire frame shaking.

The guitar geeks guffawed at Justin as Kendall stood combing his hair. The tension in the air began to ease. Kendall leaned over and put his hands on his knees, as if he'd just taken a punch. His geek friends were shaking too, and Bron realized something.

I wasn't just draining Walton. I was draining all of them!

He felt energized, alert and powerful and just a bit deadly. But his protectors were all trembling, as if they'd just lost a fight.

Bron kept his fists clenched, to hide his sizraels. "Hey, thanks," Bron said. "I owe you."

He put a hand on Kendall's back while Kendall struggled to draw breath. He *willed* something vital back into his friend, and felt a small tug as it was released. It wasn't much, but Bron gave something back.

Kendall drew a deep breath. Bron looked at the two geeks, wanted to help them, but felt too nervous. He couldn't do it now, in public. It would have to wait.

Kendall drew upright and said, "Watch out for that creep. He'll send his dad to do his dirty work."

Bron went through the next couple of hours in a daze, worried about Kendall, longing for Whitney. He went to class, but couldn't have repeated anything that was said.

At the end of third period, as the hall filled with students bustling between classes, Bron bumped into Galadriel.

Literally, he *bumped* into her. Or maybe she bumped into him. He was walking through a crowd, had turned his head while he tried to maneuver, and "slam," he stepped right into someone. He got the impression of soft, yielding flesh, long blonde hair, and he caught the gentle aroma of perfume.

He turned as Galadriel grabbed his shoulders, as if to keep from falling, then steadied. "Oh, sorry!" she said.

Somehow he wasn't surprised to see her. He was more amazed at the change in her. There was something brilliant and determined behind her eyes, and she held him with ... boldness, he decided.

"Hi," Bron said. "You coming to school here?"

"Yeah, I'm all registered." She smiled, waited for him to strike up a conversation. Finally she asked, "So, are you going to try out for the Hyperion Club?"

"Me?" Bron said. "Nah."

"Why not?"

"Because I don't want to look like any more of an idiot than I already do."

Galadriel's face fell a little. The school was electric with excitement. This was the most important club on campus. "I'm going to try out."

Bron wondered at that. "Really?"

"Yeah," she said. "Do you want to stay and watch me? You might even offer a few tips."

He didn't really, but he couldn't admit that without hurting her feelings. "Maybe I could."

Immediately he regretted saying it. He wondered how long he'd have to sit waiting for her. Still, watching Galadriel would kind of be like watching a gorgeous sunrise. Tedious but breathtaking.

"Great!" Galadriel beamed.

At just that moment, Whitney came down the hall, smiling prettily. She took one look at Galadriel and the smile faltered.

"Who's this, Bron?" Whitney asked. "New girlfriend?" Whitney came close enough to bump elbows with Bron, and leaned into him, as if to stake her claim.

She forced Galadriel back just a pace.

"Uh, this is my neighbor, Galadriel," Bron apologized.

"Lucky you," Whitney said.

Galadriel's smile faltered. A hurt expression crossed her face, frown lines and tight lips. Bron realized that Galadriel hadn't heard about Whitney.

"Well," Galadriel said, retreating just a bit, "see you after school, Bron. It was nice to meet you, Whitney."

She lunged through the crowd as if to escape, trembling.

"She's beautiful," Whitney said. It was a loaded compliment. If Bron disagreed, he'd obviously be lying. If he agreed, he'd get in trouble.

"You're beautiful, too," Bron said, turning his full attention to her. He almost felt that he had to say it. Normally he would have held his feelings in, but he just decided to let them out.

In part, he was surrendering to his desire. In part, he wanted to reassure Whitney. Maybe, even, just a little he wanted to make Justin Walton crazy.

"So what are you going to do about it?" Whitney demanded.

He gave her a quizzical look. "I was thinking about asking you out this weekend, if you've got time."

"I'll make time," Whitney said. She half turned to head for class, then did an odd thing. Her smile faltered and her expression became thoughtful. She put her hand on his shoulder and peered into his eyes, as if seeking to come to some decision.

Her pupils went wide, and Bron breathed in her scent, as if she were an orchid that had just opened in the night. She leaned on her tiptoes and kissed him.

Her lips tasted intoxicatingly sweet, and they were softer and more inviting than he'd ever imagined.

He'd never been kissed by a girl before, not like that. It snatched his breath away. He felt as if he might fall into her.

Whitney whirled with a mischievous smile and headed for class.

He stood staring as she stalked away, and fought the impulse to beg her to come back.

Two girls giggled nearby, and Bron realized that news of the kiss would spread all over school within the hour.

He glanced back, saw the girls with their heads down, exchanging excited remarks, texting on their phones.

Nah, he thought, *it won't take an hour. The news will be all over school in* ten minutes.

Bron spent the rest of the day in a daze. He kept imagining Whitney, what it would be like to run his hands through her hair, to stare into her eyes for hours. He had never taken a girl out before. The Stillmans had had a rule against dating until he was sixteen. Even once he reached the age limit, he'd been too broke to date.

Mainly, he realized, he'd never dated because he'd never been attracted to a girl the way he was to Whitney.

He'd promised to watch Galadriel practice for auditions, but realized that Whitney would be jealous. So when the bell rang, he bolted for the door.

Galadriel caught him in the foyer. "Hey, Bron," she said, as he joined the stream of students heading out the front door. Her face was pinched with worry. "Can I ask a favor?"

"What?" Students, mostly girls, jostled Bron as they passed. He felt exposed and vulnerable, like a rabbit in the open.

"My mom called, and she's sick with a migraine. I don't have any way to get home. Could you give me a ride? Pretty please? I'd owe you forever."

He looked into her blue eyes, and wind gusting outside stirred her hair. He was afraid that she might be trying to make Whitney jealous, but all he could see in her eyes was worry and an apology.

I'll be stuck here for hours, he thought. Olivia might be able to take Galadriel home, but who knew how late Olivia would have to stay? He didn't know anyone else who might be driving all the way to Pine Valley.

"All right," he agreed.

She smiled in relief and bounced a little. "Thanks," she said. "You're the greatest!" She bit her lip, as if worried, and begged, "Can you come help me prepare for my tryout?"

He didn't want to be alone with her, so made an excuse. "I can't. I have a bunch of homework. But I *will* wait for you."

While Galadriel found some place to rehearse, Bron hid in the Hafen Theater, with a math book opened on his lap, as he watched the tryouts.

As faculty advisor to the Hyperion Club, Olivia sat in the front row during auditions. To Bron's surprise, Whitney, as club president, hunched beside Olivia, taking notes as each student tried out.

Between auditions, Whitney often glanced up. She just beamed, but didn't come up to say hello. Bron realized that he was going to have to walk down to see her, if they were to spend any time together.

An hour after school had ended, Galadriel entered the theater and took a seat beside Bron. He wished that he could shrink under his seat, and somehow hoped that Whitney wouldn't notice Galadriel.

It didn't take ten seconds for some girl to nudge Whitney. She glanced back, and lost her smile.

Bron tried to think of some way to put her at ease. He wanted to pretend that Galadriel didn't interest him. He peeked to his side, and felt stunned: once again, Galadriel's natural beauty floored him. She was too gorgeous to ignore. The sweet scent of her hair tugged at him. He tried to figure out words to describe her: curvaceous, shapely, sexy, desirable.

Superlatives failed.

Thoughts of Galadriel seemed to burrow into the back of his skull. Even when he looked away, he felt profoundly aware of every little shift of her body, her chest rising and falling with each breath.

Being with her wouldn't be so bad, he considered. *I mean, she does seem to have changed a little.*

He tried to focus on the performers, and was barely aware of them. The auditions were an odd mix. The Hyperion Club was for triple threats. Over a hundred kids tried out for only five slots. Those who won a spot would receive extra training from Olivia, and that would take them a long way in their careers.

Competition was fierce. People performed who could sing but not act, dance but not sing. Everyone got applause, but some of it was less heartfelt than others.

Near 6:00, a deliveryman came in with a stack of pizzas, and auditions broke up. Bron walked down and selected a slice of Hawaiian, then climbed up on the edge of the stage and sat next to Whitney. She had her own pizza, something with steak and tomato.

She let him sit by her, but turned and began to talk to friends. He knew she was angry. She'd make him suffer. After a minute, she turned back and asked, "How's your friend Galadriel?"

"We're not really friends," Bron said. "She just asked for a ride home. Her mother got sick, and couldn't pick her up."

"I'll bet that happens a lot this year," Whitney prophesied.

"I'd be happy to give *you* a ride home, sometime," Bron suggested. "Maybe even pick you up? Like tomorrow morning?"

Whitney smiled. "I live down in Saint George, way out of your way."

"I like taking the scenic route," Bron said.

"There's nothing scenic in my neighborhood."

"You're scenic."

"You wouldn't be impressed by my neighborhood," Whitney said. "Too many cheap houses." He could see that she wanted him to pick her up for school, but she was worried.

That surprised Bron. "I like cheap houses," he said. "I've lived in them all my life." He realized that he wasn't the only one at the school hiding behind a uniform. "Somehow, I thought you were rich."

"Why's that?" Whitney asked. She inched toward him, and he felt stunned by her nearness. His heart was pounding.

"Your smile," he said simply. "That alone looks like it's worth a million or two." He was telling the truth. He'd seldom seen teeth that were so perfectly aligned, so white. Her smile spread slowly, opening like a morning glory when touched by the sun. "Then there are your eyes: you should get a patent on that shade of green. Your freckles are really cute, too. I think each one is worth at least a couple of bucks."

Whitney grinned widely and moved closer, until her shoulder bumped his. Bron had earned forgiveness.

"You're not really jealous of Galadriel, are you?" Bron asked. "I mean, she's got nothing on you."

Whitney's expression hardened. "Look," she said, "my dad died when I was eight. My mother got just enough money from dad's life insurance so that with luck we'll survive until I get out of high school. Then mom will have to try to live on her income as a waitress. The only way I'm ever going to get through college is if I can rack up a couple of scholarships, and to do that, I need parts in plays. Even better, I need summer jobs at the theater.

"Now when someone like Galadriel comes along, she's got something that's worth a lot to casting directors: she's breathtaking. I don't know if she's got any talent, but even with a little, she turns into major competition. I hear that she's rich. She's got a great look to her, and with her money, if she needs a little enhancement—a nose job or her lips collagened—she can run to the best plastic surgeon in Hollywood, and the next day she'll be twice as gorgeous.

"So ... we're in competition. I have to be worried. That girl is a dream breaker. I'm kind of hoping that she has zero talent, or that she falls off the stage and snaps an arm or something."

Bron laughed and bumped shoulders. "It doesn't have to be that dramatic, I hope."

"Life is hard enough without her. Bron, I want to hang out with you, get to know you. But time is not something that I have much of. Play season starts today, and for the next eight months, I'm going to be working my tail off each night."

"So," Bron said, "if we're going to hang out, it sounds like I'd better sign up for theater tech."

"You'd do that for me?"

"Of course. I want to hang out with you, too."

Whitney nodded toward his pizza. "Are you going to eat that beast, or just gaze at it longingly?"

Bron realized that he hadn't touched it. She hadn't tasted hers. She raised an eyebrow at his pizza, as if admiring it.

"I've been waiting for a royal food taster to come by," Bron said. "You never know what someone might try to sneak onto your pizza, like arsenic or roofies. Want some?"

He held up his pizza, and Whitney looked into his eyes as she leaned forward and took a bite, then smiled. When she'd chewed it slowly, she said, "Seems safe. Alas, I have no food taster of my own."

Bron leaned forward, took a bite of her pizza, and Whitney stifled a chuckle.

He swallowed quickly. He was surprised at how great it tasted—sundried tomatoes, marinated steak, forest mushrooms and ... something he couldn't name. "Wow," he said. "That's the second-best thing I've tasted today."

She looked confused, as if nothing could be better than her pizza. "What was better?"

"You."

She raised an eyebrow. "Hmmm. I don't really remember how *your* lips tasted."

"If you want a kiss," Bron said nonchalantly, "you don't need to beat around the bush. For most women, my lips are off-limits. But for you...."

He leaned forward, peered into her startling green eyes. Part of their attraction, Bron decided, was the size of her eyes. They were so large, he could get lost in them.

Whitney grinned, glanced around the room. At least a hundred students were milling about. She leaned into him and kissed.

Bron's heart pounded and his cheeks flushed, but he didn't dare stop. He took it long and slow, and he didn't care whether anyone saw. He reached up and cupped her head with his hand, just holding her lightly....

It wasn't until almost eight at night that Galadriel took the stage. She wore a yellow designer raincoat that went fantastic with her blonde hair, and she carried a matching umbrella. She cued up music from the sound booth, and then went into a little soliloquy that launched her into a tap routine while she sang "Singing in the Rain."

She started out a little wooden with her first lines, but quickly her voice took on a sincere tone, and she slid into the role as easily as if she'd just pulled on a sweater.

Bron was surprised to find that she had real acting skills. Her singing was nowhere as cool as Whitney's, not as soulful.

As she began to sing, he realized that she had a pretty voice. It wasn't amazing. She had probably never been trained, but it was better than average.

Her tapping was impeccable. The stage had a few leftover props here and there—stairs that went to nowhere, an overturned bucket, a barber pole.

Galadriel danced up the stairs, twirled the bucket, swung on the pole.

When she finished, there was enthusiastic applause, and Bron saw Whitney and Olivia with the other judges exchanging urgent notes. When they finished, Olivia nodded, and Bron felt sure that Galadriel was in.

The sun was setting after the auditions, when Bron walked Galadriel to the car.

When they left the school, Tuacahn had a festive air. Orange lights lit up the school and the theater. People had begun to arrive for the Tuesday performance of "Tarzan," and were lining up on the plaza, talking contentedly. The snack counters wafted a scent of cinnamon-coated almonds and caramel corn, while lights in the gift shop illuminated bronze statues and wall hangings.

"That was so great," Galadriel said. "That was so great!"

Bron said nothing. He realized that he should be on the lookout for strangers. He saw plenty, but none with the cruelly focused gaze of Olivia's enemies.

Bron and Galadriel strolled down in the evening shadows, into a parking lot that was rapidly filling. It was that gloaming time, when shadows deepened toward pure darkness. A crimson glow limned the red rock cliffs behind the school, and bats weaved crooked patterns across the sky, as if writing words that only prophets might read.

If a squad of enemy masaaks is hiding down here, Bron realized, *I'll never see them.*

Bron got in his car, as Galadriel hopped in the passenger seat. He turned the key with a sense of relief, and sat for a moment, just letting it idle. Some old people walked past on their way uphill to the outdoor theaters.

He glanced at Galadriel. She'd surprised him. He wondered, *Do I really have any talent? Sure, I played the guitar today, but that wasn't really me. Olivia loaded me with memories, taught me to play.*

296

But where does the teaching end and me begin? I'm not sure that I'm any better than a karaoke singer.

Bron didn't want that. He wanted the music to be a part of him, as natural as a laugh, as essential as bone.

"That Whitney girl has a crush on you," Galadriel said.

"Yeah," Bron said. "I've got a crush on her, too."

He wondered where he should take Whitney on Friday.

He wondered how he could even be thinking about Whitney with Galadriel in the car. His mind spun. Galadriel was pretty, and apparently talented.

He drove slowly out of the parking lot and downhill, then reached the turn at the road. He had not gone far when he realized two things: he seemed to be heading the wrong way, driving up the hills into the sunset, and Galadriel was just leaning back in her seat, staring at him.

He kept driving for a long mile, and saw a sign announcing that he was entering Snow Canyon Park. There was a ranger's shack just ahead, and the park was closed.

He pulled off the side of the road, and Galadriel laughed in amusement. "Man, you're lost. Turn around already. Unless ... you brought me out here for a reason?" She smiled teasingly.

Bron felt the blood rise to his cheeks, and he turned around, went down the hills with the sparse mesquite bushes until he reached the main road. From there he was able to follow the signs home even in the dark.

He had just reached the T in the road as he came into Pine Valley when he saw Officer Walton's squad car parked by the chapel.

Bron's heart pounded at the sight. He couldn't help think of Kendall's warning about Officer Walton. Bron made sure that he used his turn signal, then took a left and accelerated slowly toward home.

The bubble lights on top of the police car began to flash, and Officer Walton made sure to flip on his siren as he spun out of a driveway and "gave chase."

Bron couldn't believe it. He pulled over at the park, and the squad car came up behind.

Officer Walton turned on his spotlight, so that the car was lit brighter than day. He came out with his long flashlight, the weighted kind that could be used as a club.

Bron hit the switch and rolled down the window, and Officer Walton flashed his light into the cab. There was a gloating expression on his face, tinged with chagrin. He seemed displeased to see Galadriel there, as if having a witness to what was about to happen might suck all of the fun out of his evening.

"Everything all right, ma'am?" he asked.

"I'm fine, officer," she said.

Bron reached for his driver's license, but Officer Walton said cordially, "Bron, could you step out of the car?"

Bron tried to remain calm. He climbed out the door, stood facing Walton. He imagined that he might be asked to walk in a straight line, as if he was drunk, but Walton said, "Will you put your hands on the hood and spread your legs?"

It wasn't until then that Bron saw that Walton had pulled his revolver and had it leveled at Bron's gut.

"What? What's going on?" Bron asked. "Is this about me dating Whitney? I can't believe this!"

He turned and dutifully took the position as Walton patted down his back and waist. "Put your right hand on your neck," Walton ordered.

Bron did as asked, and the officer snapped a handcuff onto his right wrist. Half a second later, Sheriff Walton twisted the arm down while he clasped the cuffs onto Bron's left wrist. By putting a toe into the back of Bron's knee, Walton forced him down onto the ground, where the gravel dug into Bron's skin.

"Galadriel, will you step on out of the car, sweetie?" Officer Walton asked.

Galadriel came out, shaking. "What's going on here?" she begged.

"We got an anonymous tip," Walton explained. "Someone sent a cell phone picture into the police, which identifies Bron here as a suspect in a murder...."

Bron froze. He tried to sound surprised. "Murder?"

"There was an incident down in Saint George, on the on-ramp at Exit 8?"

Bron's heart hammered. This had nothing to do with Whitney at all. Officer Walton went to the passenger side of Bron's car, opened the glove compartment, and pulled out a pistol.

Bron blinked in surprise. He didn't recall ever having seen the gun before. He could only imagine that Olivia had put it there. But when?

"Well, well, well?" Walton said. "What have we got here? Maybe I better check into any armed robberies in the area."

Bron wanted to object, to tell Walton that it was Olivia's weapon, but his mind was racing. The only people who knew that he'd been in the car when Olivia threw out the tire traps were the people who were chasing him. They must have been the ones who supplied the police with the "tip."

He hadn't realized that anyone had photographed him.

Which begged the question, "Why?" Why would they want him arrested? He could only think of one answer. They'd been hunting for him, and they'd come up empty. So they'd enlisted the aid of the police.

Saint George was a small city. His arrest would be a media circus, and would land on the front page of the Spectrum. The paper might withhold his name, since he was a juvenile, but the enemy would learn he'd been caught. They'd know where to look.

Neither he nor Olivia would be safe.

Bron worried that if he implicated her at all, Olivia would get arrested, too.

Then what would happen? If the enemy caught him, he wasn't sure. What could a memory merchant do to him? Rip all of the memories from him? Yeah, he thought, they could do that—and probably a whole lot more.

Officer Walton stuck the gun in his belt, reached into the glove compartment, then pulled out a paper bag filled with caltrops. "Looky here," Walton gloated. "These look curiously like the custom-made tire spikes that got thrown out onto the onramp the other day. So what do you do with these, Bron?"

Officer Walton pulled out a spike. The spike was made of iron, and had four prongs. No matter how it fell, one prong would always be left pointing up. Each prong was roughly two inches long, and had a hollow center, so that it would pierce and deflate even the toughest tire.

"Those? I play Jacks with them," Bron said.

"Jacks?" Walton asked, as if he'd never heard of the game.

"You know," Bron replied, "One, two, buckle my shoe?"

"Ohhhh," Walton said. "That little kid's game?"

"Adults can play games, too," Bron suggested.

"According to reports," Walton said. "You were in a white Honda CRV at the time of the incident the other day. There was a woman with you. You mind telling me who it was? Was it Galadriel here?"

"Friday?" Bron said. "I don't remember being with anyone on Friday."

"Olivia?" Walton asked, as if confused. "Was it Olivia, maybe?" Even Walton couldn't imagine Olivia being involved in anything like this, obviously.

"She loaned me her car for a bit, to run some errands," Bron said. "I may have picked up a hitchhiker."

Walton peered at him for a long time, looking down his nose. "You sure that you want to play it this way?"

"I want a lawyer," Bron replied. On television, that always left the cops frustrated and angry, but Walton just smiled coolly, like a lizard in the sun.

301

"Okay," Walton said. "Bron Jones, you're under arrest for carrying a concealed weapon, vehicular assault, fleeing the scene of an accident, premeditated murder—and a whole lot of other things that I haven't even thought of yet."

Before Bron could say anything more, Walton read him his rights.

CHAPTER 21

CHARGES FALSE AND OTHERWISE

"Most criminals believe in their own innocence. They are so used to lying to themselves, telling themselves that they are wonderful people, they never see the truth. My job is to enlighten them—by putting them in a cage."

– Officer Rick Walton

As soon as "Washington County Sheriff" popped up on Olivia's caller ID, she knew it was trouble. She still hoped to get in another two hours on the first night's auditions, but took the call anyway.

"Hello," Olivia whispered. Her voice came shaky, and her stomach clenched. Whitney glanced up in alarm.

The girl on stage continued an interesting rendition of Hamlet's "To be or not to be" soliloquy.

"Olivia," Officer Walton said, "could you come down to the Sheriff's Office? We've got a situation. Bron is being detained." His voice was as sweet and oily as honey butter.

Everything inside her warned, "Trap." *He plans on arresting me,* Olivia thought.

He'd seen her drive her CRV around for years, though she'd never given him reason to run her plates. He knew what kind of car had been involved in the accident last week. By now, he'd put two and two together. She'd hoped that this wouldn't happen. In fact, she realized, some corner of her mind was so afraid that she hadn't completely planned for this possibility.

"All right," Olivia said. She needed to draw out details, to buy time to think. "I don't understand. What is this about?"

"Murder."

Whitney had leaned near, trying to eavesdrop on the conversation. Olivia waved her back, got up and headed out the door. The kids would have to handle the rest of the auditions.

She reached the rear of the theater. "Is this about something that happened back in Alpine?"

Walton liked to gloat. Now he couldn't help himself. "No, it's something that happened in Saint George, just last Friday. We got an anonymous tip—a picture of the killer, sent with a text message. It's Bron all right."

"I'm sure that this must be some kind of a prank," Olivia said. She decided that she shouldn't say much more. "If Bron is being accused of something, doesn't he have a right to face his accuser? I'd like to know who sent this picture." She could hear radio chatter in the background, and highway noise. She realized that Walton was calling from a car. "Can I speak to Bron?" she asked loudly.

"Not now," Walton said.

"I'll be right down. I forbid you to interrogate Bron before I get there. He's just a minor." Olivia wasn't sure if Walton would be a stickler for the law. Probably not.

In the background Bron yelled. "Olivia! I want a lawyer!"

Walton hung up.

Whitney sat near the front of the stage, her mind a blur. She'd seen the caller ID on Olivia's phone. She'd heard Sheriff Walton mention Bron's name, ask Olivia to come down to the police station. Walton had said something about "murder."

Whitney felt numb.

In her pack this morning, she'd found a little folded note. It said simply: "You smiled at the wrong boy yesterday."

The note wasn't signed, but it was so like Justin. He was so jealous of other guys, and something about him frightened her. In fact, she felt her skin crawl, as she turned around and searched through the darkened theater.

Justin was there, seven rows back, his face twisted in a superior smirk that said, "I told you so."

Whitney leaned back in her chair, bit her lower lip. Whatever was happening with Bron, she felt certain that Justin was behind it.

It was just like her fling with Nathan Sweet last year. He'd taken her down to Crave for some yogurt, and the next day at school, all of his tires got slashed.

Two days later, Officer Walton had pulled the boy over and found some Oxycontin in his car. Nathan hadn't been into drugs, Whitney felt sure. She suspected that Justin had framed him, and the charges stuck. So he'd transferred out of the school.

That day, she'd found a note in her pack that said, "You may give your body to others, but your heart will always belong to me."

Something about the note had chilled her to the bone. It was as if Justin sought to claim her, regardless of her lack of feelings for him.

He was always watching her at school—standing down the hall, sitting at a nearby table at lunch, following her when she went to the restrooms.

It wasn't stalking, exactly. At least, when she'd told the police what was happening, they said that there was nothing that they could do legally. But it was creepy.

I should have warned Bron, Whitney thought.

Walton glared at Bron as they sped down the highway. "Shut your mouth back there!"

"I want to talk to Olivia!" Bron said. "I heard her ask to talk to me."

Walton considered, then said, "You'll get that chance." He drove while he peered into the cage in the back of the car.

Bron resisted the impulse to shout "Deer!" just to force the sheriff to watch the road, but Walton didn't seem to have a sense of humor.

Bron felt a tingling in his hands. His sizraels had begun to extend. He panicked.

Sweat broke on his brow, and his throat went dry. He tried to steady his breathing.

Nothing bad will happen. Nothing bad will happen, he told himself. He knew that it was a lie. Terrible things were about to happen.

Olivia shoved her cell phone in her pocket, hitting the school doors at a run. It was full dark, and music played in the outdoor theater. The stage lights, reflecting from the rock walls of the canyon, gave the sky a surreal, bloody glow. The air smelled of popcorn. Strings of orange lights outside the theater reminded Olivia of pumpkins and Halloween.

Every muscle in her body tensed. She walked in the dark, wanting to run, but she didn't want to call attention to herself or risk twisting an ankle in the dark. An instant later her phone vibrated. She looked at the caller ID. It was the Mercers. She answered.

Galadriel's voice was hysterical. "Uh, is this Olivia—Mrs. Hernandez, I mean?"

"Hello, Galadriel," Olivia said.

Galadriel began to sob. "Bron's been arrested!" She kept talking, trying to explain, but fell to blubbering. Olivia couldn't understand her.

"I know," Olivia said. "It's all right. I'm sure that it's a misunderstanding."

"Really?" Galadriel asked, suddenly coherent.

"Yes, really," Olivia said.

"How did you find out so fast?" Galadriel sniffed. "I mean, he was just taken in, not ten minutes ago."

That confirmed Olivia's suspicion. Walton was so eager to smirk, he hadn't even taken the time to get Bron into booking.

"Officer Walton called me," Olivia said.

Olivia was in real trouble she knew. The Draghouls would soon be on her trail. Her whole world could come crashing down. There was only a slim chance to save it.

Galadriel began sobbing again, and Olivia asked, "Galadriel, have you told your mother yet?"

"Yes."

That was a nuisance.

"Can you do me a huge favor? Can you promise me not to talk to anyone else about this? Not anyone. I'm sure this is all a misunderstanding, but if news gets out, it could really hurt Bron's reputation. We wouldn't want to do that to him, would we?"

Galadriel hesitated. Olivia knew what she was thinking. She'd want emotional support. She'd want to gossip with her friends. Olivia was asking her to resist that impulse.

When Galadriel didn't answer, Olivia took a risk, asked, "Do you love Bron?"

"What?" the question caught Galadriel off-guard.

"Do you love him?" Olivia said simply.

The question was premature, of course. They hardly knew each other. But Olivia understood how powerful a teenage crush could hit a girl. Besides, "love" could mean just about anything. Galadriel could love him as a friend, as a human.

"Yeah, I really do," Galadriel said. She couldn't resist the impulse to be a little dramatic.

"Then do this for him: Don't tell a soul what has happened. I'm sure that this will be cleared up by morning."

"Okay...." Galadriel sniffled.

Olivia sighed in relief and thanked her profusely as she hung up. She reached her pickup, fumbled with the keys, hands shaking.

Walton hadn't been able to resist calling Olivia as soon as he took Bron in custody. *That might work in my favor,* she thought.

It was only a matter of time before Draghouls learned of the arrest. The more advance notice Olivia got, the better chance she had of breaking Bron out of jail, cleaning up this mess.

The Draghouls wouldn't need to rely upon such outmoded media as the local newspaper to find out about Bron's capture. They had access to their own spy network. She wasn't sure what their capabilities might be.

Olivia knew that the CIA, the KGB, and Chinese MSS all had enormous spy facilities. On the internet alone, a hundred thousand Chinese agents worked monitoring email transmissions that they intercepted using "ghost servers." One in every three emails sent in the United States got read by agents in China.

But it wasn't just the internet that was monitored. Satellites using advanced voice-recognition software listened in on every conversation for certain key words.

The average person on the streets wasn't aware of just how closely they were being watched, listened to, studied. But not all of the spies worked for government entities.

The Draghouls' efforts also used sophisticated software. If anything, their spy network was more advanced than the CIA's. Much of the security software developed by private corporations and sold to governments around the world was built by the Draghouls.

All it took to build a spy network was money, and the Draghouls had a nearly limitless supply.

Their criminal empire had flourished from the time merchants first traveled down the Silk Road out of China, smuggling stolen gems and antiques under piles of silk. They'd made a fortune selling blue lotus blossoms to ancient Egyptians eager for a high, and by rigging bets in the Roman Coliseum.

Over the centuries, they'd amassed trillions of dollars.

Nowadays, they made most of their money bootlegging prescription drugs and manipulating global stock markets.

They'd tapped into the communications satellites decades ago. That's why Olivia seldom contacted other masaaks by phone, and why she spoke in vagaries and codes when she did. The Draghouls might well be listening to a recording of Olivia's call with Officer Walton at this very moment, analyzing every word.

If so, the wisest course for her would be to throw her cell phone out the window so that her location couldn't be traced. She could drive away, disappear forever—leave Bron in his cell for the Draghouls, leave Mike to have his brain picked apart for any clues as to where she might have gone.

The fact that she froze in indecision, considered driving the lonely roads to Elko, Nevada, and hiding out in the desert, indicated just how much the enemy terrified her.

But she couldn't run. *If I don't try to save the people I love, I'll never be able to live with myself.*

She had to squash this, and fast.

Bron closed his eyes, imagined an old song called "Free Bird." He had a gift for remembering music. If he concentrated, he could almost hear a song, remember every note, every nuance to the singer's voice. He only had to hear it three or four times, and he had it forever. It was like having an iPod in his head.

The engine roared as the police cruiser raced down the highway.

The band that had sung the song, Lynyrd Skynyrd, had pretty much all been wiped out in a plane crash. Snuffed out and silenced in the dead of night.

Such a loss.

Bron opened his eyes to mere slits. The car bounced as it hit a bump. A purple light sparked in the air.

Bron hadn't meant to do anything. His powers were still untamed. He couldn't help it, but he'd just drained something from Officer Walton.

What happens if I drain too much from him? Bron wondered. Would he just crumple, clutching the steering wheel? Would he faint and veer from the road at seventy miles per hour?

Bron didn't want to find out.

He tried to calm himself, taking deep breaths, until they reached Saint George, turned into the center of town, and rolled into the police station.

It was bigger than Bron had imagined. Officer Walton escorted Bron to a front desk and told the petite receptionist, "I'm going to need an interrogation room here. The prisoner's name is Bron, B-R-O-N. Last name Jones."

The woman smiled at Bron as if she were used to working the counter at Taco Bell, rather than in a police station. She typed his name into a computer, then jutted her chin. "Room three is yours."

Dozens of officers were bustling about.

Walton marched Bron into the back room, keeping him in cuffs, and set him in a hard chair. Walton wiped sweat from his brow with the back of his hand. "Lordy, I'm tired." He turned to leave.

"Aren't you going to ask me any questions?" Bron said.

"No," Walton smiled. "You lawyered up. Besides, I'm not all that interested in you. You're just a minnow. I'm after the big fish, and you're just the bait."

Walton gave a gloating smile, turned, and left Bron beneath the glaring lights.

As Olivia reached Highway 89, she made a quick call to Father Leery, the only other masaak that she knew locally. She briefly explained the situation and asked, "What should we do?"

"First," Father Leery said, "don't be in such a hurry to get down to the police station. I know you're worried about Bron. By now, I suspect that the enemy knows that someone has been arrested. They'll be coming for him."

"That's why I want to get him out now!"

"It's almost 10:00," Father Leery said. "There will be a shift change at the precinct. Officers will be coming on duty, others will be filling out reports. The place will be busy. The enemy will send an extraction team, but they'll want to wait until things quiet down, to lessen their risk."

Olivia nodded. Father Leery was wise in many ways, and she appreciated having a man with experience in such dangerous matters.

"So what do we do?"

"They'll come for him in the dead of night," Father Leery warned. "Four in the morning would be the safest hour, but they'll be too eager. They'll strike just after midnight."

"Okay," Olivia said. That was only a couple of hours away.

"I'll reach you well before that. We'll take Bron out before the enemy gets there. Don't be afraid. I'm on my way."

"Bring guns," she begged.

Father Leery didn't answer, merely hung up.

Of course he'll bring guns, Olivia thought. But she wasn't sure. He was a man of peace, after all.

Before she could put the phone back in her pocket, Mike called. "Did you hear the news?" he demanded. "Bron's been arrested!"

"I know," Olivia said. "I'm on my way to the police station."

"Okay," Mike said. "We've got to figure a way out of this. I don't believe these charges. I don't think Bron's a killer. He's a nice kid. There has got to be some kind of mistake."

"I agree," Olivia said.

"But we don't have the money to bail him out," Mike said. "I mean, if he goes up on murder, with a full trial? We could lose our life's savings real fast."

She hadn't even considered the notion that she might get Bron out on bail. It seemed a faint hope. No, with the Draghouls out there, she really didn't have any hope at all.

"Don't worry," Olivia said. "I'm not going to put the ranch at risk. I won't post any bail."

"Do you want me to come down there?" Mike asked.

He'd want to make sure that she didn't make a mistake, get emotional and throw away all of their money, of course, but Olivia heard something in his voice: a real concern for Bron.

"This has to be some kind of stupid mistake," Olivia said. "Even if they do offer to let Bron out on bail, the best thing is to wait for a few weeks. The judges don't want to fill up the jails, so they'll keep lowering the bail every week or so, until someone springs for it. The best thing that we can do is to let Bron know that we love him, and wait."

"Yeah," Mike said, sounding reassured. "Yeah, you're right. I think I'm going to come down anyway."

She didn't want him there. This looked like it might get messy real fast, so she tried to warn him off.

314

"Tell you what," Olivia said. "Let me find out what the situation is, and I'll call you later tonight, if I need you. Morning comes early. You go get some sleep."

Olivia drove quickly to the police station, which was situated on a hill above Saint George. She glanced down over the city as she exited the car. The lights were soft and warm. The Mormon Temple, the largest building in the city, was all luminous white and gold, its central spire rising above the sleeping city.

The Sheriff's office was imposing, big and blockish. Dozens of patrol cars parked out front, their bubble lights gleaming in a well-lit lot.

Olivia would have preferred a smaller precinct—something where only one lone dispatcher might be manning the night desk. In her imagination it would be easy to subdue just one officer.

She considered waiting for Father Leery, but she was too nervous. She wanted to see Bron now, to get him out quickly, if she could.

As she walked up the sidewalk toward the doors, she glanced up at the security cameras overhead, and realized that she had another problem: there might be an electronic record of Bron's arrest—video footage, photographs, induction records, dispatch transcripts.

This incident could already be too large to contain, she decided. *Maybe I should just snatch Bron and run.*

She was trembling as she reached the door. The automatic opener let the doors slide backward, yawning into a dark space.

Like the Greek entrance to hell, Olivia thought. She peeked inside, saw a smiling desk clerk—a petite woman with dark hair. *My very own Cerberus.*

Olivia stepped inside the building, with its bland beige walls. The place was bustling. Two dispatchers handled the desk, while a corrections officer milled about, processing a dejected-looking drunk. Dozens of officers were finishing up day shift, or coming in for the night.

It was as if it were the busiest time of day. Her heart sank.

It might still be possible to get Bron out.

She imagined that the police would escort her to some kind of interrogation room. With any luck, she might overpower Officer Walton, wipe his mind, and then just walk away.

She went to the desk clerk and announced herself. "Olivia Hernandez, here to see Officer Walton?"

The desk clerk punched a call to line three, spoke softly, and moments later Walton came scurrying from the back, with a female officer at his side. He smiled, his mouth as wide as a bullfrog's. "Olivia, thank you for coming down and making this easy for us. Right this way."

Officer Walton led her down a hall. Through some one-way glass she spotted Bron sitting in an interrogation room, his hands cuffed behind his back, while a lone bulb shone overhead.

Walton led her to a second interrogation room. "Go on in and have a seat," he said, as he opened the door.

She felt certain now that she wasn't here to see Bron. Walton intended to arrest her. She had only one chance to escape. The hallway was empty except for the two officers.

She had never used her sizraels as weapons, but she knew how to.

Normally, a person's mind filters their thoughts, allows them to concentrate on only one thing at a time. But with a little burst of power, Olivia could open thousands of memories at once. The resulting "brain burst" was like an explosion in the mind. The stimulus knocked most people unconscious.

Olivia entered the room, unsheathed her sizraels, whirled, and reached up to tap Walton on the temple.

But Walton responded faster than a fat man should be able to, grabbing her wrist and twisting fiercely, digging the knuckle of his thumb into her wrist, in the bundle of nerve fibers in her ganglia. A throb of pain numbed her arm.

Walton shoved her against a wall and slapped a handcuff on one of her wrists.

He must have spotted the suction cups on her fingers, for he shouted, "What the hell?"

Olivia immediately forced herself to relax, retracted her sizraels. They were worthless anyway. The ganglia in the human wrist was a pressure point used by martial artists, but attacks to this spot were doubly effective upon masaaks. Olivia's whole arm was numb with pain.

Walton seemed scared now. Frightened people are often mean. He slammed her against the wall again for good measure and twisted her other arm up into the cuffs. For a moment he stood huffing, trying to catch his breath.

He grabbed her cuffs and pulled them back and up, so that the metal cut into her wrists, as he examined her fingers. The suction cups were gone. By now he'd be wondering what he thought he'd seen.

"Well," he said after a moment, confusion evident in his tone. "I think I'm going to pile 'resisting arrest' and 'battery' on top of all the other charges."

Blair Kardashian had been listening to a police scanner in his hotel room when a message came over the radio. "This is car 7, Officer Walton. We have a 10-82, suspect in custody, on that freeway incident last Friday. I'm bringing him in for questioning."

"That's a 10-4," the dispatcher said.

Blair leaned close to the speakers, waiting for the dispatcher to ask the identity of the subject, but she didn't bother.

Night was on, and the air was filled with end-of-shift chatter. Beyond that, someone had just called in a major accident down on the Arizona border, and emergency vehicles and police were rushing to the scene, so news of Walton's arrest got lost in the excitement.

Blair picked up his cell phone and considered calling his master.

His acolytes were out doing grunt work for the dread knights, watching store parking lots. It was a menial task, but someone had to keep watch: masaaks are nocturnal by nature. Darkness makes them feel safe, concealed. So the dread knights had reasoned that their quarry would most likely wait for full darkness to run their errands. They'd need to eat sometime. So each major grocery store in the area had one Draghoul guarding it.

The fact that Blair was relegated to listening to a police scanner was humiliating. The dread knights were hindering him from finding his quarry. Using memories they'd stolen from him, they insisted on conducting their own search, hoping to win their master's reward when they caught this pair.

It wasn't fair, Blair knew. But the dread knights were not known for being fair.

Why should I let them have the honor? he wondered. *Why should they gain a reward?*

Though he was growing old, Blair was far more capable than others imagined. He kept physically and mentally fit. Over the years he had gleaned a great deal of information from various fighters—Navy SEALS, Army Rangers, and the like. Killers all.

So he slipped into his new Mercedes and drove to Harmon's Grocery Store. There he found Acolyte Riley O'Hare in the parking lot, keeping the store under surveillance. Blair pulled up to Riley's car, rolled down his window, and said, "Get in."

The acolyte knew better than to ask why.

Half an hour later, Blair had gathered all four of his acolytes. It was nearly 11:00 by the time he reached the police station. An officer was just leaving. Civilian cars crowded the parking lot. Too many.

Blair huddled behind the driver's seat. The acolytes in the car did not speak. They'd been trained to remain silent.

"All right, my little nightingales," Blair said. "It's time to go to work. You know what to do."

"Is this a wet op?" Riley asked.

"Yes," Blair said. "Prepare to get bloody."

S o, Olivia," Officer Walton said, "our tipster tells us that a woman in a white Honda CRV was driving when the attack on the highway occurred. Would you like to tell us what happened?"

He bent his ear, as if Olivia might whisper. A female officer sat at his side, sprawling in her chair, with a bemused expression—the look that a child might have on her face when she's getting ready to tear the wings off a fly.

Olivia bit her lip and simply waited. It had been more than an hour since they had cuffed her. She needed a drink, but dared not ask. "I want my lawyer," she said for the tenth time.

"You and I have been friends for a long time," Walton said. "You're a good woman. The kids down at your school love you. So I've got to say, these accusations sound downright crazy to me. I've got to wonder what really went on?"

Olivia tried to keep calm. With every second that she waited, it increased the likelihood that the Draghouls would come. Yet she couldn't tell them the truth. She'd contacted Father Leery, but it would take some time for him to reach the precinct. She had to hope that he'd make it, that he'd be able to do something.

"I told you, I'm waiting for my lawyer," she warned Officer Walton.

He circled, scratched his head. The female officer leaned back in her chair, looking bored.

"Was it some kind of road rage?" Walton asked. "Did these folks do something to you? Were you afraid of them? I mean, if it was self-defense...."

A soft rapping came at the door. The interrogation room door opened, and the desk clerk poked her head in and whispered, "Her lawyer's here."

"Well," Walton said, clearly annoyed, "the more the merrier."

Olivia breathed a sigh of relief—until the Draghoul from Best Buy strode into the room, grinning like a skull.

"Watch out!" she shouted to Walton. "He's not a lawyer!"

She threw herself backward, hoping to break her chair, but merely landed on the floor.

Officer Walton whirled and reached for his gun, just as the Draghoul touched his temple. Walton spasmed so hard he was thrown into the air. He bounced off the wall, fell, and began to convulse and growl.

Stunned, the female officer tried to pull her gun as the old Draghoul leapt. He grabbed her head, jerked to the right. Neck bones snapped. She sagged to the floor.

The Draghoul turned to Olivia and flashed a baby-killer smile. "I love to see a woman in cuffs."

Bron sat in his chair, beneath a bulb that beat at him. Though it gave little light, it seemed to exude a great deal of heat, enough so that he found sweat dripping down his armpits, beads of it twisting down his nose.

He wondered if the government had special bulbs made just for interrogation rooms. With all of the examinations that the military made of Iraqis and Afghans at places like Guantanamo Bay, he imagined that they probably needed such bulbs.

Bron decided that he would simply endure—the heat, the boredom, the silence. He'd been in the room for a long time, and no one had come to speak to him. No one had offered a drink, or asked him if he needed to relieve himself.

It was part of their strategy, he decided. This was how they hoped to break him down.

They'd come for him in a couple of hours, the interrogators, when he'd been up all night and all day. They'd let his own fear work on him.

The problem was, he didn't really fear the police. Bron had long ago learned to turn off his feelings, not just for others, but for himself. Worry, fear, fatigue—if he concentrated, he could ignore them all.

He heard a scrape at the door, and a plastic card swiped through the outside lock. He expected Officer Walton, but instead a teenage girl entered the room, a pretty brunette. She walked toward him with a strangely mesmerizing gait, her hips rolling gracefully, her back straight and poised.

She smiled. "Good to see you, again, Bron."

He didn't remember seeing her before, until she was nearly upon him—the young woman from Best Buy!

A shout died on his lips as she reached up and touched his temple. He saw the flash of sizraels, felt an electric spark, and his vocal chords went soft. He wanted to yell a warning, call for help, but he had forgotten how.

He stared up at her, mind blank with horror.

"You don't remember me very well, do you?" she asked. "But I remember you!" She tilted his head up and looked into his eyes. "I remember our time at the group home, that football game we played on Thanksgiving, what, six years ago? Riley gave me the memories."

She tilted his head up, examined his jaw, and smiled. "Yep, you're Bron Jones, all right. Now you're ours, little nightingale. So let's take a peek at those nasty old memories you've got rolling around in that skull."

She stood just in front of Bron. His heart was already racing from fear, but the nearness of her set it thudding to a new beat. He could smell her perspiration, her perfume. She wasn't just pretty. Her face was flawless. She wore a black leather jacket over a white t-shirt, and he couldn't help but notice her curves. She smiled teasingly. "Oooh, you're going to go into musth soon! You'll be needing a mate. Wouldn't it be cool if I was your first? Would you like that?"

She smiled, leaned near, with eyes as dark as a fawn's. Despite his fear, he found himself wanting her, and as she placed her hands up on his skull, she did it tenderly, caressing him. She splayed her fingers out, so that they cupped each lobe of his brain, and then softly touched his eyes.

He closed them. "Don't worry," she said. "I don't want to hurt you. You're one of us now."

She leaned forward, and her warm breath stirred the skin of his face, played through his eyelashes. She kissed his lips.

I'm not going to tell you anything! he wanted to say, but his tongue couldn't have been any more numb and useless if a dentist had shot it full of Novocain.

His mind exploded. It was as if a thousand memories surfaced at once, bursting like fireworks:

Mr. Bell driving him to Tuacahn.
Olivia showing him to his room.
The Mercedes flipping as it rolled.
Bron handing Olivia the caltrops.
Galadriel huddled in the back of a police car.
Purple fireworks exploding from his fingertips.
His heart pounding in terror as he discovered his sizraels.
Playing the guitar.
Watching lightning arc across the sky.
Oreo-cookie cattle.
Figuring out how to flush the toilet in his room.
Mike giving him a grin.
Whitney's gorgeous teeth.
The little Stillman kids, all sneaking waves goodbye.

Everyone that he loved, everyone that he wanted to protect, all flashed through his mind at once. Every secret thought, everything he wanted to conceal, all that he held sacred came out of him in an instant.

It was like being raped, he knew, at some primitive level. He'd never felt so sullied, never imagined that he *could* feel so violated.

And this is just the beginning, he thought. *They'll take whatever memories they want from me, dispose of my friends.*

Olivia's mind would be wiped, but not before she was forced to reveal the contact information for any other masaaks that she knew—Father Leery, her family, the Weigher of Lost Souls.

Bron realized that their little community was like a terrorist cell, but once it was discovered, everyone in it would be laid bare. Olivia's people, the Ael, weren't just in hiding from their enemies, they were in hiding from themselves. How much damage would come from Bron's capture, he couldn't begin to calculate. Dozens of Ael might get rounded up, hundreds!

In another room, there was a popping noise, like firecrackers going off.

The girl lurched back, her eyes going wide, startled. She didn't bother looking toward the sound of the gunfire. She was startled by *him.*

You can't have my friends! Bron wanted to scream, but it was too late. She already knew where Olivia lived.

"Oh, my god," she said. "You're a dream assassin!" There was wonder in her voice, or something more akin to awe, and excitement. She began to breathe rapidly as she backed away, and then she shouted. "Blair, Blair, get in here!"

A moment later the old man from Best Buy entered the room.

"We've got a dream assassin!" the girl said.

"Quiet," Blair said. "The wet-work isn't done."

At that instant, gunfire popped again—three shots in rapid succession, then two more, then one. Then a hail of bullets. Cries of pain arose, and moans, and wet thuds as bodies smacked the floor.

Down a hall, someone shouted, "Clear!" From far ends of the building, two more voices called out, "Clear!" "All clear!"

Blair smiled. With grizzled hair cropped close, his face seemed to be little more than skin stretched over a skull. Yet there was brilliance in his eyes, and something more, limitless cruelty.

"Don't be afraid, Bron," he said. "I feel like we're old friends, after all those hours playing videogames in the group home."

It was creepy, the way that these perfect strangers all spoke to him so personally about the good memories they shared.

"Yes, we're going to be great friends. There's nothing to worry about, Bron. You're very valuable to us. You'll be the Shadow Lord's favorite. Anything you want, will be yours—the finest cars, the most beautiful women. I'm going to make you a promise: we won't hurt you. We won't hurt anyone that you love. Instead, we're going to welcome you into our ... family."

What if I don't want to go? Bron wanted to say, but he knew the answer. His wishes were of no import.

Bron's hands tingled. They were still cuffed behind his back. He knew that he had leeching abilities, and now he wondered if he could use them. He tried to extend the suction cups on his fingers, but he had forgotten how. He tried to draw the will from his captors, but felt only empty inside, and lost.

"Now," Blair said, "we're going to go to the car and drive away from here. Let me help you up." Blair took Bron's arm and pulled him to his feet.

Bron stood, feeling numb and empty, as Blair went into the other room. He returned moments later, bringing Olivia. Her hands were cuffed behind her back.

Bron had never seen such terror. Her wide eyes darted back and forth, and her entire body trembled. Her breaths were so shallow, she was gasping. There were red marks on her forehead from sizraels. She'd obviously been interrogated already.

Bron's heart went out to Olivia. He wanted to save her, but could think of no way to do it.

"Come," the old man said. Blair didn't brandish a weapon. Yet his commanding tone said that he would brook no argument.

The girl asked, "Aren't we going to call this in?"

"Not yet," Blair said. "Let's get them to a secure location."

With hands still cuffed behind his back, Bron was marched into the hall. A policewoman lay crumpled on the floor, blood pooling beneath her back.

Bron walked into the police department's main offices, saw two Acolytes carrying long-barreled pistols, with laser sights.

The desk clerk was slumped in her chair, apparently unconscious. Another officer appeared to be dead on the floor, his head askew. In another room, two officers lay bleeding.

Riley O'Hare came from a back room and announced, "I've pulled all of the security footage, and scrambled the audiotapes of the police logs." Riley wore gloves.

Blair added, "I've read through the memories of Walton and the others. We'll need to visit a couple of the officer's homes, if we're to clean up."

The girl added, "Bron has a friend, Galadriel. We'll need to wipe her—and Olivia's husband."

The old man nodded wisely, half-closing his eyes. "Very well. Let's get to it, people."

He marched to the precinct doors, and Bron followed in his wake. Bron considered running, but there was nowhere to go. Blair's grip on his arm was too powerful, too sure.

The pressure plate activated. Doors slid back.

A man stood in the doorway in front of Bron, wearing a Harley Davidson jacket and a motorcycle helmet. Beneath the jacket, Bron discerned a black shirt and a priest's white collar. Before Bron's captor could so much as blink, the priest whipped his hands up to Blair's temple.

At Bron's side, Riley shouted a warning and pulled a pistol.

Bron saw his chance to save Olivia. Blair's followers had taken his memories of how to talk, but they hadn't taken his memories of how to wrestle. He lunged sideways, shoving Riley with all of his might, throwing him off balance. Riley's hands flew up by instinct, to protect him from a fall, as Bron knew they would.

A single bullet flew wide, hitting the plate-glass window of the entrance. Tinted glass shattered in a hail.

Before Riley could regain his balance, the priest leapt into action, sending a roundhouse kick to Riley's face.

Olivia had thrown herself backward, hitting one of their captors—the young woman—in the face. Blood spattered from the girl's nose, rained down upon the floor. But the girl leapt forward with the determination of a cornered animal.

Bron leapt in the air, grabbed her legs with his own, and twisted, throwing her off-balance and pulling her down. The girl slammed to the floor. Her gun skittered away.

Bron adjusted his grip on his captive, clasping her chest, as she struggled to rise. He knew he wouldn't be able to hold her long, but he kept her in a scissors lock, trying to squeeze the air from her. She pushed his legs down, so that he only had her stomach, and tried to squirm free.

Olivia saw his predicament and dropped on the girl, crushing the air from her lungs.

The last of the Draghoul acolytes rushed from a back room, pistols in hand.

Bron never saw the priest draw his own weapon—just heard a shot. The young Draghoul reached up and grasped his neck. A dart stuck there, a bit of white wool at its end.

The young man touched it, then his eyes rolled and he crumpled.

The priest rushed into the room. The young woman gained her feet and tried to attack with her sizraels, but the priest's helmet foiled her. She couldn't reach his head.

The priest threw the girl against a pillar so hard that bones cracked. The girl stood there for a moment, stunned, out on her feet. The priest grasped her skull.

Almost instantly she flew into convulsions, her eyes rolling back, spittle rising from her mouth.

The priest held her gently as he let her sag to the ground, and then crouched above her as he looked for others. "Is that all of them?"

Olivia nodded wildly.

He stood for a moment with one hand upon the girl's forehead, almost as if he were feeling for a pulse, but Bron realized that he was reading her memories. "They've already cleaned the police logs for us, taken down the security cameras. But there are a couple of officers that know that you were picked up tonight, Olivia. We'll have to clean them. And we'll need to wipe this place of prints—any room that you entered."

The priest got up, took a key-card from their captor, along with some normal keys, and unlocked Olivia's cuffs. He grasped Olivia's head for a moment, like some old-time street preacher bestowing the gift of the Holy Ghost, and Olivia's mouth flew open.

"Thanks," was all that she said. She rushed back to the interrogation offices to wipe any prints.

The priest grabbed Bron's skull and held him for a moment. Bron felt something inside him click.

"I can talk!" he said.

"And you can use your sizraels now," the priest added. He unlocked Bron's cuffs.

He knelt over the old man, Blair, and just held him for an instant. Bron saw vivid blue lights pulse at the priest's fingertips.

"What are you doing?" Bron asked.

"They can't be allowed to remember that we were here," the priest said. "I have to clean their skulls out, sanitize them."

"Of everything?" Bron asked.

"By tomorrow," the priest said, "this man won't know his name, his phone number, or how to put on his socks."

"You'd do that?" Bron asked.

"They're lucky," the priest said. "I could make their hearts forget how to beat."

Olivia returned, making a final visual inspection. "I count fourteen dead police officers, and one dead civilian." Her voice was ragged with shock, regret.

The priest went from Blair back to the girl.

Olivia erased the third boy, then finished up with Riley. He was lying asleep at Bron's feet. Suddenly his eyes flew open.

Olivia suggested, "Go to your car, sit inside, and wait for us." Riley stared at the ceiling blankly for a moment, got up, and ambled out the door, as if he were a zombie.

Olivia did the same with the girl, and soon all of the Draghouls had wandered from the room.

"What are you going to do with them?" Bron asked. He could think of nothing worse than finding your mind wiped—having no memories, being unable to speak, to dress. "Kill them?"

The priest looked to Olivia, as if to ask, "Is he really that stupid?"

Olivia said, "No, Bron, we won't kill them, if we can avoid it. We'll *convert* them."

"Convert them to Christianity?" Bron asked.

The priest gave Bron an odd look. "You could say that, I suppose. I'll empty them of memories, and then insert my own. I'll turn them into copies of me."

"We'll 'possess' them," Olivia explained. "Think of your memories, your consciousness, as software. We'll just pull out all of the old programming, all of the faulty stuff, and replace it with something better. When we're done, the possessed are called *poppets*."

"I can't believe that you'd do that," Bron said. "It sounds so ... vile."

"It's not so bad," the priest said. "You'd be surprised at how quickly the poppets begin to differentiate, develop their own personalities."

"Bron," Olivia said. "What do you think they planned to do to you? At the very least, they were going to take all of your memories. They could turn you into a child, make you forget how to open a door. They could put you in a room and make you forget that there's a world beyond it. Keeping you captive would be nothing. They could keep you dumber than a cocker spaniel. Or, if they wanted, they could wipe out your mind completely, and fill it with one of their minds, one of their personalities. Their Shadow Lord would have done that, made you two people with one mind, one heart, one goal. Just one night with the enemy, and you could *become* the enemy."

Bron's face must have been a study in shock. The priest smiled. "It doesn't hurt them, Bron," he said. "I should know. I was one of them, once. I was one of the Draghouls, a Dread Knight. I served the Shadow Lord for three hundred years."

CHAPTER 22

DO OVERS

"For all sad words of tongue and pen, the saddest are these: 'It might have been.'"
                                            – John Greenleaf Whittier

Olivia sent Bron to her car to wait while she cleaned up. Bron sat nervously watching the parking lot. A few minutes later, the priest came from the police station, jumped in a car with the four prisoners, and drove away.

Draghouls, the priest had called them. Bron's head was spinning. He'd met a guy who fought like a Kung Fu master. He'd met a man who claimed to be more than three hundred years old. The strangest part was, Bron believed him.

Two minutes later, Olivia rushed out to the car. "The police will be here soon, I think. Let's get out of here." She started the ignition. The car lunged as she sped away.

"What now?" Bron asked. "What do we do next?" He imagined fleeing, driving as far away from here as they could, as fast as they could.

"Go home," Olivia said. "Get to bed, and act like none of this ever happened."

"What do you mean?" Bron said. "How could we act like none of this ever happened?"

"Simple," Olivia said. "You go to school and take your classes. I go and teach."

"But the priest said that there were some cops who knew our names, who might piece things together."

"And there are more hunters in town. The priest knows where they're hiding. He saw them in the enemies' minds. He'll go after them, first."

Bron sat in the car as she drove out of the city, peered out at the desert beneath a waxing moon. The cliffs were the color of dark blood as it pools.

Olivia shook her head. Bron could tell that she was still nervous, nearly unhinged.

"What are you thinking?" Bron asked.

"Those people scare me."

"Tell me more about Father Leery?" Bron asked.

"Not yet," Olivia said. "There aren't many of us. The enemy has made sure of that. Hiding is our best defense."

"But you know him?" Bron asked. "You know how to get hold of him?"

"Yes," she admitted.

"Is he really three hundred years old?"

"Yes," Olivia said. "The Draghouls have more than one way to ... extend their lives."

"Do all masaaks live that long?"

"No," Olivia said. "Not normally. Eighty, ninety years."

Bron considered. Up ahead, a fox was crossing the road. Its eyes glowed yellow-white in the headlights, and then it leapt into the mesquite and was swallowed by the desert.

"You should tell me about them," Bron said. "I should know everything."

"I'm not sure of you, yet," Olivia said, "and for good reason."

"What reason? Why wouldn't you trust me?"

"There's a coldness to you."

"I'm not that cold."

Olivia sighed, and asked, "What's your favorite quote?"

"From a famous person?" Bron asked. Nothing came to mind, but he seized on one: "That which does not kill us, makes us stronger."

Olivia grinned. "Nietzsche. I knew you'd choose that one." Bron realized that she really had known. She'd been inside his mind, and maybe she knew him better than he knew himself, in some ways. "He's a little grim," she confessed, "more quotable than wise. Sometimes bad things happen to you, and they leave scars—a car wreck, a shocking revelation about a friend. There's another German philosopher I like, Martin Buber. He said: 'It is possible to silence the conflict in the soul, but it is not possible to uproot it.'"

Bron considered that. It sounded like she was saying that you could never really escape the past. Even the most peaceful men bear scars: Lincoln, Nelson Mandela, Martin Luther King.

Each of them was great, yet Bron had to wonder: were they great despite their scars, or did they become great because they were forced to endure the unendurable?

Or was she hinting at something even deeper?

He stopped, struck by a realization. "You've got something you want to tell me, but you're afraid of how I'll take it. You think I'm too scarred."

Olivia peered deep into his eyes, and just when he thought she would speak, she said, "There's no hurry."

"No hurry?" he asked. "We just about got possessed!"

"And now our enemies will be *our* poppets," she said. "It only seems just. Tell me, what do you think the Draghouls will do when they find out that they've lost a bunch of their own? Will they flood the area with more agents, or back off and reconsider?"

"I ... can't even guess."

She smiled weakly. "Anyone who was sane would run away from this city forever. That's what the Draghouls will expect *us* to do. They'll probably search again, make a cursory sweep, but they'll move on quickly. So we're going to have to keep a low profile for awhile."

"There's something you don't want me to know," he pressed. "Something that you think will leave a scar?"

"Patience," she said.

Fine, he thought. *Let her keep her stupid secrets.* He was determined to wait her out.

Bron woke at dawn and showered quickly. He was just stepping out of the guest shower with his towel wrapped around him when he heard the back door creak open, the one that led to his bedroom.

He glanced to the back of the room. The old man, Blair, stood smiling his skeletal smile.

Bron's heart thudded.

"Don't worry, Bron," the old man said. "We're friends."

There was something creepy about the way that he said it. It was like a twisted dream. It was an echo of what he'd said when Bron was captured.

"Who are you?" Bron demanded.

The old man smiled. "I'm Father Leery, for the most part."

Bron stood for a moment, feeling naked and vulnerable. He clutched the towel around him. "Okay," he said, unsure what the man was after. "What do you want?"

"I just came to let you know. The Draghouls that were here in town, the dread knights—I caught them all. It wasn't hard. When they saw me coming, I was wearing the face of a trusted comrade, so it was easy to get close, touch them, take them down."

Bron's heart pounded. He wondered if he could ever trust anyone again. Would Olivia come to him someday, greeting him with a smile, as a poppet? Is that how the enemy would come?

Bron's sizraels extended, the ribs along the edge of the suction cups becoming firm.

Yes, he realized, the enemy might come to him like that. "That's good news," Bron said. He stayed a few paces back. He didn't want the creepy old man near.

Blair smiled warmly, and there was a twinkle in his eye. "Welcome to the world of the Ael, Bron. I could tell you not to be afraid, but I'd be doing you a disservice. Any time that you see another masaak, you need to be cautious."

Bron nodded slightly.

"It was a busy night," Blair said. "Even with three of us working, we've been up all hours. We visited the Walton home. I know what you did to Justin ... draining his will."

"It was an accident."

"Don't return it. The boy is a danger to you. You can't guess how nasty his mind is, how dangerous his cunning. He's all small-minded jealousy, but he imagines that he's fueled by righteous desires. With a little less will, he won't be likely to act upon his more vicious impulses."

"Is that everything?" Bron asked. He wanted this ghoulish character out of his room.

"For now," Blair agreed. "I'll be going to Los Angeles. I'm going to lead the Draghouls off your trail, call in a sighting of you there. Everything should calm down here, at least for awhile."

"Just for awhile?"

"I'm just hoping that I can get them to look for you in the wrong place. I can't promise anything."

"Oh," Bron said.

The old man opened the door. "God bless," he said, and then slipped out.

Bron went to the door after Blair was gone, bolted it. His head whirled. He felt as if reality had become slippery, and he didn't quite know what was real anymore.

Someone pounded on the front door to the bedroom, and Bron wondered briefly if Blair had gone around the house.

Mike poked his head in. He had a broad smile, as if he was a kid who'd just stolen a cookie. After the nightmare that was last night, Bron couldn't imagine why Mike would smile, but then he realized: Mike probably remembered nothing. Olivia would have taken care of that. The police had never taken Bron into custody. Bron had never been handcuffed.

"Did I hear you talking to someone?" Mike asked.

"Just myself," Bron said. "I was making up lyrics."

Mike nodded wisely, as if he'd suspected just that. "I got a phone call from Marie Mercer a minute ago. She pointed out that it's silly for both you and Galadriel to be driving to school every day, when you live right next door." Bron groaned inwardly. He could have suggested a carpool, but he didn't take the bait. "Marie has a proposition for you: if you'll drive Galadriel to and from school, Marie will keep your gas tank full. What do you think?"

Bron was not in any position to decline. He didn't have an income, and the truth was, he worried about how much he was costing the Hernandez family.

Mike grinned. "Hey, you get paid to drive a pretty girl around? Sounds like a bargain to me!"

Bron smiled sheepishly. "All right."

Mike grinned as he left and said, "I'll let her know."

Bron dressed slowly, went out into the kitchen. Olivia was frying up bacon and eggs.

"Can we talk about something?" Bron asked.

"Mike's gone out to work," she said.

"That old man just came to the back door," Bron said, "the one Father Leery caught last night?"

"Oh, Father Leery," she said, as if the old man and Father Leery were one and the same. "What did he have to say?"

Bron told her everything, somehow hoping that the world would make more sense if he just ... thought about it.

Olivia was silent a moment, then admitted, "I slipped into the neighbor's house last night. Marie and Galadriel won't remember a thing, either."

Bron suddenly felt relieved. All his problems of the last few days were ... gone, overnight. The world had reshaped, like a nightmare that twists into a pleasant daydream.

"So that's it?" Bron asked. "It's over?"

"We can't be sure," Olivia said. "With the Draghoul, nothing's easy."

"That's such a strange name, *Draghoul*," Bron said. "Blair said it with a little bit of a *K* sound, with an accent. More like *Dragh-kool*. Where does it come from?"

"It's an ancient term, from an forgotten empire that crumbled thousands of years ago," Olivia said. "It comes from a combination of words: *dray* and *gul*. It means the 'dark guild.' Originally the dark guild was a criminal organization, something like the mafia. It was a society of thieves and assassins that worked by night. Eventually, they became more of a political power."

"This Shadow Lord that the priest mentioned: who is he?"

Olivia weighed her words. "He's the leader of the Dark Guild."

"So, how exactly do you stay alive for three hundred years?"

Olivia just smiled secretively and would answer no more questions. "That's enough for one day. All of your questions will be answered: very soon, I think."

The sun was cresting the horizon when Bron went to the car. In Pine Valley, the light just sort of drifted over the hills in the morning. The sun had not yet risen above the purple mountains on the far side of the vale. The grass in the fields held hints of autumn tans, and this morning there was a slight blue mist above the creek out back. A pair of mallards circled the marsh.

Bron got into his Corolla and started it up, punched the radio on, and then opened the moon roof as the engine warmed. He drove carefully out of the driveway, avoiding the deeper potholes.

He reached the Mercer's big log cabin. It stood three stories high and was made of white pine, stained a golden brown. The cabin had huge windows on the front and sides, so that the folks inside would be able to take advantage of the gorgeous views of the valley and the mountains above.

That house would be hard to heat in the winter, Bron realized. In most of the houses he'd lived in, his foster parents had always complained of the cost of heating. But he figured that if you had enough money, it wouldn't matter.

He worried that he might have to go up and ring the bell to get Galadriel, and he worried what her mom might say. Would she tease him about bringing her daughter home on time? Or would she try to force money on him immediately, as if he were some desperate slob who needed it?

The house was still dark inside, except for one upstairs light. He hated this. He hated having to pick up Galadriel, when Whitney was the one he wanted to see. But he'd have to dump Galadriel at school before he went to Whitney's.

To his relief, he saw Galadriel through a big window come bouncing around the corner, past a dining room. She smiled as she jogged to the car, pulled the door open, and hopped in.

"Hi, Bron," she said. Her teeth were white, her breath smelled minty.

"Hi," he said.

He backed out, then went up Main Street. He wasn't sure what to say to Galadriel. Did she remember anything that had happened last night?

He turned off by the church, and crossed the valley. They had gone perhaps a mile up the road and were just entering the juniper forest, where dark green trees marched side by side, filling the air with their bitter scent, when Galadriel nodded toward a little gravel road ahead. "Will you turn on that road, please?"

He wondered what she was up to. Was she going to try to neck, or seduce him again?

If she does, he wondered, *should I let her this time?*

He did as she asked, and followed the gravel road for a quarter of a mile, before he hit a turnout. She jutted her chin. "Park here."

He pulled the car to a stop, turned off the engine, but kept the radio on. An old Dave Matthews Band song was playing, "Satellite." She turned it off and faced him.

"I want a do over," she said.

"What?" Bron asked. In his world, life wasn't normally that simple. If you made a mistake, you were stuck with it. But he wondered. His life had changed last night.

"I want a do over," she said. "I acted like a jerk the other day, and I'm begging you to forgive me."

She bit her dainty lip and sat in her seat, hands in her lap. She looked poised at a glance, but in reality she was clutching her legs nervously. Her face was like stone, jaw set. Her eyes had a pleading look, and he realized that with a word or two, he had the power to make her cry.

"There's nothing to forgive," he said, thinking that would end the conversation.

"Yes, there is," she whispered. She searched for the words to explain. "The other day, you and I talked. I took one look at you, and I sort of went crazy. I thought you were the cutest guy I'd ever seen, and I threw myself at you in a way that I've never done before. Now I feel really icky, really embarrassed."

Bron nodded. He didn't quite know what to say.

"When you didn't come out to the pond," Galadriel continued, "you don't know how that made me feel. I thought that you hated me, that I disgusted you. I thought that you would never want to see me again, and I curled up and wanted to die."

Bron couldn't understand how she could get it so wrong. "I didn't hate you," he said. "I hardly knew you. Why would you care what I think?"

"I know. It was crazy. It was the middle of the night, and I came and waited at your door. It was like my mind closed down, like I walked inside this dark cave inside my head, and got lost. I went to the pond, determined to wait until you came, and I just felt like, like something had sucked my insides out.

"I can't explain it," she said. "I just began to feel so hopeless. That's not like me. I mean, look at me." Bron had been staring down at her hands, but now his gaze flicked up to her eyes. She was startlingly beautiful, so beautiful that he felt lucky to be here with her. "Everyone tells me that I'm pretty. When I go to the store, clerks fall all over themselves trying to help me. Any time I do something wrong, my parents and teachers give me a pass. I don't think I could get arrested in this town if I shot the mayor. But you looked at me, and you saw right through me. You saw how petty I really was."

"I saw how dangerous you could be," Bron corrected.

Galadriel said softly, "When you told me that you were saving yourself for the girl of your dreams? Oh, man, you don't know how that made me feel! I kept thinking, I wish I knew a boy who was like you, someone who would fall in love with me before we ever met, someone who would remain true no matter what kind of bimbo threw herself at him."

Bron wanted to apologize, but how could he? Galadriel seemed to have gotten it. She was agreeing with him.

She flipped her hair back a little, and tears glistened in her eyes. She sniffed. "When I woke up in the hospital, you were there. You were touching my face, cradling it in your hands."

Bron's heart skipped a beat. He hadn't known that she had awakened.

"What were you doing to me?" she asked. "It felt—it felt so wonderful! I felt like ... like you were inside me, walking around in my heart, in my head, and they were rooms, dark and corrupt, and you were turning on all of the lights. I felt my heart start jumping.... What were you doing to me?"

A tear slid down Galadriel's cheek.

Bron had to make up a lie to cover himself. He said the first thing that came to his mind. "Just holding you. I whispered in your ear when you were asleep, and begged you to wake up. I didn't know if you could hear me."

She nodded thoughtfully, and said, "I saw that white rose that you brought. My mother said that a white rose stands for love, and for purity."

Bron hadn't meant anything by it, but he didn't dare tell her that now.

"When I saw that," she said, "I realized that that was what I wanted in life: love that was pure." She raised a hand in a gesture of warning. "I know, I know that you aren't in love with me. We hardly know each other. But I woke up, and I realized that maybe if I tried harder, maybe if I worked at being a better person, someone somewhere will find me worthy of love."

"I think," Bron said, "that you have to learn to be comfortable with yourself for that to happen. I knew a bishop once at the Mormon Church. He said that once you love yourself and treat yourself with respect, others will do the same."

Galadriel nodded thoughtfully. "That's what I've decided to do. Olivia once tried to get me to come to her school. To tell the truth, the idea scared me to death. I mean, there are a lot of talented people there, and I don't know if I'll fit in, or if they'll all think I'm just a fake."

"Join the club," Bron said.

"So I've decided to change. I'm going to try to do something with my life. I don't know if it will work or not, but at least if I go down in flames, well, I'll know that I tried."

"Flames are nice," Bron said. "Not that I like seeing a girl go down in flames. It's just that, well, not trying, that's *completely* tragic."

Galadriel really did seem to be changing. There was a confidence in her tone, an assertiveness that he hadn't seen before. A few nights ago, she'd been so pliant. He hadn't realized it until now, but every little gesture had been frightened. She'd sat with her shoulders slightly hunched, her expression guarded, as if with every moment, she was waiting for him to make a move, to let her know what he wanted. Now, she seemed to have made a choice, and she was unleashing herself on the world.

"The thing is," Galadriel said, "I wanted you to know something. I want you to know that I'm not stalking you or anything."

Bron let out an exaggerated sigh of relief and wiped his forehead. Galadriel laughed. With the tears still in her eyes, they seemed to dance with merriment. "I was really worried," Bron admitted.

"Don't be," Galadriel said. "I'm not stalking you, for now. That doesn't mean that I'm not attracted to you. I'm really attracted. But I promise not to stalk."

"All right," Bron said. "I'm officially at ease."

Galadriel fidgeted with her hands nervously and said in a shy voice, "I ... uh ... just wanted to thank you."

She leaned forward, took Bron's chin in her palm, and kissed him on the lips. It was more than a friendly kiss. She let it linger. Her breath smelled of mint, and he realized that she had planned this. Her lips were soft and sensual. She pulled away. He sat, stunned.

She gave him a self-conscious, questioning look. "I didn't just creep you out, did I?"

Bron shook his head. "No, that was definitely not ... too creepy." To be honest, he wanted more, and he felt guilty for wanting it.

"Good," Galadriel said. "Thank you. Now, as I said, I want a do over. I want you to know that I'm not the same person you met on Sunday."

"I can see the difference already."

She smiled confidently, reached her hand out to shake. "I'm Galadriel Mercer. My parents named me after a stupid elf princess from a book. In the past, I've always pretended to be embarrassed by the name, but to tell the truth, I think it's kind of cool. You know what my middle name is? Eowyn."

Bron laughed. "Man, they really hammered you."

Galadriel sat back in her seat, wiggled to get comfortable as Bron turned on the ignition. "To tell the truth," she said, "I like my middle name even better."

She fell quiet as he drove, and Bron began to wonder about what she'd said. He had accidentally taken her hope, and she had rationalized it. She thought she had felt depressed by his rejection. And when he gave her more hope, once again she had invented an explanation for the change that took place in her.

He wondered if that was the way that people always worked. Do they invent reasons for how they feel, getting the reasons wrong?

He remembered seeing a clip in school about a woman in Africa named Umandu who was dying from AIDS. She had blamed a woman in the village for her problems. After all, the woman was a witch, and had obviously cast a spell.

So as a dying act, Umandu had gone to the witch's home and chopped off her arms with a machete, leaving her to bleed out.

Though Bron lived in one of the world's most modern and sophisticated countries, Galadriel was still showing symptoms of "magical thinking."

Am I any different? he wondered. Yesterday I played the guitar better than I would ever have imagined possible, and Olivia assured me that I'd improve vastly this coming week.

It almost felt like magic. Yet there had to be a scientific explanation for what Olivia had done to him.

He knew that memory flows through the brain with electrical impulses, but there was a chemical component to memory, too, one that was triggered by the electrical impulses. Was it possible that all Olivia was doing was manipulating electrical fields, so that information somehow crossed the barrier from one body to another?

Yet I feel as if I have been touched by the gods.

He thought of how Galadriel expressed her own feelings about what he'd done.

Drive, passion, hope. Whatever you called that quality that he could steal from others, he had given Galadriel a great deal of it.

Was that the difference in her: hope? Could a little extra hope really change how a person acted, turn them from being unlovable to ... someone he cared for?

He'd never really thought about it much, the value of hope, but he had to admit, he was starting to care for Galadriel.

CHAPTER 23

BETRAYALS

"It is not the giant pine huddled in the midst of the forest, but the tree that must stand alone in the storm that grows the strongest."

— Olivia Hernandez

Whitney woke late on Wednesday morning. The auditions the previous night had taken their toll, but her worries about Bron took a greater toll. Seeing Mrs. Hernandez run out of the school like that, the alarm on her face, had left Whitney a bit frazzled.

If Bron had been arrested, Whitney's first impulse was to blame Justin. Yet in the clear light of day, that didn't seem reasonable. Maybe Justin might plant drugs in someone's car, but he wouldn't have planted a body, would he?

Which left Whitney with a new worry: who was Bron Jones, anyway? Other than the fact that he played the guitar like an angel and he looked really hot, she didn't know much about him.

Maybe she'd been fooled, the way she'd been fooled when she began dating Justin as a freshman.

She was still trying to disentangle herself from that relationship.

Then she had to wonder, *Do Bron and I have a relationship at all? He was supposed to call me last night. Why didn't he call?*

Whitney got up and ran down to the Bear Paw Cafe, where her mother worked as a waitress, and asked for a half-order of the cherries jubilee crepes, along with an egg for a little protein. The cherries jubilee crepes breakfast wasn't the healthiest thing she could eat, she knew, but they were sooo good!

At the other tables, people were talking about a big shoot out. A bunch of policemen had been killed last night, down at the police station. Whitney called her mom over.

Whitney's mom was pretty still, petite with red hair and smiling eyes. One look at her, and you could guess that she'd once been an actress. Her mom said that her looks were her only asset. It helped with the tips.

As her mom refreshed Whitney's water glass, Whitney asked, "So what is this about a shooting?"

"Oh, yeah," her mom said. "Fourteen officers were killed late last night. More like assassinated, from what we hear—necks broken, single shots to the heart. Some of the lucky ones were just knocked unconscious, probably with some kind of drug. They can't remember a thing."

"That's crazy!" Whitney said.

"Justin's dad was there," her mom said. "He's one of the lucky ones that got knocked out." Whitney remembered the phone call last night, the caller ID

354

from Officer Walton, and wondered if Bron had gotten tangled up in something big.

"If you ask me," her mom said, "this sounds like some kind of attack from the CIA or something. The killers were all professionals...."

She scurried off to take care of another customer.

Whitney fretted all through breakfast. Maybe Bron hadn't called because he'd been arrested. Maybe he'd seen the shootout.

A wild thought made her wonder if he could have even been involved in the shootout.

That's crazy, Whitney decided. *Maybe he doesn't really care that much about me. Maybe I was being premature when I kissed him yesterday. Some boys like to just kiss and grope, after all, and it doesn't matter much who they do it with.*

An image flashed in her mind—Justin trying to put his hand up under her blouse, his face flushing with rage as she pushed him away.

She shook her head, trying to clear it of unpleasant memories.

As Whitney dove into breakfast, her phone vibrated. She answered, saw a picture of Bron out in front of the school, smiling. A text message below asked, "Can I pick you up?"

She suddenly felt so happy, tears filled her eyes. Bron hadn't been arrested. He couldn't have, could he? In the picture he was just standing there, smiling, after all.

She texted her address, and asked "Fifteen minutes?"

He texted back. "CU."

355

She smiled, bolted down the best breakfast ever, and ran back to her house, and took a look at it from the outside. She lived in a trailer park, in the poorest part of town. The area was so trashy, most people didn't even know it existed, tucked up as it was behind a few businesses. There were only eight trailers in the park, and each looked crummier than the last.

This was the acid test, Whitney knew. If Bron could see her house and get over it, accept her for what *she* was, then maybe their relationship could go somewhere.

She stood in the front yard—a patch of dry cheat grass and milkweeds, and just waited, head hanging. There were cigarette butts on the ground. The neighbor guy had been out here smoking again. Her mom's trailer wasn't much, two small bedrooms surrounded by rusting aluminum, but it kept them warm in the winter. Not that it ever got cold in Saint George anyway.

All too soon, Bron pulled up in the driveway. Whitney felt like a bundle of nerves. She climbed into the passenger seat, and could still smell Galadriel's perfume.

Bron glanced up at her house. Over at the neighbor's trailer, their red rooster leapt up on their car, let out a "cock-a-doodle doo," then crapped on the rusty hood.

"Well?" Whitney said, afraid that he'd ask her to get out.

He turned and peered into her eyes. "This is definitely the most scenic place I've ever been." He smiled, and Whitney realized that she didn't need to worry. He leaned forward and kissed her, and by the time he was done, all her nervousness felt as if it had washed away.

Bron started the car and headed to school. Whitney wanted to warn him about Justin Walton, but she wondered if that was a wise idea to tell him so soon. She didn't want to scare him off.

"So," she said to fill the silence as Bron eased out of the trailer park, "How are you doing?"

"Great," Bron said.

"What was all that stuff about last night?" Whitney asked. "Mrs. Hernandez got a call from the sheriff, and ran out of the auditions in a panic. He said something about you ... and murder charges."

Bron didn't answer immediately. It was like he was trying to figure out what to say. Then he shrugged. "I ... haven't got a clue what you're talking about. Maybe we should talk to Olivia about that."

His answer seemed so strange. "So ... you didn't get arrested?"

"No," Bron said. "I drove Galadriel home after the auditions, then went and played my guitar for a few minutes before I went to bed. I don't know when Olivia got in. When I left the house, she was still in bed."

Whitney felt sure that he was hiding something.

"Whitney," Bron said. "I have a confession to make. Galadriel's mom asked me to give her rides to school. She said she'll keep my tank full if I do. So I gave Galadriel a ride this morning. I didn't want to do it, but I can't really say no."

"Okay...." Whitney said, thinking furiously. That explained why the car still smelled like Galadriel's perfume. She understood Bron's dilemma. She knew all about being poor.

"The thing is," Bron said, "I want to be with you. Is it okay if I taxi her around, in between?"

"Promise you won't fall in love?" Whitney teased.

"Not with Galadriel," Bron promised.

Whitney reached over and took his hand in hers.

Olivia had arrived at school early on Wednesday morning. She was just looking through the morning transfer reports when Bron walked into her office, with Whitney in tow.

"Hey, Olivia," Bron said. "Whitney here had a question for you. She said that she thought she saw Officer Walton's ID on your cell phone. He said something about arresting me, and murder charges? What's he talking about?"

Olivia peered up at Whitney, who clung to Bron timidly. Olivia knew what Bron wanted from her, what he needed. She felt sad and a little guilty.

"Oh, there must be some kind of misunderstanding," Olivia suggested. She looked at Whitney and said, "Excuse me, but you have a ladybug in your hair."

Olivia reached up touched Whitney's brow, and sent a thought pulse out. Electricity arced, and she peered into Whitney's mind—saw the caller ID, heard the accusations that the poor girl had fretted about half the night, and then pulled them all away on invisible strings. She felt the snap as the memories left.

Whitney's green eyes blanked for an instant, and then she jumped, startled.

"Oh, excuse me," Whitney asked, "what ... what was I just saying?"

"Um," Olivia said. "I ... don't know." There was always a moment of disorientation with humans after they'd had a thought stolen. "I came in here," Whitney peered toward the door, "and wanted to ask you something. It was something important." She chuckled nervously.

"Well," Olivia said, "I'm sure that if it was important, you'll remember."

Whitney smiled.

Bron stood looking down at the floor, as if ashamed, shuffling his feet. He hated having to take a memory from a friend, but at least he understood that it had to be done.

Olivia asked Whitney, "How did the auditions go after I left?"

"I'll show you my notes," Whitney said. "We found a couple of possibilities."

"Great," Olivia said. "I look forward to it."

The bell rang, and both students hurried out into the hallway, hand-in-hand.

Bron stopped at the door, glanced back at her, and his face said it all: *I don't ever want to have to do that again.*

Olivia nodded.

She'll be good for him, Olivia thought, after they left. Bron had never really bonded solidly with anyone before. She suspected that this might be his chance. Whitney was as good a girl as he'd ever find.

Olivia felt unsettled. *How many other little clues did we miss that the enemy might yet pick up?* Olivia had to wonder.... Trying to clean up after last night's fiasco was like struggling to wipe a frying pan after it has gotten burned on the stove. Sure, you could scrub it well, but you could never get it completely clean. You couldn't take out the bits of grime cooked into the metal. Every event in our lives leaves its residue.

She'd dusted the rooms for her fingerprints, but had she cleaned them all off? And Bron's?

She couldn't be sure.

Dozens of police officers had been in the room when Bron was brought in for questioning. Had the priest missed wiping the mind of someone who might have heard Bron's name?

One thing was certain: with so many policemen dead, this incident was getting international scrutiny.

By now, the Draghouls knew that something was going on. The priest might try to lead them off on a false trail, but how long would that last? A day? A week?

The Shadow Lord would figure out what was going on eventually. He'd demand answers. He'd send Draghouls into the homes of police officers, silently interrogating everyone who'd worked yesterday. He'd peer into the minds of their spouses and children, seeking answers. His agents might even scan the minds of their neighbors.

The priest hadn't had enough time to be thorough. Time was on the side of her enemies.

The human body can't be scared all of the time, Bron noticed. He felt on edge after last night, but once he got to school, he was able to go for an hour or two without worrying about the Draghouls.

He settled into school nicely, felt eager to get there, to see Whitney. Suddenly they were an item—clinging to each other in the hallways, kissing in the shadows. Bron relished every minute of it. He ate lunch with Whitney that day, out at the pavilions.

One young man who called himself 'Tuba-licious' played near a statue of some Sioux warriors. His tuba had a sweetness that belonged to a French horn, and an earthiness reminiscent of a sax. With the music in the background, and the sun on the hills, Bron and Whitney talked intently at lunch.

Bron switched out of Spanish after lunch, and into theater tech, just so that he could hang out with Whitney in the evenings.

Every moment left him wanting more. He learned a few things about her at lunch: memorized her phone number, favorite color (purple), favorite movie (Avatar). But she still held a lot of mysteries.

Bron had never been in love before. He'd never trusted anyone fully, and Whitney had a way of earning his trust.

That night, he drove Galadriel home after school, then returned to watch the auditions. At midnight he went to Whitney's home and met her mother, a tiny thing with Whitney's slim figure. She seemed to like him all right. She invited Bron to join her and Whitney on a hike to Bryce Canyon over the weekend. Whitney's mom even promised to make her special barbecued chicken and some "Saint George" salad, whatever that was.

Whitney explained, "It's a lot like a Waldorf salad, but it has pomegranate seeds instead of raisins, and my mom likes to use pine nuts instead of walnuts."

"Yeah, that sounds great," he said.

On Thursday, Galadriel remained in the shadows, getting rides to and from school, acting a bit lost but hopeful.

It felt kind of weird, and Kendall joked about it at lunch. "You are sooo close to turning into a polygamist, you know!"

On Friday morning, Bron learned that he was in trouble. He went to school, saw Riley O'Hare standing outside the office in the morning. The old Draghoul, Blair, was talking to the secretary, Allison, checking him in. Allison looked worried.

She saw Bron, bustled out of her office to meet him. "There's a new boy registering in school. Do you know him? Is it all right with you?"

Bron shrugged. "Riley? He's all right. We're old friends." He wondered what Olivia might have told Allison.

She peered hard into his eyes, as if afraid that he might be hiding something. "Okay." She cast a worried glance and retreated to her desk.

Bron was walking with Whitney in tow, and would have preferred to have ignored Riley, but he stepped forward. "Hey, Bron Jones!"

He came to a halt, just stood. "Uhhh."

Riley introduced himself to Whitney. "Riley O'Hare," he said. "Bron and I are old friends. We lived together for awhile in a group home in Salt Lake!"

"Cool!" Whitney said, shaking one of his hands in both of hers. She leaned forward in a friendly manner, turned to Bron. "We should show him around the school."

"Yeah, good idea," Bron said. "That would be really great!"

Riley excused himself. "I can't, just yet. I'll see you at lunch, though."

Bron turned to go, but Riley called at his back. "Bron, I'll introduce you to a couple more of my friends. They'll be checking into school soon, too!"

Bron turned and strode away, clutching Whitney's hand entirely too hard. All three Draghouls were coming to his school? It sounded as if they were getting ready for World War III. A chill crept down his spine, and Bron realized that although it took a lot to scare him, when the fear did come, it could be profound.

At the end of the school day, Olivia came for him. "We're going out of town," she announced, as she escorted him down an empty hall, three minutes before the bell would ring. "You'll have to cancel any plans that you have with Whitney tonight."

"Where are we going?" he asked. He worried that he had to go heal Melvina. Olivia had spoken vaguely about plans to do that. He'd already managed to find time to take care of Kendall's buddies at school.

She took him out a back entrance, where no one would see them, and they began climbing a little stairwell.

"We're going to meet the Weigher of Lost Souls," Olivia said. "It's her job to ... test you, decide if you'll be allowed to join us."

"Test me?" Bron asked. "How?"

He didn't feel ready for any kind of test. Somehow, he'd begun to imagine that Olivia would make him wait for months before letting him in on the whole truth.

"She will look into your mind," Olivia said. "And decide what you are."

"I'm an Ael," Bron said. "Like you."

Olivia shook her head sadly. "You're a masaak, but you're not much like me. Like any species, the masaaks are diverging, like branches on a tree, twigs that grow farther apart as the tree ages. There are different kinds of masaaks. I am an 'Ael,' one of the ancient gods. Others are 'Draghouls.' They've been breeding for ages, trying to become cold and cruel.

"We don't know *your* lineage. Until the Weigher of Lost Souls examines you, you can't be allowed to join us. You might *never* be allowed."

"Why not?"

She fell silent. They'd reached the top of the stairwell and now they raced downhill to the parking lot.

Bron wondered at the timing. Riley had come to the school. He was bringing backup. Had the Draghouls learned where they were? Is that why Olivia wanted to bug out?

"Don't you see," she said, "the answers to what you are, they aren't inside of me. They're inside of you."

He suddenly remembered something important. "I was supposed to go on a date with Whitney tomorrow."

"You can't," Olivia said.

He shook his head, annoyed. "Fine. I'll put it off."

"Next week," Olivia said, "we can invite her to the house for a picnic. You two can go out back to the pond, as long as you don't go skinny-dipping."

Bron grudgingly accepted. There wasn't a chance that he'd ever go skinny-dipping with anyone, not so long as he lived with Olivia Hernandez. He would never be able to keep secrets again.

"Does Mike know what we're doing?"

"I told him that we were going up to a water park in Provo. Mike didn't want to come. He's afraid of water."

"Afraid?" Bron grinned.

"I tried to get him into a boat once, and he got so scared he threw up."

They reached Bron's car, and he popped the doors with the keyless entry. He held his door open for a few long seconds, to let the hot air escape, and Olivia took the keys from him, then eased into the driver's seat. Bron got in on the passenger's side.

"Where are we going?" Bron asked when he'd settled in.

Olivia shook her head. "You'll find out when we get there."

Bron fell silent, and Olivia took the road into Saint George. When she reached the corner of Bluff Street and Saint George Boulevard, she took the steep road to the airport, which was atop a mesa that looked down over the city, with the big white Mormon temple at its heart. Moments later they reached the airport and on the tarmac Bron spotted a shiny black helicopter. A pilot in a black flight uniform stood at attention, regarding them from behind mirrored sunglasses.

"We're taking that?" Bron asked. "Why not a plane?"

"I don't think there are any airports where we're going," Olivia said.

When they reached the chopper, the pilot opened the door. "Climb in, folks," he said, "and make yourselves comfortable."

The interior was surprisingly plush, with leather seats and a quiet cab. A radio played light rock music. Bron put on his seatbelt, and sat, nervously excited.

The pilot opened a privacy window and called, "We'll be airborne in a moment, folks. Strap yourselves in. Feel free to grab a drink out of the cooler. We're a little more than an hour out from our destination. The skies are clear, and the trip should be pleasant."

"What kind of helicopter is this?" Bron asked.

Olivia shrugged. "A *fast* helicopter."

The pilot hit the ignition, and soon they were lofting east out over the edge of the city. They streamed past sun-baked mountains, rocky gorges and barren desert. The sky was a deep blue, like a flawless sapphire.

Sooner than expected, the chopper breezed above Glen Canyon Dam and they reached Lake Powell, one of the scenic wonders of North America, with its sparkling waters butting up against ancient petrified sandstone hills. With over two thousand miles of shore, there were hidden inlets everywhere that one could swim in and explore. Majestic arches rose up in places, providing fantastic scenery, and Anasazi pictographs adorned the rocks.

Bron had seen pictures of it, the surreal slot canyons where sunlight filtered down narrow cracks, glowing like gold over the sculpted stone.

The pilot flew past the marina at Page, Arizona. Houseboats dotted the lake, and long swells, blown by the wind, seemed to crawl toward shore.

Soon, there were no more roads along the lake. The chopper began dropping. Bron tapped Olivia's arm and asked, "Where are we going?"

Olivia pointed in answer—to a fantastic arch of red sandstone rising up almost from the water—Rainbow Bridge. A few boats were moored out front, tourists taking pictures.

The pilot breezed above it, to a secluded inlet, where a single houseboat sat moored. It drifted in a still lagoon upon the blue waters.

The helicopter settled onto a gently sloping rock.

The pilot jumped out and opened the doors. Bron climbed out, peering at the houseboat: it was different from anything he'd ever seen.

The first thing he noticed was its sheer size. They'd passed dozens of houseboats on the way—but none so large. It wasn't a forty- or fifty-foot houseboat. It had to be closer to a hundred.

But it wasn't just size that made it seem so ... stately. Most houseboats on the lake were painted basic white. The color reflected the desert sun, keeping the boats cool. But this one was different. At the waterline it was gold. Not paint, he suspected. It looked like real gold foil. The foil was shaped into scales that reflected like mirrors, showing every little ripple at the waterline.

A walkway encircled the boat, with fluted columns painted ruby and deep blue that reminded Bron of something from ancient Greece. But above them was a deep blue strip of tiles, and upon each tile was an ancient symbol: the eye of Isis. He recognized it from an old history book.

Not Greek, he realized, Egyptian. The houseboat was decorated to look like an ancient Egyptian pleasure barge, something Cleopatra might have taken out upon the Nile when she sought to seduce Mark Antony. Bron almost expected to see Egyptian slaves, all painted in gold, manning the oars while serving girls stood by to fan him with ostrich feathers.

Broad windows looked to be made of cut crystal, and inside, soft lights glowed an unearthly pink, as if someone kept a setting sun inside them. He could see rich cedar paneling, and a fine bar with couches and a big-screen television, and a walk-in refrigerator with a stainless-steel door. It looked almost like a yacht.

Bron glanced at Olivia, dumbfounded. "Is your friend rich?"

Olivia smiled. "It appears that her investments are doing well."

The pilot climbed back into the helicopter. He'd never turned off the engine. Now he rose up, and the wind from the props washed over them, as if driving Bron toward the water.

He headed to shore, where a pontoon bridge invited him onto the boat. The sky overhead yawned wide, and golden sunlight glinted off the waters and reflected from the stony ground.

Bron held back, waiting for Olivia to take the lead. She didn't. He said, "You've met this woman before, right?"

"Yes, we were roommates in college." Olivia suggested, "Go ahead."

He set out over the bridge, which bobbed with each step. "Where did you say you went to college, again?"

"Harvard," Olivia said, "and Juilliard." Bron glanced back in astonishment, and she explained, "Memory merchants do well in school. I got by on scholarships."

Bron walked along the pontoons, and spotted a pair of jet skis docked inside a little built-in marina near the rear of the houseboat. They were high-tech, black, with custom purple-and-gold flames painted along their bodies. Everything spoke of opulence.

Bron climbed onto the deck, and knocked at a wide door to the interior. It was dark inside, almost black after the blinding daylight. He stood for a moment blinking, trying to let his eyes adjust. Olivia halted. He glanced back.

"Aren't you coming?" he asked.

"No," she said. "You have to go alone...."

CHAPTER 24

REVELATIONS

"When a bit of wisdom destroys your world in a moment and rebuilds it just as quickly, that is revelation."

— Olivia Hernandez

Come in...." a woman called with a British accent. Bron leapt in surprise, then stood blinking stupidly into the darkness. He could see through the glass door, barely. He opened it and entered, then stood peering into the shadows.

A young woman crouched upon a black sofa. A low coffee table stood poised before her. Some glass balls upon it glowed a hot pink, providing the only interior light. She stood and skirted the table, nearly invisible in the darkness.

"Oh, hi!" Bron said, embarrassed. "I didn't see anyone."

She stood before him. She was shorter than him, and had straight black hair, a slender figure. She wore a flimsy red dress, and droplets of sweat had beaded on her chest. She obviously wasn't used to the heat of Utah. She might have been anywhere from twenty to fifty, for there was an agelessness to her eyes.

She appraised him as if he were a fine stallion. "So," she said at last, "You're the asufaak arru'yah, the dream assassin."

She raised her hand, palm up, as if to wave, and suction cups blossomed in perfect little ovals on her fingertips. Bron stood, unsure what to do. She nodded toward his hands, begging him to do the same. He raised his hand, self-consciously showed his sizraels. She smiled graciously.

"My name is Monique. I'm the Weigher of Lost Souls. Has Olivia told you about me?"

"Not much," Bron admitted. "She said you were friends in college."

"Good," Monique said. She had a commanding presence. She stared, as if looking through him, for a long time. "Olivia can't really tell you who you are. That task is left to me to discern. She can teach you about music, but my ... specialty, is people—the history of our people. Would you like to know who you are?"

Despite his clash with the enemy, Bron had been told little about the masaaks. He knew even less about the Draghouls and dream assassins. "Yes," he said.

"Knowledge carries a price," Monique suggested. "Knowledge ... changes you. With it comes responsibility, but I will demand more than just a promise to take responsibility. Before I teach you, I must lay your mind bare."

Bron's stomach tightened. He froze with indecision.

"You're afraid of what I will see?" Monique asked. "You have to overcome that fear. I'll learn everything about you—every lie you've told, every lustful thought or deed you've acted upon. I'll learn the deepest secrets that you fear to tell."

"I'd rather not," Bron said. He glanced around for Olivia, wondering what she'd gotten him into, but she hadn't followed him onto the boat.

Monique said, "Olivia is not allowed in here. Not now. This is for me and you alone." She said it in a tone that made Bron suspect that Monique wasn't just Olivia's old friend, but some sort of superior.

"Have a seat," Monique said gently. "I mean you no harm. You and I must talk." Bron felt suddenly nervous. He was stuck on a houseboat in a wasteland with a strange woman who seemed to have unnerving power. She gestured toward an overstuffed recliner, and Bron sat, found himself falling backward into its cushions, as if dropping into a cloud.

Monique knelt before him, and took his left hand in both of hers. The low-cut top of her flimsy dress was tantalizing. She wore no bra, and her small breasts reminded him of Whitney's, and so she filled him with embarrassing longings. He didn't believe that Monique was trying to tempt him. He suspected that she was dressed scantily only because it was so hot. He tried to look up into her heart-shaped face, into those ageless eyes. Monique smiled.

"You lust after me," she said. "Don't be ashamed. You're at an age when your hormones are awakening. It's not just me that tempts you, it's almost everyone—girls at your school, teachers, strangers on the street."

Bron said nothing. He wanted to deny it, because it made him feel embarrassed and out of control, but she was going to peer into his mind. He couldn't hide what he felt.

"I have seen into the minds of a thousand men," Monique said. "Some were criminals, but others were visionaries, and men of profound virtue. Even the greatest of them suffered the same temptations that you do. Some people were so craven that they could not qualify as human. Yet I've also encountered nobleness and beauty, order and insight, and longings for greatness. The mind is like a container, and it holds mainly what you decide to let it hold, what you treasure. I don't expect to find anything inside you that I have not encountered before. At your age, you're like a sponge. You take in everything you see and hear, and you're still learning what thoughts and ideas are of value and what can be discarded."

She began to rub his hand, his wrist, and suddenly his sizraels popped. She studied them.

"But I want you to know, Bron, that there is nothing you have done that others have not done. There is no longing so strange that I have not seen it before, no desire so perverse. You think that your greatest secrets, your greatest fears, are unique to you. But they're the same secrets and fears that we all share. I will leave the choice to you. I can teach you, but first I must be sure of you. The world is infinitely more vast and strange than you can imagine, Bron. You see it through a thin filter of the things that you know of and have learned over the past dozen years. But we can share with you memories of people who have lived over the past million years, through tens of

374

thousands of lifetimes. Have you ever wondered how Einstein saw the world? Or Rasputin? Or William Shakespeare? Or Jesus? The memory merchants can reveal it all to you—the secrets of those people and others vastly more interesting, ancient people whose legacies have been lost in time. If you will but permit me, I can show you something you would never have imagined."

Bron didn't entirely trust this woman. She was too intense, too strange, and the way that she looked at him hungrily as she studied his hand, left him unnerved. His mouth suddenly went as dry as the desert, and his palms began to sweat. He felt an electric tingle pass through them, a current that went up through his body and warmed him. She smiled.

She wasn't very old, he realized. She couldn't have been more than thirty, about Olivia's age. He would never have admitted it, but he suddenly wanted to kiss her, and he could tell by the way that her pupils went wide that she felt something, too.

His palms had begun to sweat, as if the heat in the room were growing. He tried to pull his hand back, to wipe it off, but she clutched it all the tighter.

Almost against his will, he nodded.

Monique reached up with her left hand, as dainty as a child's, and tenderly touched his temple, as if to sweep the hair back from his brow. He felt an electric tingle, heard a sizzling. Golden lights flashed around his head like a halo.

"I want to show you something," she said. "I won't add it to your memories, just show you something that has been passed down among memory merchants now for a quarter of a million years."

She closed her eyes and planted her fingers across half of his face, touching the eyelid under his brow with a thumb, his forehead with her forefingers, and others spread out until her pinky reached just behind his ear.

Suddenly Bron's eyes seemed too heavy to stay open, and he found himself....

Straddling the back of a woolly mammoth, his legs lost in thick hair. At this season in the year, the mammoth's fur was burnt orange on top, bleached by the sun, and hung in long ragged wisps that fell out in the slightest breeze. The mammoth was shedding, its winter coat coming in. The hair smelled rancid, almost moldy.

Ahead and on either side, the land was scarred and torn. Mastodons had come this way on their migration north in the spring, tearing down trees and eating every green plant in their path—grass, bush, tree.

It had been a hard year, and now weeds cropped up among the rocks, while broken trees with scraggly limbs clung to life. What should have been fertile ground had been trodden to mud, creating a broad highway that wound through the hills.

His mammoth suddenly grew wary, paused in its tracks, raised its trunk and waved it in the air as it sought an elusive scent. Its small ears flapped forward. Then it drew back and blew a warning call, much like that of an elephant, but far deeper.

Tutuk, for that was the rider's name in this memory, peered across a broken horizon, covered in rough hills and rocky bluffs, and searched among the rocks for any sign of a hill tiger, or a pack of dire wolves. To the left, a river ran. Wheat grew beside it to a height of fifteen feet. This was ancient wheat, Bron realized, a species that had become as extinct as the mammoth.

Tutuk could smell the autumn-ripe grain, but the air also carried a taste of cold and coming winter.

He did not trust the wheat field, for too often he had found that humans hid in there, and the humans in this area were craven things that hunted their own kind by night and wore the skins of their enemies. They worshipped serpents and jackals, and smelled of putrefaction, for they believed that if they smelled of death, death would love them and pass them by.

Tutuk dug his heels into the mammoth's neck, and stopped. He pulled a ram's horn from his pack and blew hard upon it, twice. If an animal heard that call, the horn would give them pause. If friends heard it, they would reveal themselves. If humans heard it, they would merely hide and wait for a chance to strike.

Wheat stalks swayed, and something rushed out. At first Tutuk thought that it was a tawny lion, but instead a woman with a broad nose and weak chin burst from the rushes. Her skin was pale and creamy, her hair a light red. She wore a skirt of woven reeds, and had lines running down her chest, tattoos created by poking a sharp stick in ashes and then sticking it under the flesh. The ashen tattoos circled her small breasts in double rows, and an ivory nose ring announced her wealth. There was wisdom in her eyes, and she smiled in relief to see Tutuk.

"Tcha khaw!" she called in greeting. *Come, member of my family.* "Tcha khaw!"

She was short and stocky, Bron thought. Stockier than any person he'd ever seen, and there was something odd about her face, deformed. She had deep-set eyes, and almost no chin.

Tutuk recognized her immediately. She wasn't human. She was Neanderthal, or as he called them, "the hunting family." Humans were scavengers, eating mussels and locusts and nuts, stealing dead kills from lions. But the khaw were a nobler sort, taking only fresh meat that they hunted with their own spears. They were brave in the face of danger, gentle with one another.

The woman raised her hand, palm outward, and Tutuk did the same, flashing the sizraels on his fingertips.

The Neanderthal woman smiled at that and gave a shout of joy. She was so happy to meet Tutuk that she did something Bron had never seen before—she broke into dance, leaping forward a couple of steps, then leaping back, swaying and singing, "Yi, yi, yi!"

Soon more Neanderthals came lunging from the wheat, dancing and singing. There was a young man with a scraggly beard that could have been the female leader's little brother, and old men with rheumy eyes, and naked children, and a dozen warriors with spears.

One of the warriors shouted, and girls ran out of the tall wheat, bearing fine skins—an offering of tiger hides—along with bone knives. A pair of boys came out bearing the skin of a wooly rhino, and upon it was part of a recent kill, the rhino's haunch. Last of all, the leader of the tribe motioned to the tall hay and called out the name, "Neptu!"

A girl of thirteen or fourteen crept forward. She wore a skirt of woven grass, and she had green ivy and wild pea flowers in her hair. She blushed prettily and ducked her head.

These Neanderthals had seen memory merchants before, and they knew what Tutuk had to offer. Wisdom was valuable beyond measure, and anything that he wanted in the village was his for the taking—their clothing, their weapons, their food, their daughters.

Tutuk smiled and looked the tribe over. There was a wealthy man in the back, a Maker by the looks of him. He would be the kind of man who napped spearheads from obsidian, or carved idols from the sacred oak. He was old, but not so old that Tutuk feared that he would die soon. He was the right age to craft weapons for the tribe, and to teach his apprentices his skills.

With a click of his tongue, Tutuk commanded his mammoth to kneel. Then he threw his left leg over the mammoth's neck and simply slid to the ground, slowing his descent by holding onto the beast's long hair.

The Neanderthals would want to know how to become mammoth riders, of course, but that was something that Tutuk could not teach them. He'd caught this mammoth as a calf, had touched its mind and trained it from birth, and though it might obey others now, Tutuk would not part with it.

Instead, he strode up to the Maker, hand raised to show what he was, and the old craftsman lifted his chin slightly.

Tutuk grasped his cranium, sent an arc of electricity through his hand, and showed the old man things. He showed how the Neanderthal arm was strong and powerful, the arm of a hunter, but it was too short to throw a spear far.

So Tutuk showed the old man how to make a spear thrower. Simply by carving a piece of wood, some two feet in length, he could make a base where the butt of a spear would sit. On the other end was a handle that could be gripped. By balancing the spear in the base, and then hurling with his might, Tutuk showed how other Neanderthals had been able to cast a spear for three hundred yards, making it easier to slay the wildebeests, mastodons, and tigers that roamed these hills.

By the time Tutuk finished, the old craftsman's jaw trembled as he fought back a sob. He teetered for a moment as the full implications of what he had learned struck home.

With these new spear throwers, his tribe would prosper. His young men would hunt beasts from afar, and the vicious, gangly human cannibals might at last be vanquished.

As Tutuk pulled his hands away, the craftsman's eyes fluttered, and tears began to leak down his cheeks, tears of pure revelation, tears of astonishment and hope.

That is what Tutuk had desired: to bring these people hope. The world in his age had too little hope, with giant mastodons tearing down Neanderthal huts on sight, and tigers dragging children into the night, and humans encroaching on every front.

Suddenly the craftsman gave a shout of joy and grabbed Tutuk by the shoulders, then wrapped him in a powerful bear hug. Such affection was shown only to the closest of family members, and all of the Neanderthals shouted and danced, for the old man was telling them, "This stranger is as dear as a brother."

The *vision* ended. Bron could think of no other word to describe it, except as a vision. He'd been able to see as Tutuk had seen, smell what he'd smelled. He'd tasted the foul scent of Tutuk's teeth, felt the weariness that made his aching back sag.

For a moment, he had been another person, and he longed for more.

Monique pulled back her hands and smiled. "Tutuk was one of the greatest of our kind. He was a teacher who traveled the northern wastes through what we would now call Germany. He sought to save the Neanderthals, whom he saw as a noble people, and in time he brought peace between them and the humans. For many thousands of years they learned to live together in harmony. These people understood something that in our day we tend to forget. Wisdom is survival. Wisdom is hope, and peace, and kindness and love, all rolled into one. That is what we hope to share with the world, the wisdom to live together in peace."

For a long moment, Monique fell silent, and in that stillness Bron noticed the sound of small waves lapping the hull of the houseboat, and wind hissing through the rocks.

"How did the Neanderthals die out?" Bron asked. "I mean, they were so strong."

"And wise and kind," Monique said. "But they died by attrition. The humans, with their penchant for cannibalism, wiped them out."

"The humans ate them?" Bron asked. Astonishment seemed to cover him like a sheet.

Monique nodded.

"But humans aren't cannibals," Bron argued.

"Take a look at Wall Street," Monique laughed. "Humans have always been cannibals, looking for ways to put one another to use. Whether by slavery or usury or eating each other wholesale, what is the difference?"

Bron longed to know more, and he realized that Monique had sprung a trap. She'd given him a taste of wisdom, but only a taste. If he wanted more, he would have to bare himself to her.

"Will it hurt?" Bron asked.

"I will not lie," Monique replied. "It hurts more than words can say. That's why I can only lay bare your memories with your permission."

Bron weighed the proposal, and whispered softly, "Do it."

Monique drew close, smiled reassuringly into his eyes. Bron felt uncomfortable. The day was scorching outside, and her flimsy dress revealed almost as much as it hid. Bron didn't want to think about the possibility of being with her. He wanted to keep such desires hidden, but the fact that he feared them only made them stronger.

"Don't worry," she said.

She put her hands upon his head, and began slowly. She started with his last memory, his desire to reach out and touch her. It blossomed hot and fresh in his mind, and then other memories came— every nasty little thought, every vile fantasy that he'd ever had about every woman he'd ever met.

The feelings that they engendered were inexpressible. At first he thought that he might liken it to someone taking an ice pick to his brain, driving it deep and then twisting, in order to dislodge every objectionable thought that he'd ever had.

Shame struck him first, like a physical blow, turning his face hot and clenching his stomach. The memories flicked before his eyes, like pages in a graphic novel, bright and colorful, but they were accompanied by sounds—the voices of women and girls that he'd known.

But it wasn't like pages flashing before his eyes. It was more like little explosions in his head, as if landmines in his brain were going off, and these dark thoughts were just bits of shrapnel. Hundreds of them blossomed like mushroom clouds by the second. Bron was shocked and disgusted by the enormous quantity of them.

He tried to pull away, to retreat into some dark corner of his soul and hide, but Monique whispered soothingly, "Don't worry. Your mind is relatively clean when compared to those of other men."

She probed through his darkest fantasies and learned of the time when he was a child that he let a girl from next door touch him.

He relived watching one of his foster mothers as she stood naked before a mirror, and he recalled paging through a dirty magazine when he was eight, kissing the pictures and laughing inanely.

Bron squirmed, embarrassed to the core.

Bile rose up in his throat, and he fought the need to vomit. He gagged, seeking air.

Why is she just touching these *thoughts?* he wondered.

Your memories are tied to powerful emotions, Monique whispered in his mind. Then she said softly, "Fear, revulsion, lust. Those are some of the most powerful emotions. I explored your lust."

Suddenly it seemed that she had exhausted the pornographic content of his mind. "Don't be ashamed. All of us face temptations, but you have not given yourself over to them. In time, I can tell, you can master all of your desires. You have a strong will."

Now she pulled out other incidents—quarters that he'd stolen from his foster parent's couch as a child, money that he'd taken from the table in a neighbor's house. He recalled all of the times that he had stopped and looked longingly at the neighbor's boat and wondered what it would be like to be wealthy. He felt astonished at how often he'd coveted the nicer meals that others were eating at restaurants.

Every greedy impulse that he'd fought down came roaring back to life, and for a moment it was like a fresh wound, hot and bloody, as he longed for things that he would never have.

I am a worm of a person, Bron thought, and he shrank inside himself, wishing to die.

"Not much there," Monique said. "Steel yourself. I can already tell that this next one is going to hurt!"

Suddenly, she touched his anger, and hot wrath flooded into him as he was suddenly forced to relive every insult that had been spoken to him, see every scornful gaze, hear every cruel word.

As adrenaline gushed through his veins, his muscles knotted like cordwood and a scream of outrage tore from his throat—and that is where Monique struck pay dirt, for Bron's hate was strong and unrestrained, and often as a child he'd spent long hours fantasizing about how to get revenge on older children, imagining mutilations.

He remembered his fantasies about Mr. Golper—wanting to tie him in a bag and then stab it over and over, then throw his dying corpse into a river.

He thought of Mr. Lewis, and from deep inside he flashed upon an image of the man curled in a fetal position, dirty and naked beside a refrigerator.

When did that happen? he wondered.

In the memory he knew that Mr. Lewis was dying. His wife was calling the police, and Bron was wishing that she wouldn't, that she would just let him die.

Then there were the kids at school who had all offended him, and teachers and shopkeepers.

Over and over through the years, he'd told himself that he didn't care about the insults and cruelty, that he could ignore it all, but Monique seemed to throw open the shutters inside him, letting powerful beams of sunlight lay all of his secrets bare.

He'd quit fantasizing about revenge a couple years ago, and it seemed unfair that he should see these fantasies now, paraded before him in all their monstrous cruelty.

Bron screamed and fought, began trying to wrench his head free, until at last Monique pulled her hands away.

Bron opened his eyes and struggled against the rage. It seemed to be rolling over him in waves. His muscles were knotted, his neck swollen with it.

Monique was shaken and pale. Beads of sweat dotted her forehead and rivulets stole down her cheeks and neck. Her pupils were pinpoints, constricted in shock, and her breath came ragged.

Bron wondered at her reaction. He'd imagined murder before, lots of times, in ways that were horrific and brutal, but it was nothing worse than what you'd see at the movies.

"No more," Monique said. "No more for now." She pulled her hands away, as if she would quit for the day.

Bron stopped fighting her, relaxed for a fraction of a second, and then Monique gritted her teeth, grasped his skull, and sent a shock through him.

"Show me what you love," she whispered....

CHAPTER 25

STRANGE RELATIONS

"At one time or another, each of us is confronted by the knowledge that someone who should be the closest to us, is in fact a stranger."

– Bron Jones

As darkness cloaked her, Olivia waited on the beach, crouching on the red sandstone like a gargoyle. Stars had filled the skies and begun to blow across the heavens on a wispy breeze.

The smell of lake came strong, and the dark boat sat quietly upon water as still as glass. Stars reflected like golden candlelight upon the lake's surface, and the horned moon was a sliver of platinum or pale, pale bone.

Olivia peered out at a line of hills, so peaceful in the moonlight, and she felt tense to the point of breaking.

It takes a long time to find the weight of a soul, Olivia knew. As Bron's foster mother, she was too close to him for this task. Besides, Monique was the only one trained to be a Weigher of Lost Souls. She had done this perhaps tens of thousands of times, peered into the mind of a Draghoul to see if it was fit to convert, or if it had to be destroyed.

Olivia's stomach felt taut from hunger, her mouth dry from thirst, but she just waited silently, knowing that this could take all night.

Monique must have hit a switch, for suddenly the houseboat lit up like a Christmas tree, with strings of golden lights all along its top and wrapped down every pillar, and running along the bottom near the water line. The lights twinkled in the heat, and reflected from still waters.

The forward living room lit up inside. A glass door slid open. "We're done for now," Monique said. She stood at the door, holding her stomach protectively, as if she might be sick.

"Already?" Olivia asked. It had only taken four hours. She got up, stepped lightly across the pontoon bridge. The golden lights extended across it, easing her way.

"He's not one of us," Monique whispered when she got near.

Olivia faltered. She had hoped that Bron would pass, that he'd be accepted. On some level, she'd convinced herself that he was worthy. She couldn't imagine the alternative.

Death? Olivia wondered. *Are you going to put him down?*

"You didn't tell me about the purple *canjiti*," Monique said, almost accusingly. Among the masaak, the colored electrical flashes that came out during transfers were called canjiti.

Olivia asked, "Don't all dream assassins give those off?"

Monique shook her head no. "I suppose that there's no way you could have known that, though. We haven't seen one in ages." Monique held the door open, glanced surreptitiously toward the kitchens. Olivia stepped into the boat, and Monique led her to a deep couch, opened a bottled water, and handed it to Olivia. Cold droplets had condensed on the exterior. Olivia drank greedily. She heard Bron moving about in the kitchen.

Monique sat near Olivia, and suddenly began sobbing.

"What's wrong?" Olivia asked.

Monique shook her head in dismay. "Can't you see?" she asked, then added, "Of course you can't. You're not trained to do an emotive profile."

Olivia tried to stall her. "What did you find?" She expected that Bron was a Draghoul, a purebred, and that with his powers, he might be too dangerous. She couldn't even honestly consider that possibility.

"He's a cold one," Monique answered. "He's been damaged. You've probed his amygdala? You know what I mean."

"It's not uncommon for someone in his situation," Olivia said gently. "He was raised by caregivers who gave no care, betrayed by the system that should have served him."

"I agree," Monique said. "He is a victim here, but you know what else he is: a danger."

Olivia fell silent for a moment. Yes, Bron had killed a foster father, but he hadn't meant to.

Was that what had rattled Monique?

Olivia glanced toward the kitchen. Bron was still inside the houseboat somewhere, though she could not see him. She risked speaking openly. "I've seen inside the mind of a Draghoul. Bron doesn't feel that cold inside. He doesn't fit in their world."

"Or in ours," Monique argued. "He's something we've never seen before."

"What do you mean?"

"I mean," Monique said, "he's a new branch on the evolutionary tree. There have been dream assassins before ... but he is different somehow. Those purple flashes that he gives off when he unleashes? They're unlike anything we've encountered. I know that you want to protect him, but you and I both know how dangerous he is."

Olivia didn't believe that she was being overprotective. She loved Bron the way that a mother loves her child. It was a new love, true, but it was powerful nonetheless. They'd been through a great deal together in just a week, and she had to believe that he felt something for her, too.

He wasn't Draghoul. He wasn't Ael.

"So what do you think we should do?"

Monique fell silent, considered. Bron walked into the room, carrying a cold can of soda.

Monique faced him. "Bron, before I teach you more, I want you to complete a quest."

"A quest?" Bron asked. "A quest for what?"

She peered into Bron's eyes. "Years ago, a woman was sent to me—a young mother who was forced to give up her son. She had abandoned the child, and she wanted me to erase her memory of him— obliterate it so deeply that no one would ever be able to learn what had happened to him. I was very young then, but I had generations of experience in such matters. Though years have passed, I still know how to contact that woman. Bron, I want you to meet your mother."

"My mother?" Bron said. His mouth opened in amazement. He'd given up hope of finding her years ago. "How do you know she's my mother?"

Monique said softly. "Before your mother left you, she bleached your hair, reddened it so that the Draghouls wouldn't realize what you were. She wrapped you in a blue blanket, and took you to the Happy Valley Inn. She laid a black-eyed Susan next to you. She pinned a note to you that said, 'Bron is free.' It wasn't a price tag. She wasn't offering to give you away. You were being hunted, both of you, and it was a prayer. She hoped that finally, someday, you would be free."

After their talk, Olivia joined Monique in the kitchen to help fix dinner. Olivia found a vegetarian lasagna that had been flown in from a fine restaurant in Vegas, rich with wine, sun-dried tomatoes, spinach leaves, fresh matsutake mushrooms, and exotic cheeses.

As she warmed it in the oven, Monique blended ice, sugar and fresh juice from lemons and limes to make a frappe. Olivia glanced out on the fore-deck, saw Bron sitting alone with his thoughts, staring at the starlight and the untroubled waters.

"I don't get it," Olivia whispered softly as Monique squeezed the juices. "Why do you want to bring his mother into this?"

In order to assure a level of privacy, Monique switched to ancient French. "Il me fait peur," Monique said simply. *He scares me.* "It is not the rage that bothered me. When I tried to look into his heart and find what he loved ... it was too empty. I'm thinking that Bron needs this. I'm sure that his mother needs it, too."

That stopped Olivia. She hadn't searched Bron's memories quite so thoroughly. "If we look deeply enough, we'll find some affection, somewhere."

"You don't see him for what he is. You haven't looked at his balance. Sure, there's love, but damned little of it. If he had a wealth of love in him, and rage in equal measure, it would only mean that he's passionate. But there's an imbalance here.

"Olivia, you're a loving person. You love everyone— the kids at your school, your husband, the teachers with whom you work...."

"They're good people," Olivia argued.

"No, they're not," Monique said. "You simply project your own values on them, imagining that they're good. You know the statistics. At least one in every twenty kids in your school is a sociopath. Yet you imagine that they are *all* like you."

Monique was right, Olivia knew. She loved pretty much everyone. It's what kept her working at the school for fifteen hours a day, five and six days a week, teaching during the days and helping with plays and concerts at nights. Everyone had dreams to fulfill, and she wanted to help make them all come true. And when she came home exhausted, she still had Mike to care for.

Then there was her work with the PTA during the school year and with charitable causes during the summer.

All week, Olivia had been running herself ragged, until she felt exhausted.

Olivia got it from her mother.

Her mom had worked her fingers to the bone, growing vast gardens up in Brigham City, planting melons and strawberries and corn and beans. At the end of each year, the family didn't eat a fiftieth of what they grew. Instead, Olivia's mother would drive her around at the end of each day, passing out fresh vegetables to the elderly, the indigent, and to the families of migrant laborers that came each year to harvest fruit from the local orchards.

Olivia had learned young that the lasting joy in life comes from giving, not taking.

She hoped that Bron might learn that, too. But she couldn't be sure that he ever would. How could he ever learn to love others, when the truth was that he feared them? He dared not get too close to them, let himself become vulnerable.

"If you believe that sociopaths exist," Olivia said, "then Bron might be one. But I don't buy the argument that people are born without consciences. A child who is loved learns to love in return. Bron can't help it if his first foster mother couldn't stand to be touched...."

Immediately Olivia knew that she'd said the wrong thing. Children who weren't able to bond with a mother were far more likely to exhibit sociopathic behaviors than others.

"My god," Monique said. "You *knew* what he was the day you took him in! You're ... trying to fix him."

"To help him," Olivia said. "I'll give him love, and maybe I can teach him how to love, at least a little."

"Don't get your hopes up," Monique warned.

"Why not?" Olivia asked. "You've got yours up. Your first instinct was to send him to his mother. Mine was to try to be his mother."

That stopped Monique. Olivia had her, she knew. For a long moment she worked, mixing juices and then pouring them over the ice. "This is a dangerous game we're playing," Monique said. "Bron is a killer in the making. And if the enemy finds him—"

"We'll just have to keep that from happening."

CHAPTER 26

QUICKSAND

"You can't help where you come from, but you can choose where you will go."

– Bron Jones

Though his bed was softer than a dream, Bron slept little that night. His mind was churning with unanswered questions, whirling with excitement.

Shortly after dawn, the chopper set down outside, and Monique said her goodbyes. She hugged Olivia like an old friend, shook Bron's hand and said, "Bron, I wish you well. I hope to see you again soon."

He wondered if "soon" would ever come.

"Where are we going?" Bron asked.

"You'll go to the airport in Vegas," she said. "After that, you'll take a jet to New Orleans. It has all been arranged."

"Will my mother meet us there?"

"She has been notified that you're coming," Monique said. "Whether or not she comes, will be up to her. Bron, if she doesn't show, you should know something. Your mother is a frightened woman, for good reason."

The helicopter rose above a blue ribbon of lake, following the channel as if it were a road. Bron suspected that between the roar of the engine and the baffling afforded by the privacy glass, the pilot couldn't hear anything they might say. Still, Bron turned up the volume on the stereo, and then began to grill Olivia. He said casually, "There is something wrong with Monique's eyes. When you look into them, she seems very, very old. But I don't think that she's any older than you."

"You're observant," Olivia said.

"I was thinking about the priest. He said that he was three hundred years old. If he was an old man, and he put his memories into the head of a young person that he captured ... he could make younger copies of himself. He could live forever."

Olivia's smile faltered. "That would be a very evil thing. Monique would never do that."

"Is she your boss?"

Olivia thought for a moment, bit her lip.

"You can't keep me completely in the dark," Bron suggested. "I don't want to go stumbling into something by accident. I don't think that Monique would want that, either."

Olivia pursed her lips, "No, we wouldn't want that."

"So tell me," Bron said, "what is Monique to you?"

"She's highly respected, she's ..." Olivia fumbled to explain, "special. Let me put it this way. When I was a child, I loved music, and I chose to play the guitar

396

and the violin, and to sing. You're learning the extent of my knowledge. I don't perform for others—it would draw too much attention. So I perform for myself, for my own enjoyment. Because of the narrowness of my training, I'm only a muse.

"But you should know that a muse is more powerful than many other kinds of masaaks. For most masaaks, our powers are small. Some merchants can only draw from others, learn what others know. They might at most be able to sneak into a person's mind and learn their secrets. Thus, they can discover if a man is guilty of a crime, or steal valuable trade secrets, or learn the numbers that will let them access secret bank accounts.

"People like that, they're really not *merchants*, are they? They're merely thieves. So we call them 'Thieves.' Most masaaks fall into this category.

"Others can pull memories and send memories, and these are true merchants. But they can't do what we call 'deep training.' They can't go into the brain stem and follow the impulses from your ears to your fingers, so that you can train a child to play an instrument or learn to walk. That takes a muse. Even Monique doesn't have my gift for that."

"So she's not more powerful than you?"

"No, she's *different* from me. She's more like a priestess, dedicated to a cause."

Olivia paused and took a deep breath, as if uneasy about revealing so much, and said, "Some of us never die, Bron. As you have guessed, there is a way for a merchant to cheat death. I could download all of my memories into a child, victimize someone. But there's a moral way to do it, too...."

397

"When Monique was only a child of thirteen, she volunteered for this. She wanted to learn the history of our people, as much as there was to know, and a wise old man who had stored that information agreed to give it to her.

"But there was so much information, that her mind could not easily hold it all, so much information that only the most brilliant of us could have tried. So her teacher had to erase all of the information that she had stored to that point—nearly every memory that she held dear–and then he emptied his mind into hers."

"What?" Bron asked. "So he taught her everything he'd learned in his lifetime?"

"More than that," Olivia said, "for he'd had it done to him as a child, and it had been done to his teacher as well—for three thousand years the chain has gone unbroken.

"Monique, if she desired, could tell you about her life as a prophetess in a temple in Greece, conversing with Homer. She speaks ancient Assyrian and Egyptian, and was a tutor to kings. She was there when Saladin re-captured Jerusalem, and fought beside Joan of Arc.

"More importantly, she knows most of what can be known about our own people, and holds memories from before the dawn of recorded history."

Bron wondered. "So, she gave up everything in order to do this?"

Olivia nodded. "All of her hopes and dreams, all of her aspirations. She had to surrender herself completely. She is no longer a single person. So when she took time to think about you last night, it was to consult the myriad voices in her head, compose a single plan of action."

"She wanted this?" Bron asked, amazed.

"Many of us would," Olivia admitted. "It's an honored position. She is the Weigher of Lost Souls, a creature far older and wiser than you or me. I offered myself when I was young, but I wasn't ... bright enough, and it was felt that as a muse, I had other gifts that could benefit the community."

"What community?" Bron asked, for he imagined secret meetings of hooded Ael, held by moonlight deep in the forest.

"Mankind," Olivia explained.

"But you don't consider yourself human," Bron pointed out.

Olivia grinned. "I consider 'mankind' to include both humans and masaaks."

Bron asked slyly, "But the Draghouls don't?"

"No," Olivia agreed. "They think of humans more like ... food."

"And how would they think of me?" Bron asked.

Olivia closed her mouth secretively, and at last said, "As a prize. They would honor you and fete you to your face, but as soon as you slept, they would take you. You want nothing to do with them, Bron. You cannot make a deal with a devil without becoming one yourself."

Bron chuckled. She sounded so over-dramatic.

"Don't laugh," Olivia said in a tone that spoke of despair and heartbreak.

Bron didn't want to hurt her feelings. He became solemn. "So any Masaak can become a Draghoul?" Bron asked, "or an Ael?"

"That's a tough question," Olivia said. "Most people can be on either side, but not all. You can try to convert a person who is evil to the core, one who lacks the capacity for love or selflessness, but in time they'll slip back into their old ways. And there are good people in the world, too Bron, people so giving, so honorable that the Draghoul can't really control them. All of their hateful thoughts, their selfish ideals, can never gain root in such people."

Bron had always been taught that people are basically the same. "Are you saying that the Draghouls are different from us?"

"I'm saying that some Draghouls lack the capacity for compassion. They were bred that way. Pit bulls were bred to attack, while Labrador retrievers were bred to lick your hand. The same is true with the Draghouls. They've been bred for ruthlessness. For more than five thousand years, the Draghouls have been perfecting their lines. You can try changing them, but it's not easy."

They had crossed over the dam now and were heading into the desert. Down below, Bron could see rusted-out trailer homes along a highway, where dead cars rotted in yards where no children played at all.

"That priest we met, Father Leery," Bron said. "Tell me about him. I mean, he's a priest, but once he was a Draghoul?"

"Yes," Olivia said. "He was a stalker, before he became converted."

Bron wasn't sure how he felt about a priest who could rip out your memories, one who would sneak into your house at night to do it. He wondered if the man was a true believer, or if he simply used his frock as some kind of ridiculous disguise.

"So one of your people captured him," Bron asked, "and possessed him?"

Olivia smiled. "It was the other way around. He caught one of us, one who stored special memories, and when he saw what was in the man's mind, he left the Draghouls."

"What kind of memories?" Bron asked.

"Memories of visions," Olivia said. "Would you like to know what Saint Francis of Assisi knew after he saw god? Would you like to know what Peter witnessed on the Mount of Transfiguration? Or what Moses saw in the burning bush? Or Mohamed? It's powerful stuff. That's why Draghouls want to destroy it.

"Bron, there's a war going on. A war for information. The Ael want to preserve it, to spread it among those who would use it for good. But if we're captured, the light we have in us will be snuffed out forever."

"So do you believe in God?" Bron asked. He felt odd about it, as if he was asking if she believed in Santa Claus.

Olivia bit her lip, trying to decide how to answer. "Let's just say ... the universe is far more vast and strange than humans can imagine. You're about to enter a far larger world."

"Do you think the priest would show me what he's seen?"

"I think he'd like to, but you're not ready for it. Let yourself grow a little."

Bron wondered about that. Could the priest prove that there was a God? And what if he did? How would that knowledge change a man?

"Do the Draghouls have muses, too?" Bron asked.

"They do," Olivia admitted. "You might learn music from them, if you liked—but they're more likely to train you in the finer arts of assassination. Avoid them. These people have no love for one another, no affection. If you meet them, do not confuse solicitation for kindness. They're at their most dangerous when they are at their most subtle."

Bron wondered at that. Father Leery had turned Blair's old acolytes into poppets. Could such creatures be trusted?

Bron tried to rest on the helicopter flight to the airport in Las Vegas, but he was too anxious. He'd never traveled outside of Utah, except for a short trip to Idaho. He had no idea what to expect once his plane landed in Louisiana.

The flight to New Orleans was uneventful, and they touched down a few minutes late, arriving in the early afternoon. Olivia called Mike while they taxied in from the runway. He didn't expect them home for a day yet. Olivia pretended that they were still on a lark up in Salt Lake. She didn't tell him about their trip to New Orleans.

Neither Bron nor Olivia had packed any luggage, so they simply walked out of the airport.

As they neared the baggage claim, they found people lining the exit. Some were limousine drivers, men in fine gray or black uniforms, each holding a sign with a name, such as "Mr. Brandt." Others were family members, bearings signs like "Welcome home from Afghanistan, Dad!" A few cabbies with ragged hair held signs.

Olivia halted and searched their signs, their faces. Bron looked eagerly for something that might have his name on it. At the back of the crowd, an old coot with gray hair raised his hand for a brief flash, splaying his fingers just a bit. He didn't show any suction cups, so Bron figured that he wasn't a masaak. In fact, he suspected that the man was just waving to someone behind him, but Olivia grabbed Bron's hand and headed in the old man's direction.

When they reached him, the old man said in a heavy Cajun accent, "Come to see some big gators? You picked da right spot, by gar."

He reached out to shake Bron's hand, and that's when Bron *felt* the suction cups on his fingers. Bron didn't have time to flash his own sizraels. The old man pulled his hand away as if Bron's touch had burned.

"Sorry," the old man said. "I was tinkin' dat you is someone else."

He turned to hurry away, but Olivia said, "We'd love to the see gators." She grabbed his hand, flashed her sizraels, and the man halted, looked at Bron in confusion, then shook hands again. This time Bron gave him the sign.

There was so much to learn about masaak etiquette.

The old man smiled in relief. "Le's go, then!"

Bron felt nervous. "Are we going to see my mother?"

"Mebbe," the old man said. "That jus' may be." He said it as if he didn't trust Bron and Olivia, as if he was still making up his mind.

They stepped outside, and sultry air hit them in a wave. As they headed to the parking lot, Bron studied the old man. He had a week or two of white stubble on his chin, and a large wart under his right eye, but he had the same coloration as both Olivia and Bron—skin that was slightly olive in complexion, as if they shared Greek ancestry, but this man's face was broad and heavy of brow, while his hair was as coarse as a brush.

He looked weathered, beaten.

He led them to an old red Ford pickup, dinged and rusted in spots. A couple of aluminum lockboxes sat in the back. The old fellow flipped one open and said, "Dass is whar you stow yar chut chuts." Bron had no idea what "chut chuts" were, so he just stared blankly. The old man nodded toward Bron's school backpack.

Olivia put her purse in the lockbox, and Bron dropped in the backback. Before the old man closed the box, he nodded to the cell phone in Olivia's pocket, "Toss dat phone in dare, too, beb."

Olivia set the phone in. Bron's was already in his backpack, so he got in the truck's cab.

Bron took the middle, and when the old coot got in, he reached under his seat and pulled out a huge, old revolver. The fellow took off the safety, set it down on his lap, and then started the truck with a grin.

Bron swallowed hard. He couldn't keep his eyes off the gun. He tried to break the silence.

"So, what's your name?" Bron asked.

The old fellow smiled. "It doan matta." He dismissed the question, then let out a nervous sigh.

They rode in silence for over an hour, skirting the towns, heading down back roads past dilapidated houses with huge yards. Many of the homes had tattered barns, with a swaybacked mule here and there.

The roads looked like a kill zone. Bron spotted dead turtles and frogs everywhere, with an occasional skunk or raccoon or coyote or beaver or rabbit. He'd never seen so many dead animals in so short a time.

"Sure are a lot of dead animals on the road," Bron said, trying to get the driver to open up.

The old coot didn't speak. He neither asked questions nor answered them, and so Bron figured that the old guy just wasn't the type for conversation.

Or maybe he was just too scared. The old guy didn't trust them, that was for sure.

At last the truck pulled onto a dirt road that bordered a swamp. A sign just before the turnoff said, "Black River," and soon they reached a broad river whose water was darker than coffee.

The man pulled up beside a small wooden dock, where an old silver motorboat was chained. He got out, still carrying the gun, and Olivia and Bron tumbled out of their door.

The old fellow waved his gun at them, motioned toward the boat. "Ya all go climb 'board, now."

He let them take the lead, then stood by the pickup for a moment, eyeing the road behind, making sure that no one followed.

Bron walked over the uneven ground toward the boat, a little worried. He'd heard about the dangers of the swamps—gators and cottonmouths and rattle-snakes, and he began to wonder if he'd encounter any of those things.

On the far shore, the banks were covered in saw grass and cane. On this side the grass had been clipped a week or so ago, so that it was short enough that a big snake couldn't hide in it. A few gnarled pines clumped along the bank, creating a wooded feel. As Bron stepped onto the dock, he heard a large "plock," and something dropped into the water near his feet.

He stopped cold, unsure if he should move.

"Just a turtle," Olivia said, "trying to catch some sun."

Bron hurried onto the dock. Across the river, something long and gray slid into the water. An alligator splashed its tail.

Bron peered into the river, to see if anything might be moving within it, but thick sediments, like bits of black moss, floated in the water, hiding anything below.

Bron walked to the boat and peered up toward the pickup. The old coot was just standing there at the back of the pickup, as if peering into the bed. He had his revolver in hand, hidden just behind his back.

A black sedan with tinted windows came down the road and slowed a bit, then rolled on down the highway. The fellow watched it suspiciously, gun ready, as if trying to decide whether to pop a few rounds through the windshield. By the time that it had passed beyond a screen of trees, his fidgeting had calmed.

He limped on down to the boat, as if his hip were stiff, and unlocked the chain that held it to the dock. He motioned to Olivia and Bron. "You all take de frent!"

The both of them sat on an aluminum slab at the front of the fishing boat, while the old fellow took the back. He pushed a button on the motor, and it coughed a bit, then took hold. In moments they swung out from the dock, onto the broad river.

Bron felt stupid. With him and Olivia sitting in front, the weight on the boat was distributed unevenly, so that the bow was deep in the water while the motor rose too high, almost high enough so that the propellers were in the air. The helmsman didn't seem to mind, though. He wanted to keep his passengers as far away from him as possible.

So the boat plied the dark water, slowly at first, then picked up speed. Bron watched the banks and trees. Every few hundred yards, a dead log would poke up out of the water, often with a few turtles sunning on it. Blue herons strutted in the shallows on stilt-like legs, hunting for fish, and sometimes a snowy egret would do the same. Every few hundred yards, he'd spot an alligator floating as still as a log, until the boat neared. Then the gator would thrash and dive.

Most of the gators were small, a foot or two in length, but a couple of times he glimpsed bigger gators ahead—ten-footers. The big gators never let the boat get close.

Bron's thoughts were a muddle. He tried to imagine his mother. Out here in the swamp, she'd probably be wearing blue jeans and a work shirt.

How old was she, anyway? If the old guy was her husband, she might well be in her sixties. He hadn't thought of that.

But Monique had said that she was a young woman.

What will she think of me? he wondered. Almost he felt as if he were going there to be judged.

What should I do when I see her? Say hello and stand at arm's length? What if she wants to kiss me?

He couldn't imagine kissing the woman who had abandoned him. He resolved that he wouldn't do it. He wasn't even going to touch her. If she hugged him, she'd get no hug in return.

Along the channel, a few cabins on stilts began to rise up from the water. Some houses floated on giant pontoons. Some had motorboats or jet skis parked out front, and he saw a few kids at one. Four children, ages eight through twelve, were swimming in the water. They were diving off the deck of the cabin, while one boy swung on a rope.

Bron wondered where their mother was, or where they'd left their common sense, for he'd seen three or four large gators in the past mile.

Soon a forest closed up around the river, and the channel began to narrow and wind through a swamp. In many places, the ground was dry on either side, and here the cypress trees and forests of alders and magnolia, interspersed with palms, began to darken the channel.

Trumpet vines with flowers of red and yellow hung over the limbs of trees, creating living walls, while dragonflies and linnets, gnats and butterflies and hummingbirds darted in and out of shafts of sunlight.

Bullfrogs croaked in the shadows, while strange birds emitted piercing cries.

Everywhere was the scent of water, mold, vines, and an earthy odor that Bron couldn't name.

As they began to pass beneath the shadows of trees, Olivia whispered, "Watch out overhead. I've heard that sometimes snakes will drop out of the branches into a boat."

Bron didn't have to be warned twice. Almost an instant later, he saw a huge dark snake drop out of a tree and hit the water with a splash. It went twisting through the waves. Suddenly something dark lunged up out of the water, and the snake disappeared in a flash of teeth.

Bron hated to think what might have happened if he'd been in the water. He hoped that the boat wouldn't hit a snag.

Soon the old coot had to slow the boat, skirting submerged logs as he took a narrow path. Every so often, the river would fork, and he would veer to the right or left. He did it so often that Bron felt convinced that he was only doing it an effort to confuse his passengers. He didn't want them to be able to find their way back to his lair.

After a lifetime of dreaming about his mother, wondering what she had looked like, Bron found himself trembling with anticipation. He had never imagined being here, had never envisioned a mother in hiding, out in the deepest swamps.

At last they entered a dead-end, where weeds and water lilies choked the shallows, and the old fellow gunned the engine so that the boat slid up over the foliage under some dark trees.

They got out and stood on the shore, Bron searching the trees above and the grass below for any sign of snakes. He spotted a white egg in the water, and said to Olivia, "There must be chickens around here." He thought that was a good sign. It meant that they were probably close to someone's cabin.

"Dat's a gator's egg, son," the old coot informed him. "Dere be a nest round-bouts."

He climbed out of the boat, and led them through a forest. Vines clung to the ground, and every few yards, some lizard would slink up the trunk of a tree. Bron heard a warning rattle and stopped, but it was just a big snake making the leaves of dried vines shiver as it slithered away.

The woods were baking, oppressive, and Bron found himself opening his shirt, trying to stop the flow of sweat down his front. For three miles they walked over vines, climbing fallen trees, negotiating a landscape that seemed to have no trails. Darkness began to fall, until the only light was a blush on the horizon, and the shadows grew thick. They waded through a bog, where young alligators watched from the rushes, and then finally dropped down into another swamp.

The old man waved the gun at Bron's back. "Dere is da pirogue, unner dem vines. Take care you doan get bit by no bebette."

A thick carpet of vines was draped over a tree, and beneath it Bron spotted part of a boat. He didn't know what a bebette was, and imagined that it was some kind of snake. Since the old man had the gun, Bron pulled the vines off, uncovering a long, flat-bottomed skiff. A pair of colorful black salamanders with red spots lurched away. A millipede trundled about in confusion. A long black snake went slithering under the boat to hide.

Bron checked the boat. A spotlight was attached to a huge battery, and a long pole lay in the boat's bottom. Bron shoved the boat out into the little lagoon. The snake that had taken refuge beneath it hissed and raised its head, displaying fangs and a white throat.

Olivia pulled Bron back a pace, and the snake turned and raced into the water.

They loaded onto the boat, and the old man took a seat in the back, with his flashlight, and pointed the way. "You ken punt da boat."

The pole was light of weight and rough on the surface. It felt as if the wood was rotting away, but it was strong enough to push through the black water easily.

Bron began to pole as night fell completely, with only the thinnest of starlight shining through gauzy clouds. Vines and creepers hung down from the cypress trees. The water could not have been more than two feet deep. Yet with the coming of night, the sounds of the swamp grew raucous.

Frogs croaked everywhere, millions of them. Some he recognized as deep-voiced bullfrogs, but there were several other frogs peeped or emitted high-pitched croaks. Leopard frogs, like the ones he'd dissected in biology class, were everywhere. The sound grew in volume until Bron felt as if he was in a football stadium and crowds were cheering.

The old man shined his light out over the waters, and Bron could see the frogs under the trees, each of them with a bloated sac under its throat, croaking like mad. The males were serenading females, and each of them seemed to be shouting, "Me! Come to me!" with all of his might.

As a musician, Bron wondered, *is that what I'm doing when I play?*

Yet with the frogs came the gators—many of them newly hatched in the spring, a foot or two long. Their older cousins from last year were out in force, too, and they silently cruised the waters, legs splayed for stability. Bron could see their big yellow eyes, like golden coins, and their toothsome smiles.

He'd hear a frog croaking for attention, oblivious to all else, and then see a gator float up behind it. With a snap the frog would go silent.

There has to be a lesson in that, Bron thought. *He understood now why Olivia would not play in public.*

So he poled for a long hour. From time to time, green flashed in the bushes as fireflies lit up the night.

They reached some shallows where the boat could hardly get through the mud, and Bron found that the pole sank for two or three feet in the muck. Quicksand, he realized.

They went through a narrow space, where dead cypress trees blocked the way, as white as old bone.

Their bark had rotted off long ago, and gaping holes could be seen at their bases, habitat for raccoons.

Bron was just about to push off on a tree, when the old fellow called, "Hop! Watch da han'!"

Bron halted and saw in the wan beam of the flashlight that he'd nearly put his hand on top of a giant spider, a wolf spider with a leg span wider than a tarantula's.

"Watch for dem eyes," the old fellow said, "glowin' like diamonds." The spider's eyes shone bright yellow and crystalline in the light, like gems. The old fellow shined his light about near the water, and Bron saw that at nearly every one of the cypress trees, where its base met the water, there was a bright pair of eyes on a giant spider. The wolf spiders hung upside down, with their mandibles in the water, where they could easily hunt for minnows and frogs by touch alone.

"I get de freesons when I see dem critters!" the old fellow said.

Suddenly the river opened up, broadening, and in the pool ahead, Bron spotted a truly huge gator, perhaps twelve feet long. The thing dove and the water churned.

He kept poling for an hour more, following a watery road through the trees, and the noise of frogs deepened, becoming deafening, until at last he spotted a light.

A pair of dogs began to bay and howl.

There was a cabin in the swamp, hidden away. The roof was shingled with wooden shakes, so old and mossy that they blended with the trees themselves, as did the ancient planks that lined the cabins' walls.

It would have passed as an abandoned hunting shack, if not for the light of a single gas lantern hanging from a hook out front, along with the howls and barks from the hounds.

"Dere we go," the old man said softly.

The house perched on stilts at the very edge of ruin, at the end of the world. This long lagoon seemed to dry up just down the way. They were on a watery road that came from nowhere, led to nowhere.

Like my life, Bron thought.

People who did not want to be found could not have resorted to a more desolate place.

Bron poled up to a floating dock some eight feet beneath the house, and tied up the pirogue. Two redbone hounds were chained to the porch above, and their chains rattled as they lunged excitedly. They quit barking, except for little yelps, and stood with tails wagging. As the light flashed about, Bron saw a couple of giant spiders down at the waterline. His back and shoulders were aching from all of the work. He suddenly felt weary as he peered up that crumbling ladder that reached the porch, but he placed his foot on the bottom rung and shinnied up.

One of the dogs came to inspect him, and Bron held out his hand, then petted its wet snout as it began to lick.

Olivia and the old man followed, and when he reached the top, the old man waved his pistol toward the door.

A small sign above the door said in faded letters, "Adder Manor."

Olivia took the lead, opening the door, while their guide grabbed his lantern. He unleashed both of the hounds, and they stood wagging their tails. "Gwon, then!" he told them. "Gwon and getcha them coons!"

Both dogs lunged away and raced into the woods out back, baying and barking.

Bron steeled himself. He wanted to savor the moment, the first sight of his mother. He stepped through the doorway.

The house was utterly dark inside, but a woman's voice warned, "I've got a gun, and I can see you against the starlight. Don't make any sudden moves."

She spoke elegantly, but with a Louisiana drawl. Bron had never imagined that his mother might have an accent.

Bron and Olivia entered the shack and stood uneasily, as their guide came in from behind. These people obviously didn't trust Bron.

Bron just hoped that none of the guns would go off.

In the light of the lantern, a petite woman was revealed. She sat on an old sofa, as if the better to remain completely hidden in shadow. Her thin dress was pulled over a lithe body, her breasts almost nonexistent. Her hair was hacked short, as if by a butcher's knife. She looked surprisingly young, maybe only thirty? But no, she had to be older.

If he'd seen her in a supermarket, he would not have recognized her as his mother. She couldn't be. She was too young, slender, impish.

Even now, he wasn't convinced. He even suspected that Monique had sent him to the wrong place.

Could this really be his mother?

All of her attention was focused on him. She was shaking, staring at him in terror, as if afraid that he might be a fraud.

She looked like the victim of a war, or perhaps a refugee hiding from police. Her clothes were worn to rags. Her hand moved, and Bron's eyes adjusted enough so that he suddenly spotted the double-barrel shotgun pointed right at his throat.

I'll get no welcoming hug from her, he realized. *They've got me in a crossfire.*

She nodded just a bit. "You have the look of your father about you, boy. You remind me of that sick old bastard."

Bron didn't know quite what to say, so he asked the one question that most often came to mind. "Why the hell did you leave me?"

The mousey woman stared at him, and her jaw began to work, as if she were speaking, but no words would come. Tears welled in her eyes, and she shook her head no. "Oh, god, I am so sorry! I wasn't abandoning you. I was trying to *save* you!"

"From what?" Bron demanded.

"From Lucius," she said as if it were obvious, but the name didn't ring a bell.

She frowned, then said, "Lucius *Chenzhenko*, your father." She said the name as if it should strike terror into his heart, and to Bron's surprise, Olivia gasped.

"I, I haven't told Bron about Chenzhenko," Olivia apologized. "I never imagined...."

Bron's mother peered at Olivia accusingly, her mouth widening in horror, then looked back to Bron. "Your father is Lucius Chenzhenko. You've never even heard the name?" she asked in disbelief, as if a major part of Bron's education had been neglected.

"You know what the Draghouls are, though," his mother asked, "those who belong to the dark guild?"

Bron nodded.

"Lucius is their leader, their ... king," his mother explained. "He is the Shadow Lord who rules the stock markets and the banks. He is a puppet master who controls the nations. He has held his position for the last five thousand years. Though you might not have heard of Lucius, an older version of his name has passed down through history. Certainly you've heard of Lucifer?"

Chapter 27

A Child's Tale

"The greatest leap in human evolution took place when men realized that they could use their brothers as tools to meet their own ends.

"For most people, to do this remains morally repugnant.

"But as masaaks, we need not refrain from using mankind on moral grounds. We are lions, and they are cattle."

– Lucius Chenzhenko

S ommer was Bron's mother's name, Sommer Bastian, and she did not move from her chair as she spoke. Instead she jutted her chin toward a couch, ordering Bron and Olivia to sit, and both of them took seats uneasily.

Olivia looked about the two-room shack, torn between the desire to know more, and an aching thirst.

As she settled into a seat, Olivia studied her surroundings. A wood stove sat quietly in the corner. There was no need for heat tonight, and probably had not been for months.

There was no sign of electricity that Olivia could see—no refrigerator, no microwave, no phone or clock. The only burglar alarm came from the hounds on the porch.

The only sound from neighbors erupted from the frogs outside, croaking in hysteria, and the occasional barking call of an alligator or the hoot of a great-horned owl.

Olivia could only guess at the fear that had driven Bron's mother to such a primitive existence. The petite woman bore little resemblance to Bron.

"Could we have a drink?" Olivia asked. Sommer kept them covered with her shotgun, but the old man went to a corner and opened a cabinet. He rummaged around for a moment, pulled out a couple of tin cans. He tossed them across the room. In the dim light of the lantern, it was hard to read the contents. Bron's can contained lemonade, sugar free. Olivia had a beer. Their hosts didn't apologize for the fact that the drinks were warm.

This is probably as good as it gets out here, Olivia realized. There would be nothing to drink in this swamp.

"I was only eighteen when I met him," Sommer began, as she settled into her story. She spoke guardedly, as if what she had to say pained her. Yet she was resigned to tell the whole truth. "My father worked on the bayou, fishing for catfish by nights, trapping crayfish and turtles by day. I knew nothing of the world. But we lived near the city, in a fine little house, with twenty acres of swamp behind it. Our nearest neighbors lived half a mile away, and so it was a quiet existence, until I turned eighteen."

As Sommer began to speak, Olivia was struck by something: how odd her voice sounded. Here in the swamps, living with this old Cajun, one might have expected Sommer to fall into his habits. But her voice was elegant, refined. It was as if, through her speech, she clung to the last remnants of civilization with every fiber of her being.

"We were all masaaks, in my family," Sommer continued. "I longed to see the world, but we had no money, so one year I decided to take a short drive to New Orleans for Mardi Gras.

"It seemed so grand—the parades, the music, floats and costumes. I sang and danced through the French Quarter, and someone shoved a drink in my hand.

"The party lasted all night long. I found myself among some drunken college girls, who stripped for the applause of leering idiots.

"I was slinking from the crowd when I smelled something glorious. There are many great restaurants in the French Quarter, with strange delicacies—barbecued alligator steaks and shrimp gumbo, powdery beignets with fresh café au lait.

"But this smelled glorious beyond anything, and I found my blood thrilling through my veins as I followed the scent down a side street, to a mansion with marble columns. I walked through the door into a grand entrance, then climbed a winding stair.

"By the time I reached the master bedroom, I knew what the smell was. My mother had warned me against it—the scent of a masaak in musth. But I was drunk and young, and I followed it to a door that had been left half open.

"I dreamt that I would meet a man, and that he would be the love of my life, much in the way that my mother met my father. I tried to imagine him—tall and strong and handsome.

"He was all of that, and more. When I saw the room, I knew that he was wealthy, too, beyond anything that I had imagined. He had two other people with him on a canopied bed, with silken sheets of scarlet—a dark-haired succubus, and another woman lay naked and exhausted.

"He had servants in the room, too—butlers to wait on him hand and foot, along with security guards and counselors.

"All of his servants were more beautiful than me, stronger, taller. I felt insignificant in their presence.

"He looked at me as if I was nothing, fleshy garbage.

"Compared to everyone else in that room ... have you ever seen a purebred Arabian, one with a lineage that goes back for two thousand years?"

"Like in that movie," Bron asked, "the Black Stallion?"

"Yes," Sommer said, "like that. All of the people around me were purebreds, and I ... was a beat-up draft horse.

"When he saw me, he would have mocked me, if I had not bored him so.

"I went to the foot of his bed, and by then, there in that closed room, the pheromones were so strong, that I yearned for him with an unspeakable lust. I knelt at the foot of his bed, and he was so beautiful, that I could only reach up and touch his ankle, begging for him. I felt so insignificant, and he was so grand. I wanted him. I've never wanted anything so much in my life.

"He just laughed.

"'You think that I would have you?' he asked. 'We Draghouls are purebred. You ... you're nothing. Still, from time to time, one of you feral rats holds something that amuses me....'"

It was a singularly odd scene, Olivia thought. This woman who claimed to have tried to save Bron, now sat across the room, holding a shotgun on him. She was so petite, she looked almost stunted. Olivia felt that Lucius's judgment was correct. Sommer was ... plain. She was pretty in her own way, but she had none of Bron's strong build, his symmetry, his grace.

Sommer was deep inside herself, dredging up painful memories. Her voice cracked as she continued, "Lucius turned away from me then, and would have rejected me altogether, but the head of his security team grabbed me and threw me on the bed, and pinned me down. He put his thumbs up above my eyes, and grasped my skull with his fingers. Grimacing from displeasure, as if he disliked even to touch me, he invaded my head, stripped my memories bare.

"He saw my mother, my sisters, in their little house near the bayou. He learned about my tedious life, all of my insignificant hopes and dreams. I heard his voice in my mind, laughing at me.

"When he was done, he told Lucius, 'Milord, this one is a wondrously powerful leech!'

"Lucius seized me then. What happened next, I do not recall. Someone cleaned the memories from me, so I know that they must have been filthy indeed. I remember Lucius promising to leave my family alone, so long as I bedded him.

"Lucius kept me prisoner for nearly a year. I know that I had a child, and that somehow I escaped from Lucius's compound in the Hollywood Hills, and ran all over the country."

Sommer began to weep, and her eyes filled with tears. The regret was thick in her voice. "I remember that I planned my escape for days, but I don't remember you, Bron. I'm sorry. I'm so sorry. I don't remember ever having you. Lucius caught me afterward, and questioned me. His men accused me of having a baby, of stealing it away." She looked across the room blankly, and her voice trailed off to nothing, was drowned out by the distant croaking of frogs. "After that, I can't remember much."

"You don't know what happened next?" Bron asked.

"I couldn't even remember your name, if I ever gave you one," the woman said, looking vacantly at Bron. "But I've been told that I had a son once. For all that I know, you may be him. I only remember that I escaped from Lucius again, a few years later."

Silence fell in the room, and Sommer just sobbed for a moment. When she finally looked up, her voice went cold. "Now, it's your turn: what makes you think that you're my son?"

Bron shrugged, as if he didn't quite know how to answer.

Olivia could not see any resemblance between this woman and Bron. Yet as Olivia's eyes adjusted to the darkness, she realized that her first appraisal of Sommer had been a bit harsh. Sommer was plain, but with a bit of makeup she might even have been considered pretty.

She'd worn herself out in hiding.

Olivia told Sommer, "Bron was abandoned as a child. We were told by a friend that you were his mother, but he doesn't know any more than that. She's the one who cleaned out your mem—"

Outside, the frogs were croaking like madness beneath the starry skies. Olivia had become so used to the melee of voices that she almost didn't hear the squeaking board on the porch, as someone heavy took a step.

The old man whirled in alarm and fired his gun into the wall, in the direction of the sound. The explosion echoed in the shack so loudly that Olivia felt stunned. The powerful bullet blew a hole in the old wood, and outside on the porch, someone grunted heavily and fell.

The door latch turned and the door began to swing open. Bron's mother let go with both barrels of her shotgun, and Olivia caught a glimpse of someone getting blown backward, over the rail on the porch, and a heavy body hit the water.

All hell broke loose. Someone outside shouted, "Police! Come out with your hands up!"

The old fellow beside Bron began blasting with his revolver, opening holes in the wall, each one letting in a tiny bit of moonlight.

Meanwhile, an automatic rifle fired from outside. Bullets tore through the home, up at chest height. Olivia hunched to avoid a stray bullet. A lacework appeared in the wall, and the old fellow grunted.

Olivia was peering up, mouth agape in shock, when she felt hot red blood spatter her. The old man went down. Sommer broke her barrel open and the two spent shotgun shells ejected. She was reaching into the folds of her dress on her lap, trying to grab some hidden shells to reload, when someone bolted through the door.

It was a man in black body armor and a helmet. The back of his jacket said S.W.A.T. in yellow letters. He lunged into the door so quickly that he rammed head-first into Bron's mother before she could reload. The air rushed from her lungs with a *whoosh*, and she crumbled to the floor. She tried to struggle but the man atop her was too strong.

Bron leapt to his feet, but only got a few steps toward his mother when a woman stepped through the door and leveled a machine gun at his chest. Liquid fear oozed over Olivia's skin as she watched the red dot from the laser sight slide over Bron's heart.

"Stand down!" the woman shouted. She wore a helmet and night-vision goggles.

For an instant, Olivia was confused. Could these people really be the police? Their outfits were convincing.

Out behind the house, Olivia heard the hounds growling and barking, rushing toward them, when suddenly there was a blast of machine-gun fire, and both dogs yelped. Their voices fell silent.

Bron just stood, frozen with indecision. He raised his hands in surrender.

A helmet and goggles hid the face of Bron's captor, but the line of her jaw was smooth and flawless, suggestive of surreal beauty.

That alone confirmed to Olivia that she was dealing with Draghouls.

Olivia shouted, "Run, Bron. Draghouls!" but there was nowhere for him to go. Olivia leapt up from her chair. She wasn't a fighter, and felt that her only chance was to flee. A man rushed into the cabin and slammed the butt of his rifle into her face.

She fell back into her seat with a thud, struggling to remain conscious. Even bloody and battered, she called upon some instinct and managed a high kick that put a heel right into her attacker's face. He flew across the room, and in the blink of an eye, Olivia bolted through the open door and dove off the porch, into the dark waters.

She dove deeply, afraid that she'd hit mud or weeds, and was surprised that she made it safely. She held her breath and swam underwater until her lungs burned, and she reached the weeds on the far shore. She carefully lifted her head from the water.

"Si ji!" someone shouted at the cabin. They began firing down into the water; bullets rained, splashing her face.

Weeds formed a wall before her, and though Olivia could see into the shadows of the trees ahead, she could not find a way to safety.

CHAPTER 28

LORD OF THE BAYOU

"I have never liked killing, but I have a talent for it."
— Bron Jones

Bron realized that this was his last chance to escape. The only way he could stop this Draghoul from firing at Olivia might be to knock him into the swamp.

The gunman who was shooting at Olivia stood in the door frame. Bron's captor glanced toward the shooter.

Bron seized the moment, dodged to the left, so that the laser sights were no longer on him, then shoved the shooter. The man lurched toward the railing, nearly plunged into the swamp, and lost his weapon.

The woman who'd held Bron at gunpoint slugged his neck. He saw a blue flash, heard an electric crackle, and it felt as if Thor's hammer knocked him to the floor....

T he gunfire stopped momentarily, and Olivia heard a splash in the water behind her. A Draghoul was coming for her.

She caught her bearings, saw a place far ahead and across the pond where some willows hung over the water. She hoped that she'd be able to find cover there.

She dove and swam toward the willows, guided only by memory. She could not judge how fast she was swimming or how far she traveled. She'd never swum like this in her full clothing before. She didn't dare come up for air early. Right now, she was like a submarine, hidden in the depths, and she could not risk exposure.

So she kicked and swam until her lungs felt as if they would burst, and then she kicked some more. She reached some weeds, pushed on through, and pulled herself along the bottom for a moment.

At last she surfaced, timidly, and struggling to breathe. She had over-shot her mark, and found herself deep beneath the willow's hanging fronds. A small inlet hid here, a waterway that looked as if it might have been dredged away, and it led inland. She gasped, dove, and swam deeper into the swamp.

She had no gun, no knife, and no idea where she might find help. For the moment, she hoped only to escape.

They have Bron, she realized. *They must have followed us.*

How could they have done that?

She wondered if her phone lines were secure. Had the enemy been watching Monique? Or had they somehow trailed Bron from home?

She couldn't imagine how they'd been found. Nor could she see any way to escape.

When Bron woke, he groaned and fought to recall what had happened. He remembered the sharp sensation of bolts blowing through him. He felt like he'd been hit by lightning, more than once, and as he struggled to recall what had happened, it was like trying to wade through tar. He could make no headway.

He dimly became aware that he was sitting. He had two people holding him, and they had wrestled him onto a wooden chair. His arms were wrenched behind his back and strapped together with duct tape. He could hear tape unzipping, and felt pressure on his legs.

Bron lolled his head up, tried to see. Everything was a blur. His right eye felt swollen, nearly closed, and he wondered if someone had beaten him or if he had fallen.

For several long seconds, he let his eyes adjust, even as his captors finished taping him.

"That should hold him," one man said as he stood.

Bron pulled hard, but the tape only seemed to draw back against him.

Three people were in the room with him—the woman who had first caught him, and a pair of men. They all wore S.W.A.T. outfits, but Bron realized that they couldn't be real police. He'd never heard of policemen who carried fully automatic weapons.

The woman removed her visor, and Bron saw that he was right. Hers was the face of a supermodel, with sparkling green eyes, silky blond hair, and opalescent skin that was absolutely flawless.

She was beautiful, yet she did not look like a masaak. Her eyes were too bright green, her hair too light, her skin tone too white. Though she did not look like a Draghoul in coloration, everything about her warned of danger. She did not smile or show any other emotion. There was a toughness to her that defied description.

She's not tough, Bron thought. *She's ... murderous.*

She's a Draghoul in hiding. All it took was contacts, bleach, and a little skin cream.

"What ... do you want with me?" he asked. Speaking brought an unexpected pain. His lip had been split.

The woman slapped him so hard that spittle flew from his mouth. "You do not ask the questions," she said. Her accent sounded Eastern European—perhaps Russian.

She slipped into some foreign language then, began scolding masaaks around her. The men cringed like dogs with each harsh word.

From the other room, Bron's mother called groggily, as if rousing from sleep, "Bron?"

Bron was about to answer, when one of the men grabbed him and put a wide swath of duct tape over his mouth. Bron shouted, but all that came out was a wordless grunt.

Sommer moaned and whimpered, "Olivia?" She gasped, as if she was beginning to come to.

Bron heard the electric hum of a taser, and Sommer shrieked once, and then fell silent.

Sweat broke on Bron's brow and dampened his armpits. His captors had him, and there was nothing he could do. Bron thought frantically, but could see no way to escape.

Stealthily, he pulled at his bonds, but the tape around his wrists was too tight, too sticky. His heart kept pounding, and air in the room seemed thin.

The woman, their leader, barked a sharp command in that same harsh language. She left the room, followed by one of her soldiers, while the third man squatted on the floor.

He took his rifle and merely pointed the barrel at Bron's chest. The red light of his laser illuminated motes of dust in the air before the red dot settled on his heart.

Their leader brought the lantern into the room, and left it sitting on a dresser.

The guard raised up his cell phone and took a short video of Bron. He narrated in accented English, "This is video of Bron Jones, dream assassin, captured at home of Sommer Bastian."

Bron wondered at that. How did they know that he was a dream assassin? They couldn't have gotten that information from his mother. He hadn't told her. Nor could they have gotten it from Olivia, unless they'd captured her.

They must have messed around inside my head when I got knocked out, he worried. *Who knows what they took, or what they've added?*

When the guard was done, he punched some numbers on the phone and sent Bron's picture into cyberspace.

Far across the Atlantic, Adel Todesfall studied the video. It was just after breakfast when he raced into the study of Lucius Chenzhenko.

The Shadow Lord was studying the markets, peering at a dozen screens at once as they relayed information on commodities, recent news, fluctuating prices.

"My lord," Adel said, his voice shaking with excitement. "Some hunters in America have found your lost son, the child of Sommer Bastian."

Lucius did not take his eyes from the screens. "You see," he said laboriously, "I told you that the chick would come home to the roost."

He said nothing more. Lucius did not care that his son had been captured. Rather, he was far more interested in being right.

"There is an interesting development," Adel said, savoring the moment. "It seems that this one is a dream assassin."

There was no flicker in Lucius's brooding eyes. No ecstatic shout, not so much as a lift of an eyebrow.

Yet Adel could almost hear his master's heart begin to pound faster, and after a long moment, he betrayed his mirth. "Tell the pilot to ready the Learjet. I want to see this one."

Back in the cabin, Bron worried who might see the video of him. The woman assassin studied the cell phone, flipped it closed, and pocketed it. "Jemný," she said. She whirled and left the room.

A sick fear came over Bron. He didn't know who these people reported to.

Outside, there was no change in the night sounds. The frogs croaked like madness—grunting and squeaking and making deep bull sounds. Whatever happened in the room would go unremarked by nature.

The shadowy room was undisturbed. An old mattress lay on the floor nearby, and all of Sommer's things were stowed in a couple of drawers on an ancient dresser. It was a poor and barren place.

Bron could hear Sommer breathing unevenly, fighting for air, even though she was unconscious.

In the far room, a cell phone bleeped as numbers were punched in, then the leader of the assault team spoke softly and rapidly in her strange tongue. After a brief conversation, she gave some kind of order to Bron's guard, who simply huddled down as if for the long haul.

The wait began. The guard simply peered at Bron, gun at the ready, and passed the time patiently. He hardly seemed to breathe. He had taken off his night goggles, so that Bron could see his eyes—a deep blue, his face framed by dark curly hair. As with the woman, this man was handsome, flawless. He reminded Bron of a young Johnny Depp.

In the sweltering heat, even the guard began to sweat. A mosquito hawk buzzed around the lantern, dipping and stopping for a moment, only to leap away from the heat.

The night was deadly still.

The door to the other room was closed, and Bron could not see into it. He imagined that his mother was bound like him, taped and tased. The old man that she lived with would be dead on the floor, unless they had bothered to drag him out front and feed his carcass to the alligators.

This room had no windows, not even a grimy one to let in a little air or moonlight. There were no other exits.

Bron didn't dare try any harder to break free. He imagined that he could have toppled the chair, tried to twist his arms until he pulled loose from the tape, but he knew that it would be in vain. Duct tape holds people far more securely than rope does.

Even if he could break free, there was only one exit, and it had an armed guard, a man whose laser sight bored into Bron's chest.

That left him only one hope—that Olivia might escape, might have made it past the gators and the quicksand and into the night—and might come back to help.

But that was too much to hope.

Olivia was a singer and a music teacher, not some ninja assassin. If she was alive at all, her best bet would be to keep on running.

That left him no hope at all.

Fear took Bron then, a cold and sickly terror that twisted at his guts and made his breath come shallow. Sticky sweat trickled down his forehead, onto his shirt.

The guard studied him with a cocky smile. Bron could not speak, couldn't beg for a drink, or make small talk. It didn't matter. Nothing that he said would have earned him more than a slap to the face.

They're waiting for something, Bron thought. *Perhaps they're waiting for one of their hunters to bring Olivia back. Maybe they're waiting for someone else.*

Whoever funded these people had a lot of money, Bron figured. The military gear, the training involved. They didn't need to come in a boat. They'd take him out by chopper.

Another thought hit him. *These things, these Draghouls, have been firing automatic weapons. Someone might have heard, and they might report it.*

We're in the middle of nowhere, he told himself. *Even if someone does report it, will the police come? If they do, so what? They'll find themselves outgunned, and far out-classed.*

Olivia crouched in the woods. Here beneath the trees, there was no starlight, no moonlight, only the deepest of shadows. In the distance, she heard a wild boar squeal.

She felt the ground around her, searching for something—perhaps a sharp stick or a rock—that she might use as a weapon. All she found were creepers, and something stung her hand. In the darkness, she could not tell if it was a scorpion, or a spider, or centipede.

She reached up and sucked at the venom, and found that her hand tasted of swamp mud, putrid and dark.

Not far away, she heard a limb crack.

She peered hard, saw a darker shadow moving through the night.

She crouched low to the ground. The enemy had night goggles and laser sights, she knew. She wouldn't be able to see them in the darkness, but they would see her.

Her only hope was to avoid detection—to cling to the ground and hope that the plants and creepers here might provide enough cover.

She bit her lip, and prayed.

Time plodded. The night grew long. For hours, Bron did not hear so much as a moan from Sommer, and he realized that their captors had knocked her out good. The room was so sweltering hot, it felt to Bron as if he were in a sauna. The guard swore, wiped his chin, and called out "Potřebuju sa napiť!"

A moment later, the door swung open a few inches. Bron felt a mocking hint of cooler air. A second Draghoul brought a can of beer and tossed it to Bron's guard.

The guard wiped some sweat from his brow with the back of his hand, pulled the tab from the beer, and gave a mocking wink as he downed it.

The guard said in a thick accent, "It is pity you cannot have drink."

He tossed the can to the floor, where it rolled about and settled with a hollow sound.

"You wonder what we do with you, no?" He dismissed Bron's worries with a shrug. "You are special. You have special talent. Our lord needs it. He has grown tired of living. Five thousand years is long time, no? So he needs you to give him the fire in the belly, the will to live.

"This means you are safe. Me, I would love to rip the memories from your head right now, hollow you out like a pumpkin. But we are told, 'no!' The Shadow Lord wants to sort through them first." He shrugged, as if he didn't care whether his master hollowed Bron out or not. "He wants to learn about your friends, find out where they live....

"But for you, is no worry. The master will keep you alive, maybe forever. Who knows? You will get to eat. He will give you long, long life. He will make you breed—every musth, a new woman." He smiled, as if Bron was going to be leading the good life, but then mentioned the downside. "Of course, you will not remember your own name. We will have to hollow you out every few days, just to make sure that you don't get any ideas. You will have lovers, but you will drool upon them as you grope them, and they will hate you for it."

The guard leaned back, rolled his neck so that it popped. "Your mother now, and the woman you came with, they will not be so lucky as you."

Bron's heart hammered.

"I think," the guard said, "they will be given to us as toys. This will be their punishment."

Bron had no idea what he meant by "toys." The worry must have shown in Bron's eyes, for the guard elaborated.

"Ah, you have never had toy?" he smiled. "A *toy* is person you keep, to do whatever you want. Maybe, for example, I hollow her out, and teach her only simple things, the ways to please me. Or maybe I take all her memories and teach her a thousand ways to kill—and then we put both women together in the arena. Or maybe I lead her around with rope on her neck, like goat, and if any of my friends want to have fun with her ... I let them."

A smile stretched across his lips, and for a moment the guard seemed lost in some macabre vision, as if words failed to express how much he would enjoy making Olivia his toy.

Bron struggled to break free.

Yet Bron noticed something. His guard looked haggard, worn, as if he'd spent many long hours on duty and could hardly move from weariness.

But Bron felt strong, ready to pounce. If anything, he felt more energized than ever. It was as if all of his weariness and thirst were draining away.

No, that's not right, he realized. *I'm thirsty, but I won't give in to thirst. I won't let it beat me. I'm stronger than that.*

His guard called out to the other room, almost begging. The woman called back. "Da!" Then she began calling frantically on her phone.

She came into the room again. The guard complained, wiped sweat from his brow. She cast furtive glances at Bron and made exaggerated gestures.

In that instant, he realized that behind his back, his sizraels had extended. Olivia had told him that he had killed before, used his powers to draw all of the hope from his foster father. He'd done it by instinct.

Now, he was draining his attackers, and they had done nothing to stop him. *Why?*

Can't they make me forget how to use my powers, the way that Blair did?

They know I'm a dream assassin. Don't they know that I'm a leech, too? Or is that some big surprise to them?

There could only be one answer. They were under orders not to harm him. The woman was trying to get someone on the phone, explain their problem, and she was being stifled. Perhaps it was poor reception. Perhaps her commanding officer wasn't in.

I'm so valuable to them, Bron realized, *that they don't dare touch me.*

Their commander snarled something at the guard, then left the room.

Bron wanted nothing less than to kill his captors.

So he closed his eyes, opened his mind, and imagined that his will was like a hand, a huge greedy hand that stretched out with invisible fingers, and drew the will from his enemies.

Bron waited in the sweltering heat, measuring the minutes by the droplets of sweat that stole down his face. His mind tired, and he rested silently, eyes closed, then after a few minutes tried again, and again, until at last he heard a little mewling cry.

He opened his eyes.

His guard sat in his appointed place, trembling, rocking back and forth. The confidence had deserted his eyes, and now he had a pleading look, almost as if he would beg to leave.

Bron noticed that he wasn't sitting cross-legged anymore. He'd pulled his knees up in a fetal position, and had one arm draped around them, while the barrel of the gun now pointed at the ground.

He's like a fly, Bron thought, *fighting the effects of bug poison. He's lying on his back, buzzing his wings, scooting around the floor in circles. He doesn't even know that he's dead yet.*

Bron felt refreshed, relaxed, confident.

Almost, he would have described his state as serene, but there was too much of a thrill to it. His blood was racing.

Cocky, *that's how I feel,* he realized. *They can't touch me. They wouldn't dare kill me. I'm the heir to their lord. I'm the devil's child.*

He laughed inside.

He breathed evenly, in and out, in and out.

Maybe if they act now, they might rid the world of me. But already their own will to live is nearly gone....

He heard a *thunk.* The guard had dropped his weapon. The man lay trembling, and began to moan.

From the other room, he heard the woman cry out, a little mewling snivel. He heard something scraping on the floor, a body crawling toward him, and then there was a curse, and the woman staggered to her feet and hobbled into the room.

She stood in the doorway, and grasped onto the doorpost. Her face looked like death warmed over, as pale as a corpse, a pitiful frown.

She pulled a pistol from her holster, raised it slowly, and pointed it at Bron. She said, "Damned dream assassin!"

For a long moment she seemed to consider pulling the trigger. Bron planned to kill her. She knew it, and she could not stop him—but she could take him with her.

Bron suspected it was against her orders.

She staggered across the room, placing each foot carefully, and pulled the tape from his mouth.

"Give it back, damn you," she said in perfect English, "or I'll put a bullet through your head!"

He could feel the will seeping off her, like cold sheets of air from an iceberg. The air suddenly crackled between them, and purple sparkles erupted. A thrill coursed down his spine like an arctic wind.

"You're so pretty, I don't want to kill you," Bron said. "Serve me, and I'll let you live."

She shook her head a little, as if horrified by a thought. "Just like your father."

Bron could not stop draining her. She was too close now. He could feel her body heat, warm and comforting. Sweat rolled down her neck, between her breasts.

"I will serve you," she whimpered.

"Good," Bron said. "Tell me what you've planned...."

"I only followed orders. We were told to bring you in alive...."

"Did you look inside my head?"

"No, we were told not to touch you."

"Then how did you know I was a dream assassin?"

"We were warned before we were deployed. Somebody said something over the phone. Even I am not allowed to hear all of the details."

She holstered her gun, went behind him, and stood for a moment, panting, trying to work up the energy to loosen the tape. Instead, she pulled a knife from a hidden sheath at her hip, then sliced his bonds as easily as if she'd used a straight razor.

Did Monique tell my mother that I was a dream assassin? he wondered. It made sense. That kind of information would have made his mother more prone to seek him out.

As Bron pulled his hands free, his captor crumpled to the floor and just laid there. "Please...." she begged.

Near the door, Bron's guard went into convulsions, as if his heart were about to stop beating. He gasped for breath, but barely stirred, sucking air like a drowning man. He could not even crawl.

Bron felt invigorated. In fact, he'd never felt so much ... energy. He almost felt as if he should be shining, and some inner light ought to be illuminating the room.

If I stretch my arms wide enough, he thought, *I might take flight.*

Instead, he pulled the tape off of his legs and ankles, where he was bound to the chair, and then looked down at the dying woman. He picked up her revolver, took her dagger, and then taped her hands behind her back.

She opened her eyes as he did so, staring at him sullenly, full of hate and resignation. Her eyes had been bright and lustrous a few hours ago. Now they were dull, lifeless. She didn't have the energy to move, or to fight him. She struggled simply to draw her next breath, then exhale, and draw another.

O livia crouched in the darkness. It had been hours since she'd last heard the noise of stealthy movement.

She shivered in her wet clothes.

She crawled, but got only a few feet before her hands sank into the mud, and realized that it was too soft to sustain her weight. She was on the edge of a patch of quicksand.

She backed up a pace or two, but heard a little splash at the edge of the water behind her. It could have been nothing, a catfish jumping, or a frog.

Her heart pounded at the sound. It seemed to have been caused by something quite large.

Behind her, an alligator gave a low growl. It climbed from the water not fifty feet away. With each step, its feet splashed, and she heard scraping as it lowered its belly into the mud.

It was massive.

Olivia could not see it, and she didn't dare move, for fear that she would attract its attention. She wasn't sure if it had come after her, or if it had merely come here to rest. For all she knew, it could have been a mother, protecting her nest.

Yet Olivia had to worry. Alligators have a keen sense of smell, from what she had heard, and their eyes, which were adapted to seeing in murky swamp water, were especially good at night.

She didn't dare move.

She found herself feeling sick, nauseous with fear. Her whole body shook from cold and terror.

She waited, heart hammering, for nearly half an hour.

Suddenly, not far ahead, she heard a branch crack.

"Put your hands on top of your head!" someone ordered dangerously. A bright red dot blossomed on the ground in front of her, moved up to her eye.

She saw a pinpoint of red at eye level, just a dozen yards away.

Olivia silently put her hands on top of her head, laced her fingers.

The Draghoul was focused on her entirely. He halted for an instant, and then marched forward, stepping into some shallow water.

Suddenly he yelped, and there was a larger splash as he plunged into quicksand.

She heard violent thrashing as he gasped and fought to escape. The red laser on his rifle swung about wildly.

Olivia heard the lowest of growls behind her, like distant thunder, and then the alligator lunged past in the darkness. It slammed into the back of her leg. Olivia twisted and fell.

But the Draghoul had the reptile's full attention as it went rushing in for the kill.

Olivia pulled herself to her feet and raced away. Behind her, the Draghoul assassin screamed in terror.

As Bron finished taping, he leaned close to the Draghoul huntress. She peered up at him, with eyes full of rage. He whispered into her ear, "I'm not afraid of you anymore. There is nothing that you can do to me. You can't hurt me. You can't even touch me. So you'll live."

The woman was struggling for every breath, and now she surprised him by speaking. "If you knew me," she gasped, "you would be afraid."

Bron grinned. He went to the next guard, and wondered if he should cut the man's throat. It seemed like the wisest course. These people were killers after all, but Bron had never knowingly taken the life of anything larger than a mosquito.

Only days ago he'd spoken callously of letting Galadriel die, but now he found that wishing someone would die wasn't the same as executing them.

He didn't have the heart for it.

So he disarmed the dying man, taped his hands behind his back, and went into the other room.

He found three more Draghouls, lying in disarray on the floor, as if they were human debris. They were all decked out in S.W.A.T. gear. They had no lantern in here, and so wore their night-vision goggles.

Bron taped them all up, found his mother strapped to a chair. She too was fighting for air. He put his hands on her head, brushed back her hair, and *shoved* the will to live back into her. Electricity crackled, and purple flames seemed to fly from his fingertips, bathing her.

The effect was instantaneous. Her eyes widened, and she inhaled deeply, as if coming to life under his touch.

Sommer looked up at him weakly. Compared to the rest of the people in the room, she now seemed to be in excellent health. Bron pulled the duct tape from her mouth, quickly unbound her hands.

"They must have followed you!" she worried. "You led them right to me."

It didn't make any sense. "It's me that they were after, not you." Bron said. "And if they'd known where I was, they could have come for me anytime—yesterday, a year ago. No, I don't think that I led them to you. I think they were watching you all along."

Sommer didn't argue. Her face was a study in wonder.

She stared around in shock as realization dawned on her. There was a smear of blood where the old man had fallen, and one of his shoes still lay in the middle of the floor, but the body had been dragged out and dumped into the swamp.

"Oh, Pappy!" she moaned. Sommer just sat there, weeping, and swiping her face.

I had a grandfather? Bron wondered. He felt sad. The only memory Bron would ever have of the old fellow was of him training a gun on Bron as he drove the truck and boat and marched through the swamp for hours.

Mosquitoes buzzed around Bron's face but didn't land. He felt exposed. He worried that a Draghoul might be out in the swamp, under the trees, still hunting. They could come back at any moment.

He took the night-vision goggles from one of the Draghouls, snapped them over his face, and peered about.

The room looked as if it was daylight inside, everything in shades of green. He checked one of the Draghoul's cell phones. It was 2:14 a.m. Bron found himself worrying.

I can't afford to waste a moment, he thought. *I need to find Olivia.* But what chance did he have of finding her? The Draghouls all had night-vision goggles. If she was out in the swamp, they'd have seen her, unless she'd run as fast and as far as she could.

He headed out the door.

"Be careful," Sommer said. "There may be more out there!"

Bron stepped out cautiously, peered around. No one seemed to be near the porch. The goggles magnified the light, but the brush outside was so thick that it formed a living curtain. In many places, one couldn't see a dozen yards into that jungle.

He crouched outside on the porch, peering into the night. The swamp had begun to cool, and the croaking of frogs, while still a dull roar, had lessened. He looked up. Bright stars pierced the night, and he watched an owl soar over the cypress trees, hunting on silent wings.

He searched down in the water. His grandfather was floating not forty feet from the dock. There were two rubber rafts down on the dock, too, with quiet little electric motors. Everywhere there was movement—frogs croaking like madness and making small waves, alligators floating like logs in the still swamp. They were no longer hunting, no longer sliding up behind frogs in the darkness. Apparently they'd had their fill.

Off to his left, Bron spotted a pair of raccoons tripping along on a rotten log that poked out into the water. They were dabbling about, hunting for crayfish or minnows in the shallows.

Bron wondered if he should go search for Olivia, but decided against it. There was no telling where she had gone, which direction. He might search, but even these goggles wouldn't help much. They magnified the starlight, but they didn't show the heat of living bodies, like some military goggles might.

Bron didn't know how many Draghouls might still be out there, but he reasoned that they were under orders not to kill him. That gave him a huge advantage.

Maybe there were none. He decided to take a risk. "Olivia," he shouted. "If you can hear me, come on in!"

For just an instant, the nearby frogs went silent, and then they sounded again.

He wondered if Olivia could hear him. With so many frogs croaking, his voice wouldn't carry far.

Even if she did hear him, would she come? Or would she be afraid that he'd been possessed?

Bron went into the shack, brought the lantern out. If Olivia was within sight, she might spot the light, and she'd see him standing beside it, and that would beckon her as well as anything that he might say.

He tried waiting a few minutes, and then remembered something that Mike had said. Bron went into the house, took one of the pistols, and brought it to the porch. He pulled the trigger, and it wouldn't budge. He looked at it closer, realized that the safety was still on. He flipped it into the *off* position, and fired into the air, three times slowly.

That quieted more than a few frogs.

He hoped that Olivia was alive, and that she had heard.

He waited for her on the porch for long minutes, and Sommer came out of the cabin. There was a look of fear and awe in her face. "You sure put those Draghouls down."

He nodded.

She handed him a drink, and Bron realized that though it felt a tad cooler outside, he was still sheathed in sweat. He pulled the tab, drank it down. Applebeer.

"We don't have a lot of time," Sommer said. "Lucius will get here before dawn. We don't want to be here when he comes."

"One of the prisoners tell you that?" Bron asked in surprise. He hadn't heard her questioning anyone.

Sommer tapped the side of her skull. "The girl knew, their leader. Now she can't remember...."

"What else does she know that I need to know?" Bron asked.

Sommer peered out into the darkness. "Too much," she whispered. "She knew entirely too much of evil."

They stood in silence for a moment, serenaded by the myriad calls of frogs, and Bron suddenly realized that the world had changed around him.

"They underestimated you this time," Sommer whispered. "They underestimated you by far. They should have put you out. You can't fight them when you're sleeping. Oh, you might leech them a little, but not enough to hurt. They won't make that mistake next time, though."

"Who said there's going to be a next time?" he asked.

Bron suddenly had an urge to hide, to get far away from here, possibly to go somewhere he'd never been before. The Outback in Australia sounded good just now.

Sommer's eyes filled with tears. "Lordy, boy, the things that you don't know!"

He glanced at her.

She said, "You can hide from someone like Lucius for awhile, but not forever."

Behind the house, a cry sounded above the clamor of frogs. Bron turned, and Olivia called out, "Bron? Are you all right?"

"Yeah," he said. "We're clear."

Olivia crashed through the brush.

He lowered his weapon as he shined a flashlight. She stepped out of the forest, then clambered along a thin trail.

"There was one more following you," Sommer told Olivia in alarm. "Did you lose him?"

"Yeah," Olivia said. "Yeah, I lost him permanently."

"How?" Bron asked.

"Let me put it this way," Olivia said. "If you ever get stuck in quick mud at night, don't thrash around too much. It just makes the gators hungry."

Olivia walked past him, peered into the house, and covered her mouth as if she might retch. All of the prisoners were down, but the expressions on their faces revealed utter horror, as if each of them were peering into the depths of some private hell. "Oh." Olivia went in, came out with a pistol in hand.

"They're all alive," Bron said.

"Not that they'd thank you for that kindness," Olivia said.

Just behind the cabin, in the brush up on the hill, a coyote began to howl, joining the chorus of frogs, the hoot of owls. The noise of the swamp was maddening, so different from anything that Bron had ever imagined.

"We should get going," he warned Olivia, but she looked at the Draghouls and just shook her head.

"We can't leave them," she said. She looked up at Sommer. "She should have told you that."

Bron suspected that he knew what she was suggesting, but he shied away from it. "We can't take them with us."

Olivia shook her head, looked down at her pistol, and gritted her teeth. "I don't know if I can kill them. Can either of you?"

Sommer looked to Bron. He was the man of the group, and somehow he knew that it made him the designated shooter.

"No," he said, in fear and revulsion. He'd been carrying a weapon now for half an hour or so, and he imagined that if it came to a gunfight, he'd use it. Exchanging shots at someone out in the dark, hidden behind trees—that would be a fair fight. But sticking the barrel of a gun up to a man's skull when he was tied up, and then pulling the trigger? "No," Bron said again.

The women looked at each other, and Sommer said, "I can do it. Heaven knows, they all deserve to die for what they did to Pappy. You two stay out here, if you like. I wouldn't want you getting your hands dirty."

Sommer was already holding a rifle strapped over her back. Now she took it off wearily, began to walk into the cabin.

"Wait!" Bron said desperately. "Isn't there something else we can do? Can't you, can't you just make them forget what happened here?"

Olivia gave him a patient look, as if Bron were still just a child.

"They're Draghouls," Olivia said. "You don't leave them alive. If you do, they'll just breed more of their kind—or worse, they'll come after you with a vengeance. Sure, I could rip their memories—empty them down to nothing. But Lucius's men would just load their own memories back in, possess them all over again."

"Then why don't we do that?" Bron demanded.

"No time," Sommer said. "Possessing even one of them would take hours at the least—days if you want to do it right."

Olivia pleaded with him. "You don't know what kind of people you're dealing with. They're not...." words failed her.

"Let's show him," Sommer suggested.

"What?" Olivia asked.

"We have time, an hour or so. Let *him* interrogate the prisoners."

That's what I came here for, isn't it? Bron thought. *I came to learn about my heritage, about the Draghouls.*

"I'll ask them some questions," Bron suggested.

454

Olivia gave Bron a pained expression, as if surprised at how dense he was. "You could ask questions all night, and they'd never tell you a thing. We have better ways to interrogate a prisoner, and they don't involve water boarding."

CHAPTER 29

THE MEMORY MERCHANTS

"Knowledge carries a great price. Few are willing to pay it. But who can really afford the even-greater price of ignorance?"

– Monique

Olivia and Sommer had Bron sit in the same chair that he'd been strapped to, and then together they dragged the Draghoul's leader close. She was taped hand and foot, completely bound, and posed little threat, yet she could have struggled if there were any fight left in her.

Instead, she was like a bloated fish pulled from the bottom of the sea, too worn to resist.

Olivia unstrapped the woman's helmet, and told Bron, "They like to wear these. If they get in a fight with another masaak, it gives them a little protection. Most of us can't use our powers very well unless we make contact."

Squatting on the floor, facing Bron, Olivia reached down and took hold of the prisoner, placing a thumb over one of the woman's eyes, then placing each finger carefully over the right hemisphere of the brain.

Bron hadn't noticed before just how precisely Olivia's fingers sought out their mark, but he realized now that he knew what she was doing. By some animal instinct, he also knew just where to touch.

"Close your eyes, and hold onto your seat," Olivia said, peering up into his face. "This can be disorienting."

With her left hand, she reached up and took the right half of his skull. Immediately Bron entered the woman's mind. He found himself lying upon the floor, struggling to breathe. His stomach churned as he struggled to remember what had happened here, as he wondered at the incapacitating lethargy he felt.

Bron was two people at once. He looked about, and saw the world through both his own eyes and through the slits of the Draghoul's eyes. It was disorienting, nauseating. He clenched his eyes shut.

With one hand Olivia was reading the woman's mind, with the other she channeled the memories to Bron.

The Draghoul prisoner's name was Ramira, and she growled in anger at being violated, invaded.

Yet she was no stranger to being violated. It had happened so often before.

Lucius required it of her—weekly interrogations, so that his police force might detect whether she had had a disloyal thought. After nine hundred years in his service, Ramira was proud that she no longer had any disloyal thoughts.

Bron groaned. *Nine hundred years?* Instantly, he was transported to a tiny cottage in the Principality of Galicia, and Bron saw it as their prisoner had—a wealthy farm built of stone, with a fine roof of new thatch. The family had geese and sheep on their farm, and two white milch cows. The Draghoul remembered lying awake at night as a child, while mice scurried about in the thatch overhead, squeaking, and she would pretend that they were fairy princes, telling her tales.

The skies back then were so much bluer than now, and summer rains seemed to wash the daisies clean on the wooded hill behind their home.

Then Lucius came one night, his troops of Draghouls creeping into the house, and taking it as if it were theirs, while all the family was at the dinner table.

The house was filled with the scents of a feast— roast venison covered in a gravy of wine and mushrooms, fresh-baked brown bread, baked apples with cream. Father had just bent his head to pray for a blessing on the food, and Ramira sneaked her eyes open, admiring the feast laid out on the table before her.

The Draghouls rushed in, throwing the door open, one man bowling in through a window. They had their swords drawn. They all wore tunics and breeches of black, with helms of blackened armor and leather cuirasses.

Before her father could even rise from the dinner table, a Draghoul grabbed him from behind, with a gleaming sword bared to his throat, so that he could not move.

Lucius wore armor, a princely breastplate with the emblem of a dragon emblazoned upon it in lacquer, red and black. He wore a fine helm, too, with a leather neck guard hanging off the back, and he strode into the room with supreme confidence, as if he were more than a general, more than a king.

Her father stood tall, proud. He wore only a land-owner's robes the color of red wine, with a fine cloth belt at his waist, but he dared look Lucius in the eye.

"Why do you seek to live here among the humans, old friend?" Lucius demanded of her father. Ramira had never seen Lucius before. He had dark hair and brooding eyes, a severe face, worn with lines of care. He looked to be forty or fifty, but there was a gleam in his eyes, a look of fierceness and cunning, that she had never seen before in another man.

He was older than fifty, she thought, understanding the situation on some instinctive level. He was many times older than fifty.

"Please," her father said. "I served you long enough."

"Mayor of this town?" Lucius mocked, pulling the chain of office from her father's neck. He laughed. "Is that all you've made of yourself?"

"It's a good town," her father argued.

"And you want to be its mayor," Lucius derided. "You alone could slaughter every man in here with half a thought. You could ride their women like horses, and butcher their children for food. Why would you ... lower yourself to consorting with these ... animals?"

Her father stiffened. "They are our equals in the eyes of God!"

"Oh," Lucius lamented, as if he had heard this before, "not you, too. You offered your life in my service. You cannot now give it to some imaginary god, not when I'm so much more deserving."

460

"I gave you more than a lifetime of service," her father growled.

"And each time that you did," Lucius replied, "I gave you more life as a reward."

Bron gasped and pulled away from Olivia's hand. "They can steal life?" he asked. She had not told him that before.

"Yes," she said. "That is what Lucius does. There's something in the body, something on the cellular level that he can tap into—the power to rejuvenate. As we age, our old cells forget what they are supposed to do. Pancreas cells stop producing insulin. Liver cells seem to 'forget' how to synthesize proteins. Lucius and his kind can take a healthy young person, and somehow re-teach his own cells, rejuvenate them.

"If Lucius drains enough vitality from someone, he can grow young, while his victim expires."

Bron opened his mouth to speak, but said nothing. Olivia touched him again, transported him into Ramira's memory....

"A thousand years should be enough for any king," her father retorted.

Lucius studied him regretfully, as if her father was deserving of pity. "Tell me, when you scourged Jesus, drove him through the streets of Jerusalem dragging a cross on his back, did you see anything in him that made you want to worship him? When you pounded the spikes into his wrists and palms, and lifted him up on the cross, did he not cry out like any other man? You did not think him to be a god then. I mean, really, after all of these years, what has changed?"

Ramira's father peered down at the floor, his jaw shaking, as if he might break down and blubber.

461

Guilt smote him. Until that moment, Ramira had not known that her father was one of the Christ killers.

"You are running with the humans now," Lucius said, shaking his head in pity. "If they had any idea of what you were, they would roast you and your family in this fine house as if it were an oven. If they had any inkling of the things you've done ...."

"No!" her father sobbed, as if afraid that Lucius might expose his secrets.

"You owe me your life, Cassius, and I shall have it," Lucius said. "If you will not serve me, then perhaps your wife or your daughter...."

Lucius snapped his fingers, and the guard that held Ramira's father—a man named Adel Todesfall—made a quick cut.

Her mother had been standing by, restrained by a guard, but as her husband fell, she screamed and launched herself at Lucius, fingers splayed wide, as if she might gouge out his eyes.

But it was not his eyes that she was after. They fought, Ramira's mother struggling to get her fingers beneath his helm, but Lucius butted her forehead, and she staggered. Lucius grasped her by the skull with his sizraels, then began draining her vigor away. An amazing thing happened—sheets of red fire seemed to leap from her, streaming into him, so that she was wrapped in flame. One moment she was whole and healthy, and the next she wailed in pain, a wail that echoed in Ramira's memory down through the years, and Ramira's mother struggled and began to age beneath a sheen of fire, crow's feet forming at the corners of her eyes, age spots blossoming purple on her pale skin. Ramira's mother often sang so

sweetly that her neighbors called her "the nightingale," but now her beautiful voice turned into the
croaking sobs of an old hag.

She fell to the floor when Lucius was done with
her, like a rag doll that had been cast away. She was
creased with wrinkles.

Lucius's face had changed, softened. The lines of
care had been erased.

He turned to Ramira, a frightened eight-year-old
girl, and said. "Your father owed a debt. You may pay
it, or your sister may."

Ramira's sister was still lying in her cradle by the
hearth, sound asleep. Ramira knew that if she did
not pay her father's debt, Lucius would take her sister, force her into some loathsome sort of slavery,
while Ramira herself would be discarded, just as her
parents had been.

"Serve me well," Lucius said, drawing close so that
he loomed over her, "and I shall give you more life
from time to time. You need never grow old, never die,
unless you are slain."

Ramira had tried to answer then, but her voice
failed her. So she merely nodded in acquiescence.

"Run then and get your spare clothes," Lucius
said. "You shall never forget this night, that I can
promise you, for this bargain shall define you, now
and for all of your days."

Lucius was right. Ramira never forgot that moment.

Everything else from her childhood was ripped
away by Lucius's servants, his memory thieves—
every kind word that might have been spoken by a

loving mother, every joyful moment, her memories of holidays on the farm.

All that Ramira had left was vague glimpses from her childhood home—a place at once lovely and indistinct, like water lilies painted by Monet.

CHAPTER 30

ELATION

"It never ceases to amaze me how cheap a price some men set upon their souls."

– Lucius Chenzhenko

The Learjet's engines whined softly as Lucius sat in a padded Italian calf-leather seat, peering into a large touch-screen. The Asian markets were about to open, and he wanted to get a feel for the mood of the world's investors today, not that he expected any surprises.

Adel Todesfall approached and whispered. "We've got a problem. We've lost contact with our retrieval squad. It appears that the boy is a dream assassin *and* a leech." Adel waited half a moment for the information to sink in, and then asked, "Shall we abort the mission?"

"All of our operatives have gone silent?" Lucius demanded. He couldn't quite believe it. The team was headed by a dread knight, nearly a thousand years in the making. Sure, she'd reported that they were suffering the effects of leeching, but had there ever been a leech so powerful?

Not in the six millennia that Lucius had lived. And this one was a dream assassin, as well.

Lucius's heart raced. It was too much to hope for. On impulse he said. "No, we shall not abort. I want to visit the kill site, investigate our operatives' remains. I want to see them with my own eyes."

Adel gave him a long look. "Are you sure, my lord? The swamp is a dangerous place...."

"I'm more dangerous," Lucius said.

CHAPTER 31

THE LEGACY

"History shows us that humans are incapable of becoming civilized. The fall of Persia, Greece, Rome, and China shows us that even their most dominant civilizations are considered disposable. Time and again, they invent a society, and with the next generation, the culture is cast aside.

Since mankind cannot maintain a long-standing society, we shall put them to work maintaining ours."

— Lucius Chenzhenko

Sommer appeared at the door to the back room of the cabin, doing her best to drag a man across the floor, one of the Draghouls. He was lying on his back, and there were bullet holes in the fabric of his body armor, but no sign of blood. He'd taken Sommer's shotgun blast, and though the bullets had knocked him off the porch, they'd failed to penetrate his flesh.

"This one's a techie," she said. "He might be able to answer some questions for us."

Bron glanced at a cell phone that he'd taken from one of the Draghouls. He'd been garnering memories from Ramira for twenty minutes, and he worried about the time. Lucius was coming.

Olivia glanced down at the techie. "Bron, do you want to get to know your father? We can pull memories for you."

Bron was surprised by how passionately he felt about it. His only memory of his father came from Ramira, and it was a thousand years old. Back then, his father had looked to be only thirty. His hair was receding, yet dark. He was a handsome man, the spitting image of how Bron imagined he himself might look in a few years. "Yes," he said. "I want to see more."

Olivia helped pull the ailing Draghoul over to Bron, and this time, Bron's own mother reached into the man's mind, and then placed her free hand on Bron, grasping his skull, even as Olivia did the same with Ramira.

Memories began to pop into his mind, snippets of information, collages. *Bron felt Ramira's long hours spent in her youth, fighting with the epee and dueling dagger until her calves ached and her arms felt as if they'd drop.*

Dark muses had come to her, sent at Lucius's bidding, and trained her in various styles of butchery, until she also excelled at the bow, and more arcane weapons—the sap, the garrote.

From the Technician: *In 1762, in a small counting house, the technician, a man named Stalzi, was examining some account ledgers, when Lucius came in. The bank accounts were bursting. Lucius had bankrupted a small nation and created a false trail of evidence that implicated a tyrannical duke.*

"I'm not sure I can keep up with all of this work," Stalzi said. *"The money is rolling in faster than I can count it. This was all ... so easy."*

Lucius smiled. *"Humans cannot imagine something like me. Their minds recoil at the thought. And since they cannot imagine me, they cannot be forewarned. In the old days, their forefathers knew us, and gave us names from legend. Now, they disavow that knowledge, even as we harvest their wealth."*

From Ramira: *As she won Lucius's trust, Lucius assigned her an apprenticeship—as a torturer. He did not need to torture men for information, and could have reserved it only for punishment, but he delighted in torment, and when the opportunity arose to join the crusade, they went gladly, if only to feed his appetite for war.*

The skills that she learned there were sickening. As Olivia probed deeper into the woman's mind, the scent of roasting human flesh seemed to fill the room in her memory. Ramira had once been forced to slowly burn an Arab that she loved in order to prove her loyalty.

After that, her life became a horror. How many people she had killed, even she had forgotten. She'd manned a guillotine in the French Revolution, taking a thousand heads a day for over a month. She'd set underwater mines in the Crimean War, sinking English ships. She'd mastered the use of firearms from the flintlock musket, to the privateer's hand-cannon, to the Israeli Uzi, to modern sniper gear that used heat-detecting sights and could shoot titanium bullets through the wall of a concrete bunker that was three-feet thick.

She'd been involved in a hundred wars—training Mongol cavalrymen under the Great Kahn, propping up the regimes of petty dictators in the Middle East, and selling guns and machetes to tribal warriors bent on genocide in the Congo.

Had Bron imagined how dangerous she was, he would have wet himself upon seeing her.

From Stalzi: *It was during the opium wars in China. Lucius provided drugs for an English Captain to sell, until one day the Captain had become too powerful to control.*

Lucius had ordered Stalzi, "Send an assassin. It will be your job to empty the man's accounts, liquidate his holdings."

"I don't understand," Stalzi had said. "Why didn't we do that years ago?"

Lucius had laughed and said, "Never slit a man's throat over imaginary wealth. Wait until he's got the gold in his purse."

From Ramira: *Lucius had ordered her to head security guarding blood diamond mines in Africa, and she had trained members of the Taliban in the making of IEDs. She helped run a kidnapping ring in Thailand, selling children into slavery in Malaysia, and provided security training for some of Latin America's most powerful drug lords.*

From Stalzi: *In an economic "battle-planning session" in a chateau in the Swiss Alps, Lucius had once remarked, "Our goal here is to keep world finances destabilized. With destabilization comes uncertainty, and with uncertainty in the markets comes opportuni-*

ties. When we control the destabilization, our opportunities grow exponentially."

"For years the world has been borrowing, growing fat on imaginary wealth. So we will plan a recession, move our assets to safety before it starts, and then reenter the market at the proper moment in order to capture entire industries."

This had been said in 2006. At the time, Bron's father was preparing to create a fiscal crisis, one that bankrupted millions of elderly investors, threw the poor out of work, and left tent cities springing up across the US as people were evicted from their homes.

Bron had never imagined a situation like this, one where greedy men raped and destroyed the world out of unbridled rapaciousness, but he saw that his father wasn't the only player.

There were billionaires and tyrants in every country, in every part of the world, competing with Lucius.

From Ramira: *He learned that her dark muses could teach a child to speak at three months, to walk at six. They could download information at an incredible rate, train a man to be a doctor in a day, an assassin in two.*

Bron felt stunned. He'd never imagined this—the first thirty years of life, the part when he was healthiest and most energetic, was all a waste, by Draghoul standards. With their powers, there was no need for schooling, not the way that humans did it.

He wondered why, and remembered a thought handed down from Ramira. In ancient times, the Ael had sought to educate men, to loan them their wisdom, but Lucius had realized that human insight and discoveries were nothing more than "a crop," something to be harvested. "There is no theory that can be conjured by the human imagination, no insight so vast, that we cannot own it!" he'd said. So it began, the harvesting. Draghouls had gone throughout all of Europe and Asia, pulling wisdom and learning from the minds of men, stripping away their insights and discoveries, leaving the brightest of their enemies empty.

That is how the Dark Ages began, Ramira's memories told him.

Half of Bron's life was to be wasted in a vain search for information on how to live. That is how Lucius kept people ignorant.

And soon, Ramira's memories told him, *the Dark Ages will come again.*

The Final Harvest is about to begin.

B ron found himself gagging in horror. He fought free of the women's touches. "Enough," Bron said. "I've seen enough."

Olivia shook her head. "You haven't even scratched the surface. You know what they plan. They want to plunge the world into another Dark Ages. They want to harvest its knowledge of physics, of medicine, of technology, of warfare. They've already established advanced research facilities for space exploration, medicine, cloning, spying. They'll make themselves gods, and the humans will be forced to worship their sadistic masters, or die."

Bron got up from his chair, paced the room, thinking furiously. He had never imagined such things, an assassin who was a thousand years old, with the blood of millions of people on her hands.

Yet she was just a minor player in Lucius's organization. She wasn't a ringleader. Her title was an ancient one among the Draghouls. She was a dread knight, a rare and vaunted title, but she was not Lucius's best.

The technician was much younger, only a little over two hundred years old. He'd been trained in many arts—as a forger and a counterfeiter in his youth.

But it was the advent of technology that thrilled him. With his knowledge of counterfeiting, it didn't take much to leap into various forms of wire fraud and racketeering.

With memory thieves, it had always been easy to breach the human mind. One well-trained Draghoul could sneak into a home, touch a dictator or financier on the temple, and siphon vital secrets from him.

But with the rise of technology, stealing information had become even easier. Voices could be recorded, and files transmitted to servers. Pictures could be taken from spy satellites in space.

Foolish people around the world spoke freely over the internet, not realizing that with the right resources, it was no large feat to create ghost servers that simply recorded every transmission made.

And Lucius's plans for the world were so vast and horrifying. Bron realized now why Monique didn't trust him, why she was so afraid. The Draghouls were fierce, powerful. Who would want to fight them? And for what, to save mankind?

Did Bron care about any human enough to risk his neck for them?

If he joined the Draghouls, he would be treated like a god. He'd join Lucius, become his right hand.

Or would I? Bron wondered. *They'd wipe out my thoughts, my memories. Lucius would want to control me. He'd make sure that I* was *him. He'd wipe my memory, my personality, and put his own in its place.*

Bron went downstairs to the boat dock, but even as he did, flashes of memory kept coming to him, like errant dreams that had escaped their bounds. The tech that they'd just "interrogated" had a surprising store of information.

Lucius controlled a wide number of financial institutions—investment groups. He supplied loans to many of the world's largest governments, bought land on the sly, and had oil drilling rigs all across the planet. He was wealthy beyond imagination.

He'd been into currency exchange before the Medicis, and had insured risky shipping transactions long before the Rothschilds.

He used his money to finance strange enterprises. He had hundreds of forensic accountants hired just to monitor how much various world dignitaries required for bribes.

Yet what fascinated Bron most was not the breadth of Lucius's organization, but how he put the money to use.

He leveraged his wealth to great benefit, controlling the prices of commodities. When oil prices spiked, sending the world into global recession, he was there to purchase the failing corporations. He toppled entire countries in South America so that he could buy up land, and then put it to good use in mining and oil exploration.

To Bron's astonishment, Lucius had his own technologies division, where scientists across the globe were working on bizarre new propulsion systems for extraterrestrial flight. The sightings of "flying saucers" since the 1940s had been his experimental aircraft.

With Draghoul training techniques, Lucius's scientists had leap-frogged well ahead of mankind in some fields. He remembered an astrophysicist saying, "We're at least seventy-five years in front of them, but keeping an edge grows harder every day."

There was a method to Lucius's madness, some plan that had been thousands of years in the making, and the technician knew that Lucius's plans were about to come to fruition.

But what could they be? Even the tech did not know all of the details. He only held parts to a greater puzzle.

Once Lucius had jested, "People imagine that they are wise when they think in terms of global economies. A hundred years ago, only a few men thought on such a grand scale. They were so busy trying to figure out what was happening in their own small countries. And so in the future, one will need to think in terms of interstellar economies. Mere humans do not plan on such a magnificent scope, and so..." Lucius said with deep satisfaction, "I am far ahead of the game."

Bron stood on the dock, tried to clear his head. He looked out into the waters. His grandfather's body was gone, apparently dragged off by a gator. Sommer and Olivia came down with him.

"Don't you want to learn more?" Olivia asked.

"I've seen enough," Bron argued. He rubbed his temple. "This house ..."

Sommer said, "Is bugged...." She'd seen the same memories. "Lucius's people let me go. They've been following me for years.... They've heard every word we've said. We'd better take care of it before we make any plans."

Together, they took one of the flashlights from a downed Draghoul, and went beneath the house. The house stood on stilts, in case the bayou flooded, and for years there had been wasps and swallows building nests of mud under the floor. The nests were wedged up where the support beams joined the floorboards.

Sommer held the light while Bron went to a couple of small nests and knocked them down. They were fakes, mere covers to hide the listening devices that the Draghoul had attached to the house.

Bron ripped off the powerful microphones, with their batteries and transmitters, and hurled them out into the water.

When they splashed beneath the waves, Bron sighed in relief.

"Well, now we know for sure how they found us," Sommer said. "They've been hoping that you'd come to me. They're more patient than I'd ever dreamed."

Bron looked up. Lucius had his own spy satellites winging through the heavens overhead, much like the

Hubble Telescope, except that the lenses were all pointing toward the earth. He'd be taking infrared pictures of them, trying to track them. He'd probably succeed for awhile, until they reached a city, someplace with enough people so that they could get lost in a crowd. Lucius didn't have enough satellites to get constant coverage. There would be blackouts during those times that the satellites crossed the horizon, but he still had good coverage.

"We'd best be going," Bron said nervously. He felt torn, pulled in so many directions. He felt repulsed by the Draghouls, terrified of them, and yet a small part of him wondered if it wouldn't be safer to join them.

He wanted to delve further into the minds of the Draghouls, but he knew that to do so was a trap. Even now, Lucius knew that his men were down. He might not come himself for hours yet, but he could easily send reinforcements.

"We're going to need to burn the house," Sommer suggested. "We don't want them finding any stray fingerprints or DNA."

Bron nodded. "Everything is so wet out here, will it even burn?"

Sommer grinned. "With the right accelerant, all things are flammable," she said, bastardizing a quote from the Apostle Paul. "Pappy had the right accelerants."

Bron did not want to murder the poor Draghouls that he'd drained, but it would be necessary. Shooting them would be merciful, but somehow he didn't have the stomach for it. He decided to take the coward's way and just let them burn. Creatures that were so evil deserved no mercy.

Olivia stood on the docks looking forlorn and nervous while Sommer went upstairs and poured kerosene all over the house.

She came back out with a flare in her hand, struck it, and stood for a moment.

"Who wants to do the honors?" she asked.

Bron took the flare, prepared to toss it through the open door, and had a brief inspiration.

"Give me a moment with the Draghouls," he said. "I need to know one more thing."

CHAPTER 32

THE FLIGHT

"There is no sin in running from a fight that one cannot win. The sin comes if we run forever."
— Olivia Hernandez

In the predawn light, Sommer's cabin lit up the sky with flames. Plumes of smoke rose above the cypress trees in the swamp, and smoke crawled upon the water.

Firelight reflected from the smoke, making the swamp as bright as day.

No screams rose above the crackling of flames. The Draghouls in the house had died in silence, not with a shriek, but a whimper.

"More to the left!" Sommer said. She was guiding their boat toward the far end of the swamp.

"We came in from the other side," Olivia objected.

"That's because Pappy brought you the long way," Sommer said. "There's a shortcut."

Olivia drove one of the Draghouls' rafts. She didn't need a pole. The Draghouls had left two black rubber rafts with electric motors on the docks. She'd been able to clamp both motors on the back of one boat with ease, and now they rode over the water swiftly, sliding past a huge leaning willow that blocked the channel.

"Skirt the tree, and turn left, under its branches," Sommer warned.

Olivia spotted the opening, a thinning in the fronds that trailed down over the water. She plunged through the curtain of foliage. Sure enough, there was a channel ahead, a narrow passage not much wider than the boat. A big gator was floating in the shadows. It whipped its tail and disappeared.

Olivia recognized where she had come ashore in the dark.

"That's it!" Sommer said. "Ease into the channel. The water isn't deep, but we can make it!"

Olivia realized that the hidden inlet made a lot of sense. That old man couldn't have dragged all of his supplies over miles of swamp each week.

She worried about Bron. She needed to keep him safe. She gunned the electric motor and headed for shelter, under the shadows of the trees.

CHAPTER 33

DYING TO MEET YOU

"Violence does not solve everything, but it does solve some things."

– Bron Jones

When Lucius's plane touched down at the Louis Armstrong International Airport in New Orleans, it took only moments to rush to a waiting helicopter.

By then, satellite pictures showed that the cabin was in flames, and three people had left it—speeding off in a raft until they reached an old Ford Explorer. A transmitter had been fitted onto the Explorer years ago, but it had suddenly gone inoperative.

Lucius's quarry had made it into the city, where they would soon be lost in the crowd.

Still, Lucius was eager to see how his agents had died. From the airport, he and his men took a chopper and headed along the Black River, into a tangle of trees. Half an hour after sunrise, they reached the remains of the cabin, it was only a smoking ruin.

From the sky, it looked like a black hole in the canopy of the forest. The trees all around it had leaves of dull green, as happens late in the summer, and only a little gray smoke marked the site.

Adel ordered the pilot to circle the burn a few times before landing. There was no open ground to land on—only a bit of shallow swamp, but the helicopter's landing gear was fitted with pontoons for a water landing.

So they circled.

A sweep of government radio frequencies confirmed that no authorities had come to investigate. A brush fire deep in the swamp wasn't a concern. The area was deluged by thunderstorms at this time of the year, and lightning strikes were common. But with the frequent rain, aided by humidity that normally ran at eighty percent, a fire in the swamp wasn't likely to burn long.

"Sir," Adel told Lucius, "the cover is very thick. Do you dare risk a landing?"

"Of course. Our quarry has already fled," Lucius ventured, for that was the safest thing to do. The Ael were good at running, at hiding. That was about all that they were good at.

So when the chopper dropped near the cabin, no one was there.

The house was completely gone. It had been propped up on poles, and when the main structure was consumed by flames, the floor and struts of the cabin had burned completely. Then the house had crashed in upon itself.

All that was left was the lower dock, with a black pontoon boat tied to it. Flames had scorched it, leaving it disfigured.

The chopper circled, dropping lower with each approach, much as a goose will do during hunting season, staying just out of shotgun range.

When the chopper landed, it made a perfect touchdown near the smoking ruins, and Adel leapt from the chopper onto the dock. He took a rope and wrapped it loosely around the pylons, and then two of his men followed after him.

His men climbed up to the burn and began to search for bodies. The Draghouls, in their dark assault gear and helmets, strutted through the smoking debris, taking no harm. They looked like demons in hell, tormenting the remains of the damned.

Lucius remained beside the helicopter, listening to his agents chatter through his Bluetooth, which was set to a secure channel.

"I've got two over here," one man said.

"Here's a third," Adel answered.

"I think ... yes, there's one down here in the water."

The men began to flip charred bodies.

"They're all in fetal positions, my lord," Adel said. "I'm looking, but I don't see any signs of bullet holes. Our men were burned alive, I think. They didn't die in a firefight, or in any type of hand-to-hand."

Lucius grinned widely. An entire hunting squad, snuffed out by one untrained teen? It sounded too good to be true. He had to verify it himself.

He leapt off the floating dock, then rushed a few steps until he reached land. He strode among the remains of blackened timber, while wisps of smoke slithered about his feet. Glowering embers simmered here and there like fiery carnations, lending the swamp their brutal heat. His dead agents smelled like roasting pork, scorched in a pit.

He went to one of the corpses, blackened and puckering, its hair all burnt off. It lay in a fetal position. Millennia ago, Lucius had worked as a priest in an Egyptian temple, and he'd often taken dead merchants out into the desert for burial, folding them up just as these agents lay now.

With their hair burnt off, their heads looked shaven, in a style that had been popular back in Pharaoh's court. Adel flipped one of the bodies, and knelt, studying it intently.

"No sign of a struggle," he said. "No bullet holes or knife wounds. No ligature marks from strangulation."

Killed by a dream assassin, Lucius exulted.

Lucius began to chuckle. What a treasure Bron would be!

He raised his hands high, and threw his head back in triumph. "I love my son!" he roared, and deep in the swamp, herons squawked in alarm at the sudden noise.

On the far side of the inlet, Bron knelt behind a log, with an assault rifle in hand. He'd been waiting for Lucius to step into the open. He studied his father with his own eyes: a man with dark skin, head shaved clean, a little black soul patch for a beard. He had the glittering dark eyes of a snake.

Now Bron pulled the trigger, as easily as plucking a string on a guitar, sending one sweet note to fill the universe. He had taken only a few minutes of instruction in automatic weapons, having Olivia rip the information from Ramira's mind, training his fingers how to pull the trigger fluidly, how to take the long shots while releasing his breath imperceptibly.

It all came so naturally.

The gun jerked once, and the bullet ripped from the muzzle at 2700 miles per hour, spinning as it went. The brass casing ejected, and in that instant, Bron froze, hoping that he'd made his shot, even as the gun roared.

The bullet crossed the water in a fraction of a second, slammed into Lucius, pierced flesh and muscle. The lead bullet mushroomed as it went, sending fragments through bone, slicing nerves and arteries.

Something exploded in Lucius's neck—as if he'd taken a blow from an ax. Bones shattered, and a fragment of vertebrae exited from his throat. With his spinal cord snapped, Lucius dropped even as he registered a report from a single shot.

The blast roared, then echoed across the water, and echoed back, and echoed again and again. It reminded him of cannon fire in the old days, when a cannon was set upon a hill, and blasted into the heavy walls of a castle. The echo of the blast went on and on and on.

He landed on his side in the ashes, and felt a coal blistering his right cheek.

Here in the bayou, with trees rising up on every side above the water, the gunshot report seemed to come from everywhere and nowhere, as if it rained down like a judgment from god.

His men cried out in alarm, and suddenly Uzis appeared in their hands, flashing up from their suits. They immediately laid down suppressing fire, each spraying almost blindly in a different direction.

Lucius lay choking on his own blood, gasping. He was perfectly conscious. The bullet had severed his spinal cord, paralyzing him. Lucius could not feel his fingers or toes. The only sensation below his head was a hot pain in his neck, as if someone had shattered a vertebra and then laid an ember in the wound.

He had moments to live before his lungs and heart shut down, moments to suffer. He struggled to breathe.

Adel knelt over him, Uzi in hand, and checked for a pulse. "My lord," he whispered, even as he opened fire into the brush. If he hit the enemy, it would be a miracle. Lucius worked his mouth, but no words would come out.

One of Adel's men rushed up, instantly assessed the situation, and grunted, "Leave him!"

The words were hardly out of the man's mouth when Adel leapt up and raced for the chopper. By some stroke of fortune, Lucius was lying in such a way so that the helicopter was in full vision. The Draghouls flitted into the black chopper quickly, shadows disappearing into deeper shadow. Smoke stung Lucius's eyes, and the coal against his cheek sizzled.

I'll come back, Lucius thought. *I'll come back, and I will be stronger, and I will gain the devotion of my son.*

The bayou looked so peaceful. He peered out over the dark pool where hordes of dragonflies danced above the waters, winged jewels of emerald and ruby and sapphire.

The thought of his son filled him with hope. The blades on the helicopter whirred, and the prop wash whipped up the ashes, blew them onto Lucius's tongue and into his face.

The helicopter rose no more than ten feet before a white tracer round coated in phosphorous streamed from the jungle. Such rounds presented a severe fire hazard, and perhaps half a second after it slammed into the chopper's tank, the helicopter exploded. None of Lucius's men had time to leap for safety.

Bits of fiery shrapnel slammed all around Lucius while a fireball erupted into the sky. The props and hood exploded upward, while the ruined body veered and nosed into the swamp. Flaming debris rained down everywhere, amid falling bolts that *thunked* loudly. Most of the rubble sank instantly, while some of the insulation and seat cushions floated on the water, flaming ruins.

Lucius lay there in a daze, fading from consciousness. Watching, waiting, watching....

Bron rose up from his hiding spot in the jungle. His body had been hidden behind a fallen log, and it was a good thing. Return fire from one of the guards had sprayed into the log, almost as if the Draghoul knight had spotted him.

Heart hammering, Bron hurried through the cypress trees along the water's edge. He felt lucky. Killing Lucius had been easy, almost too easy. The Draghoul guards had tried to flee, as he had hoped. The sniper shot had taken his enemies by surprise.

He'd been well concealed in the shadows, away from the blazing sunlight. His enemies had directed most of their suppressive fire across the swamp. He'd hoped that they would think he was on the opposite shore.

Few snipers in the world had been as good as Ramira, and almost all of them were masaaks. Along with the training, he'd learned all about how to field dress his weapon, an Israeli galil ACE 52 assault rifle. It was a bit heavy for his inherited tastes, but the barrel was long enough to ensure accuracy for long-range shots like this one had been, and Ramira had installed a Humboldt laser sight on the gun's Picatinny rail. With a dead wind on a day like today, the bullet had hit within an eighth of an inch from where Bron had aimed.

At only two hundred yards, it had been easy to sever Lucius's spinal cord, leave him alive, paralyzed.

Now Bron reached his father and found him breathing almost imperceptibly. Bron twisted his father's face up, so that he could look into it.

"Hello, father," Bron said.

"My son," Lucius mouthed.

"This isn't over, I know," Bron said. "I learned from your man Stalzi. You're too powerful for me to take out this easily. So I wanted to see your face, and let you know: I'm going to destroy everything you've created."

Lucius peered up at Bron, and there was no fear in the dying man's eyes: only admiration for his son. Lucius smiled broadly, and then his breath faltered, and his focus slid from his son into the eternities.

With his father dead, Bron went back to the dock and waited. The swamp was quiet by day, the air as heavy as a wet shroud. Bron's thoughts came jangled.

He crouched for a bit, and sat. In the distance, an alligator growled, and a white egret flew up out of the trees. Dragonflies were everywhere, glittering in the morning sunlight.

Stress pulled at the muscles in Bron's neck. As the adrenaline wore out of his system, it felt as if a darkness settled over him.

Was I right to kill him? Bron wondered.

It had seemed like such a good idea, to make a statement, to put the monster down, declare war. Yet it accomplished so little.

Olivia had argued against it, claiming it was too big a risk. But Bron remained firm.

He'd pulled the trigger easily enough.

Yet now an arctic front seemed to blow through the hollow landscape of his soul. Bron crouched on the dock, shaking, suddenly chill despite the heat. He peered around at the swamp as if through a haze.

There was nowhere that he could go. He didn't know the way out.

He wished that he was not alone, that Whitney was there. Today was supposed to have been their first big date, out hiking in some incredibly beautiful canyon.

I'm missing it, and for what?

He wondered what she would think if she knew what he had done.

A week ago, he thought, *I longed to know my past, to know who I am. Now I know: I'm a killer.*

He wondered if he should ask Olivia to erase the memory of the past twenty-four hours, but he knew that he couldn't do that. What was done was done, and sometimes forgetting can be far worse than remembering.

Memories can haunt a man. Memories can be a form of torture. No one had understood that any better than Ramira, a woman trained in a hundred forms of torture.

A foreboding warned that more Draghouls might be coming, and each little movement in the forest, each slap of a leaf or crunch of a twig, brought Bron more alert.

After a few minutes, Bron went and heaved up the little that he had in his stomach. Miserably, he sat and waited for Olivia to return in the boat and take him to safety. Olivia, or Whitney, or anyone.

He longed to be rescued from what he was becoming.

Back in Saint George, Whitney woke that morning to the sound of doves cooing in the backyard.

She grabbed her cell phone, checked it for messages, and found none.

She lay in bed for a long time, wondering what had become of Bron. He'd taken off early from school, and though she'd left three messages, he hadn't returned her call.

They were supposed to leave early this morning, drive up to Bryce, and go hiking through the fairy canyons. It was perhaps the most beautiful place on earth, and they could drive there for fifty dollars. It wasn't as if her mom had money to spare, of course. Her mom was making a tremendous sacrifice for Bron, for this date, and he hadn't called.

She resisted the urge to dial him again. Maybe his phone was broken, or maybe he'd gotten hurt.

She thought about how his lips tasted, and how his embrace made her feel warm and mushy inside. She longed to have his arms wrapped around her now, to be hugged.

Or maybe, she worried, *he's not as crazy about me as I am about him.*

Galadriel raced in the dawn, her feet pounding the pavement as she took the long climb above Pine Valley, into the trees.

She had wakened to a dream about Bron. In it, she had been in her hospital bed, an IV dripping into her arm, and he had told her, "The human body can be shaped by will. You can choose the figure that you

491

want, then sculpt your muscles and pare away your fat until you choose the exact form you want.

"In fact," he went on, "through will alone you can shape your entire future. You can take control of your destiny."

In the dream, he'd *shoved* will into her.

She wondered what it would be like to have limitless will. *If I could have all I want, what would I shape myself into?*

I wonder if there's a way to exercise my will, make it grow more powerful, make it respond to my wishes more forcefully?

She suspected that there was.

She'd never been a runner, but she knew that Bron had done a little racing, and she hoped that someday they might be able to run together.

The sun was still creeping over the bowl of the valley, and a pale blue fog wound along the creeks. The air smelled of bitter juniper and sweet grass. Meadowlarks sang in the tall grass at the roadside.

Galadriel raced with eyes closed, taking long loping strides. A yellow car was driving toward her, but she paid it little mind.

She'd never run this long before. Her mother had warned her that if she ran too far, she'd pay for it tomorrow with aching legs, but for right now, Galadriel was experiencing the joy of her first runner's high.

It was strange, all the energy that coursed through her. She'd never felt anything like it before.

I'm like a little car that has suddenly been given an enormous new engine, she thought. She picked up speed and sprinted with abandon. She wondered if you could make someone love you by will alone.

No, she thought, *you can't make them love you. But maybe you can* remake *yourself into the kind of person they can't resist.*

She decided to do just that. It might take a week to win Bron over, or a month or a year.

She imagined Bron just in front of her, and herself calling, "You can run, but you can't hide."

In her imagination, Bron turned back and smiled gamely. She imagined the sweet smell of his musk in the car.

Yummy!

J ustin Walton drove past Galadriel in his yellow Mustang and wondered what could cause such a beatific smile. He'd noticed her at school last week. Who wouldn't? She was the gorgeous girl who had gotten into the madrigals on her first audition.

Justin wasn't entirely sure why he was driving into Pine Valley. He was looking for Bron, and he'd heard from his dad that Bron liked to run in the morning.

But Justin could see no sign of the creep.

What would I do if I found him? he wondered. *Run him over? Beat him up? Call him names?*

Justin had been stewing all week, ever since he'd failed to deck Bron at lunch that day. It would be a shame if Bron got hit by a car some foggy morning, run down from behind.

He glanced into his rearview mirror, watched Galadriel's backside as she ran. She was all curves, sensual and languorous. He admired the way that her hips swayed as she ran, the way that the muscles in her rear bunched, then rolled, and stretched, almost in slow-motion.

Suddenly the car jerked to the right and he hit gravel. He veered hard to the left, flushed with embarrassment, and got all four tires back on the road.

Keep your eyes on the road, he thought. *Remember, it's Bron you're after.*

Epilogue

Ten thousand miles away, in Vienna Austria, Lucius Chenzhenko opened his eyes.

Around him, more than a hundred memory merchants milled in a congregation, each holding only a part of the vast store of information that made up Lucius Chenzhenko. The last two of them removed their hands from Lucius's skull.

Lucius knew that he was a clone. Experiments in Australia with human cloning had been done in secret as early as 1968, and this new body was the fruit from those experiments. Until now, Lucius had never had need of a new body. He'd always been able to extend his own life.

But Lucius was far more than just a clone—he was a poppet, too. Thus he was an exact duplicate of his previous incarnation in both genetic makeup and in memories and skills.

Adel Todesfall, the head of his security, wearing a fine young cloned body, handed Lucius a cell phone and pressed a button.

On it, a guard stood and took a shaky video of Lucius's enemy. His son. It showed a pathetic young man, secured to a chair, a piece of gray tape slapped across his mouth.

A thickly accented voice said, "This is video of Bron Jones, dream assassin...."

FUTURE BOOKS
IN THIS SERIES:

DREAM ASSASSIN

DRAGHOUL

SHADOW LORD

For more information, visit the Nightingale website at www.nightingaleseries.com.

To contact the author, email David Farland at davidfarland@xmission.net or visit his website at www.davidfarland.com.